# REMAINS

# REMAINS

## SKY JENSEN

https://www.skysmind.com

## DEDICATION

*~ Original - May 1, 2024 ~*

This story created itself, I was simply the vehicle that translated it into a digestible format. I am eternally grateful to my wife, children, and friends for providing the emotional, spiritual, and psychological space and support necessary for it to pass through me. The book is dedicated to my chosen family, each of you, and all of you, collectively, whom I hope to never suffer without. Thank you for consistently affirming me.

~

Most of the original manuscript was composed on an iPhone 14 Pro. In keeping with the creative novelty of its inception, most of the editing was performed by the best tribe ever assembled.

Special thanks (in no particular order) to:

Steve Alston

Adam "Radar" Woodall

David "G Funk" Back

Kaleb Michael Daniel

Emree Nicolette Jensen

Warren Brice Jensen

Kayleigh Lyn Daniel

Aristotle Gunnar Jensen

Carol Druppell

Jason Druppell

Cheryl Sowers

Judy Butcher-Smith

David Smith

Cathie Youngkin

Joe Panzarella

Michelle Panzarella

Jarrett Heatherly

Josh Heath

Tim Chapin

Brian Garner

Robert Liberto

Dr. John R. Lucy

Hoyt Oliver

"Dee Dee" Russell-Philipson

Stenvik Mostrum

Nick Martin

Jordan Ruback

Ian Ruskey

None of this would be possible without my father, Dr. Robert J. Jensen, for his sage wisdom and perspective ... but particularly for choosing me, over and over again. *"He said, 'I love you and I'm proud of you both, in so many different ways.'"* - The Avett Brothers -

Special thanks to Rose Oppenheimer-Curtis, for being the second to read the original manuscript and for providing the necessary affirmation to press on with the project. The best parts of Chapter Three are because of you. *"... more juicy stuff."*

Deep gratitude to Bryan Powell for volunteering his editing expertise, and for all the music, guidance, and decades of friendship. *"Boogie chillin's!"*

I understand loyalty because Zack Buersmeyer has demonstrated its worth through unimaginable patience and steadfast companionship. *"Eat my wake!"*

My partner, Kristen Jensen, is responsible for my ongoing emancipation from shame, encouraging my self-expression and vulnerable authenticity. Thank you for seeing me, but especially for looking. *"I would choose endless lifetimes of suffering with you over any amount of joy without..."* ~ Perfect Timing ~

~ Godspeed ~

*A considerable amount of this story was created within the vibe of Guild + Journeyman, Decatur, GA. You have created something wonderful.*

## PROLOGUE

Day 4

The fundamental luxuries that we most often take for granted are also the first and most prevalent things that we miss when they disappear. I have never actually considered the best place to defecate if expecting to be confined with one's own waste indefinitely. I begin with naive consideration for the optics of my decision if I am ever discovered alive. I shift into ridiculous images of being discovered shortly after dying and how my decisions would be considered. Then I recognize my flaw and consider the logical options, rooted in my knowledge of contamination and disease. Unfortunately, this process begins, in my mind, by creating a fantasy where I am discovered, dead, and my poor and hasty decision of where to shit has caused my death. The thought of this posthumous embarrassment spawns consideration for sanitation and anti-contamination in my confinement.

So, I shit in a plastic container that originally contained peanut-butter filled pretzel bites. There are 7 bites left in the container. I remove them, add them to a bag of tortilla chips, and check to be sure the container will fit in the hole in the back-right, bottom corner of the pantry, if considered standing in the doorway, gazing into my bountiful collection of dry goods and stock of paper products. The urge to release has festered to near sickness, and I regret not licking every crumb and bit of coarse salt from the jar before repurposing it. I must assume I am near septic, because the sweat and palpations climax with my submission.

There are no wifi signals. My phones have no cell signal, nor does my new phone have any access to satellite signals, that I can determine. My smart watch died yesterday, having exhausted itself telling me I need to stand and that I could still achieve my exercise goals, while warning me that my heart rate was too high. I search myself for gratitude. At least I am alive, albeit alone, and I have almost everything I need to survive, but water would be nice.

# Chapter 1

Day 1

Wednesday

The event occurred on Tuesday, but my ordeal begins in the early morning hours the following day.

I awake in the middle of the night, early Wednesday morning. I am unaware of my location, but sense that I am vertical. In the darkness, I move different body parts to establish my situation. The tactile response of the distinctive shelving and some fleeting, vague memory hint that I am in my pantry.

If a guest were visiting my home and opened my pantry door out of curiosity, they would typically discover a relatively predictable scene. The single door swings outward and the kitchen island would be directly behind the spectator. The visitor would find a small space immediately inside the pantry, with just enough room for an adult to turn around with some maneuvering. Right now, the guest would find me fully vertical in that space, with my back to the door. My right leg is bent slightly and resting on the second shelf. My right arm is out in front of me, bent at the elbow and laying across shelf four, allowing my head to rest on my biceps. My left leg is supporting me, and my left arm is hanging by my side. The five shelves are white wire, standard in all pantries and closets in the USA, spanning the width of the room, with no turns, corners, or complications. They are about two feet deep, varying amounts of vertical spacing from one-another, with the top shelf above my head. There is a rack affixed to the inside of the door, now to my backside, of the same wire material, but with upturned lips: A spice rack. These installations are great for air circulation and storage, terrible for body suspension.

Some of the shelves have sustained damage, but notably, at this time, the front left corner of the fourth shelf has fallen, lifting the opposite, rear right corner. My right arm is on top of this leaning platform, my hand being held captive by some mystery at the back of the shelf. In the darkness, I cannot determine the extent of my injuries, or the design of the trap holding me in place, so I resist the urge to yank my hand free. My right leg is bent at the knee and perched atop shelf two, offering little support for my body weight. My right arm is keeping me suspended, the left side of my upper-body dangling in space. My left leg is the only real support beneath me when I first awaken.

I have no idea how long it took to regain relative consciousness. I sense that I am awake and experiencing pain, but cannot identify its origin. Oddly, I cannot see and there is no sound. It is like the screen of a television without signal: black, but not completely, and no sound. Then I realize that I cannot hear myself breathing either. I try to make a sound, but hear nothing. I panic, try to move, realize I am stuck, feel a stabbing sensation from my right hand, and lose consciousness again.

When I become aware again and repeat the realization of being stuck, notice that gravity is present, recognize my hand, and acknowledge that the silence, this time, is replaced by a ringing. Not a rhythmic ringing: a steady, high-pitched tone. I am pretty sure it is an "A," or very near 440 MHz. My first instinct is to retrieve my phone from my pocket and play an "A" on the tone generator of my guitar tuner app to see if I am right. This is when I notice the darkness again. But I now recognize that there is some sort of light. Some light is coming from above my head and some from below. I attempt to focus on the light below, because it requires less effort to direct my gaze down and to the left. I cannot focus and the tone in my head is painful, somehow affecting my vision. I attempt to shift my weight, recognizing that my right hand is still screaming. As I move, I see the light move! I try to call out, but cannot confirm whether I am successful over the noise. I shift again and the light moves again. It just twitches, disappears and then reappears. It is blue-white and unnatural. I squint, but my eyes refuse to cooperate, so I close them, hoping for a reset.

I then experience a great calm. I exhale long and slow, and focus on my inhale, remembering to slow its draw and allow my chest to expand and fill with new air. I have a momentary memory of panic and fear, and my kitchen, and then the sound silences, and I sleep again.

I awaken: unidentifiable pain... right hand discomfort... something poking my back... right knee discomfort... gravity pulling me down... I am upright, suspended, stuck... loud ringing tone in my ears, definitely an "A," but seems to be softening... darkness... faint light from somewhere above and below to the left.

I let out a sound, a grunted "uuuuullllllgggggg."

I can hear myself! I am very far away, many aural levels beneath the tone, but I feel the vibration in my head, neck, and throat, and hear myself in the distance.

I look to the light below to the left again, and this time it looks familiar. The blue-white light is not new, I know this temperature and hue. I lean toward it and squint. It moves again. This is when I realize that I am looking at my arm and the light is my watch!

I feel a subtle awareness that my brain is traumatized and does not want to participate in that trauma. My body and mind are not communicating normally, however, it feels like my body is also determined to prevail and return to normal operational procedures. Once my mind makes the connection to where my left arm is, it starts connecting all of my nerves and limbs. I can sense the synapses re-establishing communications in my brain. It starts with my left arm tingling, then my left arm twitches. Then I feel a barrage of senses radiate from my core. I imagine that my nervous system attempted to process millions of signals at once and they bottle-necked in my abdomen, with the sensations appearing as multi-colored lines and brush strokes. From there, pain becomes the leader and radiates from my core to each of my extremities. I cannot recognize details, just the awareness of pain.

Right hand... right arm... right knee... right shin... middle-right-back... right shoulder... neck... forehead... rest of head... left foot... then my left arm begins to tingle and burn. It starts in the shoulder as a tingling that creeps slowly down to the fingertips. When it reaches my elbow, the burning begins in the shoulder and follows, at roughly half the pace of the tingle. I see my arm gently twitching, only noticeable because of the light from my watch. My left thigh feels sore, although my left leg has very little sensation, I know it's there.

The sound continues to weaken. I make more sounds, but they are still distant. I wiggle my left fingers, and every movement reduces the burning. I recognize this response and focus on movement up from there. I am finally able to turn my wrist to look at my watch, but I still cannot focus.

There is a sudden awareness of a need to shift or adjust my weight. My left leg is throbbing, and I want, desperately, to relieve pressure from it. I become aware that my right leg is bent. I have very little weight on it. I close my eyes, relax, breathe, and attempt to picture my positioning. My right leg is bent at the knee and forward at the hip. The knee and shin are uncomfortable. My left leg is straight down, throbbing, and desperate for relief. I tell my brain that I need to get my right leg down and under me to assist. My hip flexes and pulls back. There are sharp but tolerable pains in my knee and shin, and I am aware that I am dragging them across something. My foot, in its shoe, hits something behind me, and I can't lower it. I try to lift my knee to make space, but it finds resistance above. Frustrated, I try to bend my left knee to adjust and potentially pivot, but my right arm screams, and I am out again.

When I awaken next, I am able to jump back, immediately to where I was, developmentally. Hearing is improving, physical sensations becoming clearer. I look to my watch, and my arm instinctively turns and raises the face to my gaze. Face to face, I see the words, "You seem to have fallen, would you like me to call for help?"

I say, "yes," in a shallow whisper. I do not hear it, but feel the air and vibration.

Nothing happens.

I take a deep breath, and say, this time with feeling, "hey Siri, call for help!" I feel my voice, still weak, but certainly demanding and authoritative.

She hears me, the face turns red and shows "Calling Emergency Services" on the tiny screen. I expect to hear the sound of a phone receiver ringing, but I only hear the ringing in my head. The animated ellipses after the words on my smart watch indicate that it is still trying to connect. I drop my arm from exhaustion. When I raise it again, it tells me "failed to connect." In the top right of the screen, I see the three lines that indicate "no signal," and in the top left, it reads, "5:42 AM." I drop my arm and wince from the pain in my right arm or hand.

I am startled by my watch vibrating and making a chirping sound. I realize that the ringing in my head is quieter still, and I can hear my watch over it. I lift my arm, "10:06 AM," no signal, "failed to connect, would you like me to sound an alarm?" I answer, "hey Siri, yes! Please get help!" The screen changes to "OK!" and begins chiming a pleasant "timer done" notification sound. I drop my arm, grateful to hear something other than the noise in my ears, however faint. When the alarm stops, it is 10:11, which I recognize as "The Angel Number," connectedness, and other positive things, ironically. This time, when I drop my arm, I notice that I can see the outlines of objects where my watch illuminates a light field roughly 10 inches around its face. I lift my arm and turn my watch away from my face. I immediately see a toppled can of Cream of Mushroom Soup, at eye level, very distinct. My first thought is of Andy Warhol, and I recall his exhibit at The High Museum. Then my brain latches onto the idea and fuzzy images flutter across my mind's eye. There are nude bodies, from the erotic art exhibit that we visited. There are faces of other adults, silently scolding me for bringing a child to such a provocative display. I see a bent mirror outside the museum and I think I hear children laughing. The ideas are scatter-shot memories, but when I see my son's face in my mind, I panic, scream, "Nathaniel!," try to jump up, searing pain into my right arm again, and I lose consciousness.

This is when I begin to recognize pattern and process.

Awaken... reconnect to pain... then to gravity... then to position... say "ah" to determine the decrease in ringing... raise arm... check time.

9:19 PM, Wednesday

Once all previous experiences and orientations are established, I prepare to consider my situation for the first time.

I am in my pantry.

I am in my kitchen.

I am in my apartment.

I live on the third floor of a five story apartment complex.

I am in Decatur, Georgia, USA.

I realize that the pantry door is behind me, so I instinctively reach for the handle to my left. It is there. I push down to release it, but it does not move. It does not budge.

I feel behind me, there are containers of spices and other items on the door-mounted rack.

I remember my son, Nathaniel. He is 11 years old.

I remember my wife, Samantha.

I close my eyes to remember what happened.

I remember the rain outside my window. I was on the phone with Justin, my colleague. He had just called to tell me to turn on the radio. I told Siri to play public radio. The president was addressing the nation.

Nathaniel was at school.

Samantha was at work.

The man on the radio said, "the threat is imminent, this is not a matter of 'if' but 'when'."

I picked up my briefcase, grabbed my keys, and there was a sound outside. At first, I wondered what it was, then the radio broke into an emergency broadcast, and instructed listeners to "take shelter immediately." I realized that the sound was the city's tornado siren.

I stepped into the doorway of the pantry, reached back with my left hand to grasp the handle and pull it against my backside, and was overcome by a sense of pressure.

Then: Darkness.

I realize, at this moment, that my mouth is agape and my face is wet. My head is upright and I am in shock.

The replay has caused my brain to start thinking, fast, and panic invades again.

I push down on the handle behind me, shift to free my right leg, something cracks, something falls, hits my left ankle, and my right leg extends beneath me until my right foot connects with the floor. I push into it, my knee screaming, and relieve some pressure from my left leg, only to shift my stance, and twist my right arm in its trap. The pain runs through my body and shuts me down again. This time, I slowly fade into black, and try, desperately, to stay awake, but lose to the pain and succumb to the sleep that prevents the pain again.

## CHAPTER 2

Day 2

Thursday

5:17 AM

Regain consciousness.

Pain.

Gravity.

Upright.

Both feet on the floor.

Right arm up and across in front of body, numb but hot, left arm dangling.

Head resting on right biceps.

Lift head, neck pain.

I lift my left arm, slowly this time, and turn my watch face toward where I sense my right hand could be. I move my left arm around slowly to take inventory.

The fourth shelf, that is at my chest level, appears to have collapsed on the front left. My arm is not stuck, but I cannot see my hand. I decide that my hand must be stuck somehow.

I attempt to wiggle my fingers: the ring finger and pinky meet the most resistance, but my thumb, index, and birdie are relatively free. I begin with an attempt to move my hand, first in a cupping motion, which is very painful. My hand responds. Then I attempt to open my hand wide, and I find the resistance again, but everything seems to move.

I take a mental inventory of the pantry. The fourth shelf is roughly five feet off the ground. The left side is populated by three can dispensers, almost completely full. There are more cans on top of the three-tiered dispensers and also beside. The weight of this collection must have caused the front left of the shelf to break free from the wall during the event. There are some boxes of pasta and crackers around my right arm, which is pointed straight back and slightly upward, from my shoulder to my elbow, where it then turns close to the wall, to the left, and my hand is out of sight. The back right corner of the wire shelf is raised. When the front left collapsed, it must have pivoted on its diagonal axis. I reach across with my left hand to access my right. The can racks prevent access, which could be remedied, but, instead, I reach under the fourth shelf and back toward where I assume my hand should be. I begin to contort my upper body to reach with my left hand, but the pain in my right hand amplifies. I wince and let out a groan, which I hear clearly over the sound in my ears. The pain causes my left knee to buckle, and I shift, further exacerbating the intensity of the pain.

"Fuck me! How are you not in shock?" I grumble aloud.

I hear my voice for the first time in two days.

It startles me.

I have been an amateur singer and entertainer for years, so I am familiar with my voice. It is somewhat comforting to hear that I still have one. The experience is reminiscent of hearing yourself on a recording: with my hearing returning, my voice comes from outside, so it does not initially sound like me; but because of the many times I have experienced this, I recognize myself.

This is the first time I've smiled since the event.

Now my left arm is directly under my right beneath shelf four, and my trunk, neck, and head are leaning to the left, to allow for such a pose. I find the bottom of the shelf with my left hand and begin to feel around, gently sliding my thumb and index finger into the spaces between the wire supports, finding the thicker wire cross-members. I feel cans, boxes, plastic items, cellophane wrappers, and, finally, what seems to possibly be one of my fingers, but it is coming down through the wire rack. I touch it gently and can feel its features with my left hand, but receive no feedback from the right hand that is being touched. It seems to be my ring finger. I explore further and find another finger just behind that one. Less of it is protruding below the shelf, and it is smaller. This must be my pinky.

Interestingly, I have not considered any other needs up to this point. I am not aware of hunger, thirst, or any need to evacuate my bladder, excrete any waste, vomit, or anything else. All I can think about is trying to free myself, avoid pain, and stay awake. My singular focus allows me to carefully dissect this acute situation. My instinct is to survive, so I run through all of the current dangers and challenges to that goal. The most immediate concern is that a significant injury poses a critical threat if I am actually stuck in my pantry. The pain and subsequent lack of feeling assures me that the damage to my right hand is serious, but I have no idea if it is life threatening. I decide to continue with great care, remembering many examples of people stuck in collapsed buildings and the dangers faced when freeing them. I could bleed out. I could be infected by some horrible bacteria. My hand could be the only thing keeping the rest of the room, or building, from collapsing, and freeing myself could cause total devastation. This thought plagues me. While highly unlikely that the building's remaining integrity hinges on my hand's placement, it is possible that the shelves, or part of the tiny room I am in, does. I decide to explore further before attempting manual rescue.

There are at least two small boxes and multiple cans in my line of sight to visually examine my hand in the relative darkness. I feel under the first object with my left index finger, it is a small box, some kind of instant rice or pasta. I push up on the box from below until it falls onto my right forearm and partially across to the other side. I flex the muscle in my forearm to cause the box to fall a bit farther. There are still more objects blocking my view. I repeat this process with two more boxes by my forearm, one of them farther away. I have to move it in stages. I can see that my right hand is down on the shelf, as if resting on it, but there are still some cans and objects nearer to my face and obstructing my view.

The last two boxes are small, light, and shift easily across the shelf to where I can lift them and dump them across my arm by shifting space to space from below with two fingers.

The next object is a large can. I know this can without seeing it: Whole, peeled, San Marzano tomatoes. It is a #10 can, like you would use in a commercial kitchen. I bought this from a restaurant supply store, because I had begun making my own sauce at home.

I was a chef and restaurant manager in my late teens and through my twenties. While I did not win any awards or gain any notoriety, I am skilled in the kitchen and have a good sense for innovation. Recently, Samantha took a new position with her law firm, and received a healthy pay increase to help launch a new, remote, office in the suburbs. She worked in downtown Atlanta as a paralegal for Holly and Fitzgerald for more than a decade when the new opportunity presented itself. Driving to Marietta and back three days a week keeps her from home in the evenings, so I started experimenting in the kitchen more. I have the luxury of working from home. I travel occasionally, but mostly work with data and analytics from my home office. I am a consultant and set my own schedule, so when I find interest in hobbies, or obsessions, I schedule my time to allow for them. Cooking a fresh and creative dish for the three of us every evening is my most recent hobby. I can easily throw a quick meal together, and we can afford to go out, or order in, any time, but I have been increasingly frustrated with food I have been served by restaurants. Because of this, I began planning and developing a menu for my home, not unlike the work I had done in Welbourne's as a promising young chef de cuisine. Store-bought tomato sauces had not been meeting my standard at home, so I started researching and developing my own recipe. The first batch was fine, not great, and I decided that ordinary tomatoes wouldn't do, so I sought out San Marzano's. The second batch was much better, but something was still off. Over time, chefs recognize that certain items, designed for discerning palettes, are only packaged in industrial-grade portions. I knew that my tomatoes would only be the quality I expect from a particular Italian company, only available in #10 cans, found exclusively at a particular supply warehouse. I had just visited last Wednesday, the only day they allow non-members to shop, and I used all of my coercion to secure a single can, broken from a case. They didn't have it priced individually and had to do some creative math to sell it to me. The manager of the distribution warehouse was not the individual I worked with in the past, creating a disconnect regarding my intentions, his willingness to break a case and store policy, and language: Vietnamese versus English. I had just opened the case of 8 cans from the side, where the glue holds the containing cardboard lips sealed, and was carefully removing a single can for inspection when he approached me from behind the racks, spewing verbal assaults. I had no idea what he was saying, all I understood was the occasional "no." I continued reading the label, smiling, and nodding my head, when he snatched it from me, said, "no," and began returning it to the case. He was younger and smaller than me, allowing me to manipulate the can back from him, gently, and hold it out of reach long enough to retrieve my phone and show him the case price divided by eight on the calculator. He spat a few more lines in Vietnamese, that were surely offensive and sprinkled with insult, because some passersby giggled, took out a yellow sticky-note and pen, upon which he wrote the price plus two dollars, something else that I could not read, and stuck it on the can, before turning on his heel and sassy-stomping away. I was satisfied and made my way to checkout.

I had big plans for this can of tomatoes. None of my plans involved moving it 18 inches, with two fingers, through wire rack shelving, from below, forcing it onto my arm and over. It is grueling: Moving the object an inch, or less, at a time, and making numerous futile attempts to clear my right arm before finally getting it atop and shifting my right arm just enough to allow gravity to complete the job. The second to last time I got it up there, it fell back down. But I was so focused on the balancing act, I didn't move my fingers, and the giant can crushed them. It was more disappointing than painful, but the crunch of my digits was the icing on a shame-cake.

Now that the can is gone, I can almost see my entire right hand. I can see to the knuckles, but nothing appears wrong or stuck, it looks like I am loosely holding the shelf.

The only items left in my way are a small jar of artisan jam from my aunt last Christmas and a tall cellulose bag of farfalle pasta.

I check my watch: 3:47 PM. I move the pasta bag, little by little, like every object preceding it. I could have seen without dumping it over my right arm, but I am not going to veer from my process. I finish the task, and note how I have strategically positioned all of the objects at different locations to distribute the bounty evenly and avoid fall-backs. There is now a veritable feast piled along the side of my arm.

I adjust the jam jar so that I have line of sight to my right hand, and bring my watch up to illuminate the area. My middle, ring, and pinky fingers are jammed into adjoining spaces between wires of the shelf. It is ugly. It is confusing. I feel sick.

Suddenly, my watch vibrates and chirps at me. I look at it: "You can still do it!"

It is encouraging me to exercise and hit my move goals.

"Fuck you."

I bring the light back to my hand from beneath and look closer. My pinky is turned at an angle that is not natural. As I stare at it, I start to feel it. It is almost definitely out of joint at the first knuckle and possibly the second as well. It does not appear swollen, which I think is probably not a good thing.

Now my right pinky is screaming pain at me. I focus on my ring finger: swollen at the knuckle, but otherwise intact. I try to wiggle it: nothing.

I consider my middle finger, as it is penetrating part of the way through, just past the first finger joint, no apparent damage. I instruct it to move with my mind, and it twitches. That motion triggers an explosion of pain in my pinky again.

My index finger is laying flat across the top of the shelf along with my thumb. My wrist does not seem to be bent poorly, but it certainly hurts as I move.

I deduce that I fell into the pantry, leaned across the shelf and grabbed hold of the wire rack. When the front left collapsed during the event, the back jutted up and contorted my fingers, trapping them with cross-forces alone. I also figure that I could easily move my hand toward the wall at the appropriate angle, and should be able to simply lift my fingers straight up: easy!

Suddenly, I hear my breath. I hear my pulse. I notice the silence. The screaming sound, that has been distancing, has quieted to unnoticeable. I assume it is still there, but I cannot detect it.

However, my world is not silent. I can hear a droning from outside my cell: a low, grumbling, droning, barely discernible rumble. I look up toward the light coming from above my head and identify a slightly sharper audible tone coming from the light source. I start to consider this phenomenon, but decide that I would be better equipped to investigate if I could, perhaps, move from my current position.

I turn back to my right hand, bring up my left wrist from below to illuminate my project field, and begin shifting my weight forward to force my hand to bend at the wrist, bringing the back of the hand more parallel with the back wall to allow for pinky extraction with less resistance. When I have moved about 2 inches, something shifts inside my hand and a white-hot pain runs up my arm to my face, where it burns, I flush, and break into a sweat. I shift a bit more, something else happens, the pain produces tunnel-vision, and reality seems far away. My eyes shake, my mouth goes dry, and I lose consciousness.

I awaken... again.

Check my watch: 10:18 PM, in the top corner, because the message center says "time to stand!"

It is my watch that wakes me. It vibrates and chirps again, reminding me to stand up.

"Fuck you. I have been standing for two days. I want an award for sitting down, bitch! Let's do this!"

My voice seems rough and weak. It has moved further into my head than before. The droning outside continues and sounds familiar.

I illuminate my right hand again, and consider my options. I know it will require some force to get my ring and middle fingers out, but my pinky is the source of pain. I decide that a quick motion to free all three is the best choice. I start to consider, think, calculate, ponder. Suddenly, I recognize the stupidity in this behavior and take a deep breath, exhale and yank my hand up and toward the wall with everything I can muster. I generate the required force from my shoulders, hit my head on the shelf above from it, see my fingers come free, recognize the limpness of my wrist and pinky and sense the pain running up my arm. I pull my left arm back in, right arm to my face, and then I go dark again.

## Chapter 3

Day 3
Friday
5:32 AM

I regain consciousness and progress through my senses. I am still partially vertical, but half-hunched between the shelves and the spice rack behind me. I am immediately aware of all of the points of contact where my body parts have been pressing on objects in my unconscious state. My legs are shaking.

I hear the droning sound again. No light coming from above now. My watch has entered low battery mode. I can't believe it has lasted this long. I realize that I am free from my binds and I start to move my legs. I am resting my right arm on the fourth shelf. My right hand hurts, so I just leave it. I experiment with putting weight on that arm a little at a time to relieve pressure on my legs. It helps. I try to extract my left arm from below the fourth shelf, but the can dispensers have fallen forward off the shelf and do not leave enough room to bring my arm up. I begin to press my left shoulder against the dispensers to lift them and push them back on the shelf with my left hand and arm. Because its supporting bracket failed, it is leaning down and I can't release it once I adjust, or it will fall.

I get the can dispenser aligned with its original position on the collapsed corner of the fourth shelf and begin lifting. I estimate levelness with my right arm, which I am using to push down on the opposing corner, toward the middle of the back of the shelf, near where my hand was trapped. Once I estimate that it is close to level, I twist my hips to the left, to allow room to lift my left leg, confident now that my right leg, which is below me, and my right arm on the fourth shelf can hold my weight. I bring my left foot onto the edge of the first shelf and have to stop, because this is the first movement of these joints in days and my body is still deciding if it wants to participate in this new challenge or take another untimely nap. I fight through the pain and slowly work to bring my left foot up to the second shelf. Now my left knee is screaming at me, and my left ankle feels like I have been hobbled. I repeat this process, with a slight lean away to bring my foot atop the third shelf. I slowly pivot my hip back toward the shelving, and gently bring the fourth shelf, with the can dispensers, that I am still holding with my left hand and arm, down onto my left knee. I lift it again and adjust my left leg, repeat until the shelf is resting in a way that I can tolerate for now. This is not how I planned it. I had hoped my leg would perfectly span the distance between shelf three and four to keep it level, but I have to lower shelf four significantly to rest it. I need another plan and I'm not sure how long I can tolerate this position.

"This is the dumbest game of Twister I have ever played."

I chuckle. That was clever. I bring my left arm back, grab the pantry door handle behind me again to confirm that it will not budge. I bring my left arm on top of the fourth shelf, wriggle beside the can dispensers, and bow my head in a soft nook between both my biceps to breathe and rest a moment.

I decide to start shifting the can dispensers to the right, to counterbalance the shelf and free myself. I move my left arm over to the left side. I use the palm of my right hand, index finger and thumb to pull and wiggle on one side, and my whole left hand on the opposite side of the three can dispensers to start sliding them to the right, one wire of the shelf at a time, due to the weight and limited space. It is heavy, full of cans, but this is working. When I complete crossing the space where my right arm had been, originally, I start moving all of the items that I had shifted across my arm previously, over to the left side of the racks. I leave the can of tomatoes and force it toward the back right corner by pushing it and leaning into it until it will not move any further. I ignore the sensations of crushing and smashing other objects behind it. This creates another foot of space, roughly, so I repeat the process of moving the racks rightward again, methodically. After three moves, the shelf begins lifting off of my left knee. One more move and it lurches back onto its right rear bracket in the wall. I decide to move it once more before extracting my support-leg.

I close my eyes.

My watch chirps and I startle awake. I look at it, and it reads: "heart rate is dangerously high," and switches to an animated graphic of my pulse and the number "168."

Then the screen goes black.

I lay my head down on my left arm and close my eyes.

The droning sound is still there. But now I can make out an occasional "clank," very faintly. With my eyes still closed, I try to imagine what it might be.

I shoot upright: the generator!

That is the industrial generator on the office building in my complex. It is just across the driveway, ground floor, by the entrance to building 2. It is a commercial/industrial generator that I am familiar with hearing whenever the power goes out or when the technician services it twice a year and runs it for several hours. It is relatively quiet for its size and is certainly a diesel engine, judging by the base-tank, the exhaust, and the smell. The whole unit is about 8 feet tall, and likely provides life safety emergency backup power to the office building. It must utilize an automatic transfer switch that senses when the power is out and starts the unit. The clanking is the rain cap on the exhaust, meaning the flow is starting to fluctuate, and I assume that it is either running out of fuel or suffering some mechanical challenges from running for so long. As soon as I manifest this realization, the droning sound suddenly increases in pitch, slightly, and then reduces tone for about 20 seconds, surges a few times, and the large diesel engine sputters to a stop. I hear a final "clank" as the rain cap slaps closed.

I listen for a bit and hear nothing else. I can, again, hear my own pulse and breath. I lay my head back down on my arm and close my eyes. The silence takes me almost instantly.

This time: I sleep.

I awaken with a start. My knee hurts. My neck hurts. My hand hurts. I check my watch: dead.

Then, I remember that my phone is in my pocket. My right pocket, always. I know my personal phone is there, but I am not sure about my work phone. I bring my right arm, that is still on the shelf in front of me, back and to the right, pointing my elbow into the hinge corner of the door and then gently descend my hand down my chest and belly to my belt. I hook my thumb into my belt, and start moving my hand toward my pocket. My right hand is now throbbing with pain, assuredly from the blood rushing to it. I slide my thumb and index finger into my pants pocket and grasp the top of my new iPhone. I carefully slide the phone out of my pocket and begin bringing it up to the shelf. I slide the corner of it onto the fourth shelf, just below my chin, and push it the rest of the way. I bring my right hand up, then my arm, rest my arm on the shelf, and hook my hand around to allow for screen access. I touch the screen: nothing. I tap it hard in the center and it comes to life. The sudden light blinds me, and my vision goes completely white for a moment, before dissolving into clarity from the outer edges of my field of view to the middle, taking at least 30 seconds. It is my lock screen, an image of a random galaxy imaged by some super-computer. There are notifications: lots of notifications. The service indicator across the top is just dots, but says "ER," meaning there is no cellular service, but I can still call emergency services. I hold the power button on the side until it gives me the option to call emergency services, and I slide the bar to do so. It goes to the call screen and idles there for about three minutes, then indicates, "call failed."

I check the time: 11:34 AM.

I check the battery level: close to 75%.

God bless this new technology. I go into my settings, to look for the SAT-Phone options, but lose interest and decide it is wise to shut it off and come back to it.

The light from above me is there again. I decide to plan a few projects and work on them methodically. That's how I climbed the corporate ladder and how I approach any daunting task I face. I decide that my overall goals are:

1. Escape from this room, or

2. Survive until I can be rescued, if I cannot get out.

Since the door is not opening easily, I decide that making room to sit is my first short-term objective and investigating the space is second.

I quickly develop a plan to remove everything from the bottom two shelves and try to lift the shelves enough to sit on the floor or remove them altogether. My hand hurts. All of my joints are aching and have blasts of pain that force me to move them, if possible, but my right pinky is throbbing, the related wrist is aching, and I fear that I will need these to execute other tasks. I re-evaluate my objectives and decide it may be wise to investigate my injuries first. I pull my right arm out from the shelf, over to my side, and raise it up, toward the ceiling, being careful not to get it caught on anything. I aim for where the light seems to be coming from, and it provides enough to generate a silhouette of my hand. I can see that my pinky is swollen now, near the hand, and points away from its adjacent finger at an awkward angle. I have dislocated it. While I have it up there, I try to identify where this light is coming from. I start to notice that there is significant structural damage to the walls of the pantry. I am standing just inside an ordinary, hollow, wooden, closet door that has wire shelving hung from the inside of it, facing the shelving of the pantry in front of me. The shelves behind me go the entire height of the door, but only down the middle of the door. There is equal space on either side. The depth of the shelves in front of me is shorter than my outstretched arm, hand, and fingers. I am 5'10," 185 pounds, and there is enough space for my body between the rack hung on the door and the main shelving. The space on either side of the door shelves allows a bit more play when attempting to make stunted maneuvers. I can turn my head and look up with ease. There is something protruding through the sheet rock in the top left corner of my space. It is above the door and has pushed through the ceiling, and perhaps part of the wall, as it seems to be at or near the corner of the door wall and ceiling intersection. This is where the light is coming from, seemingly near the edge of the object where it meets the ceiling. The thing is light in color and has some reflective quality that augments my perception of it. I have never actually investigated the ceiling of my pantry, but I know there is a good bit of space above the top shelf. The object is pushed in about 8-10 inches at the apex and appears to be rounded. With only dim light behind it, I become frustrated from squinting to discern what the object could be. I abandon and conclude that it gives me enough light to do general work in the room and I can try to sort out its identity later.

I decide that I better get to work while I have some light in the room, remembering that it was not present early in the morning, so I assume it must be sunlight. My plan is simple: relocate all objects from the floor and the bottom two shelves to higher shelves, and attempt to remove the lower shelves so I can sit down. Fuck me. I want to sit down worse than I have ever wanted to sit down in my life. My pragmatic side insists that I take inventory and organize my supplies while in the process, and my exhausted side decides to oblige, but to focus on clearing a seat.

Box of Lucky Charms: Samantha loves these things. She claims she only buys them when they're on sale, but that would suggest that they are on sale every week.

I have not yet mentioned the yearning for my partner that burns inside me. I have, thus far, taken for granted that one might assume I miss my wife and partner in all things, but that would not approach the explanation necessary to understand how I yearn for her when she is not near me. I saw her Tuesday morning when she left for work. It was 7:35-ish and she was running late. I wish it had been the morning that she was late because I awoke with a desire to fuck and executed a not-so-subtle maneuver to let my partner know my intentions which she, as always, succumbed to, delaying her morning routine, but it wasn't. She was late because she dilly-dallies. I get it, she does not love the commute, and is not in love with her current responsibility or professional location. But she is loyal and committed to her career, so she will see her promise through. She looked amazing Tuesday morning. Because she was running late, she had her hair in a ponytail and barely wore any makeup. That is my favorite way. I am at an age where I can still get an erection, do so often, and easily for my beautiful wife, but find myself less compelled to initiate a physical encounter. I am also in good health, so keeping up is no problem. Right now, I am not missing her sexually, but intimately. It is likely because I am injured and she is very good at mending me, and our son, which is her second full-time job. I wish I could say that Nathaniel is the primary cause of strife concerning injury, but I win that award every year. He is perpetually sick, so that takes care of any free time my Samantha may have hoped for.

My name is Samuel: my wife and I are both named "Sam." We met in college, at Georgia Tech, and joked, immediately, about how funny it would be if we dated. There was a social trend at the time, to combine the names of the two people in a relationship into one name, like: "Scoffany," for Scott and Tiffany. When our circle discovered that there was a secret "thing" happening between us, they were forced to be creative, because we had successfully evaded the go-to relationship sass, and they, instead, decided to refer to us as "The Sams."

"Did you invite The Sams?"

"Are The Sams going to get their own place next year?"

"Have you heard The Sams having sex? It sounds like a bar fight!" *(No one ever said that)*

Samantha was a year ahead of me, although only 6 months older. She was a sophomore when we were introduced at a social mixer on campus. I was a freshman, still attending every event intended to ease the awkwardness of first-year American College students. Campus Life mixers, sponsored by clubs and groups, were recruiting events, but also opportunities to meet and mingle. Mixers utilize games and activities, none of which interested me, but when a stunningly beautiful woman asks you to be her partner, you either find your wits, quickly, or suffer stinging regret.

I was watching some other situation, when she slid, curiously, into my space. The music was loud, she was already pretty close to me, but leaned in further, to my left ear, and asked, "do you stretch?" My immediate assumption was that my friends were playing a joke on me, but I was witty enough to respond with, "of course I do! Why? Did you pull something? Or are you planning to?" She leaned back and presented the first of many looks that I would come to adore, this one asking, "oh really?"

"Good," she said, "I need a stretchy partner to help me win this next one!"

"Next one what?"

"They are about to start another game over there, and the winners get insulated coffee cups and Starbucks gift cards, so I need you to help me win."

"I really hate these games, what do I have to do?"

"Something about a balloon and no hands."

"That sounds terrible. Tell you what: If we win, you have to spend the gift cards with me."

"Alone?"

I thought I had blown it. "No, with our parents. Yes! Alone!"

"Like a date?"

"Sure. But I was just thinking coffee. I don't even know you!"

"Strange way to ask a girl on a date, but I will have coffee with you either way."

"Even better. Can we just go now?"

"Nope. I liked you when you were willing to help me. Game or no coffee."

"Deal."

"Just imagine how willing I could be if we win!"

Then she winked at me and smiled a big, friendly smile. I remember thinking that her face was the most inviting visage I had ever experienced. The attraction was not physical at first, I was truly captivated. The conversation felt like the casual meeting of old friends: jovial and loose. After the game, the physical infatuation was solidified. Samantha had calmly recruited me into an event that I would never have volunteered for otherwise. We had to put our hands behind our backs, hold an under-inflated balloon between each other's knees, work the balloon up to our crotches, and then pop the item with no hands. When I caught my friend Andrew's face in the crowd while they were demonstrating the rules, and he realized what I was about to do, and with whom, the open-jaw expression he returned was epic. I spent the next minutes maneuvering into an extremely intimate position with the most beautiful human I had ever been close to. I was focused on the balloon, our legs, and my positioning, when I noticed she was not really helping. I looked up, caught her gaze, and realized that she was just staring at me.

"What?"

"Nothing. I'm just kind of impressed by you."

"What did I do?"

"I don't know, but now I really want to win."

We assumed our decided positions, and when the judge blew the airhorn signaling us to start, we began working our bodies in synchronized motion, as if rehearsed. I do not remember any of the other participants. I could not tell you what I was wearing. I have no memory of time or other details, but I remember that she was in a light blue tank-top, khaki shorts, white tennis shoes, and I could see her flesh-colored bra straps peeking out at me. Her hair was in a hasty ponytail and she wore very little makeup. Strangely, we began gyrating, looked up, made eye-contact, and held our mutual gaze the entire performance. I saw her blue eyes and all of the glittery reflections within them, and I fell in love. I did not know it then, but I was hers. Our movements brought the balloon to crotch-placement in mere moments, and we began cross-thrusting toward one-another and dragging our bodies sideways across the object like professionals. I like to imagine that the audience was uncomfortable, because our first intimate experience was in front of hundreds of our peers. But we didn't know, nor care. We were alone, locked in gaze, rubbing and gyrating at the hips until the balloon popped, throwing us together at the waist. Suddenly, we were very close, and I remember feeling her breast against me and understanding something primal and unspoken. Her face was right before mine. She turned away, I tensed, completely disconnected from the actual scene, and worried about us, not the game. She saw that the other participants were still working their bodies on either side of us, stepped back, raised her hands, smiled wide, and screamed, "Yes!"

We won. I transitioned to reality quickly and took in the whole situation. Noise returned and I processed what had just happened.

"Holy shit!"

"We won!"

I was lost for anything clever or appropriate, so I repeated, "holy shit!"

She threw her arms around my neck and kissed my lips in celebration. It was not passionate, but it was significant.

We spent that day and evening together, talking, laughing, and, later, drinking. We did not solidify the relationship that day, but we honored our promise to a coffee date that week, after much anticipation. We kissed on our first date, a lot. We scheduled a second date for the next day, she invited me to her dorm room while she finished getting ready, and she kissed me again, as soon as I was in the room. That kiss led to sex, and our second date was spent in a single bed, talking, fucking, and not watching whatever was on her television. We went to Waffle House around 3 AM, and I knew that I had met my match.

Three cans of Coke Zero: We don't drink Coke Zero, but my Mother-in-law does, and we bought them the last time she was over. Nathaniel said he would drink them, but since they are right in front of him, he doesn't see them hidden in plain sight. Unless I put them in the refrigerator, they will live on my pantry floor for all eternity, like some sad homage to capitalism and gluttony.

One already-opened case of Top Ramen containing 3 units. They appear to be beef-flavored, but I do not look carefully at this moment, I just want to sit down. Ramen Noodles are likely the greatest equalizer in American society today. It does not matter how wealthy you are, you are not above instant Ramen, or a cup of noodles, and you likely have some in your home. I cannot personally attest for the uber-wealthy, because they do not invite me over for noodles very often, or at all. Our household participates in this behavior. My 11-year-old has been preparing his own Ramen since he was four. He was nine when he could finally navigate the removal of the bowl from the microwave without assistance or disaster. At ten, we really fucked with him, and swapped the plastic packs for cups of noodles, and he had quite the disaster microwaving the styrofoam/paper cup because he didn't read the directions. I pause as I pick up the box, picturing my child's face, and cry. I stare at the packs of Ramen in my hand, crying, not sobbing, but tears coming steadily, and imagine him walking through the door. At this point, I have experienced a few moments where my mind has tried to unpack what had happened, and I consciously told myself not to do that. That part is coming, I'm no dummy, but I need to get in a better head space and be ready for that mind-fuck.

Yes: I'm preparing to fuck myself, directly in the mind.

Plastic gallon jug with handle of distilled white vinegar, 1/3 full: my only thought is that I can clean with this. I'm not sure if it was a trend, or if the internet caught onto something people have been doing for years, but recently, everybody was making dilutions of vinegar and cleaning their homes with it. What's worse, is that they were writing about it everywhere online and talking about it in casual conversation. We tried it, immediately rejected the scent, and never did it again, to my knowledge. I am perfectly happy cleaning with chemicals, and not smelling like a pickle jar afterward.

One jar of coconut oil, raw, no idea the size, but it is almost full: this is a great thing. We purchased an expensive brand, in a large size, because we were using it for sensual massage. It is almost full, because we just don't have very much time to give long massages and have drawn-out sexual encounters these days. But the stuff smells great and is an amazing personal lubricant. Plus, it's edible and packed with nutrients. I make an intentional note of this resource.

One empty plastic cereal container. I assume this was going to house the Lucky Charms soon, but I plan to keep it empty until I absolutely need it. Samantha prefers to keep cereal in a container, because the bag never gets rolled and closed properly, so we have a few of these. I assume I will find another one as I continue.

I have been moving all of the floor objects, thus far, to the top shelf. I have been shifting other items over to make room, but not taking inventory. The top shelf is mostly overstock items: condiments, baking goods, and other random objects. There are some cooking utensils and three Rubbermaid containers, about 12"x4"x4", that I have lined up, so that I can place other objects on top of them. I do not open them or investigate, although I know most of the contents. I decide that they could be a simple amusement later.

I try to reach down to the bottom right, where the first shelf has bent slightly upward, and there is an object on the ground beside me to my right, blocking access to the floor beneath the shelf. It is fabric, and I can't see it, so I run my hand across the top, where I recognize a zipper, and a cloth handle, and exclaim, "oh shit! That's right!" It is my briefcase. Currently known as a laptop bag, it is soft, black fabric, with tough synthetic fiber handles, multiple compartments, and straps. It really is a pretty nice bag. Samantha bought it for me when I was last promoted at work, and I had texted her, with great excitement. I was in Savannah, Georgia, where my company is headquartered. She got home that day, picked up Nathaniel, and they went shopping. The story they told me: They saw the bag at the department store, and knew that it was the perfect gift, that it was "so Sam." This is not what happened. Samantha loves me, but she is terrible at picking things for me, and Nathaniel, that day, was not presenting helpful suggestions, according to Bryan. Bryan is one of my closest friends. He was my roommate at Tech, freshman and sophomore years, before The Sams got their own place. Bryan has fabulous taste, is very fashionable, and always has a great mind for how to flatter someone. Samantha, wisely, asked Bryan what to do. Nathaniel adores his Uncle B, so the three of them took a little trip to the mall. Nathaniel was thrilled, Samantha was not, but Bryan, being the great voice of reason, reminded her that The Apple Store is at this mall, so she could likely find something there for herself, if not for me. That sealed the deal. Bryan told me this story later, over drinks, because he could not help but take credit for convincing my wife to spend a small fortune that day. He waited until I had received the gift, and took me for drinks. Two tequila shots and he "just had to tell me" this tale. But the man is wise. He told my wife and child that I am impossible to shop for because I don't want things, and if I do, I just go buy them. I have everything I need, so you will never think of that. His solution was the fact that I am very practical, and quite frugal with needs, so I never splurge on "fancy" items. I research the market and purchase the most practical item that is reasonably priced. I do not bargain or discount shop for necessities, because I certainly value quality, so the only way to really "wow" me, according to my devious friend, would be to buy me something practical, but very nice, because I would never do that myself, but would appreciate the quality, if well-chosen. I did not need a new bag for work, but my jaw dropped when they presented this to me. It really is the nicest "bag" I have ever owned, and is practical in every way one could hope for, except its price: roughly $900. When I looked it up the next day, I almost spit my tea out. "Surely she didn't actually pay that." But yes, she did. I never asked her or brought it up, but Nathaniel knew, because he slipped up and bragged about it where I could hear him once. She also bought herself a new phone case and iPad, plus got Nathaniel earbuds and a hat. Bryan was rewarded with a bottle of cologne that he always says he loves when I wear it (he sits next to me all night and nuzzles his face into my neck, breathing deep and sighing). Samantha was not threatened by the behavior between Bryan and I, that was not the reason, but when he asked her to show it to him that day, so he could come back for it later, he made that face of satisfaction just smelling it from the bottle, and she bought it for him. He swears he didn't ask for it, but it wouldn't matter if he did. I just made him promise that he would still snuggle me.

He promised.

My bag will prove to contain many important items, and I just repacked it Tuesday, knowing that I was to take a trip Wednesday, so there is no need to rummage through it now. I place it on the fourth shelf, just to the left of the can dispensers. It slides into its new home perfectly, and stays upright, as an obnoxiously overpriced bag should, damnit.

One box of saltine crackers, with one of four sleeves left, half eaten, and secured with a sloppy twist and a chip-bag-clip, that is the same width as the final sleeve is tall with crackers. This is all Nathaniel. He loves crackers, but refuses to put them away or consolidate. We are using a whole box to store a single bag clip, essentially, because the crackers will be stale, but I won't care if needed: To the top shelf it goes.

This thought leads me back to that dark place: That place where my imagination runs a short film of Nathaniel walking through the front door after school. The place where I question how long I have been in this space and he had not come through the door outside of my pantry-home, because I would have heard him. I start to wonder if he is in some similar situation, thinking about me, and shake my head hard enough to hurt my neck. But the act works and the pain from my neck causes the vision to dissolve, like pixels, into the blackness of my minds eye.

The color of the light from the mystery object in the ceiling has changed. It is tinting toward an orange tone, but no color of sunlight that I am used to. If it is sunlight, it has a strange hue. I take this as a sign that I am losing daylight. Fortunately, as I run my foot under the bottom shelf, it does not strike anything. But I can't see, so I retrieve the phone from the shelf and make the decision to turn it on and use the flashlight, briefly, to investigate the project area. I will also check the time, and try to make a call for help again. The phone boots quickly, because it is very new, and I am blinded by the artificial light coming from the screen. It is so bright. The wallpaper is a picture of my family. I stare at it for a moment and remember my goal.

Check the time: 6:22 PM.

Open the flashlight app, turn it on. Holy shit that's bright. Turn it off. I decide to use the light from the screen. This phone can stay on for days, so this may be the most efficient method. I turn the screen to the ground, but the items on the first and second shelf are blocking my view. There does not appear to be anything, but I can see the damage to the wall, floor, and bottom shelf. The wall to my right has been forced in at the bottom. There are various cracks and chunks of drywall have fallen out all the way up the wall. The floor and the bottom 12–14 inches of wall have been forced inward, bending the bottom shelf down at the edge where it meets the wall, and up, approximately 4 inches in. The bend in the shelf is uneven and is raised about 2 inches. The floor beneath has buckled. It looks like rolling hills in places. The other side of this wall is the open space that was our foyer. The back wall is also damaged and almost looks crushed, like a giant hand grabbed it by the top and bottom and squeezed, just enough to crack in multiple places. One large piece of wall is missing, exposing the face of a metal stud behind it, just enough for me to see what it is. I always assumed this building utilized galvanized steel studs and this confirms my assumption.

I realize that I have been investigating the walls and the damage, but my feet and legs are killing me. I need to focus on the shelf. I will try the phone again later. I set it down on the fourth shelf and reach for the next item, but I catch my pinky on the second shelf on the way down and bend it away from my hand. It offers little resistance, because it is dislocated, now confirmed. I have been very careful until now, and this mistake is critical. The pain does not feel like typical forms of pain. The injury has been throbbing and hot ever since I removed it from the shelving, but my wrist and other digits were feeling much better, or they had gone numb. While hastily descending with the yoga-like maneuver that has proven successful thus far: Raising the opposite leg to the side (the only place it could go) and folding at the hip, slightly bending the supporting knee, all while holding on to the shelf with the non-active hand. This motion has become fluid and natural in both directions from working with the floor objects, which made me cocky, and I let my guard down. I actually recognize resistance in my arm and shoulder before I feel anything in my hand, but when I do, my eyes roll back, I groan, and my right knee buckles. I fall down in a space that I can hardly stand up in, and I fall hard. It is so sudden that my face strikes the fourth shelf, hard, on my way down, my right leg wedges atop the second shelf, my left leg comes back down but does nothing to support me, and I fall back against the spice shelf in the door, and then to the left. I acknowledge hitting my face and I bring my left arm toward it, instinctively. I lose all sense of gravitational direction, my left elbow hits the wall to my left, pushing my hand and arm past my head, causing a slight roll to the right, and I strike the left wall with the back left of my head, toward the top. Again: I hit it hard. There is no room for me to fall to the floor in this position, so I am wedged, contorted, and lose consciousness. I can remember the fall and I recall the jolt when my head hit the wall. If you have ever hit your head hard, you know the feeling: Like a sound you feel in your neck that spawns an immediate headache and you don't even feel the impact location until later. I lose consciousness immediately.

I feel my hand first, and then my head. I realize I am awake and recognize serious pain in multiple places. My eyes are still closed, because my head hurts so bad, I am afraid that there may be something sitting on me, and I would rather not see it.

Then something hits my face and I open my eyes.

Then it happens again: something hits my face, not hard, not heavy. I realize there is something on my face. When it happens again, I conclude that something is dripping and it is dripping right onto my face. I am able to move, but not easily. I can see, and I immediately worry that I have slept the entire night. Then I realize that my phone is still on. It is fancy and new, and only goes fully to sleep, screen off, after a long while. But it is still producing some light from the screen. Another drop on my face. I have shifted slightly, so this one hits my nose, while the others have landed on my right cheek. I try to grab a shelf with my right hand, but even using my thumb and index finger makes my pinky and hand hurt, so I stop. My left arm is crossed in front of me and upward, so I withdraw it to my left side, and reach down. I expect to find the floor, but my angle causes me to find the bottom shelf instead. I push off enough to get my left leg back under me and press upward. As I pry my head off the wall, another drop hits me in the right eye.

I do not suffer from mysophobia (fear of germs), but I do consider the high potential for contaminants, since I do not know what the substance is. I notice that it stings on impact, but then my eye waters, and the sting dissipates almost immediately. I continue to shimmy up to my standing position. Both legs are down after bringing my right knee out of the shelf again.

The phone is still on.

Check the time: 1:01 AM.

It is now Saturday.

## CHAPTER 4

Day 4

Phone battery is hovering at 55/60%. I have another phone also. It is in my bag. It is in the smaller outside pocket, in a special compartment, just for fancy phones. I decide to turn it off. I remove it carefully and see that I received a text from my colleague on Tuesday. I do not read it, I just turn the phone off and put it back. It is at approximately 20% battery, but I do not waste it looking for specifics, I just put it back in its fancy little home.

I pick up my personal phone to plot my next move and see that I am shaking. I realize that my whole body is shaking. I am trembling. I am not cold, so this must be weakness, shock, or something else. I need to sit down soon. I take quick inventory of the bottom shelf and decide to turn my phone off to save the battery.

In this new darkness, my hearing improves. This is true dark. There is absolutely no light. I stare and shift my gaze, expecting an image to manifest, but my eyes just begin creating bits of light. I know that there is no real light and my brain is going to provide some fun visuals. I hear a sound outside my cell. It is a constant sound. It is a familiar sound. I begin unbuttoning my shirt. I am donning a dress shirt over a t-shirt and I do not need both. I unbutton all of the front buttons, and begin to wriggle out of the shirt, left hand and arm first, working it backwards and leaning into the shelves. I let it fall across my back when freed and bring my right arm, carefully, across my body, and meet my left hand in front of me. I take the right sleeve cuff in my left hand and start removing my right arm very slowly. I am shaking more now and there seems to be a revolving pain making its way around my body. Once the sleeve is almost off, I grab the shoulder stitch with my thumb and index finger of my right hand, and start gently wrapping the soft material around my right hand.

"That shit ain't gonna happen again."

The pain is intense every time I wrap across my pinky, but I inflict minimal pressure, just enough to stay in place and to keep my pinky against my ring finger.

The trembling continues, but with my right hand protected, and unusable, I start working with my left to clear the bottom shelf, in the dark.

I had looked across the items before going dark, so I plan to use my memory and feel what the object is. Then I will just move it hastily up to the second shelf, because I posture that I can sit with only the bottom shelf removed. I start on the far left.

More cereal: a container with about 10% left. I think it is some sort of bran cereal, maybe with berries in it. I don't eat much cereal, but I enjoy it when I do. I have a problem with eating too much and feeling horrible, which is likely the reason I tend to avoid it. Taking a box of cereal and milk to the couch with a bowl and spoon is going to be a stomachache, and nurse Samantha will have to fill me up with bismuth and soda water. I never ask for it, she can read me, like a ridiculous book. She will sit down beside me and say, "what is it?" If I am going through some type of stress or emotional situation, she will watch from the sidelines and point out my behavior once the chaos settles a bit. But if it is physical, she sees it, often before I know. My sloppy hand wrap could use her cleverness right now. She would certainly know exactly what to do.

3 unopened boxes of frosted mini wheats: these are not consumed in a bowl with milk. We eat them like a snack: straight to the mouth, perhaps taken with you in a snack bag on a trip. My memory can only account for two, but there must have been a great sale.

A glass jar of popcorn, 1/2 full: I prefer popping corn on the stove, in a pot, with olive oil and salt. Samantha prefers microwave popcorn, heavy butter and salt, but does not like it at the movie theater, or non-microwave style. She has also been known to sprinkle ranch powder on it. We consume borderline-unhealthy amounts of popcorn. Nathaniel likes mom's better than mine, even though I make it how his "Sugy" (pronounced: "shUh-GEE," short for "Sugar," short for "Sugar Mama"), my mother, prefers it. My mother is a simple woman and my love for popcorn comes from her. It is like her magic trick, one of her great mysteries: she almost always has popcorn, somehow. Even if we are out somewhere, she carries a little brown bag of popcorn. Cooks it fresh, every day, and multiple times a day to ensure freshness. She will not eat, or serve, "old" popcorn (meaning more than two hours out of the oil). She has experimented with other oils, but swears by extra-virgin olive oil and none of that "fancy shit." Samantha and Nathaniel will eat my popcorn, if they are desperate.

2.5 boxes of microwave popcorn, "movie theater butter" style: this is theirs. I try not to use the microwave if I can avoid it. Sometimes, it just makes sense, but I always try not to. I certainly do not prepare meals in the microwave, unless they are microwave-specific meals. I enjoy being actively engaged in the cooking process, not watching it through a weird little window. I am particular about some things and this is why I have taken over the kitchen.

7 fruit and grain breakfast bars: grab and go for anyone. I'm sure these are not actually healthy, but they are better than Pop-Tarts. They appear to have fallen from the shelf above.

One sleeve of Ritz crackers, unopened. I find that Americans can be categorized by their food preferences. Cracker preference is one clear segregator. We can all sit at the table together, but if Club, Saltine, and Ritz crackers appear, the tribes will form instantly. If there is a dish that calls for crackers, the water gets much muddier. I love Ritz. I almost always prefer Ritz, and I am shocked, and quietly offended, if they are not offered when crackers are required. But you only put a raw oyster on a Saltine, if that is how you eat them. I slurp them straight, but if I do use a cracker, it's a Saltine, and you don't fuck with that. Samantha prefers Saltines. She will not eat crackers as a snack or meal, but if soup or chili is served, you better bring the Saltines and butter. I, too, will eat myself sick on Saltines and butter. I have also been known to slide a sardine onto a Saltine. Nathaniel likes crackers. He is not particular. If you ask which he prefers, the answer changes every time, but he typically eats the Saltines first, then the Ritz in our house. He gets pretty excited when there are Club crackers at a table, but I think that is simply because children get excited about small, single-serving items, in general. He drinks half-and-half shots at the diner, eats every pack of crackers at the table if someone orders soup at a restaurant, and would likely eat the sugar, and "not-sugar," packs if anyone would let him.

One fruit roll up: this is Samantha's. If left to her own devices, she would eat breakfast food and elementary school brown-bag-lunch items for every meal. God, I adore that woman.

Three unopened packs of paper napkins: yes, the fancy ones. They were on sale and Samantha knows I prefer the heavier ones. I suspect these may come in handy.

The bottom shelf is clear. I feel around with my hand to be sure, but I discover nothing. I lift the front lip with my left hand, but it is wedged from all the damage. I stand up straight and pull up on the lip with my left foot first. It budges, but does not break free of its brackets. There is a plastic bracket in either wall, that the front lip of the shelf sits in and snaps into place. I switch to my right foot, still won't free. I move my foot over to the right wall and lift: nothing. I do the same with the left foot, feel it budge substantially and pull up hard with my foot. The left lip breaks loose: now I can get the rest. I reach down and pull the left corner up, slide my left leg forward, still planted on the ground, hold the shelf up with my left shin, and kick the center-right hard with my right foot. The right front lip of the shelf then breaks free and I feel that it can lift easily. I hoped it would fold up, still mounted to the back wall, and it does.

Now I can sit. It still takes great focus to determine how to contort my body to fit under the second shelf. The simplest method is to move my body into the space to my left, where there is no spice rack, but the door handle may provide additional leverage. I move my back as far to the left as possible, and begin sliding down the wall while simultaneously lifting the bottom shelf with my shins as I descend and walk my feet forward. My business shoes have poor grip, so when I am about a foot off the ground, my feet slide out into the corner and I fall the rest of the way to the ground on my ass. I never even use the door handle. There is just enough space for me to sit in the front left corner and extend my legs into the back right corner. When I lower my knees to the ground, the shelf descends over my legs, but does not fall completely back to its original position, because of the displaced wall.

If human legs could breathe, mine would exhale a long sigh of relief in this moment. There are a few seconds of relief, peace, and calm before my brain processes the negative feelings again. Then, all of the muscles in my legs begin to complain at once. They have been supporting my weight for almost four days. My other joints are whispering complaints also.

Just as I am taking inventory of my chorus of sensations, the liquid drips onto my head again. This time on top of my head. I decide to take some inventory. I start by touching and rubbing my thighs with my left hand. I explore while hoping to ease the pain also. I am feeling with my hand to determine if there are any injuries I am not aware of yet. The muscles are tight, and massaging them feels good. I lean my head back against the wall, slide my tailbone forward, bend my knees slightly, and feel the place where I hit the back of my head. Another drop falls on my forehead and I fall asleep.

I become aware again. Something hits my face, my body is in pain, but there is no specific source right away, just general pain. The ringing is gone and it is replaced by the sound of my breathing. There is some light in the pantry, coming from the hole in the ceiling, which also seems to be where the liquid is dripping from. My face is wet. I have some other discomfort that I cannot identify, but it feels like a sickness. It's not pain. It is

deep inside and growing. My mouth is dry: I am thirsty. I
recognize the horrible thirst and understand that I may actually
be at the critical stage of dehydration. I look around for a
solution. The second shelf is still full of items, but I have not yet
inventoried them. My phone is up on the fourth shelf, I know
there are drinks on the fifth shelf that I relocated. The second
shelf is usually for breakfast foods. I can see the unopened boxes
of fruit and grain bars, and the one on its side that is the source
of the three that fell to shelf one that I have relocated. There are
fruit and nut bars. I see cylinders in the back that I know to be
instant oats, but there is also a pile of single-serve, plastic, fruit
cups: the kind that are preserved in sugar water, or just water,
depending on the brand. This is the remedy. I lean forward and
try to ignore the shooting pains that I am starting to notice. I
reach for the cups and realize that my hand is wrapped in a shirt,
so I reach across my body with my left hand, shaking
uncontrollably, and grab the closest one. I hold it tightly around
the base and bring it to my mouth. The place of the lip with the
tab for opening is away from me, but I simply tilt it toward me,
take the lip in my mouth, and work the hard plastic until the thin
membrane separates from the cup under my top teeth and bite
down on it. Then I pull the cup away with a wiggling motion
until I can sense the seal separate, I hear it inhale, feel the cup
inflate a bit, and smell something wonderful, which is the return
of my olfactory system. I don't bother with full removal. I release
the lid from my teeth, turn the cup in my left hand until I can
access the opening and drink from the space. The sweet liquid
feels thick and warm at first, but doesn't want to make it to my
throat, because I have no saliva. There are small bits of fruit in it,
so I, instinctively, start chewing the liquid. I swallow a tiny bit,

work some more, then swallow a bit more. A warmth radiates into my face from my mouth. I finish this sip and pour a bit more into my mouth. These amounts are likely less than half of a teaspoon. I work the, mostly liquid, material again and swallow, then repeat. The third sip goes straight to my throat, then a fourth. Now the liquid does not pour like I want, so I close my lips around the opening and suck as much juice out as I can. I never remove my mouth between attempts until I am getting air, with each portion containing less liquid and more air and fruit bits. The taste is amazing, sweet and soft, almost thick. It reminds me of nectarine juice, but I know these aren't nectarines. This must be the sugar water version. The warmth has spread to my neck, and it crosses my clavicles down my front now. This excites me, so I bite the film again and tear the lid a bit further away from the lip. The cup is about halfway open now. I pull my legs toward me a bit and wiggle my back up the wall. Another drop hits the top of my head. I bring the cup up and shake some fruit into my mouth. It is oranges, just mandarin oranges. The texture of mandarin oranges from a plastic cup is distinct so there is no other possibility. They are soft and warm and I can feel each juice follicle explode with nourishment. They burst and release refreshment and I am able to enjoy each one. Swallowing the fibrous remains after masticating most of the liquid out is more challenging, and it feels like my throat is smaller than before. I repeat this process three more times, truly enjoying it. I have finished more than half of the cup when my chest signals that something is wrong. There is a strange tightness. I recognize this feeling: it is my esophagus. I suffer from gastro-esophageal-reflux, so I am intimately familiar with sensations from my esophagus. This feeling is commonly referred to in my family as "slow-chest." I typically experience this after bouts of severe reflux, when my esophagus is inflamed, and I do not masticate well enough. The food gets "stuck" and it feels like I am choking, but still breathing. Your brain panics a bit and there is nothing much you can do. I tell myself to relax, knowing that my organs have gone to sleep, so the muscles required to move the food are not awake yet. The liquid can just pour through, but the solids need some assistance. When you sleep, parts of your digestive system sleep also. I believe it is some evolutionary development that prevents us from shitting ourselves throughout our lives, so now I must wait, uncomfortably, for the system to reset. I feel a warmth in my gut and know that is the liquid reaching my stomach. It intensifies and becomes a burning pain. But as it does, the problem in my chest reduces, and I feel the food moving down. Once it passes the uncomfortable location, I begin to eat the oranges again. I repeat the process until it is gone, then I tear the rest of the plastic film off and lick the cup clean. When I pull the cup away from my face to investigate my thoroughness, I see that I left something on its lip. Something dark, that I know was not there before, because I inspected it carefully before licking it, as one always should, in every situation. It is something dark. The light in the room is not the best, but I cock my head like a puppy and contemplate what is happening. My gut answers with a lurch. I try to look closer, but cannot determine. I set the cup on the bottom shelf in front of me and bring my hand to my mouth to investigate manually. As I almost reach my mouth, I notice a reddish look to the substance on the cup. I touch my face gently at first, and it is slightly wet at the corners of my nose. I look at my hand and it is there. I go back to my face and start moving around my mouth, identifying the damp locations. It seems to be where the cup contacted me. I look at my fingers and they are covered in it. It must be blood.

"Fuck."

Now I begin inspecting my face higher and higher. As I move outside of the spaces around my mouth, dampened by the cup, the dampness lessens, but is replaced by a dry substance. It is on my right cheek and the side of my face, up and into my sideburns, and becomes damp again at my hairline. The same substance is on my forehead and eyebrow on the right side, mostly dry. My eyebrow feels almost dry, but there is a good amount there. As I cross to the left side of my forehead, it seems to thin, and I can barely detect it down the left side of my face and cheek.

I suddenly remember the substance dripping on me, because a drop hits my head, on the right side, very top, slightly toward the front. I reach up to where it landed and feel that my hair is wet on top. How have I not noticed how wet I am? I slide my hand forward on my head and connect with a place, directly up from my right eyebrow, just above my hairline, that is soft, very wet, and punishes me for finding it. It hurts and my stomach lurches again. I have the sudden sensation of impending loss of consciousness, and remove my hand quickly. I realize that my mouth is wide open. The intense pain stops with my removal, but now my brain is aware of something there. I sit, frozen, unsure of what to do.

That is when I smell it. The fruit cup may have awakened my sense of smell, and this smell likely has been here all along, but I can't imagine not smelling it before. It is unlike anything I had ever experienced. It is pungent and reminds me of high school science class. Once I notice it, I cannot un-smell it. It is like formaldehyde and chlorine at the same time. With all of the other things happening in my body, I cannot figure out why this was even a problem right now, so it must be strong. I go back to my self-evaluation. There is obviously a wound on my head. Another drop on my head, this one toward the crown. I reach up and touch where it landed, and my head, again, tells me this is a bad idea. This time, the sensation comes from the back, below the crown, and slightly to the left. I adjust my hand and re-approach the spot with my fingers instead of my palm. I am very cautious. It is also wet and when I get to my scalp through the mess of damp hair, I detect the same softness and it is immediately tender; not as bad as the location on the front of my head, but as I explore further I become queasy. I can feel this laceration with my fingertips and then I can suddenly picture it. The feeling that sweeps over me is the same feeling I get when having stitches removed. I am injury prone and I have had to endure sutures many times. I do not tolerate their removal well. I get queasy and have fainted before. My instinct is to pull away, so I stop touching that spot and bring my hand down.

"Shit."

Now I'm free from restraint, but have new, more serious, concerns.

My gut lurches again. I can feel the oranges and juices in my stomach. I sense digestion beginning. It is an unpleasant feeling. It occurs to me that every current solution I pursue reveals more consequences and further problems to solve.

"Damn, that smells bad." I notice the smell again: same as before, overwhelming and distracting. Another drop on my head.

I consider getting up, but my mind generates an image of blood dripping from the intrusion in the ceiling, instead of it coming from my head. I picture a grotesque scene: I imagine that there is a person... a man... a white, middle-aged, man in business clothes... above my ceiling, bleeding from virtually everywhere. He has been crushed by some massive force like an inconsequential object, or, perhaps, assaulted by a force from someone so angry, that it was more of a slaughter. He is almost dead, but his heart is still beating and he is bleeding out, into my ceiling, and it is dripping from one location above me onto my head.

This distraction is nice for a moment, but I decide to come back to reality and think. I reach up with my left hand to grasp my shoulder/neck, impulsively, as a common social display of stress or concern. I recognize that my shoulder is wet, so is my neck. I lean forward and feel my shirt and back slowly peel away from the wall. The dampness is all the way down my back. If this is all blood, it is probably a miracle that I am still alive. But I recall hearing that head wounds bleed more than other injuries, or at least bleed substantially. I decide that I should try to get up, and if I feel uneasy, I should go right back down. My gut lurches again, lower this time, and after the movement subsides, I am doubled over where I sit from a sharp pain in my lower abdomen. This is followed by a feeling of sickness and nausea.

I realize that the rest of my digestive system is awake and I have the sudden and immediate urge to defecate, like I have been holding something in for days, which I have. I know this feeling too and realize that I have limited time to fabricate a solution.

I will need to squat.

I will need more space for that. I will need to contain this in something. I lean forward and start frantically emptying all of the unidentified objects on the second shelf up to the third shelf; no order, no plan, just moving them. Poor lighting only allows me to see that shelf three is now a mess, and shelf two is empty. But there is a plastic jar on shelf four that I can see from below. It is on the right side. It is a relatively large plastic container of peanut butter filled pretzel bites. I know, for a fact, that they are almost gone, because Nathaniel will not finish things, and he has been munching on them and put the container back almost empty.

I relax my mind and body and focus on slow, calm breaths. Then I start pushing upward with my left arm below me and walking my feet toward my torso, inching my way back up the wall behind me. I have to pivot slightly to avoid getting caught on the door handle to my right. I pause to breathe every few moments and become vertical again with impressive timing. I am quite pleased with myself when my lower digestive tract reminds me of my purpose: I am running out of time. This is going to happen whether I like it or not. I use my already-proven-successful method to reach down with my left hand and grab the front of the bottom shelf. I yank it away from the back wall, but it does not come free. I increase the angle and try again: no luck, and I hit my hand on shelf two in the process. I instinctively kick the second shelf corner and free the front. I use my right foot to hold shelf two up and back, and grasp the front of shelf one with my left hand.

I am not an idiot. But when an urge is overwhelming, it can cause tunnel vision, and one may not consider all of the variables in a situation. It is the same reason we have all been already sitting on the commode, halfway through a session, when we realize there is no toilet paper available. In this case, I need that shelf gone, so I yank as hard as I can, throwing the weight of my torso back to generate the force I assume to be necessary to accomplish the task. It does not require that much force, and when the wire shelf is suddenly freed from the clips on the back wall, I am in full throw, and pull it, with great force and momentum, into my crotch, with excessive follow-through. I am already in so much pain and discomfort, this should not, theoretically, even phase me.

Wrong.

"Goddamnit!"

The shelf is free, and my knees go together in some delayed reaction to being struck directly in the testicles. I hunch over, but to the side. I lose all sense of time, rocking, wincing, and groaning, with tears falling from my eyes.

As soon as I have any clarity, I bring the shelf out from between my legs slowly and very cautiously. I turn it vertically and bring it to my left side, set it down, and turn back to shelf two. I am not going to do that again, and I am not going to clear shelf three in a repeat attempt. I know that the shelves are actually just resting in a series of clips that are attached to the drywall. The front is loose already, so I just started kicking up at the back where it is attached. I feel it pop loose in one place on the left side, then near the middle. Then I kick it hard and it comes completely free. It falls across my right leg, and I squat to retrieve it. Same basic motion: grab with left hand and begin to turn it vertically, but then I utilize my right hand, palm side, to help direct it to my left.

My fucking balls hurt like crazy.

I notice a hole or space in the back of the room, near the bottom right corner, where the sheet rock has fallen out. I grab the phone and turn it on. I hold the locked, but illuminated, screen toward the hole and bend over to investigate. The other side of this wall was my laundry room (closet), before the event. The washing machine should be right there. No time for that. I consider how to best deal with my dilemma. I review my previously outlined concerns and decide that I need to contain my waste for reasons of sanitation and sanity. I stand again and grab the plastic snack jar from shelf four. I twist the top open, careful not to spill, because I have to hold the jar with my right forearm against my body and twist the cap with my left hand. Then I set the top down, go back for the jar, and set it in front of me on shelf four. I am sweating and feeling quite queasy: I am running out of time. I snatch a bag of tortilla chips, scoops-style, from shelf three, squeeze the clip in my teeth, and remove it. I spit the clip out to the ground and start unrolling the top of the bag. I then begin working to kick off my shoes. I lace and tie my shoes with the specific purpose of being able to slip them on and off, so I have my left shoe off by the time the bag is open. I use my teeth to hold the edge of the bag open and manipulate it into the best opening possible that might hold form. I grab the pretzel container and dump the seven bites into the chip bag. I drop the plastic jar and remove my right shoe. Then I unbuckle my belt, one-handed, because I can get my pants off while using my right hand for other things (this act is well-rehearsed). I unbutton and unzip. Next, I begin working my pants and boxer briefs down with my left hand and some creative dancing. I don't wear my pants "tight," but they do not simply fall down when loosened either. Once they are at my calves, I start stepping out of them. They invert in the process, but I do not care. I have them covering my brown leather shoes. I bend down and grab the entire pile, two shoes, khaki jeans, and black boxer briefs, with one hand, and shove the collection into shelf three. I locate the plastic jar on the ground and bend down to pick it up. I decide to squat in the same corner where I intend to store, or dispose of, my waste: back right. I hold the jar behind me and lower myself onto it. I have to remain squatted and hunched to fit under shelf three, but I am able to make one more adjustment to spread my cheeks and ensure proper anal-alignment with the container. The floor is buckled, which makes the whole act more interesting, but the receptacle wedges into a conveniently stable spot and seems relatively sturdy. I am suddenly anxious about the possibility of overfilling the container, but feel sure that I have never released that much shit at one time, nor do I think it is humanly possible.

"Fuck it."

I relax, focus on not urinating, because my penis is not contained, but I would rather deal with that mess than the alternative. When my bowels accept the situation, they release, somewhat violently, and very steadily, but without the vigor or volume I expect from all of the anticipation and foreshadowing. I consider, momentarily, how and why my movement is so cooperative. My last bowel movement was Tuesday morning, before the event, after two pieces of avocado toast, so the volume is explainable. I am a very regular person, regarding my digestive system and its consistency. If I eat poorly, my body reacts poorly, but I rarely suffer any type of constipation. After four days without a bowel movement, one must consider the effects on the body, and that there must be some sort of stoppage. This movement did not resemble the descriptions of dehydrated or overly-solid, and difficult to pass, stool. I was able to empty my bowels with ease and relief. The only time I have ever experienced real constipation was when I was prescribed narcotic painkillers after one of my injuries, and the side-effect was constipation. I realized after the second day on the medicine that I had not felt any urge to defecate and there was a sharp pain in my gut. I ate extra fiber and attempted to loosen my pathway naturally, before resorting to chemical assistance. In hindsight, the substance that I consumed, mixed in water, may actually be extracted from some natural source, but it certainly does not occur in nature in this water-soluble format. After a few hours, it worked. I cannot explain how I am experiencing this now without the aid of medicine or dietary measures, but I pass this material with virtually no struggle. I assume that my system was in some state of hibernation from the shock and recurring unconsciousness, much like a surgical patient. I recall a time when my aunt was in the hospital for a short period that included multiple surgical procedures. The anesthesia caused constipation, but her system had also gone dormant, and the medical staff insisted on a bowel movement before she could be discharged. I find comfort in this connection and decide that it is a good sign that I have awakened my guts and proven to my medical staff (myself) that I am ready for rehabilitation. The relief is substantial. I instantly shift from panicked and very sick to calm and relieved. The whole exodus lasts less than a minute, and I sit on the jar for about four more. I groan and realize that my teeth are still clenched and I sound funny: I still have the chip bag in my teeth. I take a moment to visualize the scene. I am in a white undershirt, gray crew height socks, squatting on a plastic jar, my arm wrapped in a nice blue dress shirt, face, head, and neck covered in blood, holding a bag of scoop-shaped tortilla chips in my teeth. All of my panic and concern for where to shit is immediately eclipsed by the mental image of someone opening the pantry door and finding me, looking up at them, chip bag in my teeth.

It is the eventual discomfort of the thin edge of the jar digging into my ass that convinces me to stand. I reach under and hold the jar with my left hand, lift off of it, separate, and bring the object forward between my legs. Then I kneel where I am, in a swift movement, hang my cock into the opening of the plastic jar and urinate. It is the saddest amount of piss I have ever produced, but it is done. The pleasure of relief allows me to ignore any disgust from my ordeal. I inspect the jar, and note that I have barely filled one tenth of it. I can probably use this container for a week or more. I slide the container to the back wall on a flat spot and stand. I sense some remains in and around my anus and immediately search for the napkins. I use 1/4 of a napkin to carefully wipe myself, place the paper in the jar, and retrieve the lid from the shelf. Because I do all of this with my left hand, it is even more calculated and awkward. I secure the lid and kneel again to investigate the hole in the back wall. I reach in. It is large and there are only bits of insulation behind it. There is a metal stud, in the corner, to the right, and I can easily reach through to the other side. I feel downward and there is a metal stud across the bottom also. I decide to try inserting my shit-jar into the opening, remind myself not to force it, so as not to spill it. It slides right in, bottom first, and settles back, with a clunk, into its hiding place. This began as an act of curiosity, but once it is in there, I decide it might be a good idea to leave it. I learn how to stand from beneath the third shelf in this moment. Having removed the bottom two, I find that I have created significantly more space to work with.

I notice the light from the ceiling is sharp and decide not to waste my phone battery yet. The putrid smell has not abated. I wonder why my bodily actions have not overtaken the stench, but I am no match for this. Standing in the limited space, I decide to see about escaping my prison now. I am facing the door as I rise from beneath the shelves, so I turn, carefully, and grab a fruit and nut bar from shelf three. I do not need light to find them, they are my favorite breakfast, even though I am pretty sure it is afternoon by now. I open the package, and turn back to the door. I push down on the handle and then pull up: nothing moves. It seems to be completely wedged. I push on the door, near the handle, but above, and it does not budge. It is strange, but it doesn't feel hollow, as I expect it should, but more dampened and solid, with no play. I knock on it, and while the door makes the empty sound and does not react with the force of a solid door, it also does not reverberate. It is like there is padding on the other side, so I knock up and down the door, in every space where the spice rack is not: it is all the same. Then I lean into pushing it in every place: nothing. This discovery puzzles me, but concerns me even more. How could a hollow door suddenly be impenetrable? I consider choosing a place to begin taking it apart, but if there really is that much material on the other side, the door and frame may be all that are keeping me safe. I abandon the door, and consider my other discoveries. The wall between me and where my foyer should be has buckled. If there are steel studs in that wall, it should not move that way. I run my hand across it, and it feels odd. I find a place where the drywall is cracking and start picking at it. The building is not very old, so there is not much paint to get through. I create a hole that I can get two fingers in, so I try it. I feel some insulation, and then find what feels like stone, or jagged little pebbles. When I extract my fingers, dust and tiny stones come out with them, not much, but messy and loose. I know this wall has two sides, so why would there be rocks inside the wall? Maybe it is leftover from construction. But more likely, it is from the building deconstructing rapidly.

I decide not to pick at that hole any more. Whatever force buckled the entire wall is likely still pressing on the room, and I certainly do not want to encourage it. I finish my fruit and nut bar and feel very thirsty. I have the Coke Zeros, but I am not sure that is wise. I have canned goods, and some contain water, but that will not be as good as water. The thing I do not have right now is water. I get my phone from shelf four and turn it on. I turn the screen toward the floor in the front left corner where I sat and slept. I can see the blood on the wall where my head and back were, and I follow it down to the ground. The floor is wet. The luxury vinyl plank is uneven, which I do not recall being the case before I was stuck in here. Our floors and walls are not concrete on the surface, but I believe them to be poured concrete between each unit. We can hear our neighbors when they stomp, but it is not loud. The floors have always struck me as feeling very strong, and very sturdy. The warping in this floor suggests that something beneath it was forced into, or through, it. The floor is wet, but because the flooring is dark in color, I cannot tell what the liquid is. I decide that I must look more carefully. I turn the phone over, find the Lock Screen button for the flashlight, turn my head from the pending field of blinding light, and close my eyes tight. I touch and hold the screen, but nothing happens. I look at the phone screen: my finger missed. It is actually very difficult to aim your finger at a single position and subsequently land on your intended target after you look away from it. I try again. My phone provides haptic feedback when I successfully switch the flashlight on. I open my eyes to slits and see the shelves of my pantry in what seems to be daylight. As amazed as I am by how much crap I have in my pantry once it is lit, I slowly turn my squinted eyes toward the lighted field of my intended inspection. My eyes adjust and I investigate the scene, which looks more like a crime scene than a residential dry storage area. I can even see the outline of where I sat and slept and where my blood has soaked the walls. I look to the floor, it is wet, and it is red. I decide to place my phone on the top shelf behind me so I have my hand free. But when I turn back, my shadow disrupts the field. No matter, I touch the wet ground and produce a finger with blood on it. I still don't have any pants on, so I wipe it on my leg and check my fingers: the pads are all clean. I do it again, blood on my fingertips and I wipe them all off on my leg. It is odd, but I sense that the viscosity is off. It doesn't feel like blood, alone. It seems thinner. I reach toward the wall, and a drop lands on my forearm. I stare at this liquid from beyond and then it runs across my arm and eventually drops to the ground. The visitor leaves a few small droplets behind, as liquid does when running across porous surfaces. I slowly stand and turn toward the light. The liquid on my arm is not blood, it is colorless, mostly, and behaves like water. I lift my arm to smell the minuscule droplets, and realize that I can't smell anything over the stink that surrounds me. Now I turn and look up to the source.

"What the fuck?"

I turn back and grab my phone from the top shelf and reach up with the light to really have a look.

There is a white, shiny, rounded object that has broken through the ceiling, just inside the corner where the wall meets the ceiling. There is a line where liquid has been running down the face of the curve to the inverted apex where it gathers and forms a droplet and, assumedly, falls to the ground below. We have twelve foot ceilings, so it is out of reach, but I know what it is. There is only one thing it could be: A toilet.

I feel like I have won a game. I do not need audience applause or prizes, because I just stand there and beam with pride.

## CHAPTER 5

Check the time: 4:49 PM

It is Saturday, Day 4.

I am stuck in my pantry.

There is a toilet protruding from my ceiling.

I want, desperately, to clean up the blood and mess, but decide it is not worth it. I decide to plan and process. There is something dripping from the toilet, from the front of the bowl of an elongated-style toilet.

Now … If it is water, do I drink it? I have other options. I don't have to drink toilet water. But I don't want it on the floor either.

Time to solve another problem, maybe without creating a bigger one, or uncovering a series of hidden problems in the process.

I turn back to the shelves and locate the empty cereal container. I remove the entire lid, designed with a flip-top dispenser for pouring the cereal, and place it back on the shelf. I place the container on the ground near the wet area and grab the phone. I find where the drops are landing, because they make a clean spot on the blood-water soaked floor. I place the open container atop the landing point, watch, and wait. A few moments later, I witness a drop fall directly into the center of the container. I note that it looks clear, but decide to gather more before inspecting and making that final decision.

I point the light toward the toilet again and note where the largest spaces are between the porcelain and the Sheetrock. One of these spaces is allowing some sort of light to come in. Which means there must be a clear shot to the outside.

I perform a categorical, mental, dissection of the information gathered thus far.

The toilet has broken through the ceiling only. But it is sitting in a way that the rear portion of it is aligned with where a wall should be. The apartment above is identical to mine, so I know, relative to the overall structure, how it should be laid-out. The toilet, if intact, would be penetrating the pantry-door-wall upstairs, with the bowl facing into the pantry, the "nose" slammed downward, forcing the porcelain bowl through the vinyl plank flooring, through the concrete fire/subfloor, through any existing insulation, through additional reinforcement of the floor/ceiling, and through the ceiling drywall of my apartment's pantry, in order to be visible here. Having been a homeowner, previously, in an older neighborhood in Atlanta, I am relatively familiar with basic construction and building composition due to performing extensive repairs and refusing to pay contractors for things Samantha and I could do ourselves. I am sure the object is a toilet, but this explanation seems unlikely. Also, outside of the pantry door is the kitchen. This room is just beyond the island in the middle that contains the dishwasher and sink. People do interesting things to their apartments, but I have yet to see a toilet installed in the kitchen. The master bathroom is just behind the rear, left corner of the pantry, if you are standing in the doorway looking in. But if I, hypothetically, ran through that corner, I would be in my bathtub/shower combo, with the toilet just beyond. The other bathroom is across the foyer through the opposite wall. Either of those two toilets from the apartment above would have made epic journeys to appear where this shitter materialized. None of this seems likely. But I recall that the apartment above is vacant. They have been doing work, I assume to prepare for new tenants. Perhaps the location of this toilet is happenstance. Maybe it was moved into its location, but was not yet installed. If that is the case, it would be clean, "factory fresh," as we like to say. But this theory begs a question: if it is not connected to a water supply, why is there water coming out of it? I decide to turn off the flashlight now. The room goes completely black before the screen light comes into view. I unlock the phone. I dial 911. It never connects. I find the "Emergency Text (SOS)" option and click through a series of instructions about needing to have a clear view of the sky and to hold the phone steady once I locate a satellite to utilize. I click "begin," and the phone starts guiding me to turn and adjust and pivot and direct its case in different manners. Then it asks if I have a clear view of the sky. I click "no." It tells me that it is "unable to locate a viable satellite for communications." I decide to call Samantha. It never connects. I close the phone app and open Messages. I send a text to Samantha, it pops up a red warning that says "not delivered." I read her last message: "why do people have to be such assholes?"

I try to call my mother, no connection. I open settings and look for wifi, none. I don't think I have ever seen zero wifi. There is always something. I open "Find My," and see where Nathaniel was last located: in his school. I look and see that Samantha was on the freeway, on I-75 South, just inside The Perimeter. It was too early for her to be heading home Tuesday when the event occurred, so I have to shelve that mystery for later.

I decide to forfeit this vain attempt, for now.

I check the time: 7:17 PM.

Turn the phone off.

I take my briefcase off the shelf and sit down with it. I sit, this time, with my back in the front right corner, between the door and the compromised wall on the right, adjacent to the foyer. My legs go across to the opposite corner that would lead to the bathtub of the master bedroom. I slide my personal phone into its safety compartment and feel around inside the outside pouch of the bag. I get bored, and decide that I am hungry. I stand once more and take down one of the plastic bin containers on the top shelf. I put it on the floor, open it, then carefully feel around inside. This one contains birthday supplies, but that means candles and multiple cigarette lighters. I do not need this now. I replace its lid, retrieve the next bin, and set it on top of the first one on the floor. I open the lid and feel carefully in this one. Bingo! This has camping supplies in it. I sit down. We bought a hand-operated, geared can-opener on our last trip. It is not in here, but the classic bottle-and-can-opener is. This also has a set of camping silverware that all link together, and other supplies. I locate the tool, remove it and the silverware, and close the container. I slide both, still stacked, under the spice rack, to my left, against the door, on the floor. I stand again and decide to play roulette. I find shelf four, and locate the can dispensers with ease in the darkness. I take my hand away from the units, and move it around, then return it to the shelf. There are three dispensers, linked together, meaning there are three possible options in the dispensing locations at the bottom of each. I randomly land on the middle unit, take the can that is there, and set it on the shelf. I reach up and find my clothes on the top shelf and extract my underwear from the pants legs. I have been functioning in a t-shirt and socks all day. I feel for the seam of the waistband, because I can tell right-side-out without looking. I get them correct, and get my left and then right leg into their places and shimmy them up until satisfactory. I retrieve my khaki-colored pants, in case I get cold, and sit back down. I am feeling calm, but tired. I hear a droplet hit the container to my left. Not much splash yet. I start to work triangular holes in the lid of the random can, holding it between my knees on the ground, and I work my way around until only a small piece of metal holds the lid in place. I smell the can, but I cannot tell what it is. It smells like canned meat, or dog food, which we have neither of. I remove the fork from the connected silverware and dip it into the can. I take a good-feeling scoop of mystery substance, and go straight to my mouth. It's beans, not baked beans, I am pretty sure it is cannellini beans in water, very inoffensive. I take another bite and decide this needs dressing up. I reach up behind me and feel for the spices. There is a set within reach that is in metal canisters. I take the first down and open it for a sniff: cinnamon. I repeat this until I smell the earthy aroma of cumin. I shake a healthy amount into the can and stir. I taste a couple beans, but it still needs something. I find a large container of coarse salt just beside me on the bottom shelf of the spice rack mounted to the door. I add a good bit of salt. Then I start taking down small, plastic, spice bottles until I find one that smells like garlic. I add a good bit of garlic powder to the can and stir. I take another taste and I am perfectly satisfied with my dish now. I try to eat slowly and not think about my thirst. I remind myself that there is water in this food and that is all I need to survive. I am accustomed to 100+ ounces of water a day, so I am struggling to adjust to this punishment. While I eat, I return to thoughts about what has happened.

I have taken for granted how exposed to information I am and how we are inundated by news and information as a society, in general. We assume that we have access to accurate and thorough information, particularly with regard to our national security and safety as citizens. I am not so naive as to believe that we are told everything, I believe we are told very little, but I did operate within the philosophy that our country was relatively safe from massive attack or annihilation. I did not think it was impossible, but I figured there would be some buildup or time to prepare if the end of times were near. I truly believed that the intelligence gathered by our government would trickle into society in a way that would prevent instantaneous destruction should any of our adversaries decide to attack us. World wars and international conflicts typically display warning signs of events on the horizon, but we have known that our world leaders have been jockeying for power, and firepower, for a very long time. Maybe that was the warning. We simply became numb to the fear. The logistics are relatively simple: three major adversaries of the United States decided that western culture and society was a curse and they began secretly stockpiling three independent-but-mutual nuclear, long-range, high-accuracy arsenals. The strategy since the Cold War seemed to always lie within threats and reminding anyone who will listen of your ability to develop mass-casualty weaponry and agree that "no one wants this," because the chain-reaction from an international assault against civilians in an effort to gain power would result in potential end-of-times, as every nuclear superpower would respond, in-kind, with retaliative countermeasures. Three leaders came to power, which ultimately resulted in our needing to keep an eye on "the quiet one," but in this case, there were three. The stockpiling and preparation had skirted all intelligence, as far as the general public could tell. The American public was completely unaware of the threat while they prepared. But all three nations also, simultaneously, launched social systems and propaganda that convinced most of their citizens that the fallout would be worth the result. Their "means-to-end" strategies were each rooted in different philosophies, but had the same focal point: destroying western civilization completely would save the world. This rhetoric was nothing novel to spectators across the globe, because these nations had always displayed this sentiment, but I do not think anyone, less a few people, generally considered paranoid or fringe conspiracy theorists, anticipated the level of buy-in that had been generated within all three nations.

One week before the event, life seemed relatively normal. Five days before, there was a slight increase in chatter on the major news networks, but no one thought much of this, because we had become skeptical as a nation about the integrity of our news sources. The Friday before, one of my colleagues asked if anyone was following the drama, while we were on a conference call, everyone else shrugged it off, so did I. Monday before the event was the first time it felt like something might actually be wrong, but there did not seem to be much urgency. News outlets were screaming about it, but the spokesperson for the White House was so calm, it almost diffused the concern. In the end, the actual and final catalyst was not money, or power, or greed, as we all expected... It was personal.

The stage had been set for this to be possible in every way. The three powers against us had the firepower, they had the philosophical backing, and they had the go-ahead from their secret constituencies. In all fairness, it was not only directed at the USA, but our country is certainly seen as the central and major problem to our enemies. It was also our leadership that provided the last requirement to engage. Our president, when faced with this information, and expected to address the situation, started by ignoring the request for response and referring to it as a "veiled threat." Once confronted with the details about their capabilities, he responded with doubt and insult. Finally, when all three powers revealed their collaborative strategy, he responded with immature, toxic, puffed-chest, masculine defensiveness and doubt. Not only did he insult the group, he challenged them to "bring it." This pathetic excuse for diplomacy occurred less than 24 hours before the event. Monday evening, a warning was presented with far less urgency, concern, or enthusiasm than necessary and did not cause much panic or concern. The "end-of-times" folks did take to the streets Tuesday morning, but it was basically business-as-usual for most Americans. We were used to this behavior now. So we all slept just fine Monday night. Samantha and I talked about how much it is going to suck to be at war again. We also discussed the concern for fighting three enemies who seemed pretty angry with us. I honestly do not think our defense department had any idea that thousands of warheads were already being targeted or mobilized against virtually every location in our country. We assumed it was going to be another long and annoying war, that we were against, philosophically, but supported our troops, because that is our duty as citizens. Our enemies were not concerned with any of this. Their plan was to ensure no survivors of the plague that is modern society. But they had actually prepared for this outcome in far greater detail than we anticipated and were more poised to engage than the USA or our allies than any of their predecessors. The other important factor is that all three nations had convinced their people that it would be worth dying and potentially eradicating the scourge that is humanity from the earth in order to appease their deities or save the earth itself from being destroyed. One such theory held by some of the supporters of the instigating leadership was that, even after the devastation from world destruction by atomic fallout, the earth would eventually correct and recover, and that this long-range consequence was better than what we are presently doing to it. This may not be untrue, but I am selfish, and I want my loved ones to enjoy long and healthy lives: sorry... not sorry.

I do not watch or listen to the news in the morning: it's depressing, so my family began our day last Tuesday like any other Tuesday during the school year. I rise around 6:00 to begin my stretching and exercise regiment. Depending on the day, I am either on the treadmill or doing strength training. Last Tuesday was treadmill day. She rises around 6:15, and is out of the shower by 6:30. I finish my workout when she gets out of the shower, because I prefer to bathe immediately. I am out by 6:45. She is leaving the house by 7:00, unless she is running late, which she was Tuesday, so she was kissing me around 7:10, and I heard grumbling from Nathaniel's room moments later when she woke him for a kiss goodbye. We have experienced significant loss to unexpected tragedy in our life together, although I admittedly do not know the statistics of whether ours is more or less significant than the average couple, it certainly feels significant to us, so we make a point to always tell someone we love them when we part ways, because we have both missed that opportunity in the past, only to discover it was the last one. Samantha did not miss Tuesday morning and neither did I. We always embrace tenderly when departing and when finding each other again, not because of any expectation from one-another, but because we truly bask in the joy. Taking the time to make eye contact and express sincere adoration for one another is central to the success of our relationship, and its manifestation that morning is very important to me now, but seemed somewhat typical at the time. I did not see her tell our son goodbye, but I heard them, and can imagine exactly how it went, every detail. After Samantha leaves, I go sit on the edge of Nathaniel's bed and we have a quiet conversation.

"Good morning, young man."

"Good morning, Pops."

"Did you sleep well?"

"I don't know, so, probably?"

"Are you excited about school today?"

"I think so… let me think about it while I'm getting ready."

"OK, well let's get started, so we don't feel rushed."

"OK… Dad, can I have a hug?"

"Of course."

I give him a hug and then leave him to get ready around 7:15-7:20. He leaves at 8:00 to get to school by 8:15 and I return to my preparations. I boil water for tea while I dress, boot my computer, make my tea, set it up to steep, then take my drink and headphones to the balcony to listen to music and prepare mentally and emotionally. I am back inside by 7:45, and this day, I decide to skip emails until the boy leaves. He hears me enter the apartment and peels out of the bathroom.

"Dad! I *am* excited about school today! Not really about school, but after school."

"Why's that?"

"Because they will post soccer teams today!"

"That's right! What do you think you will get?"

"Coach James again. He always picks me now."

"If you say so, but you never know? They may need to split up the rosters to keep it fair. Can't keep letting Coach James run away with the championship!"

"It doesn't matter to me, I just want to know! We have been waiting forever!"

"Well... then you do have a very good reason to be excited."

We try to find things to look forward to every day. If we ever can't find something, one of us will say something like, "well then I can't wait to see you later, and I hope amazing things happen before then, so you can tell me all about them!" Some may call it "cheesy," but it's our way. If I am not myself in the morning, my child senses it, and has played the role of "encourager" for me many times. We have a unique relationship.

Nathaniel is out the door at 7:59, and I remember this because I always look to see if he makes it. He seems to have a better day when he is in his routine and not rushing.

I was meeting a client for lunch, so I was dressed for business. Once I caught up emails, I started re-packing my briefcase. I had not performed this ritual in a few weeks, and I was leaving for Dallas Wednesday, so this was a good time to get it done.

Samantha texted me about one of the attorneys in her office obsessing over the news and telling everyone that they needed to close the office. I asked her why, and she wrote, "because he's an idiot and wants to WFH today. LOL."

I laughed back and continued my process. That is when she sent me the last communication I received on my personal phone about people being idiots. That was at 9:48 AM. At some point after, she left her office, but I didn't know that. I considered that maybe the attorney won the day and convinced them to close and she seized the opportunity to come home early. This would have allowed for afternoon sex after my meeting, which she almost never turns down. I have the awesome wife that performs strip-teases for me behind my monitors while I am on a call, and had, on more than one occasion, crawled under my desk at home and performed spectacular fellatio while I was giving a presentation online. She also surprised me at the office once, at the end of the day, and insisted on staying while I closed so we could add "my office" to the list of places we had sex, which was a long list, mostly because of her penchant for creative seduction.

I had no indication that she thought something was actually wrong. Similarly, Nathaniel was at school and the administration had not sent out any warnings, or carefully worded statements about the situation, or anything to suggest that something horrible may be coming. I admit that a giant concrete school building may be the safest place during a disaster, but we live in a world where the school feels compelled to communicate anything that any parent may possibly worry about or consider a threat. I honestly had no unusual concerns that morning.

I was finishing an email when Justin texted me about turning on the news. It was around 11:00 AM. I was somewhat distracted, but my takeaway was as follows: The media correspondent calmly explained that recent intelligence suggested the enemies to be in possession of more sophisticated weaponry than originally believed.

They used some terms that I understood and a few that were new to me. They allegedly possessed enough firepower to land a fission bomb every 75 miles across the continental United States and most of Western Europe, Canada, Australia, and the outlying regions. The warheads could, potentially, devastate a 50 mile radius from the blast each, with fallout estimated to cover the entire western hemisphere, if executed as threatened.

In hindsight, I should have been concerned about this news, but the woman speaking was so calm, I did not sense urgency or fear.

They played a soundbite from one of the ministers of war, translated, that referred to "Cloudstorm" technology, which I was not familiar with, but referred to the ability to neutralize communications and "swiftly eliminate the potential for counterattack."

The correspondent then explained that "Cloudstorm" was a technology that isolated communications systems and that we only understood theoretically, but the enemy claims to have produced successfully. Then I heard something that caught my attention: the correspondent said, "I am very sorry, but we can only assume that this threat is real, as our last attempt at diplomatic intervention was met with silence and then a pre-recorded, looped, reference to apocalyptic demise." She apologized again and said that the president would now address the nation and the world. The arrogant narcissist that we were accustomed to hearing is not the individual who spoke next. This voice was calm, quiet, slow, and strange. I did notice this, but didn't think it was a sign of looming tragedy, just defeated pride, and I almost enjoyed it. He spoke about the threat being imminent, that we may have underestimated our enemy, and that he maintains complete confidence in our military's ability to protect our citizens. I found this language odd, because this prick never speaks about defense, he is too macho and aggressive to "defend." But, again, politicians say things, and we have come to ignore them. The news anchor took over after he excused himself, abruptly, mid-sentence. I now assume that they received some new information and stopped the address to evacuate the president to safety. As I reflect on the timing, I doubt they were successful. The man on the radio was explaining that they would have to revisit the address later, but that it sounded like the president was through for now. It was 11:30, I had not received any other notifications, other than emails, so I grabbed my briefcase, grabbed my keys, picked up my water, and stopped in the kitchen, at the end of the bar, on my way to the door, because the pantry was open. I stood there and wondered why it was open, because I did not remember opening it. Did Nathaniel leave it open? He had been eating breakfast at school recently, so probably not. Had it been open all morning and neither of us noticed? That was not unlikely and I settled on that as the most probable answer just as the tornado siren sounded.

I will make some assumptions from all of this information, but after I stepped into the pantry and pulled the door shut, my nightmare began, and that is factual. I must assume that the attack was already in progress, and either our leaders truly did not know, or decided it was too late, so better not to inject panic into the equation, which, if true, is the darkest level of compassion, to allow your citizens to die in ignorance. I must assume they also had no idea how horrible this would be.

I suddenly become aware of the fact that I have not experienced any other signs of life since the event and the need to unravel this factoid.

I decide to scream for help, so I do just that. I take a deep breath, still seated, tilt my head back, and scream, "help!" as loud as I can. I am impressed with my volume within this space, so I do it again, because, honestly, it felt good. The immediate response from outside is silence, so I shrug my shoulders and keep typing. I will make this part of my routine for as long as I can. I start to consider the evidence and I begin to wonder if rescue is a possibility. Because of the light from the toilet hole in my ceiling, and that I have not suffocated already, I can assume there is a pathway to the outside above me, somehow. But I have not heard sirens or rescue workers, or... anything to suggest other survivors.

I pause to brace myself, as I am suddenly overcome by feeling nauseous. I panic, because for a moment I think I will vomit and then it passes. It does not completely subside, it lingers, but is less urgent or overwhelming. Now I just feel slight nausea and lightheadedness.

As I consider the previous information, I look up at the toilet, and how it reflects the light from my monitor, and I think about how the light changed at sundown. The color was very odd, very unnatural. This triggers the concept of "fallout" in my brain. I have heard it too many times recently, and I vaguely remember how nuclear fallout causes all kinds of residual effects. I am narrowing in on the belief that the event was almost certainly an atomic blast, or multiples, and that there may have been other factors or weapons that I don't understand. I know that my devices are detecting no trace of signals, at all. I check my laptop for signs of life, and it too returns an empty set, where no less than 12 always appeared. I contemplate the "Cloudstorm" concept and how this could be the result. My phone has the ability to connect to satellites as an emergency measure, but it is telling me that I need an unobstructed view of the sky to locate a target, which I cannot provide. I also cannot confirm whether this form of communication is lost as well. Another bit of evidence: the smell. It is definitely chemical in nature and does not feel healthy. This could be some other form of chemical warfare, or simply another consequence of the damage. The next point: the generator. Clearly, it ran for a long time, and the manufacturer should be proud. But I could hear it well enough to identify the source. I never questioned the accuracy of my answer, because it was so clear. It certainly emanated from the hole in the ceiling, but I could hear it well. It was very muffled, and seemed incredibly distant, but I could definitely hear it. If I can hear an engine, roughly 150 yards away, that was designed to have decent sound attenuation due to its proximity to residential buildings, why have I not heard any other mechanical noises? I have not heard any planes, or helicopters, or emergency vehicles, or obnoxiously loud car exhausts, or...

How did the generator survive? I survived, so there must be other survivors. Which means it is possible that a piece of equipment survived somehow. The thing that makes it unique to the many other sounds you typically experience, is that it is starts automatically, without the need for human intervention, by design.

I stop typing again because the urge to vomit overwhelms me. I assume it will pass, so I close my eyes, take a deep breath, and try to relax. Then I immediately turn to my right, lean forward, and vomit, mostly on the wall, and a bit on my leg. It is quick and disturbingly violent. I almost never throw up, so it is strange and bothers me. It tastes bad, and I want the aftertaste gone, so I wipe my mouth with my shirt-covered right hand, turn my laptop toward the shelves, and reach up to retrieve a Coke Zero. I sit back, open the can, and take a long sip. It burns my mouth and throat, hits my stomach like a brick, and immediately comes back up. This time I spray some across my computer screen and then aim toward the wall. It burns going down and coming up, which is very unpleasant. I sit back, relax, breathe deep, and take a tiny sip. I let it burn my mouth with the carbonation and chemicals, and when the bubbling stops, I swallow, gingerly. It does not feel good, but I think I can keep it down.

I check the time on my laptop: 12:17 AM.

## Chapter 6

Day 5

Sunday

Laptop: 75% battery

Both phones are off.

I consider another fact: Once I was in the pantry, I remember a vibration that I can only assume an earthquake might be like, then a rumbling, and then the "pressure." I don't know how else to describe the feeling other than "pressure." When you dive too deep in the pool or the ocean, and your ears and head send a message to the brain that "something is wrong," that is similar. This pressure was exponentially stronger, I sensed it with my entire body, and it came on so fast, that it confused me for the 2-3 seconds I was awake before losing consciousness. Strangely, I do not think the "pressure" caused any significant harm to me, but I gather it caused incredible damage to virtually everything else around me. My injuries, at this point, are from objects around me during the event, or afterward, as a result of my own actions. I struggle with the idea that my decision to step into my pantry is how I survived this catastrophe, but I do not have any other reasonable explanation right now. The compromised integrity of the interior of my cave is likely evidence that what I would find outside, if I could somehow get there, would be far worse. The buckling of the floor suggests there are objects beneath that are causing the malformation. The crippled wall on the right, now also blessed with my cannellini bean and Coke Zero vomit, suggests that great forces have acted upon this building. I have not heard the sound of water in pipes, or any equipment, that are the ordinary sounds in a large apartment building. I do not hear people screaming or crying. I do not hear anyone else screaming for help. I do not smell Indian food cooking. I cannot identify a single thing that would encourage me to believe that anyone else has survived this.

I start to consider the information I recall from the news on Tuesday. If the enemy claimed to have enough bombs to detonate one every 75 square miles across the entire continent, that would mean virtually all of North America would be either dead or dying. With a blast zone of 50 square miles, and fallout of much more, no one was safe. I heard rumors of a method in which the enemy could paralyze our ability to detect their high altitude drones that carried multiple payloads, before it was too late to stop them from launching. Then the attack would be laser-guided and released into a grid pattern, which assured instant victory. There would be additional long-range missiles with heavier payloads and more devastating power that would rain on major cities and critical military locations to prevent retaliation. One theorist recently postured that the advancement of the secret weaponry was so specialized, that our countermeasures had already been deactivated, but our military had no way of detecting the infiltration. There was rumor of our entire internet and cellular network being controlled by the enemy, and they had set up the entire attack already. This way, once the reality of the threat was realized, our ability to respond or provide advanced warning to our people would be compromised and manipulated as they chose. All of these seemingly impossible scenarios were now feeling quite realistic. I have no way of knowing what gruesome reality had unfolded out there, but I know it has managed to trap me in here, and has rendered me helpless and alone.

My mind is now spinning into various pathways and creative stories that yield no factual answers, and certainly no comfort. I decide to find some peace and consider what I have to be grateful for before trying to sleep. It is 3:22 AM when I turn off the MacBook and put it away. I turn on my work-issued iPhone and check the last message I received from Justin, my colleague, that I never read. It says, "I know you have a lunch meeting, but you may want to see if your person is still coming. Traffic is a disaster."

Ever the helper, he was simply trying to save me from a trip in horrible traffic. If he hadn't told me to turn on the radio, I may have already left when the event occurred. I also assume that he was likely in traffic when he sent that at 11:23, which means he probably did not survive. This device has less than 20% battery remaining, so I turn it off and return it to its pouch.

The considerations about casualties and survivors slid into my thoughts over the past four days like a well-lubricated finger in a prostate exam: you know it's there, you barely notice it arrive, but it's a necessary reality, so you better try to relax and accept it, otherwise things can get more uncomfortable than they already are. Again, I calculate that if I cannot hear other signs of life within my field of perception, I must be isolated, audibly, from where the nearest survivors are, or there are not any close enough for me to hear them. If there were, I certainly would be getting some sort of feedback. I picture my city from above, like a game of SIMs, and imagine how the humans would look and behave like rodents if mass-annihilation occurred. Once the dust settles, I picture them scurrying out and running around, anxiously taking inventory and sniffing each other. I'm sure that one of the first issues addressed would be internet and cellular connectivity. The fact that I can't see any access points between four devices hints at disappointing realities. Either the enemy was very good at ensuring communications were removed, blocked, or destroyed for a long time, or they were very good at making sure no one would survive to re-establish the communications systems, or both. The other possibility is that I am somehow isolated in a way that I cannot access those signals and where I cannot hear the others. The light coming from the ceiling, the horrible smell, and the sounds that have drifted into my cage suggest that this is highly unlikely, because the outside world is close enough for me to sense it in multiple ways, but human life does not populate on my list of identified or unidentified experiences, yet. As I work through these thoughts, I rummage around in my briefcase after sliding my computer in and take manual inventory of the items I chose to carry on my disrupted business trip. There are two sharpened, Ticonderoga, #2 pencils, brand new, and three ink pens: one black-clicky-ballpoint, one black-clicky-fine-tip-gel, and one blue-clicky-ballpoint. I have my black notebook, medium sized, lined, and only a few weeks old. I had recently filled my last notebook, so I figure that when my computer dies, and both phones lose battery, I can write in my notebook, like a heathen. I also brought a leather-bound executive folder, that contains various files, with about 50 printed pages that I could use the backs of, and a legal pad, yellow, lined, with around 30 pages left in it. I find various charging cables and a set of wired earbuds. Then I run my hand across an object that

I had not given much thought to yet, but decide now is the time. I carry a pistol, my sidearm. I carry it almost always, unless I know I am going somewhere that doesn't allow it, which is rare. It is a Glock 43X, with a 10 round magazine, loaded, and another magazine in the pouch attached to the holster. It is loaded with critical defense rounds. I do not keep a round in the chamber, and it is always on me, or locked. I keep a cable lock with the weapon so I can render it useless at any point, and if I have to leave it in my vehicle, it is cable-locked, and locked in the dash compartment. If I have to leave it at home, it is cable locked and in my safe. I spend sufficient time at a firing range to ensure preparedness, safety, and the reliability of my performance and the weapon itself. I like to think of myself as a good example of responsible gun ownership. I am a supporter of my right to carry, concealed, responsibly, as a responsible and law-abiding citizen of the United States of America, but I understand that there are certainly gray areas regarding gun rights. I believe in the concept of a well-armed civilian force, if trained properly, and believe that it is my duty and right to "have it and not need it," and hope that I never "need it and don't have it." I am fully prepared to use my weapon in defense of my family or other innocent civilians. I would proudly participate in an opportunity to utilize my sidearm for the right reason. I have always felt that keeping this weapon with me was one of my most strategic preparations for critical situations. Now I find myself having it, in an unbelievable situation, and not seeing any need for it, yet. I decide to inspect and qualify my weapon in the near future, but not yet. On this day, I am somewhat comforted by the knowledge that I have this resource should my situation take some unforeseen turn that would cause me to need it.

I drift off and sleep, comfortably, until the smell wakes me up... and the pain.

It is still Day 5, Sunday.

The light from my ceiling-toilet is enough to feel like morning, but I admit to myself that it is probably midday or later. It is autumn, so the weather is pleasant most of the day and night. I have not felt temperature as a problem yet. Another thing to be grateful for: I am not freezing to death, dying of exposure, or desperately searching for things to keep me warm. When it gets hot, I can take off my clothes. But if the weather turns the other direction, I could have a problem. Similarly: I am not starving. I have enough food in this room to sustain myself for a very long time. I do not have much of an appetite anyhow, and if I am confined to this space, I will not burn many calories, so I can intentionally eat less, in order to ration, but also to maintain healthy behaviors and be prepared for my escape or rescue. I am consciously deciding to maintain a healthy optimism about not perishing in this room. I am going to eat, drink, and explore potential ways out. I look at the cereal container that is collecting water beside me and it has a good 3/4 inches of water lining the bottom. I hold it up to the light to inspect its clarity and visible characteristics. There are a few tiny particulates in it, which is to be expected, but it does not appear to be tinted in any way. I am not shining a bright light on it and I'm not sure I want to. I smell the container, it smells slightly like plastic, but the object is not new, so it is faint. I smell more of the putrid local aroma that I cannot escape. The water does not seem to give off any "don't do it" signs, other than knowing it is coming from a toilet above me, that appears to have been thrown from a plane and landed in my pantry ceiling. I close my eyes and tilt the container up to allow me the tiniest bit of the water into my mouth. I roll it around on my tongue and across my teeth. It does not taste bad. The viscosity seems normal, and it is on the hard side of water, but not any more than many tap water sources. I swallow that bit and have a bit more, then return it to its place. I choose to eat some lucky charms. I get up and grab the unopened box. I open the lid, but before I open the bag, I decide to stretch. I can't lose my momentum now. I perform a truncated version of the stretching routine that I start every day with. It requires the motion of all major joints beginning with the face and ending with the toes. The whole ordeal takes less than 5 minutes. This version is much less effective for my larger limbs, due to the limited space I have for execution, but I definitely feel better when I am done. I am warmer and decide to, finally, remove my socks. I am now comfortable in a white undershirt, that is getting pretty ripe, and black Hanes boxer briefs. I am still wearing my watch, so I use my teeth to remove it and place it in my bag. I use my left hand and my teeth to open the bag of cereal inside the box. I chuckle when I see part of the box and know that it says, "They're trying to get me lucky charms!" which my brain processes in an Irish accent. I eat a few pieces successfully, and start to eat three or four pieces at a time. I have awoken quite hungry, so I remind myself to pace it. After about 10 handfuls, I shove the bag down inside the box and set the box on the shelf again. I decide to unwrap my right hand. If there is any way to correct this, I need it to happen today, because my plight is not getting any easier from here.

My dress shirt is a light blue, with, almost unnoticeable, dark blue diamonds every few inches. It is a long-sleeve, non-button-down-collar, 95% polyester, 5% spandex, flowing shirt that helps me appear sophisticated but not stuffy. It has been wrapped around my hand for days, keeping my pinky mostly immobilized. I remember the pain that caused unconsciousness and proceed to unwrap my right hand with great care. The material is still relatively soft and the blood on it has dried, but is not causing any overall material stiffness. The spandex in the material allows some stretch, one of the marketing features of the product that led me to purchase it. It suggests that flexibility in material is somehow better, because it stretches. I certainly appreciate flexibility in relationships and casual commitments, but I have no idea if it dictates higher quality in clothing. It certainly performs well as a makeshift medical wrap when a bandage was not available. I slow down when approaching the end of the wrap and the density of material around the injury reduces significantly. My other digits shift and wiggle slightly when they sense freedom, which sends jolts of pain to my pinky and up my arm. The pain comes from the knuckle and I do not feel the finger beyond. When I reveal the hand, I see that it is bad, but not horrible. The outside of my hand is swollen and the pinky looks misplaced. I place my hand, gently, on my right thigh and contemplate my options. I could fashion a splint, and use the folding knife that I know is in my bag to create a proper brace, and wrap, but I much prefer the possibility of regaining the use of my right hand. Dislocation can be corrected and will typically instigate healing to begin, but the hand is virtually useless as it is now. I have never corrected a dislocated digit before, but I have had my right shoulder corrected after a roller-skating accident when I was 14. It was unpleasant, but I recall the situation improving very quickly once the joint was reset. I remember the pain at occurrence being pretty bad and the ride to the hospital was blurry. My father told me I was in shock and not to look at my arm. He later explained that the brain will ignore feelings it doesn't like and refuse to acknowledge them unless you insist or confront the realization. Then I remember looking over at the doctor when they were about to "pop" it back in, which was a mistake, but was instinctive. I had no idea that my arm was bent in the awkward direction that I found it. He stood behind me and to the side and asked if I was ready, I just turned to make eye contact and saw a strange form where my shoulder should be, and my arm twisted back. I must have gone pale, because he said "uh oh," quickly pulled, and threw his body into the effort. I don't know how it went after that because I passed out. I take this moment to acknowledge that I am a fainter. Once I regained consciousness at the hospital, the pain was minimal. I was able to move my arm again, but they made me wear a sling for a week. I didn't; I removed it every time I left the house the next day. I was sore, for a good while, maybe three weeks, but I do not remember avoiding any activity. This memory convinces me that I need to try to set my pinky back into its joint. The finger looks like it is offset, to the outside of my hand. I can picture how the phalange is stuck, just outside of its intended location, while being pulled by the connective tissues against the end of the metacarpal, and just needs some encouragement. I know that I will have to pull it away and then guide it to fall back into its proper position, but I will have to do this in one swift motion, and without passing out mid-process, which is unlikely, given my history for fainting. I picture a cartoon princess, in a beautiful blue evening gown, in a beautiful ballroom, throwing the back of her hand up to her forehead in a dainty display of fainting, as her head tilts to the side while her body begins to collapse in a three line folding motion, just before a handsome prince catches her. He looks at the camera, winks, and says, "not again"...

No rush, I decide to eat another fruit cup, assuming the sugar and nutrients might help somehow. I retrieve another cup and repeat the process of tearing the film lid away enough to drink the juice. I don't nurse it this time. I drink it all in one go, then I remove the lip the rest of the way and start eating the fruit a mouthful at a time. It is mixed fruit today. Pears, peaches, and some other type of object. Then I get the much anticipated little cherry. It is always part of a cocktail cherry, but the roundness is a giveaway, plus the strange tingle that it leaves on the tongue. Samantha would remind me that is because they use bug guts to color those cherries.

That thought is the next pivotal moment in which my desire for companionship begins to close in on my emotions. I yearn for her comfort. It is selfish. I have, thus far, refused to accept or face the likely finality that all of the evidence suggests. In this moment, I wish my partner were here to help me. I wish she could collaborate with me on a solution. I wish we could discuss all of the options. I wish she could finish the job if I pass out or back out. But mostly, I just want her to tell me that it's going to be ok. I close my eyes while chewing the next bits of fruit and picture her face. I try to make my brain imagine her giving me a comforting look, and maybe saying something encouraging, but my brain just makes her stare at me. Then she melts into the "really?" look that is also encouraging, but less comforting. This is the more realistic of the two possibilities, because she would not shame me, but she would certainly downplay the situation, knowing it would help. I try to accept that this will not be that bad, and then my mind imagines the sharp and overwhelming pain that I know awaits me. I consciously tell myself to change that thought and I go back to calm and less anxious. I look at my right hand and feel queasy again. This time, I say out loud, "come on Sam! It won't be that bad!" I recognize that, in my situation, battling conflicting emotions is expected, but for the first time in my life, I truly experience the feeling of representing two different people, disagreeing about an opinion. Both personalities are completely entitled to their stance, and as I slide into the pessimist, unconsciously, and then coerce my psyche back to the optimist, each position is whole and complete, and the contradicting point is distant and impossible. I realize that I am also witnessing myself as these two people, which provides a third, more cynical presence, that is embarrassed by his own behavior.

It is time to get on with the procedure. I set the, now empty, fruit cup on the third shelf and notice that I can make out a display of significant chaos on the shelf behind where I wriggled it in and decided that I better organize my shit.

"It's not an infinite amount of shit, dumbass. You better take inventory and have a plan." I decide that I will work on that after I fix my hand, nurse myself after, and make my next attempt at escape. Plan for pinky relocation in knuckle joint: turn both arms toward each-other in front of my body, while seated. I will grab the entire right pinky with my left hand, then I simultaneously pull my hands apart and throw them away from my body. This should provide the cooperative forces necessary to dislodge the misplaced digit from its current entrapment and relocate the bone into the proper joint alignment. I pick up my arms and hold them across my front, left on top of right, my hands going to opposite elbows. Then I straighten both out and return them.

I repeat this exercise 10 times, then slowly separate them, to gauge the angle where my left hand will be able to properly grasp my right pinky. I twist and align my arms as they approach the ideal position, so that my hand will be at the optimal angle to grab the finger with its palm and assure adequate pressure. I consider the dual motion as I make the final approach, which began as a practice run. The intention was to run through the plan a few times and stretch more between rehearsals, when I decide that an attempt at surprising my subconscious may be the best idea. I recall my shoulder problem, and how the doctor chose to act swiftly once I caught on to the truth, because the brain may have inadvertently objected and caused additional challenges. In the split-second that I manifest this concept, my hands approach what I have decided to be the optimal position and I commit.

I snatch my pinky with the opposite hand, with no time to judge the efficacy of the grasp, and pull it hard. My left side did exactly as planned and I think I feel the separation occur. My right arm pushes away from my body and I release when I can no longer keep hold. This is an excellent plan. I do not register pain, at all, until moments after release. Then I yelp, make some kind of squeaky noise, and the sensation turns my stomach. I might have yelled more, but I instantly choke and retch, again, turning to my right, just in time to miss most of my legs and cover the wall with fruit and other masticated food and liquid. I choke on some and swallow it back. My eyes water, my nose clogs, and I immediately pour snot onto my upper lip. I begin pulling air through my teeth and huffing from the pain and general discomfort. It is amazing, my brain didn't have time to prepare for what I planned, and I realize there could be some benefit to losing my fucking mind and slipping into some form of acute, trauma-induced multiple-personality disorder. Once I wipe my face with my t-shirt and can see a bit, I check my handiwork. It is incredibly painful and I immediately recognize that it looks the same. The swelling around the joint makes it difficult to gauge the result with accuracy, but the general alignment suggests that I failed at completing the mission. I try to move the digit, but only the adjacent fingers respond, and it all screams at me.

"You have got to be kidding me!"

I am instantly frustrated. I am overwhelmed by feelings that only Atlanta traffic was able to conjure in me before now. I bite down hard, overwhelmed by the urge to scream. I scream. I scream out as loud as I can. My voice shifts between notes in a scratchy, desperate tone that is almost pathetic and disturbing at the same time. I remember my commitment to yell for help regularly, and immediately scream, "help!" as loud as possible. This execution would be heard through walls and across great distances. If there were anyone alive within 8-10 blocks, they heard a very disturbing sound.

Pain is temporary.

Most emotions are fleeting.

An overwhelming sense of defeat and disappointment in myself reveals itself in this moment and I don't think it ever leaves. I fight hard to destroy it, and I even try to ignore and deny it, but the self-loathing from my inability to execute what is necessary feels crippling. I cannot believe that I came so close to a solution and failed to complete it. I consider that perhaps my approach or plan were flawed, but I cannot imagine a better plan. I settle into the realization that I have simply failed. I lay my head back against the wall and close my eyes. I shake my head in disgust and decide to rest and relax a bit. Then I will stand, stretch, and repeat this process until I am ready to try again. For now, I just want to crawl into an even smaller hole and die.

I spend what feels like an eternity preparing myself to attempt my procedure once again. I try to find that perfect headspace where I can fool my own brain, which allowed the first try to proceed without anxiety. But my brain is onto me this time, so I decide to spend more time sitting straight and arranging my hands for the moment. I focus on the knowledge gleaned from the first time, and that dislodging the finger from its incorrect perch felt like a deep breath. Perhaps I am holding mine, but I can feel anticipation within the actual bone of its potential for returning to the correct alignment. It feels as if it wants to go back and I failed it. I can use this new intuition to sense exactly when to make the swift motion to the side. I fight back the feeling that I am doing this all wrong and decide that it is time again. I position my body at the angle where I have the most clearance toward the corner of where the shelves meet the wall to throw my right hand in stage 2. Then I position my right leg to be near the plausible finish point as an easy place to rest my traumatized hand after. I do a breathing exercise to flood my system with oxygen in an attempt to muster energy for a burst. Then I cross my arms again, but find the starting position sooner. I ensure proper grip and ignore the pain that occurs as I slide my left hand as far up my right pinky as possible. I close my grasp slowly, to ease into it and adjust grip, then visualize the procedure in my mind, with my eyes closed. I am picturing it, and realize that I almost feel like both the doctor and the patient while I review the steps in my head. This third-person sensation offers the opportunity. This time, I start to pull my pinky away more slowly than last time, but still at a decent clip. As soon as I feel the joint "breathe in," I give it one more tug away from the knuckle and throw my right hand away from my body while focusing on keeping it flat and level. This time, there is a sudden and jarring pain, specifically coming from that knuckle and I feel, and hear, a distinctive "pop." It is like a deep, quick breath in, followed by the fastest exhale ever. I avoid hitting the shelf or wall, exhale my own breath, and set my hand on my right thigh. Then I lean my head back, feel the blood rush to my hand and up my neck, and let the pain come like a massive wave. I admit, there is something resembling relief sprinkled on the pain. But I do not lose consciousness and the sensation generates visual hallucinations. As it swells in me, my vision is inundated by yellow light, closing in around my field of visibility, and pulsating with the rhythm of my heartbeat.

The vision disturbance prevents me, briefly, from knowing whether my eyes are open. I look for the light by the toilet hole, but it is not there. Maybe I did pass out. The yellow glow is subsiding back to the outskirts of my field of vision, I realize the room is dark, and that's why I can't tell if my eyes are open. I presume it is still Sunday, Day 5, but I am not going to torture myself with the phone right now. I am also not going to clean the vomit off the wall. Fuck that wall. I feel around to my left for the cereal container. But I do so carefully, because my clumsiness is starting to become a nuisance. I contact the middle of the container and pick it up. I slosh it around and decide, blindly, that there is about 1 inch of water in the bottom. I do not have a real idea, but this seems reasonable. The drips had increased at

some point during my silence. They make a distinct sound when
the water is less than 1/2 inch deep, it has more of a "slap-
splash." I have heard it, twice now, change to more of a "plop-
splash." I deeply inhale the top of the container again and still
only detect the faint aroma of plastic most certainly from the
container itself. I also regret taking long breaths right now
because of the smell in the air. I had hoped it would either
become my new normal and I would no longer notice it, or
perhaps it would begin to subside or dissipate. Neither: it seems
to be getting worse. Or it is new again every time I awaken or
pay attention to my sense of smell. It is horrible. I decide again,
that the water is fine, so I take a small sip, roll it over my tongue
and around my mouth, like one would experience a fine whiskey,
inspect it for any questionable characteristics, and, when I find
none, I swallow. Then I repeat the process with larger sips and
less inspection, but make sure not to drink the rest. I decide it is
wise to always leave a little bit: "Never finish the cup."

The metaphor in my mind, the act of tasting the water, and
the pain in my hand all direct my mind to the bottle of Talisker
in my cabinet, a mere 5 feet away. It is a rare 25 year-aged
Scotch Whisky, a gift from my father before he passed. I rarely
drink, so I don't keep much alcohol around, but I have been
saving that bottle for a special occasion. I moved it twice, when
we moved homes, before Nathaniel was born, and when we
moved into this apartment. It has never been opened. My father
passed just over 12 years ago. He never knew we were going to
have a baby. He was older than my mother and they separated
when I was 10. I don't think they ever divorced, but it didn't
matter. She never moved on, claimed that she was "better off,"
and he had very little regard for social norms and expectations,

so I'm not entirely sure if they were even legally married. He was not absent from my life, but he always wanted me to join his campaign to avoid work and hustle any way necessary to get by. "Have less, need less," he would always tell me.

"I don't need to work a normal job because I live a life that does not require normal things."

But I admit, he certainly enjoyed his life. He would take up with various entrepreneurs and consult them until it started to fail, or thrive, and then move on to the next hustle. He always had and sold, pot. I prefer to refer to it as cannabis, but he would correct me and say, "I'm no doctor, I actually help people."

He contracted hepatitis from a blood transfusion following a freak accident with a combine in Kentucky, while day-laboring at a wheat farm. The pot and bourbon could not stop the progression of the illness, so he seemed to welcome it with ever-increasing amounts of brown liquor. He was not a bad drunk either. I actually preferred his company after he had at least two, decent, drinks, preferably bourbon. He did not get on with gin. It made him "ornery," he would say, but he told me once that his grandfather drank gin and beat his grandmother, so I guess he just thought it wise to avoid the stuff. He didn't do the holidays that most Americans did. He would always visit me a few weeks after my birthday so that we could actually be together without all of the "fuss." He did not buy presents for birthdays and Christmas, mostly because he didn't have extra money, but also because he thought that these things were frivolous and needless. As a child, it hurt me, and as an adolescent, it pissed me off. When I turned 15, and he showed up the next week to take me to dinner and fishing for the weekend, I told him I didn't want to go. He asked why, and I told him that I just wanted a normal birthday for once. He said, "what, exactly, is a normal birthday, son? You are only actually born once. You mean: you want a birthday like everyone else. You want a life like everyone else. You want to feel ordinary. The best gift I can give you is a glimpse of life that is extraordinary instead." I didn't think dinner at a BBQ joint and fishing a pond in Greenville was very "extraordinary," but I understand the sentiment. I really did love my father, because he taught me how to be simple and practical. My pragmatic side is mostly from him. His health declined quickly after he turned 50 and he just poured brown liquor all over it. Once the doctors at Emory gave him a year to live, I asked him if he would quit drinking and try to live a little longer, and he said, "why would I punish myself for dying? I'm going to enjoy this last year, really take the gloves off!" It was like he had been waiting for the final countdown. Suddenly, he had money, which was strange. I was not ashamed to ask him either, because he had always bragged about not working and not needing money, so he never had a career or anything that would allow for a pension or retirement plan. But suddenly he had a new car, and stayed in hotels almost every night. We went out to eat no less than 50 times before he died. When I asked how he came to have all of this money, all of the sudden, he would shrug and say, "oh, you know...."

But I didn't, I never did, and I still don't. I also never felt like he was "sick." He invited me to parties all the time, mostly in other cities and states. But he would call me and say that so-and-so was having a get-together to celebrate his life while he was still living and I should come. I went to a few, when I could. Samantha did not go with me. She loved my father, because he adored her, and he was very kind and gentle with her, but she saw through his facade and had little interest in participating in his demise. She felt that joining the team was enabling his self-destruction. We did not disagree about it, but I participated. I admit, sometimes I wonder if the hepatitis was a fabrication, and he just drank himself to death. He never allowed anyone to accompany him to appointments, so it was all just his word until he entered the hospital at the end. Then it was just "acute liver failure," with no mention of hepatitis, or alcohol, for that matter. I found him on my front porch one morning, shortly before he passed. It was a Sunday. He wasn't sleeping or anything weird, he was just sitting at our patio table, staring at my yard. I made the coffee and walked to the front windows, as usual at our little house in Edgewood, and there he was. I opened the door and said, "Dad? Are you ok?" He said, "yeah! Why wouldn't I be?"

"Why are you just sitting on my porch at 6:30 on a Sunday morning?"

"What else should I be doing? I wanted to see you, but I didn't want to wake you up!"

I invited him in for coffee, but he asked if we could sit outside instead. He always preferred to be outside, so I fetched him a cup, warned Samantha of his presence, and sat with him. I thought this visit was odd, because he was usually more excited or had some sort of plan. This time, he was content just sitting. He did tell me that he had accepted his life was ending and wanted to make sure I had also accepted that. But then we just talked about The Braves, his recent trip to Colorado, and other normal things. When he offered me a drag of his joint that morning, I obliged. I rarely smoked pot, or ate it, or used it in any way at the time, but I was not against it. My instinct was to politely decline, but I realized that he had never really offered it to me before. We had smoked together before, and recently, because I was at his friend's "going away" party for him, and cannabis was really the substance of choice that day, so when he offered to "have a number" with me that morning on my porch, I realized that this was new and that I should partake. This was a very important part of his life, so we got very stoned, and laughed, and let the world go by in front of us. We spent the whole day out there, just talking and laughing. Samantha had come and gone twice, and we were oblivious to her intentions and movements, but when she appeared near sunset and asked if we wanted steaks, my father raised an eyebrow at her and said, "what kind?"

"Strips, from Wilkes'. I was in Snellville and thought you two might want a real steak for dinner."

He said, "I don't know why on earth you would ever need to go to Snellville, but I would love a steak."

She said, "Well, only if your son isn't too stoned to cook them, because that's the only steak I will eat."

So, they drank bourbon while I cooked dinner.

We had a great dinner, and a great evening, and never thought for a minute that it might be our last. In retrospect, he obviously knew. We offered him the spare bedroom, but he said he still had visits to make, and bid us farewell. This is not just an expression, he literally said, "I bid you farewell," before he left places, but only if it was a true departure, not running to the store or anything trivial. Then he remembered that he brought me something and that was the whole reason he came over to begin with, 15 hours ago. He went out to his Volvo and brought back a brown bag, obviously with liquor in it. He produced the bottle of rare, 25 year scotch whisky, proudly, and handed it to me. I was perplexed. He said, "drink this when the time is right. It waited 25 years to get its bottle, it can wait until you decide it's time to drink it." This was a strange gift from him, but also just odd that he was giving me a gift at all. I said, "Dad, what's this for?" He replied, "I asked the shopkeep what bourbon to give your son to honor him. He said, 'scotch!'" Then he let out a huge burst of laughter. I chuckled and said, "why are you honoring me?"

"Because I'm proud of you. A bottle of bourbon would be a selfish gift. You are more sophisticated than me, so you deserve a sophisticated drink. I hate scotch, in flavor and in theory. It's what professors drink, so I got you a bottle that you could drink with your smart friends and be amazed, or that you could put on a shelf and admire."

I was shocked. We embraced, and he passed in palliative care 2 weeks later. I did see him right before he died, but he was truly just a vehicle then. I still have no idea where the money came from at the end, but I inherited his car, a box of papers, including all of his vital documents, a box of other items, his pistol, his watch, and roughly $12,000 cash. I guess he had squirreled money away like a hood-gypsy, and when the end was near, he blew it out. But he had been so simple for so long, he still couldn't spend it all. I like to think he kept some intentionally for me, but I know that to be untrue. He died 9 and 1/2 months after they gave him a year. I'm sure he was on track to spend it all when his body gave him the old "fuck you! I'm not doing this shit anymore!"

I didn't drink that scotch when Nathaniel was born. I didn't drink it when I got my masters degree. I didn't drink it when I got promoted, any of the times I got promoted. I didn't drink it on our 10 or 15 year anniversary. I don't know what I was saving it for. I don't even keep it on display, but I think about it all the time. And now, I could really use that scotch and I'm not sure if I can get to it. I decide to fetch the can opener and fork from the shelf to open and consume another random can of food. I perform this task without light. I know where everything is and I just need to feel around for it. I knock the tortilla chip bag off the shelf in the process and decide to have some of those as well. I cannot wait to find out what meal I have chosen for dinner tonight. I feel the can in my hands and contemplate its contents. I guess it is diced tomatoes. I get the can open and reach in with my index finger first. It is a watery liquid and I immediately find a cut green bean, which is another distinct object. I am very excited about this good fortune.

I eat slowly this time, one bean at-a-time, and I take breaks to chew and think. I whistle between bites. I find the melody for The Andy Griffith Show to be the simplest, and I get through it a few times.

Halfway through, I hear something outside. It is not a sound that startles or worries me. It is another constant sound. It is familiar. It is almost a hissing or rasping that is perpetual, but increases and decreases in volume. It also changes the smell about 30 minutes after I first hear it. It is faint. I am seated in my new location to the left of the door, so I grab my personal phone out of my bag, and turn it on. I search the room with the Lock Screen light and then check the ceiling. Nothing is out of the ordinary. I adjust the water catching container and notice that the bottom is almost covered, which suggests that it is filling too quickly. Then I notice that the drops are more frequent. That sound must be rain. I made sure to align the container perfectly, so as to not waste the manifesting opportunity, and turn the phone off. Once I know what it was, the sound is obvious. It is far away, but now it is unmistakable. That's when I see something move to my left. It is pitch black in the room, and I see something swing past me. It is not too fast, but I sense it and see it in space. I quickly turn the phone back on, but there is nothing there. I do not turn on the flashlight, because I can see clearly that there is nothing there, and no possibility of something where I sense it.

I turn the phone back off and close my eyes. I find the spot in the wall where I had previously picked a small hole to investigate, and pick at it some more, gently. I start taking more paint and drywall away from the edges of the hole, with my eyes closed, and eventually, I drift off to sleep, the sound of the rain providing some ancient comfort.

## Chapter 7

Day 6

Monday

I awaken, slightly cold. I find my pants on the floor and lay them over my legs. It is still dark, and I drift off again.

I awaken again and it is still dark. There is no light from the toilet hole yet. My right pinky is sending me a signal that it is hurt, but seems less intense and possibly even better. I decide to prepare myself for inventory, and decide that I should stand, stretch, maybe exercise if possible, and then put in a full day of work. I set my can of green beans in the back left corner of the room on the floor with the empty can of cannellini beans. There is still liquid in the green bean can, probably with bits of bean floating in it. I decide to save that, if possible. I also decide that I will likely need to organize the garbage that I am creating. The empty cans and other non-biodegradable objects could prove useful as tools or containers for other things, but they will need to be stored in a way that does not overcrowd my limited space. For now, I locate the two empty fruit cups on the shelf, which I had placed them both near the edge of shelf three, and stack them with the bottom of the rounded base nestled in the top of the green bean can in the corner. There are now two cans and two cups. I have not eaten much, but I have not needed much either. I decide to find my breakfast while I organize and take inventory, and that it would be wise to eat small meals throughout the day instead of gorging myself when I am hungry. I am not hungry yet, so a little workout should cure that problem.

I have almost perfected the act of getting from my preferred seating position to standing by leaning left, onto my left hand and arm, pulling my right leg up under me first, then rolling to the right to catch myself with my right palm on the third shelf edge, while also pulling my left leg up, and then determining which way to turn. I can turn around between the shelves and the spice rack on the door, but it is easier if I move into the space beside the door on the right, if facing the shelves. I am avoiding the space to the left, because my water collection container is there, and I dare not risk that accident. Plus, that corner is very bloody. Even though this is not a real issue for any particular reason, it bothers me. Now, unfortunately, there is vomit on the other wall. I'm sure it would smell in here if the chemical odor were not so dense, but as it stands, I cannot sense the vomit or feces. I stop to acknowledge that I got up smoothly, and check myself in the dark. I start with my head, and determine that the laceration on the front right behind the hairline is the worst of the two, and is still quite tender. The hair around it is matted and crusty with dried blood. This is not ideal, but I am not going to waste any resources on cleaning up just yet. Wiping my ass is one thing, washing my hair is another adventure entirely. I feel that most of this cut is scabbing, but it still feels soft in places. I estimate it to be about 2-3 inches long, running away from my hairline at an angle, from directly above my right eyebrow, an inch back from the hairline, and at an angle pointing down toward my ear. It is parallel to nothing, and will certainly leave a scar. I start to consider when this happened to estimate time of healing, but decide it is frivolous unless I can get out of here. The best course of action now is to not re-injure or open it back up so it can fully heal. I have dirty blonde hair, or light brown, depending on who you ask and how long it has been since my last haircut. I get my haircut every 2-3 weeks, if possible. I walk to the Great Clips in town and get the same haircut. Basically a flattop, but I don't spike it. My hair grows forward, and parts to my right. I do not use any product, and if I keep it cut, I only have to wash it every few days and it has looked the same for almost 20 years. If it is short, freshly cut, 2 on the sides with a fade to finger-length on top, it appears more blonde, but not "tow-head" blonde. When it is freshly cut, I am often referred to as a blonde. If I am in need of a cut, it could be mistaken for brown. My driver's license says "blonde," because the last time I renewed my license in person, the nice lady at the DMV asked what color my hair is, and I said, "blonde," to which she replied, "are you sure?" I told her that I don't care, so she listed me as blonde. I just got a haircut last week, so I figure my hair should look blonde right now, but then I realize that was actually almost two weeks ago. I feel the hair on top of my head and determine that I am not yet ready for a cut, but will be soon. This also means that the blood on my head will really stand out. I could use one of my phones to look at myself, but have decided, numerous times recently when my phone was on, that no good will come of that right now. I move my hand toward the back of my head and find the second wound. The small cut has closed into a stiff scab already and has hairs dried into it with the hair around it crusty and crisp with dried blood also. This injury has produced a convex lump just beneath and around it. I remember hearing that "a bump on the head is fine so long as it's going out and not in," and hope it to be true. It's not a large bump, but enough to feel around a few times and mouth "ooo," in response. I imagine what a bump going "in" would look like. I feel like I have seen that before, but never during a traumatic injury, just noticed when a person has an indentation on their skull that can be easily seen. I imagine that if you hit your head, and there is a concave location from the impact, you would instinctively be worried. But people have delivered babies and claimed to have never known they were pregnant, so there must be a good reason for the "rule of thumb about head bumps." I check the rest of my skull and then my face. I can feel the caked blood in different places on my face and in my eyebrows. I do not sense any injuries to my face.

"Thank goodness," I think aloud, "I'm going to need my good looks in the post-apocalypse to make the challenges of global repopulation easier." The actual humor in this bit of monologue is that I am not a particularly attractive person. This is not a statement intended to highlight my humility: I truly am not very good looking. I undeniably married way up and out of my league. I do not think of myself as average looking, but I can honestly say that I do not remember anyone referring to me as an attractive person in any of the typical ways. I am never referred to as "the handsome one" in a group, or sexy, gorgeous, or anything else that could be perceived as a compliment on physical appearance. Other than my wife, I do not think anyone finds me attractive. My personality doesn't help the situation either. I am a rather dry individual. I find myself to be in good spirits most of the time, but my face tends to display little emotion or enthusiasm, and I was taught not to feign interest or excitement, so long as I don't insult someone. I tend to come across as unimpressed, which I usually am. My son and my wife tend to get the most visible emotions from me, because they are usually the most common cause of them. The rest of my life tends to be rather uneventful and that's ok. I am confident that my rather basic face is unscathed by my recent trauma and move on to my neck and shoulders. My shirt is quite dirty. It is a white undershirt, but it is now stained around the neck and shoulders with what I can only assume to be diluted blood. But I have wiped my face and hands on it also, so there is definitely vomit on the front. I decide to take it off and ensure I do not have any other injuries. I hang my shirt over the top of the spice rack on the door behind me. I start to move my hands in crossing patterns across my neck, shoulders, chest, sides, and abdomen. I find places where I am a bit tender, and identify what seem to be bruises developing on my left side, mid ribs. I reach around to my back and do not find anything of major concern. My pinky is starting to complain from all of this activity, but I ignore it and carry on. As I come to each place, I move it around a bit, if it is a moveable body part. I twist at my waist and bend at different points in my torso. I remember to go back and rotate my head in each direction ten times, slowly, letting it reach its terminal stretch point in every direction. This always makes me a little dizzy and queasy, and today is no exception. But I am already nauseous, so this just makes me more ill. Then I begin investigating my midsection. I check my hips, my pelvic area, my cock and balls, which I pause for a minute and hold, because it's comforting. All little boys do this. They all go through a phase where they hold their "junk" whenever they are still for more than two seconds. Men do it too, most of us have just learned not to do it in public. I have this thought while holding my junk. It's not a sexual feeling, it's just comforting. My penis, scrotum, and testicles are all in place and seem unharmed. I inspect the surrounding areas, and make my way down my thighs, careful not to use my pinky, and find my right knee is warm. It does feel a bit sore, so I lift my thigh to my right and pump my leg a few times. I assume my knee is having trouble from being bent under me for so long right after the event. Considering I am just noticing it, I'm sure it will heal. I am a runner, so my knees always have problems. Beyond my knees, I am forced to inspect my lower legs one at a time, because I am standing, and the space necessary to fold in half is limited. Nothing noted on my shins or the tops of my feet. I make my way back up the backs of my legs, one at a time in the lower portions, and then both thighs and up to my buttocks. Samantha says she likes my ass, but I, again, know that she is flattering me to get what she wants. I welcome this behavior, always. I am a stern advocate for integrity and honesty, unless it threatens to harm those involved, short and long term. So, my wife's consistent efforts to flatter me are an honorable breach of integrity, in order to attract the physical satisfaction she desires. This benefits everyone involved and I cannot imagine a negative outcome.

I am satisfied with the inspection, so I continue my stretching. Roll the shoulders, both directions, rotate elbows, rotate wrists, I hesitate with the hand extensions, but go for it. My right pinky is hurting, so I barely stretch that hand, but I do my best otherwise. I work my hips and lean as far as possible at the waist in every direction. Then I work each joint in my legs in alternating order, so that neither tires too quickly. This is a slightly truncated version of the stretch I do every morning. After six days of lethargy, injury, and defeat, it exhausts me. The light has started seeping in more, and I can see silhouettes of objects around me now. I consider timing the light in my space, to have an idea of how long I have to work each day, and decide this is a waste of battery for any of my devices. Instead, I retrieve that water container, and sip about half of its contents. It is around 3 mouthfuls that I divide into 8 sips. I try to savor each one. I still do not detect any signs of contamination.

I turn my attention to the shelves. I am inclined to organize by foods or meals, but that is the chef in me, I need to organize by usage. I will make no discrimination between general categories like "food" and "tool," but rather attempt to organize by least needed or used on shelf three and most needed on shelf two. Shelf one should hold things that I would like to be able to reach while seated, so I can just slide under that shelf and still access tools and such. I may even utilize my briefcase as a tool bag so I can take it under the shelves with me to work. My computer and other items will be vacating the bag when their batteries die anyhow. I bring the Rubbermaid container with camp supplies down from the top shelf, but the container with birthday supplies can stay in the top shelf even though it has candles in it, which I can fetch when necessary. I do not worry about organizing the shelves as I distribute, that will be determined when I manage each supply center at the granular level it deserves. I begin to move the objects away from the wall and to whatever shelf they belong on. I relocate a large can of tomatoes, instant rice boxes, two mushroom-flavored brown rice boxes, a box of stuffing mix, a burlap bag of popcorn, one yellow rice with peppers, a paper box of beef broth, a large bottle of local honey, 1/2 full, and six cans of sliced white mushrooms in water. The jar of jam from my aunt goes to shelf one, easy blood-sugar fix, and once opened, it will need to be eaten. I start shifting the three canned good dispensers all the way to the right of the second remaining shelf. A can of green beans pops up from its housing. I retrieve the can and set it, as it is, on its side, just to the left of the dispensers, and turn my attention back to the task at hand. I am just lifting the subject to make another rearward shift when I hear and see the can of beans rolling to the edge of the shelf. There is no lip to catch the can, and as I realize this, I try to set the dispensers down so that I can catch the can. I get my left hand down from the top shelf in time to get under it, but the weight of it gets past me, I fumble, and it falls. I react with a little hop and spread my feet, the can hits the floor and misses me. I reach to retrieve the can, but it has rolled between my feet to the pantry door. I have to maneuver strategically to get a hold of it. The whole ordeal only takes a few seconds, but I consider what is happening the whole time. It rolled off the shelf, no surprise, because this shelf has been compromised. But it rolled fast and then continued again on the ground. I decide to place another can and get the same result. I catch it before the fall, and feed both cans back into the top of the dispensers. I push down on the front left of the shelf and see how it pops down through where its support bracket has broken but is still connected to the wall. I will need to fix this soon. I take another can out, pinto beans, and set it on its side on the lowest shelf. When I release it, it rolls toward the edge but gains momentum faster than the others.

"Well that's interesting."

"Did you see that? They really did a horrible job installing these shelves."

I set the can of pinto beans on the ground, not in the same direction, but with its top and bottom facing the back wall and the door. It just sits there, staring up at me like a stubborn teenager, "what, old man?"

I reach down, using my newly-perfected yoga maneuver, and turn the top 45 degrees to the left, and it turns until parallel with the door, then rolls slowly, but steadily, to the door and bumps to a stop.

I never checked my apartment for level before the event, I just assumed it was, because it is a very large building, composed of concrete, steel, and brick. I own a level that I use for hanging pictures, leftover from being a homeowner, but it is in the hall closet, behind my toolbox and the vacuum, doing me absolutely no good now. I am perplexed, but I remember that iPhones have a level feature. I don't know if they require cellular signals to work, but I know they have gyroscopic capabilities. I turn on my phone, and while it is starting, I stand up, and can suddenly sense that the room is leaning. I misinterpret the sensation as dizziness at first, assuming I stood up too fast, which I often experience, and my current condition would amplify this, but when my brain settles into being vertical, it highlights that I am not standing perfectly parallel within my immediate surroundings. I unlock my phone with my passcode, because it doesn't recognize my face. I locate the "measure" app, because I haven't used it in a long time. I toggle to "level" and acclimate to the functionality. I work fast, the battery is at 35%. I measure in different places and at different angles. I determine that the room is certainly not level, being at a pitch of 6-8 degrees in different places.

This discovery only exasperates my nausea, because now the world has shifted, and my brain is struggling to process it. The phenomenon absolutely amazes me: The fact that many experiences do not exist in our realities until we become aware of, or sense, them. It is similar to the scientific principle of observation influencing the behavior of particles. Now I am slightly dizzy, very nauseous, and struggling to remain upright. I decide to sit for a moment and gather myself. This time, I come down a bit harder, and now I can tell that I am on an incline. The sickness that has been lingering in me begins to strengthen, like a motor that is spooling up to speed. It no longer feels like I may vomit, but there is a sick feeling, somewhere behind my eyes, that manifests throughout my torso. My ears feel heavy, the sensation tightens my jaw, my mouth is dry, and my eyelids feel puffy.

This is similar to the feeling I get when I am sick with a virus. We all have sensations that trigger an awareness that we have been infected by something. This could mean that I have a fever, and I am overcome by a suspicion that I might be sick or getting sick. I begin to gather the tools needed to repair the shelf. I fight back the urge to vomit. I investigate my subject that is in need of repair with the flashlight on my phone, carefully taking mental images, planning to work in the dark. I turn off the flashlight and allow my eyes to adjust.

I see my son, Nathaniel, in front of me. He is not smiling. He is just looking past me, through me.

"Nathaniel? Nate?"

He does not respond. I notice that his gray hoodie is torn by the collar and also that I can see some red at the neckline of his shirt. He still does not move or respond. He is just there, in front of me.

My eyes start to regain focus, but I continue to stare where my son is sitting, like a wax figure, in front of me. The image of his blank expression worries me, and I expect his face to change, or for him to react.

Why is he just sitting there?

I blink: He is gone.

I check the time: 11:21 AM

I turn the phone off and place it back in its compartment in my briefcase. I position myself to begin working. I have enough light to see what I am working with but not enough for the detail, so I will rely on my hands for that. My pinky hurts, but I am now just ignoring it and being mindful not to re-injure. I fetch the old folding knife from the camping equipment and my fingers catch what feels like paper in the box. I dig around for it, and discover that there is a piece of paper under the package of bamboo skewers. I withdraw the paper item from the box and bring it close to my face for inspection. It is a folded piece of yellow legal pad paper. It is folded down into a small rectangle. Something is written on the outside of it. I think I know what this says, but I can't be sure. I try to make out the writing on the outside, but it is very faint, so I grab one of the cheap plastic cigarette lighters and flick it to life on the second try. The paper, still folded, reads, "POPS," in all caps. I release the lighter and quickly and carefully unfold the paper. I relight the lighter, and find a sloppily written message inside. It is my son's handwriting, much like mine. He has written larger than the legal-spaced lines of the yellow paper, so he was doing it hurriedly. It says:

"Pops,

Thank you for taking me to the little river camping. I had much more fun than roller coasters. I like fish now.

I love you pops.

Nate"

And there was a cute smiley face and a heart below his name.

I release the fuel lever on the lighter. The page goes dark. The room goes dark. I see him sitting before me again. I think it is him, same position, same shirt, same dusty blonde hair. But now he has no face. He immediately fades away as my eyes adjust to the sunlight in my room.

I wonder when he put that note in the box? I have never seen it, so I guess he stuck it in there when we were packing up the campsite. I don't remember him writing anything, but he loves to make little notes and make cards for people. He also draws and writes when he is bored, so maybe he had a moment of boredom and found some paper and pencil, but I didn't notice. Since it was on the bottom of the container, and the box has random objects in it, I may never have found it. We went camping at Little River Canyon two years ago, when he was nine. We had the trip planned for over a month when one of our neighbors, two days before, invited him to go to Six Flags. It was a no-brainer to me: we had a campsite reservation, we had been planning this trip for a while, camping is a thing we do together and is important to us and he loves it, he doesn't like roller coasters, and he doesn't really know the child that invited him very well. I actually think the other parents were trying to help their child make friends and this was a lifeline. I explained the logistical reasoning to Nathaniel and the other parents. He never really brought it up, but I guess he pondered it quietly, and realized, at some point, that it was a good decision to go camping. I break down the details in my mind, and remember that he didn't like to eat fish at the time, but on this trip, he caught a beautiful rainbow trout, which we prepared and ate for dinner. It was truly delicious, but also, catching fish, and eating your catch, is an important way to expand your palate and accept a new food item. It is a primal desire that removes barriers of preference. He connected with this principle and it obviously had a great impact on him. The whole trip was great and we spent more time sitting and talking than we had ever before. He had reached the age where he liked to explore, adventure, and liked to be entertained, but could also have a good conversation. He caught the only fish of the weekend, and it was a whopper. He wanted to do "fancy stuff" to it in preparation, but I showed him how to fillet the creature and prepare the meat, then season lightly with salt and pepper, and cook it in vegetable oil in a hot, cast iron, pan. We had it in the pan within 2 minutes of cutting it, which is the real secret to preparing delicious fish. We also saw a bald eagle on that trip, which was an awe-inspiring and peaceful moment. He noticed it by the river, and we both stood, motionless, waiting for it to move. It was 50 yards away, on the other side, doing the same thing we were: fishing. We stared until it flew away, which seemed like an eternity. Then we looked at each other and said, at the same time, "whoa." I told him at dinner that the bird only wished it had caught a fish that nice.

I imagine that, if Nathaniel were here with me now, this could somehow be a little bit more of an adventure than a struggle.

I open the side pouch of my briefcase, refold the note, and place it inside. I close it up, and try to turn my visual and emotional attention back to the abandoned support bracket of original-shelf 2.

I use the various tools and objects to remove unneeded brackets from the wall and repair the shelf in need. The project takes a long time and requires creative engineering, but I finish, set my tools on the repaired second shelf, and eat a fruit and nut bar while I admire my handiwork. I wonder more about the fact that the room is at a substantial pitch. What does this actually mean?

I can make more assumptions, and I can consider the evidence carefully, but what I come up with is not very comforting.

I know that the event was some sort of catastrophic and violent attack with weapons of mass-destruction that offered no substantial warning to the victim population. The immediate result was enough to compromise the integrity of my building. I will investigate this further next. I must assume that the "pressure" I experienced was related to the type of explosion that impacted us. I assume this was "nuclear," or "atomic," although I admit that I do not know the difference. I recall hearing or reading that one of the weapons was an arsenal of "fission" bombs, and perhaps that is what I experienced. Also, either the same weapon, or some other factor, has rendered my multiple forms of communication technology utterly useless.

I sit down with the bag of Scoops Tortilla chips that also contain seven peanut butter filled pretzels. I am eating them very slowly, with no discrimination.

I have been able to hear outside of my space, even detecting a sound as subtle as rain, but have heard no indication of other humans. I have not been visited by any other living things, either. I have not seen any flies, or roaches, rats, mice, squirrels, etc. nor have I heard any scampering or scratching that would suggest their unseen presence.

I decide to perform my ritual scream for "help!"

I have not heard any emergency vehicles, or the tornado siren that warned me of the impending doom that befell my world. If other people survived the attack, they are not within my earshot, or are not making sound that I can detect. I have considered, but will not express, a concern for "fallout." I am aware that it is a part of nuclear war, and that the residual radiation is perhaps more dangerous than the explosion itself. I am sure that the smell in my world is related to the attack, and I consider that my continued sickness and exhaustion may well be related to the result of exposure to radiation. The smell is so putrid, I consider that it may be from some type of "dirty" weapon, that unleashes more than just the explosion and radiation, but also chemical or biological weaponry. I also acknowledge that if the enemy (I decide to consider the alleged joint force a single unit) intends to obliterate the western world, they either plan to invade and finish off any survivors, or have factored that into the attack. If they released all of this by drone attack, it is likely because there are elements that they do not want to be exposed to. Physical invasion may be moot, if thorough evaluation of the potential stages of deterioration were planned and calculated thoroughly. Now I consider that some of my good fortune may soon become less favorable. The access to air and water may also be my access to radioactive exposure and other dangerous materials. I feel sick again, but I do not vomit.

I become aware of a pain at my neck. I reach up for it, and find a wound, just below my jawline, that is surrounded by the stubble of hair growing on my face. It feels like a scratch. It also itches and burns slightly. I scratch it, instinctively, and it feels better and worse simultaneously. I have a thought that I may have been scratching this spot already but I have no recollection of doing it. It feels wet and I do not need to see it to know that I have scratched myself down to blood. I note this discovery as another piece of evidence. I consider that it has been two days since my bowels moved or I have urinated, so I consider this to be in the near future. Next though, I will search for a way out. It suddenly dawns on me that I may be waiting for someone to rescue me, when there may be no one to do so. I also have a sickening realization that if my son is alive, he too could be trapped, and I would very much like to help him, even though six days is a long time without food or water. But I would much rather say that I did everything possible, instead of suffering in my tiny cell.

I begin working on a hole, mostly for investigative purposes with the folding knife that I carry everywhere in my briefcase, with a small blade, and serrated toward the handle. It should be perfect for cutting through Sheetrock. I choose a place, nipple height, near the corner. I remove a highly imperfect circle of drywall and paint, and a good amount of dust and pebbles falls into the room, revealing an off-white insulation. The light in my room is not only dimming, but has also turned a strange orange hue, which seems odd. I investigate inside the hole with my finger and find rock, or concrete, within the wall. I cannot fathom why or how it came to be inside the wall, but I will need more space to figure that out.

I get my work phone out of my briefcase and turn it on. Once it boots, I note the time: 3:55 PM. I also note that it is too early for sunset, so the light change must mean weather. I turn on the flashlight on the phone from the Lock Screen, uninterested in any other features. I shine the light into the hole in the wall as soon as I am no longer blinded by it. I decide that there is more debris inside the wall than I would expect. I know construction is messy, but this is excessive. I find the concrete and try, in vain, to move it. I look beyond that and I do not see another wall where one should be. I turn off the phone. I cut and extract more until a large amount of material decides to fall into the room on its own. I escape being struck by any of the falling debris, but I am shocked by the scenario. I retrieve the phone to investigate, turn it on, and immediately hold down the flashlight button from the Lock Screen.

My hands are shaking as light explodes into the room. I am blind for about 30 seconds, and before my eyes can adjust, I see another figure before me. This person, or creature, is unrecognizable. It is humanoid, but I do not see any arms. It has a distinct head and torso, but the abdomen is much narrower than I am used to seeing, almost like a starved and emaciated figure except with a broader, almost round, chest area and no arms. It looks as if it is shaking its head at me, but the light makes it hard to focus. I am terrified at the distinct reality of the image, because I see it clearly before me, in the lit space, but as my eyes adjust, it fades out and I know it is not there.

Now I am shaking and it is hard to settle my eyes on the actual space before me. On the ground, there is a collection of debris, most of it dust, chunks of drywall composition, like soft rocks, and unrecognizable objects that could be paper or pieces of paint. Atop all of that is a large piece of concrete. In the space left open in the wall, there is another large chunk of concrete, with pieces of rebar sticking out. It is almost centered in the hole, near the bottom. Another large piece of concrete above is suspended in the space and large enough that it, too, could fall in if I cut around it, but I have no idea how much is behind it. I can get my hand above the chunk that has fallen in to the right, and I am careful not to catch it on the twisted rebar that is also occupying that space. I pull chunks of rock and dust out, and try to brush as much as I can back into the void beyond, to save my space if possible, but there is not much play. I get much of the insulation out of the way, and direct the light into the 1 inch gap between the rock and the wall, to see what lies beyond. The wall on the other side is gone around the stone, obviously, but I can only make out a tiny space where there is no debris. I turn down to the camp supply bin at my feet and get a bamboo skewer from the bag. I return to the discovered space in the hole and start pushing the skewer in. I continue to hit hard, immovable objects and shift directions to find another entrance. I retrieve the stainless tongs and wedge them between the two pieces of stone until I reach the wall on the other side. I molest the area until another large chunk cascades into the room. This piece lands on my foot.

"Fuck me!"

The piece that falls in does no significant damage to my foot, but it hurts. I step back, leaving the tongs in the wall and lift my right foot to check it with my hand. I rub it a bit as I lean against the spice rack to my right. Gravity now exists and that is the natural direction to lean if cooperating with my environment. I shine the light at the ground and see that the object is a brick. It is not a pretty brick. One side is painted white and the other five are an ugly gray and brown. It is some type of construction brick that gets painted instead showing off its natural beauty like finer specimens. This brick belongs on the face of my building. The exterior of our complex is mostly this type of brick, as is the large office building across the lot. I cannot recall which is this color, but I doubt I would be able to determine anyhow. The exterior of our building is painted brick, like this, some architectural siding, and some, assuredly, prefabricated concrete. This brick is likely from the exterior wall that is outside this room, across the kitchen, and beyond Nathaniel's bedroom. It spans that side of the building, five stories up and the entire block back to the next crossroad. The apartments are divided horizontally by internal fire walls: Large, concrete sections of the building that go the entire height, divide the units of each floor, and can be identified outside by their edges, marking the dwellings by creating sections of brick. They are designed to segregate a fire to portions of the building, protecting access to internal fire exits and stairs in each section. The building also has concrete floors dividing units from the apartments above or below, so if my downstairs neighbor has a massive fire, I am not immediately fucked. I pick up the brick and decide it has been blown from its place with incredible force. The four sides that would connect it to other bricks in a wall all have bits of mortar still attached. It is sharp and oddly shaped. I am lucky it didn't hurt my foot more. One corner of the painted side is missing, but the object is otherwise intact. The pieces of concrete and rebar are even more concerning. I shine the light where the tongs are sticking out, but I can't see anything. From my current perspective, outside my room is a complete rubbish pile of construction debris. Again, my imagination runs wild. Did I accidentally choose the one place outside my room that is piled with this mess to attempt my escape, or is this sample representative of the whole area? It is unlikely that I am unlucky enough to find the most unnavigable location surrounding me for escape, but also highly unlikely that I accidentally chose the only place in my building seemingly not reduced to waste when the event occurred. I cannot decide which is less likely, so I just grab the protruding handle of the tongs and yank away with my left hand. They come out with some effort, but on the first try, forcing more dust into the room, illuminated by the light, and not settling at all. The cloud puffs upward into the space above and lingers. I start to consider the possibility that the physical evidence around me would suggest that my building has collapsed, but that my pantry did not. I think about the clichéd question: "what would you do if you were the last person on earth?" I have never considered the question enhanced by being trapped inside a tiny room: How unfortunate.

"I guess I would eat... and shit... and die," I exclaim, out loud.

I decide that this escape hatch is not the path I seek, and so I decide to have a sip of water. In my haste, I slid the container back toward the wall, but, fortunately, did not spill it. I pick it up and examine the contents, now there is some debris in it, floating around, but I'm sure that is from the mess I have made in the room. I consider my decision and have a hearty gulp of my ceiling-toilet-water. It is a little bit gritty, but certainly quenches my thirst. I replace the container in the correct location and keep the light on it for a moment until I see a drop fall. I decide that I need to sit and rest and turn the light and phone off, when I notice that this phone, my work phone, now only has 5% battery remaining. This time, I squat where I am, and turn my back to the shelves, reach up to navigate my clearance, plop down on my ass, and slide back under the shelves. My pants are on the ground and I grab them as I roll uncomfortably over the protruding lumps in the floor. I can now feel confident that what is below this floor is similar to what is beyond that wall: a veritable mess of rock, brick, and nonsense, making a very uneven foundation that is causing the floor to buckle. The vinyl likely allowed more play than other materials might have, and it makes for a smoother trip across the hilly terrain for my ass than if it were tile or wood, which would certainly have left sharp and dangerous spots. I turn off the flashlight and hold down the power button until the phone offers to shut down. I slide the button that I can barely see, and I am completely blind for a few moments.

I think I see that dim light is starting to illuminate the room, but the image before me is not this room. It is a tree. It is still foggy and dreamlike, but I can see a large oak tree with light behind it. No colors enhance the image, but I can tell what it is. There is no logical backdrop, it is all just a black and sepia tone image of the tree and shifting pattern beyond. I have no sense of time, or how long this image lasts, but instead of fading away and yielding to the reality around me, the image intensifies, and the pattern behind it increases in definition while remaining formless and colorless, but the pattern is moving. The tree is not moving. There is no wind rustling the leaves. There are no birds fluttering about in its limbs. It looks like a photograph, or a painting. It is very high definition now, but frozen, completely still except for the backdrop, still shifting and morphing. It behaves like oil in water, but with broader coverage and less fluid. The shifting and changing reminds me of Mandelbrot sets, representing fractal images of mathematical sequences. I stare, dumbfounded, into this visualization before me. I would reach out for it, but my mind knows it is too far from me. The tree is at least 50 yards away. I set the phone in my lap without looking down and stare. My hands are resting on my legs and my back is slouched. I stare into this strange world before me and I have no desire to make any sense of it. I don't even question it. There is a captivating beauty that also haunts and disturbs me, and I am almost afraid to look away from it, for fear that something awful is somewhere within it that I cannot see or detect, but if I don't monitor closely, it will reveal itself and threaten me. I reach for my bag while staring and pull it closer. I open the large section where my computer is, and retrieve the MacBook Pro. I set it in my lap and keep staring ahead. I reach back into the bag and find my pistol in its pouch. I leave it where it is, but explore it, still in its holster, and locate the snap that restrains it and the extra magazine on its flank. I sit for a long time, staring at the tree, trying to make the image dissipate like all the other images before it. I wonder if I am asleep. I wonder if I am perhaps slipping into some sort of coma. I wonder if I am already approaching death, and this is what it looks like when the other side beckons you to join it. But these meaningless thoughts simply flutter past my consciousness and I don't attach to any of them.

I start to fade back into the darkness. I have no idea what time it is, but the light from the ceiling is fading. I realize that I am scratching the place on my neck and it is bleeding. I wonder if I have been scratching this spot every time I fade into oblivion like this. I shudder as I think about the moment I just had. I stop scratching, but only because I realize how bad it hurts, even though it is an itch that will not stop. The tree is gone.

The dark room is eerie and I decide to light a candle and eat something. I have lost interest in rearranging the shelves and I don't want to waste energy or batteries on light. I wiggle out from under the shelves and stand so that I can reach the top shelf. I get down the box with the birthday supplies and bring it to the floor with me as I sit. I take out one of the already used birthday candles and a lighter. I get back to my feet again, wondering why I sat, and recognize that I am not actually hungry, but I should be. I forgot in the time it took to get the box down that I had planned to eat something. I flick the cheap plastic lighter and it takes me three tries to get it lit properly. I hold the candle's wick over the flame until it lit. I search the shelves for something I want to eat. I have little interest in the options, so I decide to eat peanut butter. I have a spoon and decide I do not need any other vehicle. I set the jar of peanut butter on the ground beside my laptop, that I have balanced atop my briefcase. I feel the wax drip over my fingers, but I don't react. I work my way back down again, and slide back under the shelves. Just to my left, now, is the small hole in the wall where my shit jar resides. I fit perfectly under the shelves. I take a handful of the dust and debris that came out of the wall and insert the little bit of the candle that still burns into the top of the mound. I find the camp silverware in the box and detach the spoon from the butter knife. The knife has two pegs that stick up from the handle on its flat front. The spoon and fork both have slots in their handles and are shaped just right so that they nest, fork within spoon, and spoon atop knife, and the slots allow the pins to pass through and lock down on them. The fork is now on one of the shelves and the spoon will feed me, the knife with the pins goes back in the box. I open the jar of peanut butter and fill the spoon. Before I begin to indulge in the creamy pleasure, I retrieve my computer and place it in my lap. I open the computer and boot it. I log in and open my document to begin writing. I take my first lick of the peanut butter and decide to eat the spoonful and gather another before I really start writing. While I type, I lick enough to keep my mouth busy while I write.

This time, I begin by writing in my journal, and then stop to compose a letter to Samantha.

My beloved joy,

I fear that I write these words after the ability to say them to you and I hope that we have been wrong about the afterlife so that I can deliver my sentiments to you in the beautiful hereafter that the devoted speak of.

I am sorry.

I wish I could have apologized before, but I must beg your forgiveness now.

I know that I did not love you the way that you deserve and that you tolerated my shortcomings even though you could have traded it all for a more favorable life at any time. Thank you for staying, but I wish that you had found freedom and happiness, because your patience with me was only a deeper insult to my misery.

I have always loved you, but I admit that my capacity for expressing that emotion has been stunted and has never proven itself, otherwise, you may not have ventured out.

I also forgive you, because I know you are plagued by guilt for having chosen to betray instead of confront and divide. I am not angry, or disappointed, because I also know that you chose this path because you do not want to disrupt our child's life in spite of your own needs. While selflessly noble, it is not fair to you. I knew this was happening and I chose not to confront you, because I hoped that you had the release you needed to maintain some resemblance of happiness.

Thank you for continuing to give yourself to me when we were together and for trying to preserve what we once had by whatever means necessary. Your affection toward me was never in doubt. I know that my affection in return was simply not enough. I don't blame you.

I will always love you,

Your Sam

I continue to write in my journal, then I go back and read this letter. Then I read it aloud. Then I weep.

I cry quiet, soft tears.

Then I eat more peanut butter. I take one bite that is too big and struggle with it in my mouth. I briefly panic, imagining the irony of surviving this long just to choke to death on peanut butter. I try not to laugh and slowly work the material until I can swallow bits of it. I decide: that is enough.

I check the time: 10:44 PM

# Chapter 8

Still Day 6

Monday

Something rumbles outside. That is thunder.

I decide to erase the letter to Samantha and turn off my computer. It shuts down, I find my bag in the dark, and put the machine back into it. It has 60% battery left.

I put the lid on the peanut butter and set it beside me. I hear the water dripping into the container. I count between drops. I have no idea what a second is any more, so I count in a comfortable tempo. It may be close to seconds, but it doesn't matter any more.

More thunder.

94 seconds between drops.

I do not hear rain yet.

88 seconds between drops.

I begin to see shapes form in the darkness.

More thunder, closer.

91 seconds between drops.

The shapes in the dark become forms, they twist and change like amoebae. There is a brief flicker of light from the ceiling-toilet. It disrupts my count, then more thunder. I actually wonder if it is thunder, or some new threat that mimics thunder. I do not rule this out, because I now have no idea what a follow up attack would look like. I hear a buzzing or humming, and realize it is rain, then more thunder.

89 seconds between drops.

I lean forward, find the water container, and drink three mouthfuls. I replace the object before the next drop.

90 seconds between drops.

Another flicker of light, another clap of thunder, and I start to generate forms in the darkness again. The space that allows the light in is smaller than a pencil is wide and the light is so faint it must be distant, even within that space. My eyes struggle with light. The next flash is startling, because my mind is wandering from its current reality again. When the flash illuminates the room there is a figure in front of me. I put my hand in the bag and find my pistol again. Now I become still and I don't breathe, the next drop is deafening in the silence, and I become aware of my breathing. I await another flash, because I am too terrified to move or find the lighter to illuminate the image of my visitor. Another flash, and I see that the image before me is my wife. Thunder claps and I jump in my seat. I can still see her image in front of me. She is facing me, squatting, wearing jogging shorts and a tank top. Her eyes are closed.

"Samantha?"

My voice sounds weak and fearful. If my wife is in this room, I have nothing to fear, but still, I am terrified. There is no way she could be here, but I can now sense her presence, even in the darkness. My brain tells me that is not actually her, so someone or something else is in here with me and has assumed her form.

I focus on the drop in the container that resounds in my space. The splash sound tells me the container is not very full. Another flash, I have not stopped staring at the space in front of me, and there she is. Her eyes are open this time, and she is looking right at me. But the dim illumination is fleeting and she is gone again.

"Samantha, please."

Thunder claps and I tremble. This does not feel like a hallucination, but also feels like an imposter. Samantha would answer me. She would touch me. She would send me a sign that it is really her. I am shaking and there is a tear running down my cheek. I am terrified. Of all the fears that could haunt me in my loneliness, the image of the one person that could comfort me is the visage that descends upon my inner fears.

"Samantha, if that is you, please answer me."

Another flash, and she is there, seated in front of me, with a calm smile, looking right at me. Thunder sounds again and I shift in my seat. I close my eyes in the darkness and take a long deep breath. I repeat the breath three times and listen to the drops in the container. When I open my eyes, the room is perfectly dark, but I can see her outline immediately. Then her figure begins to populate inside the silhouette. She is not as clear as she was in the flash of light, but she is the same, only seated. She is in a black tank top, showing off her perky breasts. She is wearing jogging shorts, the tight gray ones that she knows I love. She is sitting and it is dark, but I can imagine how her body looks in those shorts. Her blonde hair is in a ponytail, and she has "gym makeup" on. I always asked why she wore makeup to the gym and she would tell me that she always wanted to look her best, then I would tell her that her best was under all of that. But gym makeup was minimal and I love this look. She is still smiling at me.

"Samantha, what are you doing here?"

"This is my pantry, too."

She answered me. It is her. I try to sit forward to reach out to her, but I am frozen. I stop shaking and I am no longer afraid. She shifts in her seat and looks around the room. When she turns to the left, the right side of her face disappears.

"Please don't leave!"

"I'm not going anywhere. What's wrong with you?"

"I have been alone for days and I can't find a way out."

"You have not been alone for a single moment."

"Well I have felt alone."

"Have you? You seem to have been pretty busy, honestly."

"It's the only way I know how to beat the panic."

"Why panic? Don't you like being alone in the quiet?"

"I always thought I would, but now I am not so sure."

"Well I guess you had better be careful what you quietly wish for then, huh?"

"I think I am more worried about Nate… and about you."

"Well, what good has come of that worrying?"

"None. But I can't help it."

"You can help it, you're just being weak."

"I think I am also anxious about what's next and if I can get out of here."

Now her face comes back to meet my gaze. The comforting but condescending smile has faded into a stern look.

"I will tolerate mistakes. I will forgive carelessness. But I have little patience for foolishness."

"That's not fair. I am really scared, that's not foolish. I am alone and afraid."

"You're not alone. You just won't accept your company."

"Why can't I touch you."

"Because I'm not here."

"See! I am alone!"

"No, you're not! But instead of accepting yourself as company, you have to make me join you. The only one that has ever thought you're not good enough is you. Here you are, feeling sorry for yourself again."

At this, I bow my head. I am ashamed. She is right. I look back up, and she's still there, but now her face is gone. Just like how Nathaniel's face had disappeared, she was exactly as I saw her, but there was a blurred image where her face should be.

"Does that mean you're leaving?"

"That's not up to me."

"I wish I could touch you."

"You can."

I try to sit forward again, but my body is frozen. I try to lift my arms but they feel too heavy. I become frustrated and start to feel helpless. I notice that she is fading around the edges, disappearing into the darkness. She turns her head again, and the right side of her face is covered in blood. It is fresh and even in this dark, as she fades, I can see the blood clearly.

"Are you ok?"

She continues to look away and fade into the darkness. She does not answer me again. I try to squint my eyes to see her as she fades, but then she is gone. I hear the distant sound of rain fade back into my room and I smell the horrible smell again. I realize that I still have my hand on my pistol in the bag, so I withdraw my hand and place it in my lap. I consider that I may have to accept myself as my only company. I think back to when I was trying to reset my finger and how I was shifting between the perspective of the healer that was trying to set the digit and the patient trying to maintain composure. Then I remember the third person, watching the interaction between the two. I don't know which person is the real me, but I consider the benefit of being able to shift between the three. The healer is the methodical one, the scientist, the contemplator, and the realist. The patient is the empath, the sensitive one, the needy one, and the one most in touch with my emotions. The watcher is the voyeur, the listener, and the reporter, simply recording and preparing to explain the observation in detail. I decide to work on being able to choose which Samuel I want to be whenever it benefits me. The patient suddenly populates my body. He says, "I feel quite sick."

"My insides are churning and burning."

My organs begin to bubble and I feel a rejection swelling up into my throat. I feel instantly weak and I instinctively turn and lean to my left, toward where the shit container is in the wall. Unfortunately, the sickness strips my body of any other ability and all I can do is fold at my gut and attempt to direct my face away. The vomit comes slow now and feels like it is slithering up my esophagus. It hurts the entire way and never moves any faster. It is like throwing up in slow motion. The peanut butter comes up my throat and out of my mouth like toothpaste from a tube. I spend the rest of the night shitting out of my mouth, essentially. It is the most uncomfortable sensation imaginable and I am otherwise paralyzed while I am moving it from my body. I suffer through a cold sweat and my body trembles. I lose all sense of time and it seems like hours before I can move again. When I can, I decide to retrieve the shit container from its nest in the wall and scoop as much of the oral-feces into it as I can. I struggle with the container, as it is nestled so perfectly that I have to tilt it toward the hole while I lift it out to accomplish the task. I am shaking the whole time, because the excretion experience was so exhausting and has left me in a state of temporary shock. For the first time in days, the open jar allows me to smell something other than the rancid odor of chemicals from outside that is assuredly killing me. I use my hands to scoop the waste on the floor beside me into the jar. It truly feels like I am picking up fresh, soft, shit with my hands. I gag multiple times from the experience. Then I add the dust and debris pile that I used to hold my candle to the jar and replace the lid. I return the plastic jar to its home.

I get to my feet and find my pants on the shelf. I decide to put them back on, because I am shivering. I get my white t-shirt that is hanging over the spice rack and put it back on. I fumble around on the shelves, locate the napkin bags, and take two whole napkins from the open bag and the 3/4 of the remaining napkin from the bowel movement cleanup and shove them in my pocket. I find the bottle of distilled vinegar on the shelf and pop it open. I dump a bit into my cupped right hand, set the bottle back on the shelf, and rub both hands together. I can smell the vinegar and the fumes burn my eyes a bit, but my hands feel clean, or more clean than before, so I bring the bottle with me to the floor and pour a bit onto the spot where I shit-vomited. Then I take out a napkin and clean the floor some. I lean forward and do this again on the floor and wall to my left, closer to the door, where I vomited previously.

As I wipe and clean, I contemplate whether I am getting any nutrients. I think I have held down some food and a good bit of water, but I am worried about my inability to sustain. I finish cleaning and almost don't mind the smell of the vinegar. I decide to wet the partial napkin and clean my face with vinegar. This seems to be going well until I inadvertently touch my neck wound with it and yelp in pain. I finish cleaning my face and decide that a sip of water would be nice. The drops have increased, although I am no longer counting. I retrieve one of the fruit cups from the corner beside me, and take the lighter in my other hand. I flick the lighter until I get a flame, then I set the empty fruit cup beside the water container that has more liquid in it than I have seen yet, and I do the "Indiana Jones" swap. I am excited to see how much water is in the container. I take a sip and realize the lighter is still lit when it burns my thumb. I jerk my arm as I drop the lighter and water splashes on my face and some up my nose. I place the jug beside me on the ground and sniff and snort and blow out my nose onto my face. I decide to pour a bit of water in my hand and wash my face with water. I blow my nose at the same time while wiping my face and feel instant relief in my head. I repeat this process until my face feels somewhat clean. Some residual blood, sweat, and vinegar get into my eyes and burn like fiery-hell, but I just wiggle in place and don't really care much. I consider washing my hair and wounds on my head, but decide that risking the softening of head wound scabs is not worth it. I take two more large sips and swish the last one around vigorously before swallowing. I light the crack-lighter again and prepare for the dangerous swap back. I make the exchange and drink the sugary mouthful that the fruit cup has collected. It is a strange treat. I sit back into my new spot, with my legs toward the hole I created. I pull the piece of concrete in the ground toward me to use as a prop under my knees. It is not completely uncomfortable. The taste in my mouth is horrible. The room smells very strange. I wish one of my neighbors would suddenly yell at me about awful the smell emanating from my apartment so I could beg them to get me out of here. At that moment, I remember that I have a tin of Altoids in my bag. I reach into the bag and find the tin right away. I open it to find there are only a few left as I feel around in the dark with my fingers. I take one in my fingers and close the tin carefully, it is a red tin, peppermint. I place the mint in my mouth, the burning and refreshing sensation is immediately overwhelming. Then I remember something incredible. I feel around in my bag, because I know that I had an internal debate a week ago when I thought that I had my medicine bottle in my briefcase, but it was actually in my travel toiletry bag. I prefer to keep it in my briefcase, because I rarely leave home without it and I never know when I will need one of the two medicines that I carry with me. I just cannot recall if I moved it to my briefcase last Tuesday before the event. I find it in the wrong compartment, but I find it. It is in the main compartment with my laptop, my charger, my sidearm and my small notebook. It should be in the outside pouch with my pens, name tags, and business cards. I bring out the bottle and cannot believe I have suffered as much as I have until now and I never considered searching for medicine. I open the bottle, and take out two, 100 milligram ibuprofen capsules, and 1 omeprazole tablet. I grab the water container and hastily swallow all three pills and a mouthful of water. I also swallow the Altoid without thinking. I replace the water jug again and return the pills to the correct compartment.

Now I can relax. I am dressed, cleaned, and have taken medicine. I expect to sleep soon. I start counting again:

49 seconds between drops.

I have two hopeful thoughts as the medicine begins to take hold and I drift off to sleep. I consider that the wall to my right, opposite of the wall I surgically damaged today, might still be in good shape because the refrigerator is on one side of it. I decide that exploring this may be a good idea tomorrow. Maybe I am digging for gold on the wrong desert island. I also consider that the light, and presumably the air, is all coming from the ceiling-toilet area. Sound seems to emanate from there also. I need to find a way to get up to that space to explore if I can. That may be the only other way out. I have no idea what time I drift off, but the last count is 71 seconds between drops. The rain must have stopped some time during my cleaning and nursing and I didn't notice.

# Chapter 9

Day 7

Tuesday

The event occurred one week ago today.

I awaken from the sudden urge to urinate. I do not delay with processing anything else around, but it is still dark. I rotate to my knees in some creative form of yoga and reach into the hole in the back right wall to retrieve the pretzel jar-toilet. I struggled with it a bit yesterday when cleaning my peanut butter vomit, but today, I know exactly how to lean it toward the hole to extract it smoothly. I bring it toward me a bit, remove the lid, and unzip my khaki jeans. I bring out my penis only and spread my knees to hang the head closer to the opening and release into the jar. In the dark, I can only gauge fullness by how heavy it feels and how the piss sounds entering and landing. I do not feel any splash back, and decide I still have a significant portion of the jar left. When I finish, I realize that I may need a better place to urinate to save space. If I cut a properly planned hole in the wall, I could use that. It will smell eventually, but I can smell the jar when I open it this time, and with the lingering chemical poison in the air, I'm not sure I care how my room smells any more. I replace the lid and return the jar to the wall-hole. I complete my yoga in reverse and return to my seated position, this time, more aware of the tilt in the room. I have to assume the perfect angle from the wall in order to lean my back, shoulders, and head without effort. I recognize that 8-9 degrees is a significant incline in road sports, like running, and it is starting to seem more significant in small-room-survival applications, as well.

I acknowledge that the medicine truly helped with the pain and settled my stomach enough for me to sleep soundly. If it had not been for the need to excrete urine and my body's willingness to share that urge with me, I may still be sleeping. I decide to take more medicine and try to rest more. It is dark and I have little interest in performing any escape attempts. I am overcome with a sense of exhaustion, not unlike when you have walked long distances and desperately want to sit down. I locate the small pill bottle in my briefcase, which I can picture in my mind's eye perfectly: an old Tylenol bottle, the smaller size, with the label almost completely rubbed off. It is a white bottle and the remnant of the blue label with black writing is still visible. I decide that the reflux medication is not necessary right now, so I only take two ibuprofen capsules out. I lean forward to grab the water jug, which feels really full, and I swallow the two pills. I replace the water container and find the lighter in the open camp supply box on the floor. I flick the lighter and look to where the water container is. I continue to flick, but never fully light the lighter, adjust the container on the floor until it seems perfect, and note that it is about 1/3 full, which is the most I have seen yet. I do not need to drink more, because I want to sleep as long as possible. I slide the lighter into my pocket and lean back. I wiggle and adjust until I find the position with the least amount of pain in my buttocks, lower back and legs. I acknowledge my right pinky is throbbing a bit, but it is tolerable. I am now in the recognizable state of "medication as a factor" and decide that I will calculate my rationing and not continue this practice until absolutely necessary. But right now, I know that I need rest, and perhaps that will help with healing. I close my eyes, allowing my mind to generate some light forms in my vision field.

I awaken, or become aware of my surroundings, but I am confused. I feel softness under my body and I do not sense the tilt of the room that I am expecting. When you fall asleep in an uncomfortable place, like a train station, you can reach deep sleep, but you are immediately aware of the discomforts as soon as you become conscious again. I do not recognize the feelings around me and I am instantly confused. I am also hesitant to open my eyes, because I am afraid of something. I hear whispering. I cannot make out the voices. They sound as if they are trying to speak in a way that they do not want me to hear. I do not recognize the voices. The two I hear sound like men. The softness beneath me feels like a bed. I should welcome this sensation, but the unknown causes me to be afraid. The voices sound anxious and one even sounds angry, or frustrated, but I still cannot make out any words. I wonder if they are speaking a language other than English, but there is no way to know. All I can sense is the heated or intense emotion behind the conversation. Inflection seems to be universal, or in this moment it presents that way. Some languages sound more intense than others, and I consider that as a possibility. I try to manifest my "reporter" personality, so I can see where I am from a remote perspective, but I cannot seem to embody the consciousness I desire. I deduce that I have not had enough time to rehearse this act. I am careful not to move, as I do not yet know what experience I have awoken in. I can see that there is some light, through my eyelids, but there is no movement that I can detect. I will have to open my eyes to know more. I try to crack my left eyelid without actually opening the eye, because that seems to be the direction the voices are coming from. I sense that my eyelids shake as I attempt to control a subtle movement, and light floods my left eye when the lids split apart ever so slightly. The image in my single eye is blurry and bright. I know that it is not actually bright, but light is foreign to me, and my eyes must adjust. The talking stops and I sense that the voices have noticed my eye movement. I keep my left eye just barely cracked and the fuzzy image is a background of gray and a light to my left rear. I sense someone approaching and then I see a figure beside me. I am terrified, but I am too curious not to look. I crack my eye a bit further and make out the basic form of the man to my left. He is directly in my view, so I don't have to move my head to see him. He is light-skinned with dark hair. I can't seem to make out his facial features, but he is certainly looking at me. He is wearing a dark colored, short-sleeved, shirt that has some sort of accessories on it. There may be a name tag.

"Samuel?"

No accent, I do not answer. I just continue to look through my tiny slit at this fuzzy and indistinguishable figure. I may be holding my breath. I try to remain frozen. His voice is not familiar, but does not sound threatening.

"Samuel, I know you are awake, because the monitor tells me, so I know you can hear me."

I still refuse to respond. This is somewhat disturbing. What monitor could tell him that I am aware of him and can hear him? How could he possibly know that?

"It is a brain wave monitor. It is a single lead attached to your head."

Can he also hear my thoughts? How did he know I was thinking that? Maybe I am actually saying what I am thinking. I try again to shift into the third-party observer self that would be able to look down onto the scene and report what is actually happening. I feel like my consciousness starts to leave the body that is lying on this suspected bed, when he speaks again.

"Stay with me. We need to discuss some things."

Now I am getting angry, because I want my thoughts to be my own, but I am completely transparent to this person. I open my left eye a bit further and try to make eye contact with him. I cannot seem to focus on his face. I open both eyes and look harder, but the face will just not come into focus. He appears middle-aged and has dark, almost black, hair. His dark colored shirt is either blue, black, or charcoal, but the space I am in is dimly lit from an overhead light behind me and colors do not seem to materialize effectively. The background from my reclined position is gray. It is a light gray, and I can make out the corners and seams. It resembles the inside of a tent, but the size of a large room. I am cold. I focus on my visitor again but I still cannot see his face. His shirt has a name tag, but I can't see what it says. I realize that he is wearing a surgical mask, and that is part of why I can't make out his face. He is also wearing glasses, ugly ones. I think they might be safety glasses, and I recognize this as some sort of PPE. Americans are very aware of Personal Protective Equipment since the recent Pandemic. I do not know why he is wearing it, but it explains why I can't make out his face. I don't think he was wearing all of that when I first saw him, but my mind leaves that thought immediately when he speaks again.

"If you aren't going to answer me, I will just begin."

"I am Dr. Tomlinson. You are in a medical tent. You are in Atlanta, Georgia. You have been asleep a long time. If you have any questions, please ask them now."

I still refuse to speak and simply stare into the extremely stoic figure's face area.

"Very well… We have determined that you are fit for combat, so we will need you to prepare for engagement immediately. We do not have time to discuss anything else, because we are losing quickly and simply need bodies that can help. You are one of those bodies, effective immediately."

Now I am worried. This reality is very different from where I fell asleep. I start to allow myself to move toward the outer-consciousness again, and I can feel my awareness leaving the body on the bed and lifting away from the space I am currently possessing. I feel light, and there is a calm sensation as I start to lift away.

"Please stop doing that."

I am immediately jolted back to the body on the bed looking at the man in PPE. How did he do that?

"We have administered a substance that will force you into consciousness, so there is no use attempting to sleep again."

He thinks I am trying to sleep.

"Please sit up."

I silently refuse.

I see him reach behind me and as he approaches, I feel myself recoil away from him. But he reaches beyond me and I hear him handling something out of view. Suddenly, I hear a mechanical noise, and my back begins to raise. He is raising my bed, it is a hospital bed. I turn to look at the bed, to my right. There are other beds in the room and I can see four to my right. There are bodies in two of them. Neither are upright or moving, and neither have a visitor harassing them. I see some tables around the room and a few other workers in the distance, but I have no idea what they are doing. Now I am almost completely upright. There are two beds in front of me also. I can see the one directly in front has a person in it, but the next one up is raised like mine, so I cannot tell if there is anyone in it. All of the beds have metal posts off the back right and bags of fluid hung from them. They have a computer-looking device on the back left and various leads and tubes going to the person. I look at my arm and see a tube in my arm. I try to reach for it, but my hands will not move from my position beside me. I get an inch from the bed with my hand and my wrist prevents it. I am bound to my bed.

"Please do not try to move your hands until we can establish your intentions."

I cannot tolerate this one-way conversation any more.

"How was I supposed to sit up if you had me bound?"

"Good."

"How is that good? What the fuck is going on?"

"As I told you, we need you to go fight the enemy."

"What enemy?"

"We know that you can remember what happened, so I will not waste time with that. Are you lucid enough to fire a weapon?"

"Probably, but I won't."

"Then you will be killed immediately."

"I don't even know who to shoot."

Why am I participating in this?

"This tent is the only place you are safe, but if you do not volunteer immediately, we will send you out without a weapon, where you will surely be killed within 5 minutes. If you suggest a threat to the personnel in this tent, you will be sent out without a weapon to be killed. If you become aggressive, we will simply finish you here and move on. If you cooperate, we will arm you and send you out to fight for your country."

"But who am I supposed to shoot? I honestly have no idea what is happening!"

"Fine: you are severely outnumbered, so basically anything you see that moves you will shoot, or it will likely kill you. If you are unsure, destroy it. You will fight in 4 hour shifts with one hour to rest. You will attempt to make it to the next tent. Nothing will harm you when you are in the tents. It is quite simple. Do you understand?"

"Yes, but..."

"Will you cooperate, or do we need to prepare your replacement?"

"I... I don't... I'm..."

"There is no time for this: yes or no?"

"Um... Yes..."

"Good, you are already dressed in your identification suit. The eyewear that you have on will be switched on and you will see every living thing as either red or blue. It will enhance your vision, and you will shoot all of the red objects. Do you understand?"

"Um... yes."

"You will have a loaded weapon and there are additional magazines and ammunition in your bag. You have three explosive devices, you can use them at your discretion. There is also an additional firearm in the bag, in case it is needed. Both items utilize the same ammunition and magazines."

I start wondering if I will be able to make an escape attempt. This is happening so fast that I don't know whether to go along or plan my rejection. I look around for the door and consider the number of people I see. I start to wonder what actually awaits me.

"There is no time for this. If you decide to retaliate, I can press a button and you will be rendered useless immediately, then we will shut your body down and remove you. This is your last chance to comply. I can detect your brain and know what is happening. There is no point in plotting. I have explained more than is necessary. Will you comply?"

"Yes."

"I am going to release your binds. Then you will sit up completely. Do you understand?"

"Yes."

I feel my wrists and ankles free from their restraints that I could not sense until they were removed. I instinctively lift my legs out of the objects and my hands move to my lap. I sit up the rest of the way. I can see the room now. I start to look around.

"Turn to me. "

I do.

"Turn your body so that your legs are off the side of the bed now."

I do that.

"Good. I am going to activate your eyewear so that you can acclimate to the augmented reality you will exist in for the rest of your service."

Suddenly, my vision is augmented and I understand why they call it that. The room around me becomes overlaid with a subtle grid and objects are accented. I notice that Dr. Tomlinson is highlighted with a blue tint. I look around and see that everyone in the room is highlighted the same. It is strange how they just "glow." I look at myself and see that I, too, am glowing blue. I acknowledge that I am wearing pants that have multiple pockets, I have no idea what color they are, because of the blue glow. I have a t-shirt on. My vision identifies me in the top corner as "ID683972504523" and if I look at someone else it identifies them by a similar ID mark that floats near them almost as soon as I see them in my central field of view. All identifications and markings are translucent and do not seem to interfere with my natural vision, it is more of an enhancement. Right when I have this realization, my host says, "right, let's get on with it."

He moves toward me and I recoil again. He leans in slowly and removes the tube from my right arm, then removes a cuff from my left arm. Then he reaches over my head and is fiddling with something on the back of my skull, but I cannot feel anything. I realize that I do not feel my pinky and there is no sense of dried blood or wounds on my head. I reach up and find that the sore at my jaw and neckline that I have been scratching is gone. It is just gone.

"Time to stand up. We expect you to take a moment to acclimate once vertical, then the injection should take effect and you should feel quite invigorated."

I stand. There is no challenge to it. I simply tell my body to stand and it does. I do not have to maneuver in any strange way or perform any type of yoga to do so. I slide forward on the edge of the bed, recognize that I already have combat boots on and my pants are tucked into them. I place my feet on the hard ground and stand. I feel tall. The ground seems very far away, but then I look up, see the doctor in front of me, holding a weapon that looks very much like some type of assault rifle that I have seen in science fiction shows and movies. The barrel section is almost square and I immediately want to hold it, because it looks comfortable and safe. He looks at me and extends the weapon with both hands. I take it from him with both hands and say, "thank you."

"Do not rack the slide until you leave the tent, or you will be terminated."

I see that my visual identifies the weapon as "Armed - LTA4045." Below those letters reads, "72 - chamber clear." I understand that this is my weapon's information. I am overcome with anticipation, not excitement, not anxiety. Without thought, I say, "I am ready."

"Good. You are not required to follow the navigation in view, but it will always direct you to the closest tent. Expect danger to intercept at all times, your enemy has more advanced technology than you, but lacks intuition."

"I understand."

"The exit is just there. Godspeed."

Dr. Tomlinson points toward the end of the tent to my rear, I nod, and start turning that direction. I see two armed guards, soldiers perhaps, dressed how I presume I must look, on either side of the flaps to the tent. If there is another entrance or exit, I do not detect it. Everyone in this tent glows blue. I begin to move toward the exit but I do not sense my steps. I feel like I am floating and my movement is guided by intention. I am no longer concerned about the situation or a way to escape. The guards look at me as I move toward them and when I approach, they both nod, and I nod back. I reach the door flaps, which are less than a foot from my face and I hold my weapon up and prepare my left hand to rack the slide. My hand instinctively knows where this mechanism is and I brush it with my fingertips gently. My movements feel completely calculated and deliberate and I act with more precision than I have ever felt. The flaps open and I can tell the world is substantially darker outside the tent than within. I step through the portal and my vision flashes momentarily. I see the word "ENGAGE" in the center of my screen, only just long enough for me to understand. I immediately rack the slide, and the count changes to "71 - chamber loaded." I instinctively toggle a small switch with my right thumb and my screen flashes "ARMED." I take the barrel end of the weapon and assume a position that you see soldiers in: slightly crouched and viewing the world ahead down the barrel of your two-handed weapon. My vision identifies buildings and vehicles and the curb of the road in front of me. All of these things exist but are not highlighted in any way. I begin to move in a deliberate and methodical stride. There are dim arrows that are directing me straight ahead. I move about 20 steps when I notice that the buildings and other objects all have distances in dim numbers superimposed on them. My screen identifies objects and distances in meters. The nearest building is 42m away and I head toward it. The right side of my vision begins to illuminate in a red glow and I understand that there is danger in that direction. I find myself moving behind a vehicle, a sedan, to my left, and looking toward the red glow. I see the glow intensify from the intersection that is beyond a building 96m away. I take cover behind the front end of the vehicle and direct my weapon toward the intersection. My vision is full of crosshair visuals and color indications. The red glow intensifies and I see the edge of a figure appear around the corner of the building. It is glowing red, in a slightly more intense saturation than the blue of non-enemies. There is no doubt that this is an enemy by the identifying color. It is not identified with a number, ID, or name like all of the people in the tent. I have the crosshairs on the target but I do not pull the trigger. Something bothers me about it. It is smaller than me, smaller than the other people I have seen so far. The size of the figure is that of a child. The gait and stance are also childlike. I can see that they are not holding a weapon. I can see both hands and arms. They are not wearing a pack nor do they look like a soldier. This looks like a child, perhaps 9 or 10 years old. My screen flashes "ENGAGE," but I hesitate. I can't shoot an unarmed child. The figure turns in my direction and the red glow intensifies. It seems to lean or recoil away from my direction momentarily, then, before I can react, leans toward me and begins moving in my direction faster than a human can move. It does not even seem to be walking or running. The speed of it closing in opens a fear within me that I have never experienced. I feel absolute horror. I can't see the being or its features, but now I understand that it is very dangerous and I am very afraid.

I squeeze the trigger of my weapon with the creature still in my crosshairs and it "pops" a round. I see the figure fall back slightly and then continue its approach. It is now 19m away. I start squeezing repeatedly. I hit it every time and the impact walks the figure back, but it does not go down. Suddenly there is another glow of red coming from the intersection. I aim again, squeeze and hold the trigger. It fires repeatedly, faster than I could squeeze manually. After 12 hits, the creature falls down. Its red glow diminishes but does not go out. I adjust my aim to the intersection just in time for a smaller figure to come around the corner, glowing red. I do not hesitate, I start walking toward the intersection and lay the creature down. I continue to close in on the intersection. The red glow is almost extinguished in the first creature, not 5M from me. I keep it targeted as I close the gap. With the glow diminishing, I can make out the figure. I get to its feet and see that it is a childlike figure. I aim at its head and it opens its eyes.

It is Nathaniel. Before I can say anything or react it comes back to life and flies from the ground toward me. It has my son's face, but is horrifying and angry. My heart sinks and I sense my demise as my vision goes black.

I jump awake.

I am sweating, shaking, and absolutely terrified. I immediately feel sick. I cannot seem to comprehend what has happened and I am frantically looking around and shifting in my seat. I feel like I am on fire and the horror is still very real for a long time. I scan my space, looking for danger. It is daytime again and the light from my ceiling-toilet-light is full strength. I can see that my pantry has not changed since I last saw it when flicking the lighter last night. I have made a good mess of the space, but recall the amount of cleaning I completed and understand how much worse it could be. I am still reeling from the nightmare that I just awoke from and trying to get the image of my son as a monster out of my head. My brain is telling me there are sounds coming from all sides and I keep darting my eyes, head and upper body toward the sounds every time I register them. I think they sound like "clicks," like when one of your joints pops, and you can hear it inside your head. It takes what seems like hours to finally calm down and focus on anything else. The sounds finally stop and the image playing on repeat in my head finally subsides. The first thought I have is to check my pinky: still injured.

"That was a dream. That was only a dream. That was not real."

My mind decides that this was a "fever dream," which I have had before, but not like this. I am very cold, but I am sweating, and the achy, sick feeling is similar to the last time I was infected with a communicable disease and struck a fever. But this is much more intense. The shaking has become a tremble that radiates from my core. I have been cold to my core before, and this is the shiver that accompanies that experience. You are cold and cannot get warm and you have a shiver that is from the very center of your mass that radiates throughout your body in alternating levels of intensity. But my tremble is not from the cold and the cold sensation is one that feels like I am pale and must look shiny with perspiration.

I begin to consider why I would have a fever. I suspect that either one of my wounds has become infected or I am sick from the effects of some form of nuclear fallout, radiation, chemical, or biological weapon. None of these options are good, nor do they offer anything resembling comfort. I know that I could take ibuprofen, but I am so sick and weak, I struggle to focus on what it would take to accomplish this. I lean forward, slowly, and try to focus on the water container. Yes... I am definitely thirsty. I take the container, which is pretty full now, and start to drink. I do not put the container down, and have spilled a good bit of water after taking 5 large mouthfuls and swallowing. Once I stop and pull the container away, I can smell the chemicals in the air again. The odor has progressed. There seems to be another feature to the noxious fumes, and it is not the vinegar, or my waste, or vomit. I can't place it, but it is familiar. I carefully return the water container, formerly known as: cereal container, to its place and squint to see if it is in the right spot. I make a few small adjustments and give up. I can't see clearly enough to decide if it is right. I have a distinct spinning sensation, similar to vertigo, except that when it comes on, it feels like I have spun quickly upside-down and back again, like someone is trying to get change from my pockets. I feel like I could fall down, but realize I am sitting. I sense that I am swaying in place and struggle to gain composure. This is a very disturbing feeling. I hold my hands out in front of my face and try to look at them. I can barely focus. I feel inebriated. I recall that my college roommate always told me to put my feet on the floor and close my eyes if I had the spins after a long night of drinking. I pull my legs up toward my ass and place my feet flat on the ground. I close my eyes and attempt to steady my mind.

"I am so sorry Nathaniel."

I realize that I can see his face in my mind again, but it is twisted and distorted.

"Help!"

I don't know what to do in this moment except yell for help.

"Oh Samantha, please help me!"

Suddenly, my vision rushes my perspective out of my body and above the room. I am no longer spinning or dizzy and I can see clearly. It is as if there is no ceiling, and I am looking down at myself below. I also see another figure in front of me. It is light enough that I can pick out a few features, but dark enough still to prevent details from developing. The person under the shelves is clearly me. I can see my pants, and my bare feet are pulled up toward my body. My back is against the wall but my head is hung, my chin resting on my chest. I look messy. My short hair is discolored from the blood and my white shirt is stained and gross. I can see the cut on the back of my head and I am rocking a bit. The figure in front of me is also me, but much cleaner. He is wearing the same clothes that I had on when the event occurred and his hair is still neatly washed and naturally in place. The blue dress shirt is clean and he still dons the expensive-looking but modest brown leather shoes. He is seated upright and looking directly at the sick and pitiful version of me. The "me" that is looking on has zero emotional or physical sensations and is merely reporting the information back to my mind. I am not thinking about what is being witnessed, I am somehow reporting it to myself without speaking. The clean Sam says, "what's wrong, Sam?" The dirty Sam says, "can't you see that I am sick?"

"We are the same body, but I don't feel sick at all. Are you sure we're sick?"

"Why in the hell would I make this up?"

"Maybe you just need to stop feeling sick and simply be better."

Sick Sam looks up now and says, "if I could just stop being sick, don't you think I would have by now?"

"I don't know, but I think it is weird that we are the same person, but you are so miserable."

"Obviously, something is wrong, but if we are the same person, sharing the same body, why is it only making me feel this way? Why are you so happy?"

"I can't answer that, but I am watching you and I really don't like what I see. I think it is time to do something about this."

"What am I supposed to do?"

"Do you have any idea what is actually wrong?"

"No. I think I have a fever. That would suggest that I have an infection."

"Is the fever the problem then?"

"Yes... I think so. Is this a trick question?"

"I'm not sure how you think you could trick your own mind, but no, I don't believe it is."

"I tricked myself before, when you, er, I, was getting ready to fix my pinky. Is this the same?"

"That doesn't matter right now. If the fever is the problem, is there anything you can do about that?"

"I suppose I could try to cool my body, or take medicine."

My consciousness drops from above into my sick body as I utter the word "medicine" like a rocket. I am instantly back in my body, alone again, and I reach for my bag. My eyes are still closed and I fumble around with the zippers, trying to locate the one that holds the medicine bottle.

"Relax... Calm down."

This voice is in the room with me and I can hear it clearly, but it is definitely not my voice. I take a deep breath and locate the zipper I need. I open the pouch and reach in to find the medicine bottle. Eyes still closed, I open the bottle and retrieve a higher dose than before. I count out four ibuprofen capsules that feel distinctly different from the omeprazole. I throw the pills in my mouth and swallow. One of them sticks to my cheek and I have to tongue it free. I lean forward and open my eyes. I grab the water container again and bring it to my mouth. I drink a large gulp and swallow hard. The room has thrown me upside-down and back again and I am sick with confusion. I have never experienced a fever like this. I am too confused to be afraid, but there is something like fear mixed into all of the chaos of my world.

"Chaos. My mind feels like chaos. Why can't I get control of it?"

The voice I heard before, not mine, answers me again, "because you are trying to hold water."

"Fuck you! This is no time for Confucius!"

"Bullshit! This is exactly the time for meditation and reality."

I feel panicky, and the voice getting forceful with me is unnerving. If that is me in the room, why would I get frustrated with myself? I realize that I am frustrated with myself. I try to shift my perspective over to the other "me" in the room.

"You can't force that to happen, you have to simply let it happen."

"How am I supposed to do that, smartass?"

"Now, who is getting frustrated with whom?"

Damnit! I can't even win an argument with myself!

"This existence, over here... This is mindfulness, not frustration and chaos. Stop allowing the chaos and be mindful. Then you can be over here."

I am right. I know that most of our emotions and physical sensations are simply our brains recognizing stimuli. I try to manifest peacefulness. I have never been very good at this. As quickly as I try to find the calm, I recall the concept that it is there and I simply must "let it come." I close my eyes and clear my mind. I focus on emptiness. Then I take a long breath in and focus on slowing my breath. I am acutely aware that I have been huffing and panting, breathing quick and labored. I understand that this is a panic behavior, so I focus on releasing my next breath slowly. I try to make my exhale as long and thorough as possible. I continue forcing air out of my lungs until my chest hurts. Then I pause and begin to inhale again. I constantly focus on slowing the breath in more as I continue. I force my chest to expand and allow more room for air while sitting up straight and keeping my mind on my breath. Just as my lungs scream that they can't take any more, I pause, hold, and feel the spin approaching. I immediately begin the exhale again. I focus on slowing it even more and dragging out the act in excruciating detail and drag. When I succeed in slowing my breath out, I try to slow it even more. I never allow a gap in the act that will leave room for the sensations that I don't like to manifest. I am fully focused on my breath and I leave no space for negativity. Breath has no positive or negative, it just exists in differing amounts. It is an action. I continue this rhythm for a long time and become completely saturated with the smelly air that surrounds me, but I am no longer panicked. I release my attention and open my eyes. My vision is still not clear, but the room does not throw me over this time.

I am on the other side of the room. I am seated, cross-legged, hands in Dhyana Mudra. I do not remember moving. I am almost sure that I did not move, but I am definitely seated now where I saw my other self sitting before, and I feel more like how I imagine he felt when watching the scene from above. I was right... or... he was right: I simply have to let myself "be" the other "self."

I am typically a very logical person. I do not believe in a great big man in the sky that toys with us and allows us to suffer the way we do. I do not think that a loving god would allow us to hurt one-another like we do. I also believe that science can explain all things and mathematics is the language of nature. If we have not yet figured out how to explain something with science yet, it is because there will always be mysteries that we need to pursue. I believe our universe is infinite in all directions, including inward. It can be explored outward, into space, indefinitely. But, it can also be explored inward, smaller and smaller, and everything we find will be made of smaller things, and subsequently composed of even smaller things, for eternity, no matter how far we go. The experience of mindfulness, meditation, and consciousness, for me, must be rooted in fact. There must be an explanation. Right now, my existence is becoming very difficult to explain, and the longer I survive this ordeal, the more I wonder if this is reality, or if I have found myself already within some other horrible reality or existence that could be my next eternity. This realization, or suspicion, will haunt me. I stare across the space of my pantry, ripe with all of the detail and information, just how I left it the last time my eyes could perceive it, and contemplate if this is even real. Could I be in some dreamlike state, possibly in a coma in some other reality?

"Let's unpack some of this, huh?" This is the other voice that is now in the room with me. This voice does not seem to come from within my head or my imagination, I hear it, clearly, in the air around me.

"Is it actually possible that this experience is not reality? Are you dreaming when you sleep?"

"Yes, very clearly."

"So, should we assume the dreams are the reality, and this is just a dream?"

"I guess I am wondering if it is possible that none of my recent experiences are reality, and I may physically exist somewhere that I cannot experience right now, for some reason."

"When would that reality have paused to begin this 'imaginary' world?"

"I don't know, but this does not seem to follow the rules."

"What rules?"

"The laws of nature."

"How so?"

"It does not seem possible that everything else in my general vicinity has essentially disappeared, or been reduced to rubble, and this godforsaken room has been spared."

"I would suggest that it does not seem probable, but would argue that it is, theoretically, possible."

"Good point. But what if none of this is real?"

"Do you know how to make the 'dream' stop?"

"No."

"Then all you can do is continue to participate."

"I guess so."

"Remember that the possibility of this experience being 'unreal', suggests that there are infinite possibilities of what is 'real', and how you define it is an individualized experience."

"What the hell are you talking about?"

"If you don't know if this is real or how to make it 'end', it is possible that you have to survive and escape to return to the 'reality' where Samantha and Nathaniel are available to you."

"Like a game?"

"Sure, if that helps you to understand my theory. But, more importantly, I am highlighting the thing that you are not talking to yourself about."

"What's that?"

"You have everything you need to survive, technically, for now, but you are still trying to escape."

"I don't want to survive like this!" I gesture around me to the small space we are in.

"Why not?"

"Because this is miserable!"

"I get that, but why is it miserable?"

"Because all I can do is eat, and sleep, and exercise, and piss, and shit... that's no kind of life!"

"So, what is missing? Is there anything that, if it suddenly appeared here with you, would make it the kind of life worth living?"

"Maybe? But that's not going to happen, so why are we wasting time on this?"

"I would like to remind you that you have, quite literally, nothing else to do."

"I could be trying to escape."

"Fine, but we will revisit this when you finally accept your fate."

"What the fuck is that supposed to mean?"

"It means that I am your logical self, and I plan to infiltrate and assure that you face reality, eventually."

"I feel like I am facing reality, just fine. Getting out of here is definitely more productive than having an internal dialogue about imaginary possibilities."

"You were the one asking if this all might be a dream. I am the one pointing out that it will not affect your actions, if it is."

"So..."

"You are the one saying the life within this room, as it is, is not worth living. I am the one that is trying to make you understand that: if this is a dream, manifesting other items to make the experience more tolerable, or pleasant, is not impossible."

"Still feels like a waste of time."

"Time, you dolt, is the one thing you seem to have plenty of. Also, if this is 'reality', figuring out why the situation is miserable could help you to deal with the psychological problems you are avoiding, but are closing in on you."

"What psychological problems?"

"Who are you talking to, Sam?"

"Shut up."

"So, what thing or things would make this more tolerable?"

"I don't know. I guess, if I were not alone, I would probably be less concerned with getting out. I really wish Nathaniel were here. I would give almost anything for Samantha to be here with me."

"Good. Now... What is 'out there' that you assume will make all of this effort to get out so worth it?"

"What do you mean? I won't be stuck in here any more!"

"Yes, but what is 'out there' that is so much better?"

"Freedom? Daylight? Maybe other humans, somewhere?"

"But, not the ones you are hoping to have in here?"

"Maybe... but I definitely won't find out while I am stuck in here with no way to communicate."

"All I am trying to get at is that you are unhappy with what you don't have in here, but you are trying to get out to somewhere that may not provide what you want either. At least you know what's in here. I just don't want the weight of the situation falling onto us at once. Better to ease into it."

"Sure, I am also slightly concerned about the weight of things falling down on us, but I am being more literal. If the rubble outside that wall is on all sides, above and below, there can't be very much preventing this room from simply collapsing on us suddenly."

"I agree, it seems unlikely that this room is the only space that withstood almost complete annihilation, but statistically, something probably survives, and there is no reason to believe that it absolutely can't be this room."

"I agree. It could happen. But that also is not very comforting."

I still have no idea how I came to be on the other side of the room, but I decide it is now time to get up and begin my next attempt at escape. I think about films where prisoners have to hide their escape attempts under posters or behind their beds, and how fortunate I am that I can simply destroy a giant section of the wall, in plain view, and not care if anyone sees it.

"I probably won't get my deposit back now."

I laugh, aloud.

I turn my attention to the wall on my left. I moved both bottom shelves together to that side when I was opening the hole on the opposite wall. Now I take them, one at a time, and move them to the wall on my right, where I have already ripped a giant hole that is doing absolutely no good. I remember that I plan to use that hole as a urinal, and smile at my frugality, but realize that its location may be a bit too tall for that. I retrieve my sharp knife, tongs, multi-tool, and work phone, and move myself to the wall nearest the water container. I want to see if I can get to the refrigerator on the other side. I know that I don't want to contaminate the water supply again with my messy demolition projects, so I find the top of the container and place it on the object. I find the empty fruit cup in the waste area, back left of the room, that I already used for temporary water collection before. I move the large water container (cereal) over to the holy side of the room, covered and secure, now almost half full, and place the tiny, by comparison, fruit cup in the space where it will catch the, now much less frequent, drops of, hopefully clean, toilet water from above. The choice to design this portal lower than the last is to plainly allow easy access for my penis. I measure by standing near the wall and sloppily marking the height of my member with the sharp end of the folding knife on the wall. I chuckle, wishing I could tell Samantha that I have decided to install a glory hole in our pantry that would be hidden by the refrigerator when not in use. Then I pause, because that is really not a terrible idea. We never pursued such deviance, at least the Sams didn't, but I cannot speak for what Samantha might have explored with her friend. I doubt that I would actually participate if faced with the opportunity to have illicit sex, or sexual encounters, with strangers, simply for the thrill of it. I am enamored by the idea, in theory, but I lose my pride when I remember that I could have explored such interests any time and never ventured from the comfort of my marriage, simply tolerating her behavior with silent contempt.

My goal here is to see if the refrigerator, which was previously just on the other side of this wall, has survived the event, or provided some structural support to my sarcophagus, and possibly offers a passage out. My plan before was fruitful, although thwarted by the destruction beyond, the hole that I opened certainly provided access out of this one, the destination was simply full. I begin, similarly to the other wall, by choosing a location, away from the corner, but not too far. I begin the incision approximately 6 inches below my cock-height, which I decide should be a standard measure of a male-presenting human's attributes. It does not indicate the length or girth of his member, but will identify the measurement at the base of the penis from the ground. This measurement is extremely important when shopping for a bed for sex: a sex-bed. A person should also know the perfect height of a piece of furniture for their partner's support whilst being penetrated from behind. This object height is a ratio of one's cock-height, and is expressed as either: "bent-over-exposing-opening-at-ideal-cock-height" or "knelt-upon-exposing-opening-at-ideal-cock-height," will allow a tolerance of one inch for the former and three for the latter, due to "knee-spread" factor, and will also tolerate more or less than this, relative to the "pitcher/catcher" height ratio of the couple performing the acts. "Standing-missionary-ideal-cock-height" is a calculation of "bent-over," minus a few inches to allow for proper penetration, but is recommended to be measured independently to allow for precision and determination of multi-position furniture options or accessories to raise or lower by specific amounts.

I continue to saw the hole in the wall. I have good light, and see no need to cut a decent circle, because I will either abandon after this initial hole is thoroughly determined to be evidence of a futile endeavor, or the hole will be opened wider if further investigation or optimistic results are observed. I end up with a pathetic oval-shaped hole in the wall, roughly 4 inches wide by 6 inches tall, and not a decent curve in all the form of it. I remove the drywall figure, shake my head at the terrible cut, and place it, and the knife, on the shelf. Significant dust and some bits of rock fall out. I see the same insulation here as was discovered in all the other holes. I do not see any large pieces of concrete or brick yet, no light coming through either. I reach in with my left hand and grab a chunk of insulation. I decide that it is dusty and has some pebbles in it, but it is not scratchy at all. I wonder if this could be used to improve my comfort when I am resting. I pull that handful out and throw it behind me and toward the shelves on the ground. I reach in and tear another handful out. I throw it down with the first. I repeat this three more times, before I realize that I am pulling stuffing out of the wall when I could reach right through to the other side of the wall. I do just that and become excited that I find solid sheet rock there. On the other wall, I had already discovered a veritable disaster within, so this is encouraging. I take the work phone, and turn it on. It boots and shows "Low Battery Mode," and I realize this will be the end of this device. I check the time: 1:31 PM.

## Chapter 10

Still Tuesday

Still day 7

I turn on my work phone's flashlight and bend down to look into the wall-hole. The inside is typical inner-wall, as one would find within any commercial building. I have avoided all support structure, and cleared most of the stuffing out, so I can see right through to the off-gray, pale, dry wall on the other side. It is intact. I stick the phone in my pocket and stick the knife into the wall on the other side. I start to twist and push, attempting to fully penetrate. I hit something hard, as expected, and pull the knife back. The place where the knife penetrated pours some dust into the wall as I bring it back out. I move the knife up about an inch and try again, yielding the same result. I move far to the left from here, and push in again, twisting and working the blade to make a hasty hole. I succeed in going deeper here than I had in the other locations. I straighten out the knife and press on the butt of the handle to submerge the blade directly in. I get it in, down to the handle, about 4 inches. This means I was being rejected immediately outside the wall a few inches away, but I am able to fully penetrate here. I wonder if I might be in front of the fridge now, but was hitting it in my attempts to the right. I do not think I am far enough into the corner for that, and this is the first bit of evidence that I am not finding what I expect to be here. I start to saw downward, as the blade is already facing that direction. The serrated part makes easy work of the drywall, but after three passes, I hit something on the other side and I cannot move it further in the downward direction. I remove the blade and invert it, and with the sharp blade facing up, reinsert into the incision. I begin sawing upward. I make about 6 passes when I hit something. This object gives some as I push against it, but it does not make way for my slicing and cutting effort. I have a vertical cut, about 2 inches high. I start to insert my blade, perpendicular to this cut, as close to center as possible, with the blade facing left, assuming the object to the right will prevent progress in that direction quickly. I work the blade in, creating a 1 inch horizontal line and begin sawing to the left. Every withdrawal pulls dust into the inner wall. I make it as far as I can reach and start cutting vertically to complete another hole above, but I do not make it far, and turn the cut toward the vertical line where I began. I repeat the process downward and complete even less distance. I start attacking the wall now, working to remove the small section I have identified. I end up removing a section that is approximately 2" by 2". I stick my index finger, left hand, into the hole. I bend my finger to the right, and find something very hard almost instantly. It feels like rock. I turn my finger clockwise, and locate this hard object all around my little hole. I have found a space where there is no rock, but there is dust and bits of rock everywhere I can feel, and some returns with me as I withdraw. I take the phone from my pocket and hold the light to the hole. I angle my face and the light so that I am aligning the angle of the light to reach the secondary hole while also looking in to see through to it. There is nothing on the other side. The light finds gray rock just beyond where my fingers reach, and I know this is just a small pocket in a pile of rubble similar to what was found outside the other wall. I sigh deeply and stand upright. The flashlight turns off, and the phone dies. It shows the Apple logo and spins the wheel a moment, then goes dark. I stab the knife into the wall right beside my new hole. I turn to my left and kick the door with my left foot. It does not react and feels solid, immovable. I don't care. I kick it again. It sounds solid. I am not kicking it expecting results, I am fucking angry. I keep kicking it, then I slam my hand into it. I ram my left palm into it, just above the handle, with my weight behind it, and then alternate between kicking it at the base and hitting it at the latch point. At some point, I hear the door crack when I make contact. I pause, because I wonder if it is my foot or the door. I am using the ball of my foot, and it does not feel like anything is wrong with my part other than a bit of throbbing from impact. I assume I cracked the outer shell of the door by striking in-between frame pieces and decide that I don't care.

"Where is my refrigerator?"

I had put more faith into this plan than was probably frugal considering the evidence mounting against my escape. I had a small fit of anger and I am now feeling a bit defeated. I look around and sense the smallness of my space. I have never personally suffered from clinical anxiety, although I am familiar with the feeling of general anxiety in certain situations. Samantha suffers from intense anxiety attacks and I know how that looks. When I begin looking around myself, somewhat frantically, I can feel my pulse increasing, and I start feeling warm. Then it seems like the room is closing in, not in a hallucinogenic sense, but I feel emotionally "trapped" in my room. I assume that being physically trapped does not help this feeling. I don't think the refrigerator could be working, or still cold, or provide anything useful other than escape. In my mind, this wall appears less damaged from my perspective, so perhaps the appliance provided enough structural support during the event to create a pocket or hall that I could make my way out from. I am stunned that there is no trace of it when I access the space it once occupied. This evidence only continues to support my assumption that, whatever the details of the event may be, it generated mass-destruction and left, what seems to be, very little behind.

"Help!"

I remember that I need to yell for help occasionally, just in case. My brain hurts and I can't tell if it's from the disbelief or if the ibuprofen is wearing off. I reach for my head and accidentally land on the laceration behind my hairline. I recognize the mishap before causing any damage, because I notice the bloody hair and pull back. I decide to investigate very gently with my hand. The wound still feels soft and may still be a candidate for opening up and becoming infected. It seems like a fresh wound, not a week-old cut on the head.

"Why aren't you healing?"

I explore the hair around the cut, crispy with dried blood, it feels like I am touching someone else's head. The sensation is far away from me and perplexing. I am interested in the hairs that are stuck in the wound and I am trying to gently separate as much as I can from their glue-like binding when I feel some of my hair stay in my hand as I move my hand to another location. I instinctively look at my hand and see that the mass of hair I was trying to adjust has pulled out of my scalp. There is no cringe-sensation from the hairs being pulled, at all. I actually feel it in the cut more than my scalp.

"That's odd."

I reach back up, avoiding the perimeter of the partially-healed spot, and brush my hair right at my peak, center of hairline, straight back, simply to feel the length and condition. I feel more hair in my fingers when I lift off halfway back across the top of my head. I look at my hand again, there are hairs, chunks of hair, between all four fingers. This is not the typical shedding when your hair is unhealthy, it seems wrong. I have a recurring nightmare that involves my teeth falling out where I am shocked and disturbed, but they continue falling out. I am mostly disturbed by the vivid sensation of them separating from my gums in the dream, rather than the sensation of missing teeth after. This is the same kind of feeling, I just sit there staring at my hand, confused and disturbed. My hair is falling out.

"What the fuck?"

The realization that your hair is coming out, actively, in your hands, at first causes shock. But then it is like coming across an animal in the wild: you're not sure if you should move, or do something, or if it is better to be still. I sit there, frozen, afraid that if I move too suddenly, more hair will fall out on its own. Eventually, I brush my hands off on each other to my side and touch my head where the hair came from. I can't tell where it came out, but it feels thinner, somehow, so I reach with my left hand to the back of my head and find the hairline at my neck. I pinch a tiny tuft of short hair and begin pulling it away from the scalp at my neck. There is no pain and barely any resistance as the bit in my fingers separates from my neck. I bring it around and look at it and it's definitely my hair. Even in the fading light, I can tell it's mine. I rub my fingers together briskly while shaking my hand to release the little hairs to the floor beside me. I am suddenly overcome by frustration. This insult to my injury is very real. War-mongers do not consider the individuals and the suffering they cause. They may think about it and just carry on with the plan because they have no empathy, but they certainly do not consider the reality of the lives that are destroyed. If I can't find a way out of this space, I am going to live out the experiment that was some scientist's theory of how to assure no one survives the attack on my world, in real time, with total immersion. Did the nuclear and chemical explosive specialists intentionally utilize molecules that produce all of my symptoms? Or is this the unknown factor when creating a large explosion? Perhaps the methodology was to create big enough bombs to make sure virtually no one survives, but also that anyone who did, would not make it very long, and would probably wish they hadn't.

That is the first time I have had that specific thought.

It is starting to close in on me: the feeling that surviving the event was not some sort of incredible luck, but rather a horrible curse.

I look around my room, in the fading light, and take a short inventory of the supplies. It's really rather remarkable: I have enough food and fluid to survive in the room for at least 4 or 5 more weeks, longer if I inventory and organize and ration with methodical design. The irony starts to seep into my brain: I can barely hold down any solid food. I have even been vomiting water at times. I must be starving for nutrients because my digestive system is not operating properly. I have plenty of food, but I can't seem to process it. I assume it is related to the same issue causing my hair to fall out. A food source is one necessity for survival in any extreme situation. I have this, but I'm not sure my body is accepting it.

Another thing you need is water, and my incredible luck has provided a seemingly endless supply that continues to increase. Ironically, it is flowing, like a mountain spring, from a god-damned toilet sticking out of my ceiling. I have never really taken the time to emotionally unpack this wild piece of fuckery until now: the universe decided that I can have water, and plenty of it, but I have to drink it from a toilet. I have convinced myself that the toilet is clean with a clever story about the renovation of the apartment upstairs, but, in reality, I have no notion of the condition of that toilet. The evidence suggests that nothing outside my pantry is as I remember it, so that toilet could just as easily have come from the supermarket down the street, and have just been used by an incontinent construction worker who can't stop eating local BBQ and biscuits, and his digestive system unleashed in that commode as the world erupted around him. For all I know, he's still sitting on it up there. That toilet could have been used as a still for a moonshine operation in the neighborhood behind my complex. But I decided, as soon as I saw it, that the water was perfectly clean, because it looked and smelled fine. It tastes like water with a hint of plastic... "but it's in a plastic container!"

If the enemy detonated half of the firepower they threatened to have, the fallout and residual nuclear leftovers would certainly be settling into the water. I don't know where the water is coming from, I assume it is rain that is somehow reaching the bowl of this toilet and then dripping from the front of it. I can imagine that larger particulates are settling to the bottom of the bowl, and the clean water on top is what drips down to my container, but that is wishful thinking. I also understand that the dangers of atomic energy are rarely visible following the initial, massive, explosion. The radiation will infiltrate everything in its reach and it is generally unseen. I think about the lead vest that covers you, and particularly your gonads, when you get an x-ray. You have no sensation that you are being radiated, but you are. You can't smell the radiation in a microwave, but it definitely exists. You also can't taste the radiation. Yet, I seem to think I can identify radiation in my water supply without any tools.

The next crucial concern for survival is air. The "rule of threes" says that I cannot make it very long without air. Specifically, I cannot survive without clean and processable oxygen available to my lungs. I also cannot survive if my lungs won't process the oxygen. I know there is air and I know there is a replenishing supply. I also know the air is ripe with particles so foul, that I have been sick from the smell. I can occasionally smell other things mixed with it, but it is always there. The odor of my wasted world is a new baseline that all other detectable odors are forced to cooperate with. Nothing could possibly overpower it. I have generated odors within my confined space that certainly enter with greater voracity, but the nasal-rape perseveres. I suspect much of my supply is coming from the small spaces around the toilet, where the light comes from, but I will have to get up there to sort that out. I now assume that the air keeping me alive is also helping the water to steadily exterminate me. I am sure that I am being poisoned by my necessities. I am now confident that my good fortune is all truly a Trojan horse. All of the survival resources miraculously being provided to me are going to kill me.

The other item that I know one needs to survive is shelter. Amazingly, the structure providing my shelter is not even designed to shelter a human, but only his food. It is only a small part of my designed shelter. The destruction outside these walls tells me that there is very little shelter left. I have no reason to believe anyone else has survived, so I guess I have the only shelter left. Again, ironically, my shelter is also my prison. There is a chance that it is actually protecting me from other, more imminent, dangers, but I am approaching an emotional state that makes me willing and eager to escape and take that chance. There are many possible scenarios outside of this room. The world as I know it could be a terrible wasteland with no other life to be found within my reach. The event may have obliterated everything: all living things. That world could be a nuclear desert and that much firepower is likely going to spawn a nuclear winter. These possibilities could make my current situation a preferred option. There could be other survivors out there, but I just haven't heard them yet. They could be looking for each other so they can band together and survive through mutual resourcefulness. While this is possible, it is more likely that any survivors are desperately searching for supplies and resources like the ones I have in my room. They are also probably getting very sick, possibly more sick than me, and, at this point, getting desperate. I can more easily imagine a world of few survivors, and they are more prone to take from one-another than work together. If they are grouping up, it is to defend themselves, so there may be gang violence and cutthroat behaviors while groups work to eliminate others in order to salvage resources. If any animals survived, they may be sick and desperate, becoming more bold and violent than usual. I certainly have a good resource to help with this problem, but if others have been out there since it happened, and the hierarchy is already established, walking out with a loaded Glock may not end well. The other possibility is that the enemy has deployed ground troops or some other form of automated or air assault that is seeking out survivors for immediate elimination. I know that the previous attack violates almost every international law about war, so there is no reason to hope for capture and tolerance if that is the state of things. I would be facing a horrible future of hiding, running, and constant paranoia. I realize I am scratching the place on my neck again and I have caused it to bleed and smart. It burns and throbs.

"Why can't I stop doing that?!"

I compulsively scratch at this lesion and it continues to grow. It is probably 2-3 inches across now and festering. I am anxious. That is the only explanation. Every time I sit and really contemplate my situation I scratch this sore open.

The thing our mentors never told us about survival is that we truly need companionship. Philosophers have proposed the vitality of love and companionship from the perspective of society and relationships, but rarely have we considered how important it is when it is suddenly gone.

Loneliness is the starvation of the soul.

I have lived a spoiled life, surrounded by loving family and supportive friends. I can admit that I am privileged. I have never had a time of tremendous loneliness in my entire life. I have experienced loneliness, but it has always been acute and temporary. Often, when I have felt the nip of loneliness at my heart, I know that I have caused it, and I instantly recognize that I do not like it, and I seek to reverse the situation and take measurable steps to avoid it in the future. As I consider the possibilities that may await me outside of this room, I am overcome by grief. I may find the same state, devoid of interaction and become psychologically and emotionally devastated. I also may find other creatures, but they may be the opposite of the connection I am yearning for. The lives that I am hoping for would provide support and partnership, but the reality I discover may be violent and unforgiving. They may even be so far gone into their own survival realities, that there is little or no opportunity to negotiate or discuss options. The thing I desire most is trusted companionship, but I am suddenly terrified that I may not find it out there.

"That's exactly what I was worried about."

"What's that?"

"That you would spiral into this paranoia and lose hope."

"That is not at all what is happening."

"Stop scratching."

I was doing it again.

I try to ignore the alter-consciousness that has again welcomed himself into my room, or my mind. I also remember Samantha, or the ghost-visitor of my wife, questioning why I would not allow myself to be enough company during this struggle. I have always prided myself in being a loner. I am content in the peaceful serenity that I find in moments where no other humans are interrupting my thoughts. I think that is only a desire when we are being perpetually inundated with information and sources of interaction, albeit superficial, and often virtual. If a person is tethered to a smart device or has regular access to the internet, they are most likely connected to social platforms that provide constant reaction and response.

This also allows for infinite stimulation. Society leaned into this realm heavily during the pandemic, which marks another predictable chapter in the history of life on earth. Our world struggled to outrun and outsmart a virus, and was relatively successful. Governments executed varying stages and depths of isolation and lockdown strategies to mitigate the spread, but were not altogether effective. The results have been profound, and like most global crises, lingering response and long term effects are only just being realized many years after the climax of the disease. Younger generations, who were raised in digital environments, were well-prepared, technically, to adopt strategies that prevent direct contact with other humans. They almost seemed to enjoy the challenge. But no one was prepared, emotionally or psychologically, to grapple with the effects from being physically isolated. Depression and anxiety runs rampant through communities. I remember the first time we visited a grocery store after quarantine, and how people were cautiously avoiding entering the forbidden personal space identified by "social-distancing" guidelines. Everyone I saw was paranoid, but you could only see the tops of their faces. I admit feeling panicked by this. Everyone looked angry to me. I don't think they were actually angry, but not seeing their entire expression left me with a sense of intimidation from almost all of them. But there was one person that day, an older woman, whose eyes did not convey animosity. Her eyes looked sad. She seemed lost and pitiful. I don't think she was even shopping, she certainly was not collecting any items, pushing a cart, or carrying a basket. She had only her handbag. She seemed nimble, but was visibly weak, and trudged along, searching the store for eye contact, clearly yearning for interaction. That was the first time I recall ever recognizing the dark loneliness. I scanned the half-faces as I passed them and began to feel anxious and nervous, as if something horrible was about to go down, until I saw her. Then I became instantly depressed. I knew this person lived alone, had been asked to isolate for many weeks, and was not digitally fluent enough to compensate for the loss of direct social interaction. My soul shuddered as we stood and stared at one-another. I felt like I, personally, let her down.

I wonder what she saw in me. Neither of us spoke. We just stood there. The look of defeat in her eyes was dark. I had a horrible sense that this adventure was a last hope for her, and now I wish I had spoken to her. I consider all of the struggles that our world had to overcome in that time, and how much of that success may have just been wiped out in a matter of minutes. But, the world missed a great opportunity to unite around a singular enemy. All theories and assumptions aside, this global infection, at the scientific level, was oblivious to the human condition. It certainly highlighted inequities and the cracks in the foundation of global health efforts, primarily witnessed in the markedly pronounced availability of healthcare to certain populations. The lesson that should have been learned before the event that has now unfolded, but wasn't, is the false sense of security that Americans have garnered about health, security, and general safety. We should have learned that we are not as safe as we feel and behave, that we are completely vulnerable to attack, disease, and many other threats. People fought hard to make it through that experience, only to now be obliterated. Families were torn apart by a virus, forced to say goodbye to one-another via FaceTime. Medical professionals were pushed to their limits and asked to make decisions at a rate and of a content that is impossible to comprehend, even to those who lived it. World leaders and decision makers were tossing experimental ideas at the public in a fashion that was unimaginable. All of our research and technological advancements were virtually helpless against a microscopic invader. Our most useful defense was to stay away from each other, with most of the medical treatments and procedures ending in death. The world disconnected from the concept of mass-casualty, and began gauging the infection by death tolls in the thousands, then tens of thousands, then hundreds of thousands, and then millions. We were, as a global community, desensitized to death and loss, and yet we somehow did not heed the inherent warnings.

With all of the knowledge at my disposal, I still have no real information about the event or what actually occurred Tuesday. I am left only to ponder the intricacies of this new and merciless situation, leaving me in a state of confusion and wonder. I wonder how many people died instantly. I wonder if the devastation that I have inferred is representative of the greater population of the United States, North America, or the western hemisphere. Did the attack kill 80 percent of the country? Could it be more? How many more have perished in the slow aftermath? Was their overzealous planning of the attack too much, and they are starting to see the fallout and radiation in unintended parts of the world? Did the western allies counterattack? Was this a global annihilation? I imagine there are very few living things near me right now, which, if widespread, means a looming "nuclear winter." I have read of such devastation and it sounds horrible. How terrible it must be, for anyone who struggled to survive the pandemic, then possibly survived this attack, only to be alone and awaiting the world to fall into a horrible winter because the fragile ecosystem has been shaken from its foundation.

I am suddenly overcome by a horrible vision of Samantha being incinerated at the steering wheel of her Audi, on I-75 South, stuck in a strange midday traffic jam, not uncommon in Metro Atlanta, but peculiar on that day. I flash between the image of a heat/shock wave rushing through the city, cinematic in imagery, unreal, and jumping from one perspective to another, as it rushes from the elevated point of its inception across the vast metropolis. My brain chooses different vantage points and tortures me with the images. One begins with a scene in Midtown, on Peachtree Street at Fourteenth, bustling with business people, heading to lunch and scurrying to meetings, all on their earbud calls and laughing. The people are faceless, they look like architectural renderings, artistically drawn to suggest movement and busy-ness, but in motion, actual motion, not like the drawings. Suddenly, there is a distraction, it comes from above, and everyone looks up. The camera/perspective pans out and up and shows the underside of a rapidly-expanding explosion, bursting down toward the earth below. Suddenly, the image shifts to a high altitude perspective and there is a massive cloud blasting outward, in a donut shape, and the infamous mushroom cloud. Then the movie zooms back into the street view and presents the image of a shock wave, rushing out from the initial scene and leveling everything in its path. The massive high rises and skyscrapers throughout the city begin to collapse onto themselves, with pressure from above and all around. The camera chases the shockwave as it rushes through the city, allowing just enough delay to capture humans, trees, bushes, buildings, cars, trucks, cranes, and anything else, in rapid succession, being reduced to dust in a flash. I watch the horror unfold before me, in a dizzying flight up and out of the city, flying along the interstate, disintegrating everything before me. The picture slows as I focus in on my partner's vehicle in the road, surrounded by all of the other unsuspecting victims in their helpless shells that provide so much false security until this moment. I am suddenly ahead of the shockwave and watching Samantha, as she stares with horror at the destruction heading toward her. Just before it reaches her, the look of shock fades to a strange calm, then she is sprayed with glass, instantly set aflame, and turned to dust, in slow-motion, but still within a blink, and then blown away, like sand. I have seen this in a movie, maybe one of the Terminator films, where someone is watching a child at a playground, holding onto a fence, and is instantly set ablaze, reduced to ash, and blown away in rapid succession. The problem is that I watch this happen to my wife, my lover, my passion, with vivid detail, and my mind has created it and forced me to witness it. Then the image starts over, but from the perspective of a point on the Perimeter, I-285, where the gridlock has people frustrated, honking, and yelling at other drivers. The event is the same though, but the explosion is closer to the road, and the initial shockwave plows the cloverleaf interchange downward, instantly crushing everything. Then we follow the shockwave south toward my wife. We come upon her vehicle from behind, and this time can see, as time slows, that the alternate wave is approaching from the south, and the place where my beautiful city once was, is a massive cloud of dust, with a plume rising above it, reaching for space. The magic of imagination allows both waves to meet right at Samantha's car, and we watch her disintegrate, exactly the same, but this time some sort of conflicting force is blowing her remains away in alternate directions. Her death, in my mind, is painless and instantaneous.

I wonder if she thought of me, or her lover, or our son.

Our son... Nathaniel...

Children have been rehearsing for terrible events in their schools for many years now. We grew up learning to sit in the hallway, with our bodies curled and our heads between our knees, thinking this would save us from a tornado. Children now learn how to hide in their classrooms in the event that someone decides to invade their school and begin shooting innocent children, because it has happened so often. They learn to hide in the classroom, lock the doors, place themselves where they may not be shot from through the door, turn off the lights, be very quiet, and pray. All of our preparations are to tuck and pray so that we don't meet a merciless fate. It is much like the plan for a plane crash: "head between your knees and kiss your ass goodbye." This is not survival training, this is victim training, passive tolerance. I don't think it is bad or wrong. I also can't suggest better preparations or solutions. I do, however, cringe at the thought of my child, my brave and brilliant wingman, hiding under his desk, in full rehearsal mode, because a siren sounded and they were told to "take shelter." A good friend of mine, Daniel, who self-identified as a "prepper" and often shared interesting research and information with me, had once, at a party, shared some recently obtained knowledge regarding different building designs, styles, and materials with relation to how they withstand thermal and pressure blasts from nuclear explosions. He had acquired some sort of government text that cataloged much of the data compiled during the United States government's nuclear weapons experimentations. He was thrilled that his meager bungalow, composed entirely of cinder block, built in the middle of the 20th century in the Atlanta suburbs, was the most "blast-resistant" typical housing design on record. I recall commenting on the comfort in this fact, because most public schools were also designed with the same structural components. Now, I want to believe that the cinder block structure of my son's middle school would offer sufficient resistance and spare the innocent lives within, but the state of my building suggests otherwise. My wicked and clearly decaying mind now forces me to watch a similar scene as a warhead detonates just above the ground in our old neighborhood, in Edgewood, and the houses and shops are wiped from the land so rapidly it is dizzying. This shot is from above, and the wave is visible as a disturbance in the air like a wave in the sea, and everything it meets just goes away, leaving a blurry image that is dust and debris in the air. The matter is not being destroyed, it is being broken down, instantly, to microscopic particles, and my camera zooms in and slows time to explain this science to the viewer. Objects can be seen igniting and disappearing instantly, even in slow motion. In real time, the fire portion of the destruction is virtually unseen, as there is but a flash as the wave passes through things. We follow the wave East, and when Nathaniel's school comes into view, the perspective shifts to his classroom. I can't see specific others in the room and the walls are blank blocks. The children are all seated along the inner wall, away from the windows, and facing the wall. A few are laughing and playing, but my child, and the children closest to him are in position: knees pulled up with head between them and arms over the head. My camera is suddenly beneath Nate, looking up at his face. His eyes are closed and he is saying something. The world falls silent, and I hear my son's voice say, clearly, in a whisper, "oh God please, please let this be a drill."

He is praying. My son, who has never been to a church service in his life, is praying to a God that he, in this moment, has complete faith in. As the video of my sick mind slows to a pause, I ask it quietly to stop... It does not. I watch the perspective snap back out and I am forced to watch his body breathe in deeply and his back rise as the windows implode in super-slow-motion and the wave reaches him. The rest of the room is a blur while I am forced to watch him ignite, disintegrate, and disappear into a cloud of dust as his remains blend into the blocks around him as they also become nothing instantaneously.

"Stop! Help! Help!"

"I can't watch this any more."

The emotional torture is too much. I finally regain some control of my brain and realize that I am sitting, legs pulled up, facing into the pantry, rocking, and sobbing. Tears are running down my face. I am crying like a child, blubbering and whimpering. I see my mother's face, and the image begins to zoom out.

'Stop it!"

I don't want to watch my mother die. I realize that her eyes are the eyes of the lonely woman in the supermarket during the pandemic. She is in her apartment in Marietta, reading a paperback with the news on. She is rocking in her favorite chair and looking dismayed, shaking her head at whatever she is hearing on the TV. I'm sure it is the same broadcast I was hearing as they rushed the president to safety. I wonder if the country's leadership made it to their bunkers. I wonder what the actual state of my nation is now. My mother was a very free spirit. Neither her nor my father had any business being tied to another person, and they both enjoyed great happiness after separating. My mother was always there for me, but she lived her own life. She supported me and made sure I had everything I needed to thrive, but we just stayed out of each-other's way. I rarely knew her plans, didn't much care, and she rarely asked mine. The only real problem this posed was if we needed to coordinate something together. If I had some sort of appointment or commitment that I needed her for in my childhood, I would have to corner her and force her to assist. It taught me not to need that kind of attention if at all possible. But she certainly had the ability to materialize when I suddenly needed her, if injured or the like. She worked as a salesperson for various beauty supply organizations, then for medical supply companies, and then pharmaceuticals, so she was very rarely at an office. She was terrible at the job of selling, but was so annoying, her customers would buy things just to make her leave. That was her career. She saved enough to retire and had been enjoying it for over 5 years. She was in her 70's, still drove if necessary, and did whatever she wanted. Her life was very much the same as it was before retirement, just without that pesky "work" problem interfering with her plans. She, like my father, was a woman of little need, so she refused to enter relationships that involved expectations, and she seemed to enjoy doing things alone. When we would travel together, she would warn me not to slow her down. I learned to keep up at a young age and discovered how to travel light and see more of the world by needing less. That is a great theme of my life: need less. I rebelled against both of them in my twenties by wanting shiny, new things and surrounding myself with belongings. We bought a house and collected things, always wanting the next fancy item or trendy knick-knack. Eventually, after Nathaniel was born, we got tired of buying things and decided to sell most of it. Not at all surprisingly, my mother did not visit us in the house often, and we would have to head up to the suburbs to see her. She was still working and getting very sick of it. To reach retirement early, she downsized her living arrangements little by little until she was renting a room in someone's basement for $100 per month. This allowed her to save so much money, so much faster. Once her grandchild was born, she would come see us much more often, because "Sugy needs to see her baby." Once, she stepped into our house in Edgewood and before greeting anyone, she exclaimed, "please, son, do not die before me!"

"I mean, that is the plan, Mom, but may I ask why you are demanding this? I assume it is not because the pain of losing your only child would be too much to bear?"

"Because I really don't want to have to deal with the collection of bullshit that you have accumulated!"

She really knows how to flatter me, but this really did plant a seed. I admit, this was when Samantha began losing interest in our life. She was definitely responsible for a large portion of the "shiny-things" syndrome, but we were both trying to find happiness outside of what had originally been the only thing we needed to be happy. I am sure there was some serious postpartum depression chipping in, and I was busy trying to fix everything. Sugar-Momma knew exactly what was happening and told us regularly. She would appear at the house on a day when she knew Nathaniel would be there and tell us to "go figure

out whatever you need to figure out while Sugy spoils this angel."
Nathaniel grew up always hoping for his Sugy to appear at the
door. She did not spoil him with material things, Mom and Pops
had the overindulgence of stimulating items under control. She
would always have a plan for what they would be doing. This
type of spoiling is equally as disastrous to a child's upbringing. By
the time he was walking and talking, he was asking "what are we
doing today?" Once he started asking Sugy that when she
arrived, she stopped taking him places, and they started playing
games and crafting at home. Then, once he entered elementary
school, she lost interest, because he resembled society at large.
My mother never helped with childcare on a regular basis, but
she was definitely the grandparent that was local enough to be
our clutch-play in a pinch. When we had emergencies or
situations that required a babysitter with short-notice, she was
almost always willing to cover. She would ask us to keep it under
a few hours and, only once did Nathaniel ever spend the night at
Sugy's house. My mother certainly struggled with some
emotional and psychological issues, and as a child, she was the
object of other parents' criticism. She was referred to as
"eclectic," or "over-the-top," and came into every social situation
with high-energy to compensate for her extreme social-anxiety.
She self-medicated with various substances and never hid it from
me. My earliest experiences with drugs were always "borrowed"
from my mother's collections. I loved exploring her bathroom
when she wasn't home. In high school, I had the opportunity to
experience many types of sedatives, antidepressants, stimulants,
and hallucinogenic chemicals, all in the safety of my own home.
I never shared them, and I never took too many. Later in life, she
finally connected with a doctor that got her meds "just right,"

and she seemed relatively content, almost all the time. This was a welcome change from my childhood, because she was almost always "searching" for something, and never really landing on her feet, emotionally. Once we decided to move to Decatur for the schools, we began shedding property. My mother did not want anything we had and Samantha's parents were in Charleston by then. She had grown up wealthy in the suburbs and her parents simply wanted to live somewhere quiet. Once her youngest sibling was independent, they ran for the coast almost immediately and we began selling items and giving things away. My mother retired just before we sold the house and moved to an apartment. She came over as we were moving and asked Samantha if she could have one of our serving dishes. Samantha said, "I didn't know you liked that dish, mom." My mother said, "I don't, but I am having company over this weekend and I really can't stand buying dishes just for one night. I will probably ruin it or never bring it back, so I figure I better just ask you if I can have it, instead of borrow it." Samantha was happy to release the dish to her, but interactions like this were very foreign to my wife, and I don't think she ever settled into the idea of a parent that would be so brutally honest and dismissively abrasive.

My mind pictures my mother in her little apartment within the complex in Marietta, and then I see the windows implode toward her and the walls fly in like pieces of paper, coming apart into smaller and smaller pieces before reaching her. The shockwave causes a disturbance in the visible field around her as it connects and then she, too, ignites and disintegrates instantaneously.

I shift back to Nathaniel's face, and I see the raw fear and concern in his expression. Time rewinds and puts him back at his desk, or the desk where my imagination decides he sits in the stark, plain, classroom of my imagination. The siren sounds, the school alarm follows, and his face scans the room for something. He looks lost and concerned. I decide that he knows, in that moment, that this is the end. There is some force that children can sense that tells them disturbing news. If ever my child were nervous about something, I would take it seriously, because I believe they know things that we lose as we mature. I believe children can hear things in the air and feel forces in space that are too simple and fundamental for adults to experience. Once you stop experiencing them, you can never learn how to again, except for maybe with drugs, but rarely do you make sense of them again. He has the look of a wise person, knowing that something is amiss, and then he follows the instructions and moves to the wall. He is still afraid, but he already knows that it is the end. This image provides no comfort, it just reminds me that I am sure he is gone.

I weep fully now, knowing that my child was taken, and that I couldn't protect him like I promised I always would. I think the idea of letting him down, of lying to him, is possibly worse than losing him. But in this moment, I miss him terribly, and would give my own life, absolutely, to salvage his, unless he would have to endure the agony that I am experiencing now. Maybe, in this way, it is good that it is my struggle alone, and not my son's.

Through my tears, I recognize that the light is fading. I feel hungry and instantly sick. I reach for my throat and catch myself, I put my hand back down. I get up from the floor and grab a can of green beans from the dispenser on the left. There are still at least 30 cans of food left. I hunt for, and locate, the can opener in the container and sit back down to begin opening the can. I stop to have a few sips of water and now the taste and texture of it bothers me. I can feel when the water enters my stomach and I feel sick again. I continue opening the can and I contemplate drinking the bean juice instead, although I am unsure if it matters what I eat or drink, but when I focus on a task, I don't care that I feel sick or that I have pains. My head hurts. This headache is familiar and bothersome. It feels like I have intentionally crossed my eyes to be funny but held it too long. There is a pain, or discomfort, behind my eyes, that almost feels like my sinuses. It seems the nausea and sickness is coming from this place and it seems like something is wrong with my brain. As the pain increases steadily, my vision goes blurry and my eyes feel heavy. I eat the beans one at a time with my fingers. I don't care about my hands being dirty or that I am dropping juice on my clothes. I try not to scarf the food, but I am distracted and just continue the motion. I eat half of the can and the sensation is too much. I tuck the open can into the front right corner and put the can opener back in its container. I know that the ibuprofen has run out, and I would like to take more so that I can feel better, but I am very concerned that I am going to run out, and decide to save the medicine as long as I can stand it. I am under the shelves again, and I am watching the light on the spice rack shift to a strange red hue. I imagine that the particles in the air outside are generating amazing colors as the sun rises and sets, and that the tiny bit of light I receive in here is a representation of one of the upsides to nuclear fallout: beautiful sunsets. This feels like a great metaphor for what it is like to survive a nuclear attack and be witnessing breathtaking images from the toxic air that is killing you, the "sunset" of your life. I realize this is very likely what I am experiencing. My sun is setting and I only get a tiny snippet of the beautiful part. The color in the room shifts to a darker red and a fog starts to envelope my vision. I have a type of tunnel vision that is very slowly closing in, where the outer rim is a blur, and growing. Soon there is only a tiny oval of clarity in the middle, and the silhouette of the rack on the door and its contents morphs into the giant oak tree, the same one from before. I am closer to it, and as the blur closes in, I can see its form clearly through the haze. Then I start to pan out until I am at the same distance I was. My vision starts to clear and I can see the details starting to materialize in the tree. The dark, murky, red light that fills my field of vision seems like something from space. I imagine other planets have atmospheres like this. There is no wind and there is very little else to see as the tree comes into focus. This oak tree seems more broad than tall, which is typical of lone trees in fields, where they have not been forced to compete for sunlight or water, so I assume this is an oak tree's natural state. It will spread its limbs wide to generate a more vast solar cells with which to capture the sun. The mighty oak represents the strength of solidarity, but its evolution has supported and encouraged this behavior. I want to latch onto the image and representative message that this regal organism expresses to me, but I still see the loneliness. I start to recognize the pattern of oily water behind the tree. Everything is a reddish hue, and the pattern is there, beginning to come into focus, forcing the tree to become a foreground unnoticed. I cannot control where my vision lands and focuses. The oil-on-water background has taken the color of blood, but it is still. There are beautiful spirals in it, creating luminescent shades of red, with one very large spiral toward the top left. None of it is moving. The scene itself is calming, but the stillness is unsettling. I feel the overwhelming edge of my seat sensation like watching a car teetering on the edge of a cliff. I know there should be motion and I expect it to occur any moment. Then my eyes go back to the tree. Something flickered in the branches on the right. Still red, I see it again. It's like a tiny light in the leaves. Then I see another one. I can see the details of the tree now, but the tiny flash is momentary, and moves every time. It also makes a sound, like a tiny splash. My focus shifts back to the background, and I feel like the pattern has changed, but I can't tell how, and it still is not moving. I can now recognize the minuscule flashes in the branches while I am focused on the background. My focus shifts back to the tree, there is a gentle sense of movement in it, and I recognize this as a breeze. I see a flash and know that it is a leaf, moving slightly from a breeze and catching the light, creating a reflection. It is subtle, and if you were on Mars watching this scene, you might not even notice the breeze at all. I feel something on the back of my neck and reach for it, when I connect, I know it is an itch, maybe from the breeze, and I scratch it. Then I feel it on my right thigh, so I reach down and scratch there. It doesn't help, so I rub it a bit through my pants. I am now seeing the breeze in the oak leaves and feeling it on my body. It is gentle, like the soft brushing of fingers across skin. The movement in the branches is almost unnoticeable, except for the flashing. Then my focus shifts to the background, and I see the oily pattern begin to swirl and move, very smoothly, very calmly. It looks like a ride at Disney World as it starts to spin, like it's winding up. But the oily pattern never gets up to speed, it simply morphs and mesmerizes me.

This hallucination carries on well past dark. Fortunately, I know that I am hallucinating, but I can't seem to make it stop. The images are disrupted by coughing. I start coughing. It's not a fit of coughing, just every once in a while. Because I have lost touch with time, I have no idea how often, nor do I know what time it could be. But every time I cough, it is sudden, I can't control it, and when it explodes from me, the whole red image flashes white. My vision goes back to the tree and trippy background immediately, until I cough again. This begins to cause the images to blur and fade away. I start to come back to the reality of the completely dark room. I realize that I am scratching all of the places on me that itch, and I am not aware of the intensity. I have scratched the back of my neck to blood, along with two places on my left forearm and one on my right. I can feel the blood in my fingers as I pull away and feel the painful burn at each location. I can't see the blood, but I feel it between my fingers. I try to stop scratching.

I can't remember what day it is. I find my briefcase leaning against the wall to my left, the foyer wall. I locate my personal phone inside. I push the power button until the apple appears. The phone comes on.

Check the time: 3:41 AM

# CHAPTER 11

Day 8

I am sick to my stomach, I might retch, but I try to remain calm. I choose not to drink water, because I am sure it is poisoning me. I cough again and feel something drip from the corner of my mouth. I wipe with the back of my hand and hold the screen up to it: Blood. My mouth is bleeding. I am instantly defeated. I know this is a bad sign. I take a very deep breath and slowly exhale: My lungs feel ok, no pain or tightness, so it seems my throat is the problem and my mouth is bleeding. I close my eyes and tongue around inside my mouth. I can feel sores inside my lips, one near the right corner is very tender. This is where the blood is coming from. My mouth itself is bleeding. I recall one of the many documentaries I have watched about World War II, where they colorized all of the footage and retold the important stories of the time. I remember the images from Hiroshima and Nagasaki after the bombs were dropped and how the survivors suffered. One of the reports from the American scientists, who studied the victims like experiments, referred to the observed delayed effects. At some point after the initial horror and burn trauma, gamma radiation started destroying people. Some were said to sporadically bleed from their mouth, nose, and rectum, then "just suddenly died." I thought this was horrible at the time, but now I realize how truly inhumane atomic warfare is. I don't want to feel sorry for myself, so I decide to change the subject.

"Oh Samantha, I wish you were here with me right now."

I decide to look at some pictures on my phone. I unlock the device, quickly scan for wifi, cellular, and then satellite signals: no luck at all. Still absolutely no other devices or signals found. The phone is down to 15% battery. I open the photos app, and start scrolling, one at a time. The first ones, as I scan from most recent backward, are of a classic car show that I stopped by over the weekend. It was in a large parking lot, so I just stopped and walked around. I don't waste much time with these. I find the first picture of my son, looking over his shoulder in line to get a hot dog at a local baseball field. I had just said, "do you know what they make those out of, Nate?"

"Nope! And I don't care!"

The picture makes me smile.

I back out to the thumbnails and start scrolling faster. I am watching pictures of trees and forests and my son and my wife and our community and art shows and random pictures of mushrooms fly up the screens, when suddenly, I spot bare breasts. I go back.

Holy shit, I forgot.

I tap the first picture, it is my stunning wife, topless, staring at me, with one suspicious eyebrow raised. I asked her, a few months back, to let me take some "sexy" pictures for a business trip I was planning. She had no problem, or made no objection to, posing for these and a few even more risqué shots. There are 17 in all. She dons a silky cover-up in a couple images. They are sexy, but I can only see some cleavage, and a well-defined, sub-lace, nipple. Then, there are a few of her completely nude. In one, she got down on her knees and looked up at me while I took the photo. I can see her breasts perfectly from above and she is making convincing doe-eyes at me. I can also see the top of her vulva in this shot, and just make out the beginning of the slit. Her legs are spread, and the focus is just right to make the shot super-artsy. I scroll away to the topless pictures, and one of her laughing and partially covering herself with her arm, whilst holding out the other toward the camera in a "no paparazzi" pose.

I smile wide.

She is so fucking gorgeous.

I instinctively return to the begging mistress picture. I love this picture. I stare at it and realize that I am becoming aroused. My penis is slightly erect, "chubby." I track down to it with my left hand, and feel it through my pants, confirming the condition. I stare at my wife, who is staring back at me.

"Are you thinking what I'm thinking?"

"I'm always thinking that," she says.

This is how it always goes if I am horny.

I remember that there is a jar of coconut oil on the shelf right above me. I set the phone down and skootch out far enough to twist and feel around on the shelf. It is on the fridge side, near the back. I must have moved it there in my vain attempt to reorganize. I retrieve the plastic jar and bring it to my lap. I return to my place under the shelf and I feel like I am hiding, which creates an interesting sense of deviance that further excites me. I imagine being mid-stroke and someone opening the door. I would be so blissfully embarrassed.

I ask her, aloud, "you forgot about the pics I have in here, didn't you?"

"Nope," she answers, "but you did until just now."

"Jerking off has not exactly been my top priority."

"Well, I'm glad you are thinking more clearly now."

I fold almost in half at the waist and remove my t-shirt, then I unzip my pants and wriggle them and my boxer briefs down to my thighs. I push them a bit more, considering the potential for ejaculate stains, which is an absolutely ridiculous concern. Even if I was ever going to see anyone again, what would I care about a white stain on my pants? I'm disgusting, covered in blood and other waste. If someone found me and the first thing they said was, "is that a cum stain on your britches?" I would happily admit to my tasteless behavior. Maybe a better answer would be, "no, it's toothpaste." I unscrew the jar of coconut oil and set it on the ground beside me. I take a small amount on my index, middle, and ring fingers and bring the thick, petroleum-jelly-like, substance straight to my cock. I start to cover my half-hard member with it, immediately remember how it behaves, and enjoy how it warms and turns to liquid oil almost instantly. It is wonderfully soft and warm and the viscosity creates an amazingly erotic sensation. I am experiencing many sensations at the moment my penis becomes completely engorged, and I look down at the image of my wife, looking up at me. I am still covering the head of my penis with oil when I say, "you like that?"

"Hell yes."

This excites me more. The eye contact from my phone is vivid. My cock is covered and the skin is smooth and slippery from the lubricating substance. I am now stroking it, not a full grip, still encircling and distributing oil. I realize that I want more and have a serious "fuck it" moment. I reach over, remove significantly more thick oil than before, and bring it back to my crotch. I slap the gathering onto the webbing where the shaft of my penis adjoins my scrotum, and I work the oil downward over my entire sack and upward on the underside of my cock all the way to the head. In the next pass, I cover the entire ball sack and the area around my package and all the way to my gooch. I play there for a moment, then make my way back to my cock.

"I thought you might give me a little ass play," she whispers from my phone, maintaining the eye-contact that is the primary provocateur of this escapade.

"Nope. But I love teasing you with the idea."

She always wanted to experiment with these things. I always talked a big game and then chickened out. I am staring down her front in the picture now. My mind can imagine how her freshly shaved vulva would feel as I approached and brushed it with my hardness. I can clearly feel the lube between us, and my mind leans into that fantasy while I stroke my shaft in a more intentional manner. I am fully aroused now and can feel myself building toward climax. I decide to slow down.

"What's wrong?"

"Nothing, I just figured I better enjoy this."

"Why did you decide to wait until this moment in our relationship to slow down and enjoy it..."

I ignore her snarky jab at my reluctance to make intentional and contemplative love to her in recent times. I continue to stroke myself, slowly and very intentionally, as if I were performing the act. I return to my balls and surrounding areas briefly, then back to business. I stare into her eyes, occasionally drift to her tits, and continue down to her pussy. I continue to fantasize about the feeling of our lubricated skin together. I increase pace, tighten up my muscles, and escalate toward my climax. I am curling my lips over my teeth and holding them together.

"I'm almost there."

"Do it for me."

My breathing becomes labored and I am making a throaty grumbling sound. I can feel the release move through my body as it begins. There is a colorful explosion from my core out toward my extremities. Then all sensation zooms in, high-speed, to my cock and balls. I feel the hot rush of ejaculation welling up and time slows down.

I release onto myself in multiple explosions. My body trembles throughout impressive amounts of cumming and violent shivers. I make low and deep sounds in my throat and feel my face melting into an open-mouth expression of relief and satisfaction. I feel all of my muscles relax into soft, worthless chunks of meat, after flexing in unison to reach climax. My cock stays erect for a moment and I consider trying for another round, when I realize that there is no possible way I could do that again. I can barely lift my hand from its grip. I slide up the wall a bit and start rubbing the warm mixture of semen and coconut oil onto my belly, all over my chest, and onto my arms. I catch a whiff of the combination: the sweetness of the oil with the musky smell of fresh male ejaculate. It might be my imagination, but I enjoy it for a moment as a break from the usual odor.

"That was fucking hot."

"Thanks, I know you love watching me."

"I wish you would do that more."

"I know, and I wish you would stop seeking opportunities to chastise me for being less than adequate."

"I never said that."

"You didn't have to."

"All I ever said is that I want more than you do."

"Then you started fucking that guy."

"That's not fair."

"Really?"

"Why didn't you say something?"

"And lose you? No thanks. I can live with it so long as it doesn't cause drama and I still get to fuck you when I want."

"It never caused drama."

"Exactly. But only because I didn't let it."

"The fuck does that mean?"

"It means that I know it was him at the mall when Nate and I went for pretzel bites and saw you two chatting. I could have blown the whole thing up, but I decided to spare Nate from your bullshit."

"That's the most fucked up fishing for gratitude play I have ever experienced."

"Well you can thank me later."

"Did he know?"

"Nate? I don't think so. I admit you were pretty good with your stories and lies."

"I didn't want to hurt him."

"How noble of you..."

"I didn't want to hurt you either."

"Well, you failed there. It hurts plenty, I just decided to turn cold and keep you as my mistress."

"That's messed up."

"Touché..."

This is the conversation we should have had hundreds of times before over the past two years. I don't rifle through her phone or snoop. I see that she stops at the same parking lot at least twice a week and regularly leaves that location to go to the apartments next door. She also lies regularly about going out at night with her friends. I don't investigate, the lies just land in my lap. I bumped into her friend Melissa at the grocery store once when they were supposedly out together. I investigated and saw that Samantha was at the same apartment. Melissa was completely unaware that she was the excuse. I didn't say anything, just played dumb, wondering if she would ever tell Samantha that she saw me. But it never came up between us. She picked fights with me from time to time that felt like she was, perhaps subconsciously, seeking an easy-out, or yearning for her lies to find their way into the open, but I never gave her the satisfaction. There is an incredibly passive-aggressive satisfaction to my behavior. It is true though, I had just grown cold, and almost didn't care any longer. The fact that I could just tell her I wanted to fuck, and she would play along, is all I wanted, physically. There was a genuine gratitude that she found some peace. I don't know if she was happy, or loved him, or hoped to actually be with him, but that would have to come from her. We were still a happy family. Nate knew something was wrong, but he enjoyed each of us individually and seemed to love when we were all together. Once Samantha accepted the situation, months after I did, our entire dynamic improved. I spent plenty of time contemplating the layout and wondering if I should approach a confrontation from an angle that might allow me to see other people as well, but decided against it. Actually, I have zero interest in pursuing any other relationships. There is no way I would waste that effort seeking another person to spend time with. I am perfectly happy with the few close friends I have, the somewhat limited sex that I need and receive any time I want, and my time alone. I do not need a shift in that timetable. Relationships are easy for me because I am so agreeable, but it is truly exhausting, so I decided that I would just ignore her indiscretions as long as my simple needs continued to be met, unabated. I even tested the waters with my physical yearnings by asking for nude photos and more frequent fellatio. She always obliged with, almost too much, enthusiasm. Honestly, my wife cheating on me is probably the best thing that could have happened for my sex life, from my perspective. I don't know how she managed the safety of the arrangement, so I am left to assume it was by traditional methods. We certainly never used prophylactics, she was on birth control, and was very careful never to miss a dose from the absolute terror of any possibility of turning up pregnant. I don't think Samantha ever wanted children, and I suppose she had even more reason to be cautious later. I did some casual research about my situation, but only out of curiosity. I discovered that I am some type of "cuckold," because my wife is fucking another person, I know about it, and tolerate it. This is some people's kink, but not mine.

I don't think it is.

I never thought it would turn me on to think of her with someone else, although, I do enjoy the benefits.

Maybe I am a cuckold.

I recognize my thirst and scoot forward to retrieve the water container. I pick up my phone and take one more look at my naked wife. I use the light from the screen to help get the water, take a good few drinks, and return it to its place. The battery is low, showing red, and warns me about "low battery mode." I decide to sit back and turn it off. I'm not sure it matters any more. I rummage around for the birthday supplies container. I find it and locate a lighter within. I flick the flint and the object comes to life. This is a "good" lighter. I notice how the room looks remarkably different in the light of a tiny flame. I release the fuel lever and plunge into darkness again.

I don't even check the time before the phone turns off. It's dark, still before my room's dawn. My pants and underwear are still down around my lower thighs and my shirt is somewhere behind me. I decide to wriggle my clothes back on, but I doze off before I can get my shirt on. It's just sitting on my lap.

## Chapter 12

Still day 8

I awaken to a faint flash in the otherwise perfect darkness. Then I start to see some forms. They are so faint that I can't make anything out. There is light, but it is perhaps the dimmest illumination I have ever experienced.

Then thunder.

We instinctively know when we hear the timbre and pattern of distant thunder. Even though every clap is like a fingerprint, with the variables slightly differing from any previous thunder in history and never to be repeated identically again. But the sound is obvious. It is distant and begins with a deep growl that rumbles into a groan. It never snaps, maybe because of the distance, but it is thunder.

There is another faint flash, and the momentary illumination causes the field in front of me to play games. I know precisely what I am looking at, but that is not what I see. The silhouettes remain, and I can sense there is a dog, or maybe a wolf, in front of me. It is looking right at me. It looks like a wolf, but somehow less menacing. I wait for more light, afraid to retrieve my own.

Thunder.

No movement.

Then another flash. I see the wolf again. It is definitely a wolf. It has not changed at all. If a wolf has found its way into my room, I will need to kill it and use its way in to get out. Although I'm really not sure why I want to get out.

Thunder.

Another flash.

It's still there, but since my eyes haven't veered from its location, I can now see that it would be levitating above my legs, and decide that I am definitely hallucinating. I'm still terrified, because my hallucinations are so vivid now that my psyche can't separate from the horror of the sight. I close my eyes and breathe deep a few times. Then I open them and reach for my lighter, the good lighter. I flick it and see the wolf.

That's unfortunate.

I flick it again.

Still there.

I instinctively reach up to my head to scratch it out of confusion. I realize that my hair had been falling out without instigation. The place on the left side of my head, just above the ear, is almost bald after I make contact with it. I accidentally move my fingers around from confused curiosity and feel more hair come out from the trauma. I pull my hand away.

"Damnit!"

I consider all of my symptoms again. I reach up to my mouth, and note that the sore in the inside corner is festering and still open. Once I acknowledge it, I can taste the blood in my mouth. I run my tongue around the inside of my mouth and find various sores and tender places. It also feels like some of my molars are loose. They have that popping feeling as they wiggle more than they should from a light brushing of the tongue. This is one of my worst nightmares. I panic inside a bit while I ponder if there is any way to prevent this from happening. If it is from bacteria, I need alcohol, and I don't have any. But if it is from radiation, I'm fucked.

I flick the lighter again.

No wolf.

The drips in the water container increase in frequency, as does the thunder, lightning, and their intensities. This is the third thunderstorm in eight days of being stuck in my tiny, well-stocked, tomb, and I feel like that is unusual for Georgia in the autumn, but I can't remember and do not have an almanac in my pantry. I try to focus on whether the temperature is something uncomfortable in either direction of a thermometer, but I don't really know. I start to wriggle in my seat and decide to get up. I need to stretch, because I am sure my primary discomfort is from sitting and sleeping on the hard ground. I draw my legs in occasionally throughout the night and lay sideways in a fetal position to change posture. Then I sometimes shift to my back with my feet drawn up. There is no comfortable way, but the exhaustion from which I suffer is so relentless that I only awaken for moments at a time to shift and then drift off again.

I recall when Nathaniel was much younger, he would confuse hunger with stomach pain. I believe that children struggle with differentiating between sensations, because our nervous systems, for all of their complex design, are actually quite simple. He would complain that his stomach hurt, and we finally realized that it was always near mealtime. I finally moved the meals forward slightly on our schedule and the complaints abated. If we missed meals, and then ate a large meal to make up for it, he would also complain of stomach pains. He was not a fussy child: "complain" in this sense means that he would only mention it and carry on playing or exploring, but because he was our only child, we would note his report and obsess. Similarly, I think the sensation of food reaching the stomach is a shock to the nerves after unanswered pleas for something to digest, and they send panicked signals that are very similar to pain. Discomfort is different than pain, but our brains struggle to differentiate between the two. I recognize, at this point, that this is the discomfort I am struggling with. I am constantly nauseous. The nausea can shift into queasiness suddenly and I feel like I may be sick. It has been happening for days, but the intensity is increasing, much like the storm outside. Occasionally, it will become a sharp pain in my gut, toward the left side, just under my ribs. It bends me in half when it happens, much like a bout of gas, or when you have eaten something disagreeable and an unpleasant bowel movement is preparing. Unfortunately, my body has not produced any waste for a few days. I assume it is because I am barely getting, and keeping, anything down. I have urinated into my cock-height hole on the fridge side of the room twice, but that doesn't seem enough, especially since both were feeble, disappointing, dribbles.

I fidget with my t-shirt and figure out how to get it onto my body. I contort myself around to get my legs under me, stand, and unfold myself, being careful not to lose balance or knock anything over. The room is slightly more lit than before, but the storm outside is keeping the light very dim. The sound of the rain is more noticeable now, and the drops from the toilet to my container are frequent, almost every 30 seconds. The light, the general color of the room, and the sounds remind me of storms from when I was a child. There is something eerie about it, making me feel vulnerable and alone. I remember, as a child, that storms made me uneasy. My mother was driving once, during a daytime rain shower, possibly after a storm, that felt like a common summertime occurrence, when we came across a fresh disaster. This was before cell phones, so there was little she could do. I do not remember there being emergency personnel or other people helping. I saw, out of our station wagon window, a small house that had been reduced to rubble by a large tree that fell directly through it. My brain immediately latched onto this image, and I never felt that being inside of a house during a storm was enough safety.

This storm triggers feelings of unease and my stomach is agreeing with the sensation. My brain jumps between telling me that I need to eat, that I am thirsty, and that I am going to vomit, faster than I can react. The pain below my ribs hits and I bend over quickly, careful not to strike my head or face on the shelves in front of me. As soon as I do so, I regurgitate something acidic. It is the most instantaneous bout of reflux I have ever experienced. I spit the contents toward the back corner, fridge side, where the empty cans and food waste are being collected. The pain subsides and is replaced by nausea again. I stand upright and become very faint. I reach to the right and find a place beside the hole in the foyer side wall to support myself. My legs and torso tremble slightly, almost a shiver, but deeper. I have only just stood and my body begs me to sit again. The nausea returns to queasy discomfort and I prepare to repeat the process. My plan to stretch my joints and begin my day on a positive note has been delayed by my rebelling digestive system. I can feel that I have a cold clamminess to my skin and there is sweat gathering at my shirt collar. I assume there is more elsewhere, but this is where I notice it. I know that I am sick, but not the exact cause of the illness.

I squat where I am, capitalizing on a moment of clarity. I spit the next round of acid that comes up toward the same location, not really caring where it lands. I decide to find my bag, so I lean forward and feel around. There are many objects and items strewn around the floor. My bag is leaning against the foyer side wall. I bring it closer and open the outside pouch where the medicine should be. The bottle, when shaken, seems less than half full. I have not taken inventory, but I know there is much more ibuprofen than omeprazole in it. I open the bottle, which proves more difficult than it should. I am still squatting, and the effort necessary to press down and loosen the cap is almost more than I can muster. I empty some of its contents into my hand and use my opposite index finger to rummage through. I can tell the omeprazole capsules, which are oblong and stickier, from the ibuprofen tablets, which are round, flat, and a matte finish. I pull four ibuprofen and one omeprazole into my palm and hold them with my pinky and ring finger while I return the other pills to the bottle and affix the lid. My right pinky is screaming at me from being asked to perform such a dextrous task after the trauma it has endured, but the pain in my gut and general discomfort far outweigh its pathetic complaint, and I ignore it. I toss the closed bottle toward my briefcase and pop the five pills into my mouth. I reach for the water container beside me and find it after a few swipes of the hand. It does not shift as easily, because it is quite full. I pivot in my crouched position and use both hands to lift the large container to drink. I take enough water in my mouth to swallow the pills and it feels like a chore all the way down. Strangely, I can feel every bit of my esophagus opening and allowing the contents to pass through as the cylindrical organ comes to life. It is unpleasant and I brace myself for the next inevitable feeling. When the water and pills reach my esophageal sphincter, the pain begins. The material enters my stomach and I am doubled over in pain. I can feel every detail of the process, and it is like knives through my internal organs. I regain my composure as best I can, bring the container to my mouth again, and drink in multiple gulps, sucking air through my nose between each. I set the container down and dip my right hand into it, in a cup shape, bring the water to my face, and meet my other hand. I rub the water all over my face and then repeat this process with the other hand. The second round of water on my face causes me to shiver again. My brain reminds me that if I don't put something of substance in my system, the digestion of the pills will be horrible. I force myself to stand, carefully. I am dizzy, and the lean of the room is more noticeable now. I fall back against the spice rack and try to convince the spinning to stop. I can see the shelves, but only where they are. I know the cereal is on the first shelf, so I start feeling around for it. I find the container of lucky charms and pop the lid open. I take out a few bits of cereal and bring them to my mouth. As I begin to bite down, I feel my teeth, right side, toward the back, shift. I bend down and scoop some water in my hand and bring it to my mouth. I begin to soak the objects in my mouth in water until I can work them with my tongue and swallow. The process of digestion begins again, and the sensations return in small rushes. I close the lid and decide crunchy food is not the best idea. I replace the cereal and feel around for more options. I feel a cylinder on the back of the first shelf and get my hand around it. This is a small tub of instant oatmeal. I bring that to the floor and feel around on the edge of shelf two for the camp silverware. The pain in my gut is becoming horrible. I find the silverware set and bring the whole thing to the floor. I sit where I am and reach toward the corner for the empty cans. I find the first one and bring it to my makeshift kitchen. I can't read the label, but it is probably the green beans. I imagine the residue inside and possibly the acid that I spit in the corner lurking somewhere on or inside of it. I begin to gag. I am not typically very squeamish, but this combination of feelings, images, and sensations is too much.

I open the oatmeal container's plastic lid and tear away the plastic seal affixed to the paper top of the cylindrical object. I hold the tin can in my left hand and shake some of the instant oats into the can from the container. I set the can on the ground beside me and reattach the plastic lid to the oatmeal container. I place the container back on shelf one and pick up the can. I scoop some water directly with the can. I have no idea how much water I get, so I have no idea what the oat-to-water ratio is. I could find measuring devices and make these cold oats properly, but there is no time for that. I swirl the can slightly and sense movement inside, meaning I have, at least, achieved a consistency that still flows and moves.

I lift the unidentified can to my mouth and cringe from the mental-image of bean juice and bloody spit. The pain in my gut plus the acid reflux make me flush and feel funny. I get a long chill up my spine from mid-back that dissipates in the rear of my skull. I swallow hard and lift the can at my lips to take some of the contents into my mouth. Uncooked instant oatmeal at room temperature is relatively inoffensive, but there is this strange sensation of wet-dryness as the oats have not yet fully absorbed the water. I move the substance around my mouth a while, then swallow hard. It feels like it is sliding but not making any progress in my esophagus. My stomach lurches again, and I try to relax, praying I can receive some sustenance and help the medicine metabolize. I feel the flush sensation run through me from my sternum out and decide to take more oatmeal while possible. I repeat this process three times. I have consumed four mouthfuls of uncooked oats in water. The sharp pain in my gut has transformed into an aching throbbing discomfort. My stomach lurches and I feel my chest begin to close in on itself. This is a familiar feeling. Reflux is distinct if you have suffered it long enough, but this is different. I am going to vomit. All of the energy left in my limbs and torso drains away. My arms fall by my sides and my neck goes somewhat limp. My head falls back against the wall. This sudden draining of energy from my body is new and I imagine this is what it would feel like to "bleed out." I often practice meditations where I picture air entering my lungs as a blue color, to keep me focused on breath. This feels like that, but I imagine the blood draining from my arms as they hang to the floor on either side of me. I picture the blood from my body pooling around me, then the slow, calm, regurgitation begins. It is very disturbing, but I am completely incapable of stopping it. I tilt my head to the right and vomit down my chest and shoulder. It drips and falls from the right corner of my mouth. It rolls down my face and onto my neck and clavicle. This is a pathetic vomiting session. My body convulses, slowly forcing the substance up and out. It is gentle and slow, but I can't stop it. I make gurgling noises as I try to catch my breath between sessions and gasp for air. There are tears streaming down my face. I sit, unable to fight it, miserable, pathetic, and worthless, losing all of the food and drink I was so proud to have consumed. Once it is done, I dry heave repeatedly, and produce some foamy material that is very bitter and sprinkled with tiny chunks: this must be the pills. I heave and reject the medicine for a good time, tears streaming and my abdomen convulsing. I finally feel my right hand come to life and I reach up to wipe my mouth. I am covered in it. I feel disgusting. I mistakenly tongue around in my mouth and find my teeth are loosening more. Multiple molars and others wiggle from minimal pressure. This causes another shiver in my chest that extends throughout my entire body.

I am completely exhausted. I have been slowly accepting my situation, but now I feel disgusted by my own state. I am so completely ruined. I muster another "help," but my voice is weak. The scratchiness in my throat must be from the acids burning my flesh on the way out. I finally find stillness and silence, and hear the drips in the water container. They have slowed. I do not hear rain or thunder and the flashes have subsided. It is not bright enough to be the full daytime I have seen seeping in over the past week. As I sit, feeling defeated, I consider why the light would be dim. I remember the concept of "nuclear winter" again and if it may be beginning. I picture a wasteland outside, a scene with a yellowing hue all around, leveled buildings, and piles of debris where my town used to stand. I see the sky above is completely overcast and the sun's location cannot be determined because the atmosphere is so densely polluted by the dust, chemicals, and material from the blasts. I imagine that there is some type of wind, and there is a substance floating all around that looks like snow. This seems like a reasonable explanation for the strange dimness and color of light coming in through the tiny hole in the ceiling. In my defeat, I decide that I need help. I have been calling out for help, not understanding why it is so important. I need someone to help me survive this. I need someone to tell me I'm going to be ok. I need to understand what happened outside and what is happening to my body.

I want someone to hug me.

I want to be the person you see being rescued from a disaster, wrapped in blankets, and embracing all of the emergency workers. I want to express deep gratitude to my heroes and have the news media express disbelief that I survived as long as I did.

I want things. I want company. I want my family. I want to cry because I am so relieved to see my wife. I want to hold my son in my arms. I want to see the outside world. I want to feel sunshine. I want to stop smelling this putrid smell. I want a fucking shower.

At least the pain in my gut has subsided. I admit that the sensation of being so hungry that you might consider eating a piece of lumber, while simultaneously being sickened by the thought of anything being ingested, is unbelievably frustrating. I squirm in my seat. My digestive system is so confused. My head feels very wobbly on my neck. It is like I can't keep my head upright. Much of my behavior feels like inebriation. I may actually appear drunk right now. I can't keep my head upright, I am covered in vomit, and there is no way I could get off of the floor. When you get so drunk that you wish for sleep, or death, and swear you will never do this again: I am that pathetic.

Even more frustrating, is the realization that I have trained my whole life to need and want very little, and now I am stuck in a virtual prison, full of want, surrounded by my needs, and absolutely miserable. I know that peace resides in a place where you want very little and understand that happiness is within you, but I am now brimming with want. The icing on that shit-cake is having everything I need and being unable to utilize most of it. I have trained for this. I carry a knife and a sidearm so that I am prepared for almost anything. I keep rope and medicine handy just in case. I am trained in CPR and have fundamental medical knowledge so that I can respond to emergencies and treat minor injuries. This is all from free courses offered at the local YMCA, and I seize the chance, flexing my opportunism. I am very handy, relatively strong, in good shape, excellent health, and possess a deep understanding of numerous topics, and a basic understanding of an even more vast collection of somewhat useful information. I have, admittedly, considered many scenarios where I might have to survive with very little and I have plotted and planned how to overcome obstacles and run down potential challenges in each. I also factored my family into all of those possibilities, so that I could calculate necessities for all three of us.

I never prepared myself for the possibility of being alone and losing hope. I never considered loneliness a threat. Actually, in hindsight, I planned for the survival of my family with the underlying philosophy being that if I were alone and trying to survive, it would just be easier. But the basic concept of survival is that you are fighting to reach something. You are working to persevere, with the reward being: home, loved ones, society, or anything familiar and welcoming.

Survival is intentional.

If there is nothing at the end of your journey, there is no reason to fight, no reason to continue. As this understanding materializes, I picture myself walking along a desert highway, with no one around and nothing in sight. I imagine learning there is nothing at the end of the road, or in any direction, that there is, somehow, nothing left. Then I stop walking, sit down in the middle of the road, in the heat, in the blistering sun, and cry. I also begin to cry again in my pantry.

I still have not heard any sounds that would provide a glimpse of hope that anything exists outside of my room. I listen carefully. All I hear are the drops of water in the container. They are making a deeper sound than I recall hearing yet. I assume the container is very full, so I reach over for it with my left hand. I find the edge of the top and move it slightly to judge its weight by resistance to my feeble force. It feels very heavy. I reach inside and estimate that it is almost three-quarters full. I wiggle my fingertips in the water. It feels good.

Holy shit.

That felt good.

"Damn, that feels good."

"Do more of that, then, dumbass."

I sense my other, more logical, self sitting across from me again, but this time, he is under the shelves. I dip my whole hand in the water and move it around, enjoying the resistance of the water in the six inches I can push in either direction. It is cool. It is almost refreshing. I remove my hand and wipe it on my face again.

"Shit. That feels good too."

"Stay with that feeling. Keep doing what rewards you."

I go back to the water with my hand and scoop some in a hand-cup. I bring it over to my face, very clumsily, and slap it against my face and rub it all over.

"Aaaahhh…"

"Yes. More of that."

I repeat this until I am soaked on my front, from my nipples up. I don't know if it is doing anything productive, but I don't care.

"Good. You shouldn't care. Just do more of what feels good."

"It almost bothers me that you can hear my thoughts until I remember that we share them."

"It almost bothers me that you are leaning so willingly into the concept of conversing with yourself, but I recognize that we share that also."

"Why am I constantly creating you and engaging in this? I know that it's a bad sign and I must be losing my grip, but I keep allowing it."

"I assume it is because you are lonely."

Shit. I am lonely.

I emerge in the third-self, above the scene, in some virtual space that allows me to look down on my "selves," and I see both below. The physical manifestation that I see is quite disgusting. My psyche has provided some light, so I can see that I am soaked and my hair is only a few patches of blonde scruff. I can see the festering cuts in my scalp. They look painful and disgusting. I am immediately disturbed by how unhealed and painful they appear. If a person were to show me wounds like that in the outside world, before the event, I would insist they seek medical attention, right away. My khaki colored, slim fit, jeans are covered in stains and dirty in ways that would embarrass me if I were seen in public before the event. I look skinny.

I look sick.

I am slouching, my posture representing defeat and depression.

My companion-self is dressed exactly as I was when I entered my chamber. He is clean-cut, dress shirt, tucked, clean shoes, clean pants, hair perfect, and full of vibrant color and good posture. His composure is one of confidence and poise. From above, these two people could not be more different and separated. My perspective allows for some extra space in the room, but they have their legs outstretched, each together, and beside one-another's. The clean me is beaming at the dirty me. The dirty me is head-bent and staring at his lap. His shoulders are slumped forward and his back is curved in a way that looks uncomfortable. Strangely, I can feel that discomfort, even though I am not in that body at this moment. I see the confidence and poise across from him and it is almost insulting. I feel like the clean me is looking down at the sad and dirty me, like some privileged person side-eyeing the homeless man on the street and taking note to discuss this situation with his friends over an overpriced bourbon at the bar later.

"We are all just one atomic disaster away from being a worthless sack of shit on the floor of our pantry."

"That is the saddest and most inappropriate humor out of you yet; but I appreciate the effort."

"See! You are demeaning!"

"What is that supposed to mean?"

I realize from my third perspective above that the clean me is only aware of the inner thoughts of the dirty me below. The thoughts I am having from above are isolated somehow. The two across from one-another below share some sort of mental space and I now possess the passive observer.

"It means that I feel helpless and pathetic and I can sense that you are judging me for it."

"Well, I am struggling to understand how the strong and confident person that stepped into this room 8 days ago has been reduced to the miserable creature in front of me now."

"I can't help it. You have played this internal mind game with me already, so I am onto your methods."

"Well it worked before, so..."

"That was different."

"How so?"

"I still had some hope last time we did this."

"So, now you don't have any hope?"

"Wrong: now *we* don't have any hope."

"Ok, so let's manifest some hope!"

"We have been through this, but if it will get you to shut the fuck up and let me wallow..."

"Your cynicism is noted and not appreciated."

"Then please: what do we have to be hopeful for?"

"You haven't tried all of the ways to escape!"

"What am I escaping to?"

"I don't think that's relevant."

"I am almost positive that there is nothing positive waiting for me out there. Again, if our enemies went through the trouble to design an attack strategy that leaves virtually nothing, the only things that have survived are likely suffering a slow death. Which is how I feel in this room."

"But aren't you even curious?"

"Of course I am. But I am also terrified."

"Let's unpack that."

I smirk from above. There is no need to unpack anything. We all share the same mind.

"Fine. Even if I find a way out, it is likely that I will become more sick out there. After this much time, and hearing absolutely nothing that would suggest life outside, it is likely a wasteland that is killing everything left."

"That's depressing."

"That's reality! Plus, at some point, they are going to execute some other strategy to finish the job."

"You don't know that."

"It is the only logical conclusion."

"I would suggest that it is just as likely that there is hope out there, that you could find other survivors."

"And I would remind you that: even if there are survivors, they will be competing for resources and pack mentality will make it a very hostile place to step into unawares and alone."

"So, you're not even going to try?"

"I can probably survive in here longer than out there."

"So, try to make the best of it?"

"Save your platitudes. I think your ability to internally mind-fuck myself is running out of fuel."

"I would like to remind you that you are participating in this willingly."

From my viewpoint above, this debate is becoming uncomfortable for the bystander. I'm not sure I can allow myself to continue goading myself into this defensive behavior, but I'm not sure how to stop it. I have yet to attempt to intervene in my trinity of dwindling sanity, yet every time I fall into deep sadness, this happens. I understand this to be some primal form of defense and expression of desire to overcome the daunting defeat that overwhelms me, but I am afraid that it may not be effective.

The internal battle playing out like some disturbing reality show beneath me is worrisome.

"So, you think I should just investigate another wall and see if it produces a different result?"

"Maybe be just slightly more creative than that."

"Please stop patronizing me and just say what you mean."

"Your light, water, and probably air are coming from the ceiling. I would think that is a wise place to explore."

"That's twelve feet away."

"I don't have *the* plan, just have *an* idea."

"And you will probably take all the credit too."

My vision rushed me from my vantage point above into the dirty me and I feel the clean me rush into my body, reconglomerating all of my personalities into the one reality that remains in what I can only deduce to be the reality of my life. The feeling that manifests is not hope, but it is also not defeat. I feel curious. I look toward the ceiling and see the yellowish light coming from the space around the toilet that protrudes from where the ceiling meets the wall. When I was in my trinity headspace, there was an artificial light, but much of my setting was missing also. Now I am back in the real pantry. It smells horrible. My skin crawls. The sickness that has taken over is worse than any I have experienced. I can feel my bones, not the joints, but the bones themselves. I feel empty. The hunger is painful and must be my system trying to digest itself. It is becoming difficult to identify where the pain is coming from. If I try to focus on any one pain, my mind jumps between different locations as quickly as I can recognize one. It is time to stand and make my final attempt to escape.

I pull my right leg under my body and lean to the left to position for lift. I am very weak, but I am able to maneuver back to my feet slowly, utilizing the discarded shelving on either side of me for leverage. My joints and bones scream at me as I unfold into a vertical stance. Any part of my body that touches another sticks to it and disgusts me. My skin feels tacky and dry at the same time. I touch my right forearm with my left hand to judge the tackiness, and I am, indeed, slightly sticky. I assume this is some type of dehydration, but I am actually afraid to ingest anything, confident that my body will reject it. I lean and stretch in all directions and with every joint that I can move without excruciating pain, and this, fortunately, does not reveal any novel injuries. I find my briefcase in the semi-dark and gather my personal phone, which has very little battery left, and a small, pen-sized flashlight. It was a promotional item from my bank last year and I keep it in my bag. I have not used it yet, but know that it is there, so I have been saving it for when I really need it. I have the ability to use fire as a light source also, so I retrieve the good lighter that I discarded to the floor during a fit of pain and put it in my pocket. I find my folding knife and add it to my pocket. My front left pants pocket now contains my personal phone and the small flashlight. My right front pocket contains the lighter and my knife. I find the grill tongs that came in handy when creating a hole in the wall before and affix them to my brown leather belt by crossing one side of them between my belt and pants and sliding them all the way down to where their joint meets the belt. These hang behind my right butt-cheek, so I should be able to retrieve them with one hand, if necessary.

I close my eyes, lose my balance slightly, immediately sense the leaning of the room, and click the flashlight on. I lean back into the spice rack behind me, instinctively. Once I gain composure and feel like I can stand, I remain leaning and slowly crack my eyelids. I start to look around my room before I fully open my eyes, and as I scan the floor covered in dust, small rocks, liquid, and vomit, I decide to ignore this mess and try to remain focused on my goal. I have decided that I need to check as near to the ceiling toilet as possible without compromising the integrity of whatever structures are holding it in its strange place. I stand upright, steady myself, acknowledge the leaning of the room once more, and direct the small light to the ceiling. I have twelve-foot ceilings, and I am six-feet tall. I open my eyes fully and gauge the distance. Then I reach up with my left arm and pivot to allow that shoulder to elevate as much as possible. I estimate that I can reach up close to eight feet, so the distance to the ceiling is approximately four more feet, and the front of the toilet bowl protrudes down from the ceiling about 8 inches. I need to have some space to work and I know that working at full reach above one's head is challenging for a healthy person: I estimate that I need to gain at least four feet to be working where it could be comfortable to develop a new hole. If, for some reason, I can escape this way, I will come down and prepare before leaving, so I am only taking what I need to produce a hole in the sheet rock, either in the ceiling or the wall nearest to the ceiling. My first instinct is to climb the spice rack, so I turn toward it and find my footing again. This sensation of instability is similar to walking in an airplane during turbulence: it's accomplishable, but tricky, and I find myself pausing to regain stability often. The room is not actually moving, but the tilt makes it difficult, plus, I think my faculties are compromised, including my sense of balance. I gently push down on the lip of each shelf, judging its strength and how much it gives with minimal force. They seem stronger than I initially anticipated. I push down with my left hand while holding the light with my right. I experiment with each shelf, at either side, and monitor the 14 brackets that hold the rack onto the door. These small white plastic brackets are surely the weakest links in the proverbial chain and certainly the highest-potential failure points. If one of them gives, the whole thing will come off the door. I guess that I can probably climb the shelves like a ladder, but I should remove it from the door first. I turn the flashlight off and return it to my pocket. I let my eyes adjust to the darkness, with only a dim yellow glow from the hole in the ceiling. I begin taking all of the spices and other ingredients off of the six shelves and move them hastily to the three pantry shelves. I stick them anywhere I can find a space, with little regard for integrity, contents, or placement. Every time I turn from the door with items to the shelves or back to the door I lose my balance and have to pause. This makes the process even more frustrating. I feel very weak, frail. The process of moving these objects is exhausting and when I get to the top shelf, my arms don't want to lift to gather the few items contained there. These are small cans of spices, I assume: cloves and other, more-seldom utilized, flavors. I finally get all of the shelves of the spice rack empty and start applying upward pressure onto the edges of the shelves at chest level, hoping to feel one of the wire braces pop loose. The unit does not budge.

My general plan is to remove this rack and use it as the platform of a crude scaffolding with the two removed shelves as the legs. When I can't immediately remove it from the door, I decide to test its ability to hold me while still attached to the door.

I have never been a very heavy person, but I am certainly thinner and lighter right now than I have ever been as an adult. I estimate that I may currently be less than 160 pounds. I give a shrug to tell the room, "it's worth a try," although it comes out sounding unsure, almost a question.

"Even if the thing falls off the door, that's what I was trying to do anyway."

"I just hope the door doesn't collapse into the room when that happens."

"Thanks. Do you have a better idea?"

"No."

I am still shoeless, and I decide that I should put them on, because the thought of the wire shelving digging into my feet seems like it will be uncomfortable, at the least. I find my shoes and socks on the shelf and spend tremendously more time navigating this menial task than at all necessary. Having to lift each foot across the opposite leg to work my gray socks onto is a chore. I have to lean against the rack for each foot. And instead of performing the sock and shoe, I alternate: sock, sock, shoe, shoe. Again, my bones do not appreciate the exercise and they use the nerves of my joints to object. I complete the arduous act of dressing myself and sigh aloud, stand up, and look about as if I expect some sort of reward or recognition. I turn back to the spice rack on the door and sigh.

"Fuck it."

There are six shelves on the spice rack, now dimly illuminated, with the lowest about six inches off the floor. The rack spans the height of the door, so there is roughly 12 inches between each shelf/rung. Even if it falls off the door, the room is tilted toward the door, so the whole object will drop about six inches but likely stay, generally, in place. If it falls away with me on it, there is only about a 2 feet gap to the pantry shelves, so I would simply fall back against them.

I put both hands on the fourth rack, just above shoulder height, and gauge the stability of the object. I decide that this might work. I step onto the bottom shelf with my right foot, making every effort to slide my shoe as far into the space as I can while also turning my foot pigeon-toed to disperse my weight along the wire lip as much as possible. I begin to lift myself slowly, trying to focus on dispersing my weight across all three points of contact. I am able to get my left foot off the ground and acknowledge that the rack has barely budged. The tall lip surrounding each shelf and tighter rung design, intended to more effectively contain small spice bottles, also provides more substantial structural integrity. I gently lift and place my left foot onto the second shelf and start lifting myself until my right foot leaves the bottom shelf. The shelf bends down slightly, but not in any way that concerns me. This will certainly work as a ladder if I continue to be gentle. I tire from hanging off the rack and decide to step back down to the floor. I concoct a plan to use the two discarded shelves, one as a leg, one as a platform, and create a crude scaffolding to stand on, which should take me close to five feet up into the air. I take one of the spare shelves and prop it up. The top of it is between shelves two and three. I take the other discarded shelf and work its end between shelves two and three and slide it in until it contacts the back wall, on top of the first one. It takes some wiggling and adjusting, but now I can wedge it on top of a shelf in the spice rack. At first, it doesn't want to cooperate, so I take the small flashlight pen in my mouth and sense my front teeth shift when I bite down. I loosen my bite and sense liquid escape my gums. I have placed it upside-down, so that the lip is pointing up. If I can get up there, I should be able to work easily. I inspect all of my scaffolding materials with the flashlight and decide that I can do this in minimal light. I click the flashlight off and return it to my left front pocket. I am quite pleased with myself, so I retrieve my phone from the same pocket and decide to check in.

## Chapter 13

Day 9
Thursday
3:23 PM
No cell signal, no wifi, no Bluetooth devices detected.
No signs of life, no satellite signal acquired. Phone battery = 6%

I power down the phone.

I have no idea when the day shifted, but I have been in and out of reality numerous times. I decide not to turn it on again unless I think I might be able to acquire a signal. I return the phone to my pocket and mentally prepare to climb my crude structure in an attempt to find a way out. I begin the same way as before and pay attention to weight distribution. I step up with my right foot onto the lowest shelf. I have to stick my ass out because I am already keeping my shoulder under the newly-installed platform. I plan to wriggle around on the left of the platform and get up to it as efficiently as possible. I want to begin while I have some daylight in the room, but I also want to conserve energy as much as possible. I note that the shelf seems to maintain stability during my repeat attempt. I skip the bottom shelf with my left foot and go directly to the second shelf. I'm already contorting myself as I choose to lean to the left during this maneuver. I release with my right hand and twist my right shoulder back and away and lean toward the wall on my left. This allows some straightening of my back, I clear the platform, and begin to lift onto my left foot, off of my right. I hook my right hand and forearm over the top of the platform. The inverted shelf has a lip that is now pointing up, but it is on the opposite side from where I will attempt to summit. This was strategic and intentional during design and installation, because it could also provide a "toe-guard" when I am standing atop. I pull up and to the left, shifting most of my weight to my left foot and right forearm that is now across the shelf. I continue this plan: I release my left hand from the fourth shelf and reach up to find the sixth spice rack shelf. I step up with my right foot, to the third rack, my legs are now together, and I begin to creep toward the left side of the structure. I will attempt to summit in the next move. I disperse my weight between both feet and turn my chest completely toward the platform so that I am fully facing it, with my head now completely above and my chest at the edge. I begin to adjust my weight onto my right arm and try to sense if the other side is going to cooperate while I attempt to conquer my challenge. I sense no compromise, but remember that this is my only chance, so I would be wise to continue to focus and stop worrying.

If it fails, it fails.

My next adjustment requires multiple calculations. I bring my left foot up beside my right foot while lifting up with my right arm on the platform. Then I continue my turn and release my left hand from the sixth rack, crossing it over to the opposite side of the platform. This completes my full turn toward the back wall and my right foot starts to release from the third shelf. I bring it across my left leg and push it against the fourth shelf. This forces my left foot off the third shelf while I lift with both hands in a partial push-up. I am careful not to fall across myself to the left with that leg free, but the tilt of the room actually assists this effort. I balance, precariously, and bring my left knee onto the platform. I make a couple adjustments to get my thigh over and walk my hands toward the back of the room to allow for the final pivot. My arms are shaking from the shoulders, I can't hold this much longer. I release my right foot and try to guide it below me with minimal swing. At this moment, the platform that I am climbing onto, shifts and complains. It feels like it has decided to settle into one of the supports in front of me, in the back of the room. Either where it is perched atop the other shelf, or where it is wedged into the back wall, something set further into place.

I freeze: half pressed on my arms, with my bent left leg pulled beside me and sticking out off the platform at the knee. My right leg still dangles below me. I pause a moment, trembling, to be sure I'm not falling, then I lower my chest and belly to the platform, gingerly, release my hands, and extend my arms.

I did it.

I lie there, head up and forward, looking at the shelves just in front of me. I must look like a half-squished frog with my leg out like it is. The wire shelf is digging into my scrotum and I need to shift. I push up again and tilt left. I bring my right leg up and onto my knee. I wiggle it to where my foot is all the way back and against the top rack. Now I tilt right and bring my left leg in and up until my knee is under me and bring it back and beside my other leg. There is just enough room for both. I am not shaking now, with my weight across four points and two of those points are the length of my lower legs. I start to walk my hands back and bring my torso vertical. I walk my right leg forward until my twist allows me to find the third pantry shelf in front of me. I remind myself that I need not put too much pressure on these, because their collapse would certainly mark the end of my efforts. I walk my left leg forward now, straighten up, and reach behind with my left hand to find the top rack behind me.

Now the real test: I bring my right leg forward and my foot underneath. I push up slightly and attempt to lift with my right leg, only just enough to repeat with my left. My right leg can't quite do it and I have to shift some pressure to my arms. I execute and have both feet under me. I start to stand, my knees and thighs are screaming at me, but I try to use them as much as I can. As I stand upright, I turn my body to the left, counterclockwise, release my right hand from the pantry shelf, and bring my left foot back across and behind. I turn and grasp the top rack of the door with my right hand. Now I am in a sort of sprint-runner's starting stance. My left leg is behind and I am on my toes. I bring my right foot forward some. I am bent over with both hands holding either side of the top rack. I release and reach out with my right hand first, find the door frame and shift weight to that hand. I do the same with the left hand, just above the right. I start to walk my hands, one over the other, up the wall while tip-toeing forward with my feet. When I reach what I think is halfway up the wall, I stop to take inventory, because I feel less strained. I have lost balance a few times during this performance, but have mostly been well-distributed. I know what will happen when I reach full vertical extension. My head is pounding. I take a few slow breaths and decide to finish. As I continue standing and moving forward, I reach up with my right hand to find the ceiling. I straighten my knees and back slowly. I feel like a moth unfolding from its cocooned existence. My platform is approximately five feet off the warped ground, and I am about six feet tall, so at this moment, fully extended, I confirm that my ceilings are actually twelve feet tall. There is about one foot of space above my head.

I've done it.

While somewhat menial relative to normal life, this process has exhausted most of my remaining energy. I decide to spread my legs so that my right foot is over the shelf that is acting as a leg, and I keep my left foot directly in the spice rack space. I inch my toes forward until I find the lip of the platform, my makeshift toe-guard, for physical reference. I keep my left hand on the wall just about shoulder height. Directly in front of me and to the left, obscuring the crown edge, the ceiling-line, not quite into the wall-corner of the ceiling, is my life-sustaining ceiling-toilet. If nothing else is accomplished, I will finally have the opportunity to investigate this phenomenon up-close. I reach out and can place my hand on the portion of the bowl that is protruding from the ceiling. The bowl opening, the portion we regularly utilize, is not accessible, and is completely enclosed within the ceiling space beyond. The portion I can access is the curved outer part of that bowl, and it has been shoved through the ceiling. I still don't understand how this is happening. The position of the object would place the platform, or "foot," of the toilet just outside the front wall of my room. And the upward curve toward the bowl would be straddling the top of that wall, which should not be possible, if the wall were still present above my apartment. If that is so, how did the toilet survive but the wall disappeared? I know the apartment units are separated by concrete fire walls. That is part of why we chose this building. I watched the construction. I saw the concrete walls being fabricated in place. I witnessed them assemble the brick walls on the outside. I was engulfed in a project in Decatur throughout this portion of my town's mass-gentrification, and this building was a major part of that overhaul.

The porcelain of the outer/under bowl feels cool and wet. I rub my hand all around on it, like a rotund man rubs his belly to direct attention to it in conversation. I smile and enjoy the lack of texture, that is somehow sensual, as if I am rubbing a freshly-shaven and lubricated body part. Then I bring the water back and rub my face with it. I mistakenly move my hand up to my head only to find a patchy and almost bald scalp. I feel some remaining hairs release into my wet palm. I also find the cut in my head, still not healed, and it smarts with the contact.

"Damnit! Stop doing that!"

I reach back up and push against the ceiling above me. I lean forward again and investigate the toilet situation. I take the small flashlight from my pocket and click it on. Now that I am closer, I can see that the drywall of the ceiling is wet, or was wet. This is not surprising, since so much liquid has rolled down the front of the bowl to my container below, I assume it must have made its way through at some point. I inspect the ceiling around the bowl with my fingers and it gives way at the gentlest touch of my fingertips. It is still very wet. I choose a spot, on the inner portion of the protrusion, and push in. The material gives in completely and my finger goes right through. I hit something hard and cold. It must be the steel ceiling joist. I assume there is concrete behind it. I move my hand around the front of the bowl, knowing the side of it must be sitting in the space between joists. My finger goes through again, it is very wet, and there is some other material behind and no joist. Some of it feels soft, and some of it like rocks. I wiggle my finger and the wall starts to come apart. I want to see how far the wetness extends, so I pull out my index finger. This experiment was poorly planned. A six inch section of drywall disintegrates as I pull out. Wet material pours out of the ceiling from the crude hole. I instinctively press my hand against it to stop the flow. I keep it there for a moment before deciding it's pointless. I let it go and listen to the material fall below. I can barely see it, but can imagine it is similar to what I found inside the other walls, but wet. This room is surrounded by non-load-bearing walls on all sides, but the ceiling and floor should be concrete behind the steel joists. The only way the space behind this Sheetrock would be filled with debris is if some, or all, of the concrete is gone. Unfortunately, if I investigate further, I risk the ceiling falling completely, with my living quarters below. I will continue to wonder about the mystery of what happened, physically, outside of my pantry, and why, excluding a few minor details, the inside of the pantry has been left relatively unscathed. I turn my attention to the space from where the light is entering. Without seeing the top of the bowl, I can't tell if the toilet is sitting flush, but I am almost sure it is not, as it seems the front of the bowl is facing downward at a noticeable angle. This is deduced because I can see where the bevel of the top of the bowl begins toward the outermost part where it protrudes from the ceiling. It looks like it is slightly "nose-down." Near the front, most in-the-room portion of the toilet, on the door-side, in the ceiling, there is a gap, where the porcelain and the drywall do not meet. It is very thin, and you would likely never see the detail of the space from the ground, standing, six feet away, even if you were using a light to investigate. The only reason it is even noticeable up close is because there is light coming through it. At night, it is invisible, but there is sunlight protruding at this solitary place. It is daytime now, and I can see the yellowish light very clearly. My mind assumes this light is warm, and it is the nearest place to me on the edge of the bowl, so I reach for it. Surprisingly, I do not feel warmth as I approach with my right hand, still firmly resting my left on the wall above the door. As I near the gap, I feel a cool sensation. There is a draft. This small hole is, indeed, my lifeline. The air in my room, as rancid and horrible as it may smell, is reaching me and replenishing itself through this tiny space. I touch the gap gently with my index finger, it is not soft and wet. It must be far enough back from the lowest part of the lip of the toilet bowl that the water is not soaking it. I decide not to push too hard, because I do not want to disturb the delicate state that is providing fresh air, or at least new air, regardless of whether it is fresh or absolutely toxic. I lean toward the light and squint, attempting to peer into the tiny void, but it is too bright, and I can't see anything except bright yellow light. I know that this place is a path to the outside world, but I am terrified to perform surgery on it. I decide to start on the wall, but my energy is depleting rapidly. I question how I am continuing to perform these tasks, while I repeat the process of creating a crude hole, as before, only higher up. Every breath feels like a sigh and every movement feels like peak energy. I work through the inner wall and on to the outer wall. The space on the other side of this hole, before the event, would have been open and empty air: the wall space above my pantry door. I finish the hole, close the knife, return it to my pocket, and retrieve the flashlight. I click it on and place it gently into my mouth, only to sense my front teeth shift from the pressure: Blood.

I wince and grasp the flashlight with my fingers, relax my jaw, take the light in my lips, and slide it in as deep as possible without gagging. I make a tight "O" with my mouth and support the back with my tongue. This is not something I am experienced in, having never enjoyed the company of a man, not that I am against the idea, I have just never been in the situation or felt the desire to pursue such an adventure. I consider my oral positioning and think of Samantha instantly. She was quite skilled with her mouth and I am sure she would take great pleasure in witnessing my attempt to grasp this cylindrical object without using my teeth. I fight the urge to smile, so I don't drop my light. I bend toward the hole and reach in with my right hand. I can see so much better with the bright LED coming from my face, but its aura distorts my vision significantly. Outside at this location is the same as the other holes, as if someone smashed everything and dumped it into my apartment. I find more concrete, brick, and rebar, but there is no hope of escape here.

I need to rest. I take the flashlight from my mouth and turn it off. I let my eyes adjust, very slowly, to the lack of light, and recognize that I am rapidly losing the day. The yellow light, as it begins to populate my vision, has turned a shade of orange, and is fading into red. Strangely, I can almost see the change happening. I wish I could see the sunset, as I'm sure the colors are incredible, even if they are only possible due to the toxic and destructive forces causing them.

I am hoping that the air and light entering the slit by the toilet means there is a pathway to the outside from there. I predict that if there is, I can cut a hole in the ceiling large enough to pull myself through and escape, but I am afraid of working there and compromising the source. I knock and try to find a joist. In the quiet, the sound is loud and bothersome, but I find it easy to focus on with so little ambient sound. I also adjust my stance and feet to allow as much stability as possible, so that I can focus on the ceiling and not be distracted by the platform or thinking about my legs. I feel around with my right hand, still avoiding my pinky that refuses to heal, and decide that I have located the general area of my hole. I should be able to look toward the toilet from here and possibly escape. I don't want to get overzealous, so I decide that this cavity is solely for exploration, the escape attempt will depend upon potential positive discovery. I think of how Samantha explained the importance of "discovery" in legal proceedings and how the request itself could determine the outcome of a case. I thank her, silently, for providing yet another gem of wisdom that translates into my present challenge.

"You're welcome," she says.

I stop and look around the room. I'm not startled by her voice, because my mind knows it is not real, but it seems so authentic that I am shocked by it. There is no one there, of course, but I was really hoping some hallucination of her might be visiting to help me.

"Don't stop now, stay focused," says the other voice of my wiser self from the space around me. I can hear the muffled but noticeable reverberation when these voices materialize, and it truly sounds like I am hearing my own voice within the room and I shiver unexpectedly. The voices in my room are really there and I am fully prepared to stop questioning them. I turn back to the plan and take the knife in my right hand. While I can perform tasks with my left hand, I typically choose to use my right for activities that require fine dexterity. The ceiling is flat, because we live in a "luxury" apartment that was built long after the design style of dimpled ceilings had fallen out of favor. I appreciate this, because I am not presently fighting the particles of paint and dust that dimpled or textured ceilings drop at the slightest touch, and I would already have plenty in my eyes. I think about my building compared to other buildings in Decatur and decide that my ever-worsening impression of the post-apocalyptic world suggests that my pantry could someday be the basis of design for disaster shelters. I work carefully, with great respect for my shelter. The only major difference now, is that I am sawing vertically, over my head. I tire easily like this and avoid letting go of my knife, for fear of it falling to the ground below, and possibly ending this adventure. I regularly inhale and exhale a few times, to flood my lungs with oxygen, feed my muscles, and continue. I switch hands often, in an attempt to conserve energy. As I approach the final cuts, I pull the blade out further than rehearsed and accidentally lean my hand away from the direction of the cut, pointing the tip poorly, then it strikes something hard on the next insertion, causing my hand to slide off the handle and across the exposed blade. I feel the sharp, serrated, edge slice into the meat of my index finger.

## CHAPTER 14

I know and can immediately comprehend how quickly it happens, but time slows and I can sense the blade slice the skin and then continue to submerge deeper as the error progresses. It is a strange sensation when you cut your own skin with a very sharp blade, because the first sensation is interesting, almost satisfying. The blade penetrates with such smoothness. The body suffers a highly-delayed reaction to what is actually happening, then sends a signal to the brain. The brain processes the signal and sends a message to the rest of the body. This final leg of the chain-reaction materializes, in this occurrence, from the nape of my neck, up the crown of my head, pausing at the wound on the back of my head, just to acknowledge that "this is not what we are worried about," and lets it throb for one moment before rushing across the head, face, neck, chest, and bursts into all of my extremities. I believe that exhaustion and shock serve to prevent sudden movement while I process everything. I am still holding the blade. I freeze, close my eyes, and clench my teeth. I await any other signals or sensations. I feel the meat of the first segment of my right index finger begin to warm and something changes inside my fist. There is no pain, just shock, and I wonder about what may be coming. I recognize the feeling of blood filling my fist and decide to keep my hand still, primarily to avoid dropping the knife, but also to contain the injury as long as possible while I sort out what else I need to do. It is simple: I am going to bleed, it is going to be painful. I also know that if I investigate this now, it will hinder my progress, provide more pain, and possibly stop me. I have no idea how bad the cut actually is.

I choose the most rational response in this particular situation: fuck it.

"Fuck it."

My other hand, left, is trembling, but I have virtually no sensation from it. I gently loosen my grip on the knife, but stare only at my left hand. I feel the warm liquid run down my palm, and then my wrist, as I shift my grasp back to the handle. I know where I am wounded now, as the sub-flesh is exposed and the handle is cruel and cold against it, while the nerves scream at me with total rejection. I refuse to respond, clench my teeth and breathe deep, mindful to exhale and not hold my breath. I return the pressure of my grip on the handle where I think it is most natural. Everything that was muscle memory: where to hold the grip, how much pressure to exert with each digit, how to position my hand around the object, etc., is now a new and foreign concept that requires concentration and intentional decision. This also forces me to focus on my freshly-wounded hand and encourages the throbbing sensation and processing of the trauma that has assaulted my primary digit. Once I have succeeded at re-learning how to hold a knife, after not thinking about it for over thirty years, I continue sawing. I abandon my desire to act with any precision or delicacy, because I know that my time is short, and something is coming that I will not be able to prevent or avoid; so I carry on sawing and clenching and breathing and, now I realize, crying. I feel the tears on my face as a subtle breeze passes over me. I don't know if it is my breath or the gentle air current from my toilet hole, but it chills the tears and I know them, I understand them, and I accept their existence. I have long-abandoned shame and self-consciousness, but my tears remind me, in this moment, that I am only human.

"You can't stop now," says the perfect impersonation of my absent wife in my mind-room.

"I know," says my cleaner and not-destroyed other self that occupies the ever-solidifying false space where all of my recent encounters and conversations have taken place, "but it is scary, and I wish you could be here with me."

I continue sawing, and understand that I am still clenching my teeth and the voice that is clearly mine is coming from my mind-mouth and not my physical mouth. It sounds so real in the space between reality and my auto-generated safe-space that I have come to manifest when traumatized.

"You have spent so much time training for this, do not waste your time wishing for physical manifestations if you could enjoy that time sharing spiritual space with me."

It is Samantha's voice, undoubtedly, again, and so real that I am tempted to look around for her, but this is my inner-self creating the words and thoughts, because she would never say those things.

Almost there, almost done.

"I'm not sure what you mean."

Insert, pull-out, insert, pull-out...

"You know! You trained yourself to accept your hallucinations and to welcome them. You developed this amazing headspace for tripping that allows you to control your emotional places and journeys through spiritual understanding. You told me when you are fucked up that you can control your emotions. You said that most people start to worry and it can be very difficult to reverse the negative inclination."

"So?"

"The important thing is to be present with whatever you manifest in your hallucinations. That's what YOU told me."

"I know that!"

"So, why are you asking me to be here with you? I am here with you!"

I shift my attention back to the situation, feel the blood reaching my armpit near the back of my biceps and cringe. When I am sure that the job is complete, I withdraw the blade from the incision and bring it to my body. I refuse to look away from the project area and decide to close the blade with physical sensation only, as I have done a thousand times before. I bring the object to my hip and as I lift my index finger off the handle to execute the performance, I feel it tear from the metal with substantial resistance, surely from the blood starting to congeal in my body's vain attempt to mutate into some strange, blade-handed, cyborg. Fortunately, the fusion was not given adequate time to complete, and I will continue to be a boring, ordinary human, for now. The feeling does not generate much pain, but it is uncomfortable. I have to curl my finger in to pull the blade lock and I continue to fold the knife closed against my waist. When I remove my finger from the path of the closing blade and feel and hear the satisfying snap of the steel as it finds its place in the guarded sheath of a folding knife handle, I turn the object in my hand and slide it into my pocket. I sense wetness, ignore it, and dive into my pocket for the flashlight. I bring out the small metal object and mentally prepare to hold it in my mouth again, remembering to treat it like a delicate phallus.

"You're right... That does turn me on..."

"I know."

"You would do it, wouldn't you?"

"Do what?"

"Suck a dick!"

"I am not having this conversation right now."

"Why not? You have something better to do?"

"Yes."

"Fine. But I know you would."

"Jesus... Really?"

"Just let me have it, and if you ever do it, let me watch."

"Sounds good... like a pretty easy promise to keep, considering my present circumstances."

I close my eyes and click the flashlight on. I can see the light beyond and through my eyelids as if the sun had burst into the room and exploded in a grand supernova. With my eyes still closed, I bring the object toward my mouth. I begin to release my teeth, which are still fully-clenched tight from when I cut myself. When my jaw relaxes, I realize that this has been held tight for a long time. Then, when I start to open my mouth, I feel something abnormal in the back, left, bottom side: A foreign and disturbing feeling. There is no pain, but something moves or shifts when the pressure between my upper and lower teeth recedes. I know this feeling: The most horrifying nightmare of my life, that has become a regular occurrence, typically when I am stressed, is some rendition of a dream where my teeth begin falling out. The dream is typically not at all about my teeth and then they just start falling out. The nightmare involves a vivid sensation that I have only, until now, imagined to be accurate, and I always awaken somewhat traumatized. I move my tongue to my lower-left jaw and confirm my suspicions. My tongue pushes one of my molars out of place and, with almost no resistance, it slides out and falls between my jaw and cheek. I shiver, and it fades into a slow tremble. I am instantly cold and can feel what I am sure is blood seeping from the void that remains. My eyes are still closed, so I work the tooth into my inner mouth and spit it into my bloody right hand that is also holding the flashlight. I tongue around a bit more and it seems that every tooth I find now feels loose. I swallow the blood and saliva in my mouth and shudder. I choose to drop the tooth before I open my eyes and get back to work. I am disgusted and disturbed. I have existed in some deep anxiety for many years that this nightmare could become a reality, and now it manifests, only within another, wholly unimaginable, nightmare, as if sent from hell to crush any morale I have left.

Although bothered, I am reaching a place of distinct indifference toward everything. The pragmatist decides that I need to keep working and the empath decides not to argue, because he is defeated and the pragmatist is lacking emotion, meaning that he could become dangerous or unruly if denied his wish to complete a task. I start to open my eyes, careful not to do so too quickly. I have shocked my vision numerous times throughout this ordeal, and it significantly delays all progress of whatever job I am working on. I bring the flashlight up to my mouth again, gently insert the shaft into my orifice, close my lips, bring my tongue up to hold it steady, and guide the beam of light. I open my eyes wide and look directly at the hole and my left hand holding it in place. I see that my whole left arm is shaking violently and there is dust falling from the severed places in strange downward puffs. My arm is covered in the white substrate, but I somehow had not noticed my shaking or this feeling until I looked. I bring my right arm up to provide relief and when my hand enters my field of vision, I see the bloody mess that I have been ignoring until now.

"Fuck me."

The first reaction is heat. I do not feel or register pain, I simply feel a strange and sharp heat, like a burn from an aluminum sheet pan that has been in a 450 degree commercial oven for many hours and grasped with an unprotected hand. The pain is a bright light in my mind. Even in the fresh brightness of the room, my brain flashes, and my vision goes white, momentarily. When it dissipates, my focus lands on the blood all over my hand and arm. My hand is turned upward to push the ceiling and I can see where the incision occurred. I did not feel that I had cut the meat of my middle finger also, and it is not as bad, but now I take inventory of the trauma. I have cut my index finger, almost perfectly across the center of the first segment of the digit from the knuckle, in a deep, but relatively clean wound. The blood has run all around, but I can see the white of the newly exposed sub-flesh. The same cut is on the middle finger, but only part way across from the index side, and not nearly as deep or gruesome. The burning becomes a throbbing. I can feel my pulse in the wound, and every time it pumps, it produces a little more blood. It is only seeping blood from the index injury now and only from two small places near the middle. I almost clench my teeth, and catch the mistake before it happens, but my front teeth do touch the flashlight shaft, and I feel them shift from the pressure.

I am hurdling toward day 10 as a total disaster and I can't seem to not hurt myself or succeed at any efforts: It is time to get out of here.

## CHAPTER 15

I extract the piece that I cut and drop it, and all that it is containing above, to the ground below, with complete disregard for the consequences. Curiosity and excitement overwhelm me. I reach my left hand into the hole, and disturb some dust that gets in my eyes, and I blink wildly. I decide that I need to clear the worst of this debris before sticking my head up there. I start wiping my hand around inside the hole and allowing the dirt to fall into the room. More dust assaults my eyes and frustrates me. I close my eyes and continue the process. I decide that my concern for infection or bacteria is frivolous, and bring my right hand into the space to join the party, with a fleeting thought that, perhaps, the dust might pack the wound and help to stop and prevent further bleeding. With both hands rummaging around, I make quick work of the space immediately surrounding the hole. I open my eyes and the air is still cloudy, but I risk it. I lean toward the hole while holding the edge with my right hand and peer into the hole, initially expecting to see a solid piece of concrete that separates my apartment from the one above. I consider that this may not be the case, because I should have felt it already. The toilet is also good evidence that the slab is likely not present. Considering the amount of immovable objects in the other holes, I expect this as the most likely scene, instead of solid concrete. What I actually find is completely unexpected. As my light violates the darkness beyond the hole, it illuminates an open void. I can see objects further inside, but the immediate space is completely devoid of tangible material. I lead with the end of the light and follow with my face, taking a moment to allow my eyes to adjust. The hole I cut allows room for my entire head and its placement is also conducive to this activity. Once I clear the ceiling and my head is fully inside, I take in the image with great deliberation. There is a space around my head, which somewhat confusing. The first thing I see is the rest of the toilet, as expected, resting quite precariously, from this vantage point, wedged at a downward angle in the ceiling. The pantry wall is its primary support. The back portion, the basin, is missing. I cannot tell if the pedestal is intact, because of the angle, as it would be behind the wall. I do see that the bowl is, indeed, full of water, and water seems to be dripping into the bowl from above. The toilet looks relatively clean, but the rim and the places where the seat and basin were once attached are cracked and large pieces are missing. Actually, the portion that I can see from below is not wholly representative of the overall quality of the object. No, finally, face to face with this enigma, I find it quite miraculous that the part needed for my water provision is intact and that the object has not fallen through the ceiling, yet. The bowl is full and I witness a drop of water splash into it, near the front lip. The bowl is not only tilted toward me, but also slightly to the left, providing a good angle for me to see inside. I notice another drop splash into the reservoir and follow its path up, behind the toilet, where there is a slanted mass of gray. I see where the gray slab disappears behind the toilet and the wall, like some terrible concrete background, dropped, mid-placement, and left in this precarious way. The slab of fabricated stone rises at an awkward angle above the toilet a few feet to a jagged apex, where it meets another slab that falls to my right, toward where my bathroom and kitchen would be. I continue turning my head to investigate and I discover more and more wreckage. This broken slab must be the piece that once separated my apartment from my upstairs neighbor's unit. It has been lifted from its original location and split into three large pieces. The main point of separation is above the toilet and to the right. One piece is behind the toilet and falling to the left, the second back and to the right. The third, and largest section, is behind me and to my left. The last piece is the lowest, and when I turn that direction, I can see the steel joist just to my left, mangled by the slab being ripped from its attachment, a twisted form of near artistic rendering. The force that ripped the giant concrete mass from its perch and tore it away from the steel joists must have been so massive and instantaneous that it left the more delicate objects in place, but everywhere it was once connected, the framing is bent and disturbed. There are other pieces of objects and scattered, random, material, that are difficult to identify. In one spot, behind me, I think I can make out the dryer vent material, but it is unrecognizable. The overall design looks like the worst a-frame attic space I have ever seen, as if built by a child with random objects. I see what seem to be pieces of wood, metal, rock, brick, electrical conduit, and wire in every nook and cranny. I look back up to the point where the three main pieces came apart in a horrifying and jagged three-way split. There is significant space between them and I can identify where the water is protruding, because it has darkened the concrete where it enters and runs down the face, collects at a spot with some type of imperfection, forms a droplet, and subsequently falls to the bowl below. There are various other places like this, but this one is dropping directly into the toilet bowl. Every time it does, the toilet overflows a bit more, water trickles down the front, through the gap at the sheet rock to where I know it pools again before dropping all the way to my collection container. This process would be impossible to design intentionally and I can certainly appreciate the incredible coincidence that has befallen my situation. I look back to the largest space between the concrete and try to focus on the darkness in the void beyond. I can just barely make out a few large objects, so I move the flashlight back and forth, slowly, to shift the angle of the light and cast its shadows in alternating directions. This allows me to see that it is just another mass of debris. The only thing preventing this junk from crushing my room, is the, menacingly precarious, concrete slab, holding it back. As I explore with the light and make crude estimations, I decide that there is certainly not enough space to stand, and initially no obvious exit opportunities. I keep searching, feeling that there must be something else here. I start to panic and my mind becomes blurry and confused as the feeling sets in. The only thing I have yet to sort out is how any light is getting in. I turn my head toward my right hand, partially release my grasp on the edge, and take the flashlight out of my mouth. My hand hurts, but I really don't care any more. I hold the flashlight and the edge of the hole with one hand. I click the light off and wait for the darkness to invade, hoping there may be some light left to quell my curiosity.

While I wait for my vision to adapt, my heart slows and my breathing steadies. In a few simple moments of temporary blindness, a strange calm washes over me. My eyes are wide, and I can only see residual light spots and glowing strangenesses that I know are my eyes trying to make sense of the drastic change. I breathe deep and begin to accept that there is no way out of this room. My only hope now is that the explanation to another mystery may be revealed. I am backstage at the magic show, anticipating the promise of a magician's secrets, hoping that the explanation will provide some comfort or relief, and yet somehow knowing there is only frustration ahead.

I have now learned the sequence of events that are necessary when re-acclimating to darkness. My eyes create amazing images for a relatively long time. It actually seems that the sicker and more exhausted I have become, the longer they last and the more vivid they present. Suddenly, in front of me, I see my mother. This time, it is completely surreal. I see only her bust, from her chest up. I could describe the image as floating, except that her entire visage is simply superimposed onto the dark background of the room. Much like my mystery oak tree of visions previous, there are fascinating colors forming all around and behind her. The tone of the color is the dark and rich red of the sunset whose light is being scattered and distributed by the many unknown particles in the air outside. But the color is pulsating and shifting in wavelike patterns all around. The rich red is blending and mixing, actively, with the total darkness that was there before. As it appears, it replaces the strange white and yellow splotches that my eyes hold onto from the flashlight. The face before me is of my younger mother: the mother of my childhood. She is in her late twenties or early thirties. She looks young and vibrant, as I remember her from my youth. Her skin is tight and her eyes are closed. Her mouth is relaxed, forming the unimpressed emotion that I learned not to question so long ago. While my mother expresses joy and elation with great, animated intensity, her resting face lands somewhere between bemused and indifferent. This familiar expression has taught me not to expect comfort in the form of a smile, which I have come to realize that many people expect from society. I am staring at this strange image for so long that I cannot tell if it is simply a mental picture of her, or if some version of her is visiting with me now. Her eyes open and we connect. She looks deep into me, never changing the expression on her face. The only change is that her eyes are now open and she is peering into me, satisfying my query regarding her presence. Neither of us moves or speaks and I am genuinely disturbed by my present situation. I am unsure if I am conscious, until I blink, and the image remains. This causes her mouth to move.

"What have you done, son?"

At first, I am shocked by the question. I pause to consider my answer, partly because she is still expressionless, and I hope for some clue to the nature of her inquisition.

"What do you mean, mother?" She continues to stare for what seems like an eternity, then finally shifts her look to one of condescending questioning. One eyebrow raised and her head and lips slightly tilted.

"Where is my little baby boy?"

"I don't know, mom. I wish I knew."

"You have one job: take care of him. How can you be so careless?"

"Mother, there is nothing I could have done. I had no idea this was going to happen. I can't get out of here and I have no clue what has happened to anyone else."

"You have excuses for everything, just like your father."

This statement catches me off guard, because it is not something my mother would say. Actually, she almost never speaks of my father.

"I don't want to talk to you right now. I'm not sure what manifestation you are, but you are not my mother."

As soon as I complete the statement, she vanishes. There is no theatrical puff of smoke or animated swoop or swirl effect, she simply disappears. The red forms of the backdrop for the condescending visitor that is not my mother shifts to the foreground and the patterns within the colors fade into the strange and shadowed forms of the ceiling space where my head pokes up to investigate. Everything looks different in the dark, which is true for most objects in differing intensities of light. Because the area is no longer illuminated by my small, yet substantial, flashlight, the objects and spaces all feel ominous. When I was visually exploring the space, I was lighting the corners and crevices with purpose, but now I am staring into a mysterious space where it seems there could be things hiding in the shadows that were not there mere moments ago and I have to remind myself that there are none. The instinct to click the light back on suddenly overwhelms me, like some childhood fear, and assuming the light will eliminate any threats lurking, perfectly camouflaged, in the corners. I must intentionally choose not to simply click the light on and take one more inventory, remembering that I am trying to answer a mystery that requires this darkness. My eyes dart to the top of the space. I cannot, in good conscience, call this a room, because it is simply a void created during devastation. Rooms are conceptualized, designed, and constructed. Plus, rooms must include portals and this possesses none. I can see where the light is coming in from the apex of the broken concrete slab. That location is the life-sustaining source of my prison. I know that light, water, and air are all entering through a pathway to the outside, but the crude fractures are merely a few feet from my face and the diminishing light does nothing to encourage any possibility of escape from there. I accept, at this moment, that this is likely the grandest cock-tease of my life. When something leads you to it with hope and possibility, then opens up into a grand space, and offers more and more hope with every subsequent discovery, only harboring the final gatekeeping until the final moment, there is no more appropriate description than "cock-tease." I am tempted to cut the hole larger, climb into my crowded escape hatch, and search more intimately for pathways to freedom, but decide this plan will certainly prove frivolous. The red light emanating from the three-way split above and before me is fading. I can't see the sky beyond, and there is no bright hopeful light shining through, presenting an image of the outside, it is still only a suggestion. I realize that the red light in the room is like none I have ever seen. Everything around me that is a lighter shade of the spectrum in white light has shifted to a crimson, almost blood, red. Theater lighting specialists would most appreciate the simulated tone of red that has engulfed my vision field now. The dry and plain gray concrete slabs surrounding me are the most disturbing, and the locations where water is penetrating make it look like the objects are bleeding. I hold my fingers in front of my face and I can barely see them. The light is almost gone now. I visually explore the room a bit more, knowing that I can't stand here much longer, with my head in the ceiling, peering into the void and teasing my hope. I notice movement. I see something move a few feet in front of me. It is not living, living things have distinct, albeit diverse, movement patterns. I squint into the increasing red darkness and see that it is a trickle of water running down the concrete slab toward the toilet. It is trickling in from the top, where the light is. I can't call it a droplet, or a stream, because it is somewhere between the two. But once I see it, and follow it the short distance to where it loses its grip and falls into the toilet bowl, I think that it looks so much like blood, that I wonder for a moment if it may be. My mind jumps back to the recurring mental creation of a dead body above my room, dripping blood onto me, from days ago. I can picture the man immediately, annihilated and bloody, in the space above me, but this time, he is lying outside, contorted, across the concrete slabs above, bleeding into the space. He is not specifically familiar, like a movie extra. The images that my mind shifts to now are so vivid, it feels like my brain is changing channels. My vision can completely shift from the scene in front of my eyes to the mind's-eye with a snap. I fear that my brain is losing its ability to stay on task or distinguish reality. This entire scene occurs while the water is falling through space, shining and refracting the red light, until it lands in the toilet bowl with a splash-plunk, and I can hear every detail of the sound, in vivid, unreal detail. I picture how much liquid is in the bowl. I can see the pitch of the container and can gauge it by the angle of the water's edge against its walls. Everything within the bowl is red from the environmental hue, but I question whether I am seeing the details of its contents, or if my mind is fabricating the information for my satisfaction. The liquid's performance is all in slow motion and seems impossible, because I do not sense that I have slowed any. The tone of the droplet connecting with the collected water does not seem manipulated in tone, but it is extended in time, like a magical audio production trick, and I question reality, much as I have done on my many journeys with hallucinogenic substances.

## Chapter 16

My professional résumé is simple and somewhat impressive, but my drug use résumé contains vast and versatile experiences that would certainly garner callbacks and second interviews if ever utilized. Although I regard myself as a rather dull individual, with little remarkable contribution to the world, my personal experience has been quite profound. Outwardly, I am generally unassuming and uninteresting, but a deeper exploration of my spiritual and emotional existence will prove intriguing to the mind-explorer. I learned to appreciate inebriation early in life. I watched my parents enjoy intoxicants and experiment with substances in, sometimes vain but often effective, efforts to remedy the symptoms of adulthood. I came to understand, while still very young, that certain substances are extremely effective at altering one's experience and others are specifically for altering consciousness. I was expected to be "seen and not heard" as a child, but I was an extremely inquisitive child, and learned, during my expected silence, to be highly perceptive. I studied the varying delivery methods of substances and cataloged detailed mental inventories of the different possibilities and the outcomes. I would explore the names of the drugs, if labeled, otherwise, would pretend to be enthralled by something else, like television, while actually listening intently to the conversations that would often explain what the adults were partaking in. Then I would note, carefully, in my mind, what effects presented in the participants. I would also listen to the arguments and conversations that certain adults had with regard to the drugs and intoxicants and how they did not like certain outcomes. Most of the arguments I witnessed were related to alcohol. I decided early that alcohol is a mysterious chemical. It was the constant source of escape, acceptable in almost every situation, but the cause of much drama throughout my childhood. After my father left us, my mother began seeking support from varying sources. She was seeing a doctor who prescribed her so many medicines that she could barely keep up with the bottles and related instructions. I was always noting the expectations and monitoring her intake and behaviors. Some of this was out of a concern for her safety, but mostly out of curiosity. I remember when she was prescribed Valium for the first time and being amazed by the effect the pills had on her. She was in a constant state of frustration at that point, and I recall feeling like she was always sad or angry, but almost never happy. The first time she took Valium in my presence, the drug took effect, she exhaled, visually relaxed, and smiled. That was the first time I remember thinking that some drugs truly are miracles. I was young enough to be concerned for my mother's emotional state because it was a direct determinant of my forthcoming experiences. I wanted her to be happy, but I was incapable of providing this relief myself. Valium accomplished the feat in less than 2 hours. Her smile was the beginning of her ability to relax and let go. She shifted from concerned, panicked, worried, and unhappy, to calm, peaceful, and relaxed. The first time I "stole" her drugs, it was Valium. I counted them every day, sometimes multiple times, and concocted a plan to take one after she was asleep. I knew that she would never know, even if I hadn't been as meticulous in my planning, but I wanted to truly enjoy it and not be distracted by worry. I had no idea how little "worry" is tolerated by a dose Valium during a session. I did not see myself as a "worried" individual, nor did I think that I was stressed or anxious about very much. I was a pre-teen, what did I have to worry about? But I can vividly recall the sense of calm that overcame me as the Valium took hold of my emotional state. All of the previously unidentified stress that was in my body and mind melted from me in a conspicuously physical way. I could almost picture the concern melting from my psyche, like chocolate from a freshly dipped strawberry. In a way, I had a near-psychedelic experience on Valium the first time I experienced it, because my mind painted images of the effects in cartoon-like clarity. I found myself on my bed, late on a Friday night, perhaps early Saturday morning, focusing on my breathing and chuckling from time to time. I could sense a smile across my face that I could not force to fade. The serious and stoic young man, who was constantly evaluating every situation, was finally carefree. I instantly understood why the doctor prescribed this to my mother, because she was very stressed, and the effect of this drug was instantaneous decompression. That night was the beginning of what I would consider to be a very fruitful and healthy relationship with intoxicants and hallucinogens.

My father was always high and always had excess cannabis in various forms throughout any space that he inhabited. There were brownies in every freezer, roaches in the ashtrays, pre-rolled joints in the bathrooms, and assortments of hash pipes and glass implements, typically accompanied by grinders and containers, beside every comfortable seat. I could have smoked marijuana my entire childhood by just scraping a little from his remnants during my occasional visits. As it was, I did not need to hide it or perform any sort of devious methods to enjoy cannabis. When I was a young teen, I simply walked into his temporary home, picked up a roach from the ashtray, the lighter beside it, and lit it up. I inhaled deeply, coughed myself into a fit, until I was laying on my side with my eyes closed and watering. When I found air again, I opened my eyes and saw my father standing there, across the coffee table, smiling.

"Feel better?"

"It has been a tough week, pops."

"I'm sure."

Then he just walked away, chuckling. I do not think he knew that was my first time. Because it was so available and such a prevalent and normal part of my life, I never gravitated to it from desire or pursued it as a regular activity. Weed was what other people in Georgia considered "drugs" at the time. To me, it was as common as someone drinking a beer. I do not consider my relationship with cannabis to be one of intoxication. Sometimes I would welcome it as a casual release, but I never craved it. My parents both kept the best weed available. The first time I smoked pot socially, with my peers, I was disgusted. I was convinced that it was not actually marijuana, and my friend had been duped by a bad actor. My mother had not yet warmed up to the idea of my using, or I just wasn't comfortable confiding in her, because she was the actual and functional "parent figure" in my life, so I waited until my next visit with my father. I told him about the joint that I smoked with my friend after school, and he told me that "most people smoke dirt weed and have no idea." I was spoiled. I very rarely smoked or consumed weed unless I knew the source or had a chance to inspect it before preparation.

In the new age of legal and medical cannabis, I have had many opportunities to enjoy the fruits of regulated production, which is wonderful. Cannabis is not my drug of choice, I don't even consider it a drug, but the effects prepared me for a lifelong exploration of hallucinogenic adventures. I ingested so many different types of pills from my mother's collections over the years, that I would consider myself a primary source of information on the recreational use of prescription medications.

In my mid-teens, my mother leaned away from traditional, western medicine, and dove, head-first, into alternative methods of relief and healing. These alternative methods were typically not synthetic-chemical in structure, and are not actually "alternative" methods, as society has come to name them. Many are the oldest, best-documented, and most understood forms of escape and spiritual/psychological stimulation and introspection. Plant-based hallucination soon became the path to escape and satisfaction that I most desire and practice.

I came home from a party one night, slightly drunk, but quite frustrated with the requirement of adolescent social immersion in order to acquire and consume intoxicants in America. I truly, at that point, preferred to do it alone. I found my mother, in a very good mood, sitting, cross-legged, on the floor of our small kitchen, with uncooked brown and white rice in two piles on the linoleum. She was very happy, giggling, and was using the rice as her medium for "rice-painting" on the floor. The floor was 70's yellow and I'm sure it had some sort of pattern, but I just remember it being a yellow that seemed to be the color of choice for southern homes built in the 1970's, and provides the filtered hue of my visual memories from my childhood. She was taking handfuls of rice and pouring them out in a semi-controlled method of releasing differing amounts from the opening made between her pinky and the back of her hand, making two-tone designs on the floor. She was laughing at a freshly-created smiley-face when I arrived. She was also very excited to have an audience to share this accomplishment with. I was bemused. In all of my research, I had never seen her in this state. I did not ask how she had come to be this way, because I was always careful to never give her any reason to question my innocence, and potentially jeopardize my source. I knew that I would discover the explanation soon. I spent some time with her, quite enjoying her elevated mood. I left her to use the restroom, and to smoke a little of her pot, and returned feeling slightly closer to her mood than when I left. On my way back, I discovered the source. There was a large bag of brownish-gray mushrooms on the kitchen table. In retrospect, my mother had, somehow, acquired a startling amount of psilocybin. The bag was on its side and some of the shrooms were spilling out onto the table, reminiscent of D.A.R.E. program photos of illicit drugs that children were to avoid and report if ever discovered. I had never seen magic mushrooms in person but had been warned about them in that and similar programs that were obviously designed to make kids want to do drugs. Also, this item was clearly out of place. I had recently noticed that her stash of pills and liquid medications in the medicine cabinet had not been replenishing, and I was getting pretty nervous that she would soon notice that I was skimming. I had not determined what she was replacing these drugs with until now. Within the hour, she had moved into the living room and was in a deep state of spiritual contemplation when I decided to leave her again and take a few of the smelly little mushrooms to my room. Usually, I would wait to make sure she did not discover my heist, terrified of inebriated confrontation, but I felt compelled to explore this newly-realized opportunity right away. I waited until she had gone to bed and immediately ate the three large mushrooms all-at-once. They were strange in form and texture but did not have any negative taste like others have claimed. To me, they seemed natural, normal, and honest. The pungent, earthy flavor was exciting. The first feeling I had was while I was chewing them: I considered that if these made me feel half as good as my mother was behaving and were actually just mushrooms, I would welcome the opportunity. I was overcome with a relief that, perhaps, nature was just as supportive of my desire to enjoy extra-conscious experiences. I had been practicing, alone, to control my mind and behaviors while inebriated, and the rehearsal time had paid off, because over the next six hours, I explored places in my mind that are inarguably some of the most beautiful and disturbing locations in the universe. The experience was so profound that I began reading and studying about mind-altering substances and their place in history the next day. I quickly decided that what happened the night before was definitely a spiritual experience. I was not raised in a religious environment, so my turning to spirituality was more organic and comforting than people forced by religious dogma. Psychedelics would continue to be my medium of communication with the spiritual realm for all of my life. Strangely, I almost never tripped or journeyed with other people. Psychedelic experiences are intimately personal and I have little desire to share that. Much of my life, from then on, was spent on a personal journey that almost no one knew about or understood. My father knew, because we got in an argument about it once. When Samantha told him that I was out of town on one of my "spiritual journeys," he laughed at her, and she told me later that it bothered her. She knew that I was aided on my journeys, but we never discussed what the aids were. She knew that I would occasionally solicit the help of a trusted person, that was typically not a close friend, to monitor my experience and ensure my safety. I presume she was smart enough to deduce the reasoning. When my father expressed his condescension by laughing at the idea of a spiritual journey, she ended the interaction with him right away. I confronted him by phone almost immediately upon hearing her story and told him that it bothered her, and I would appreciate it if he would curb his elitist behavior about life in our presence. He dragged it out of me that I was tripping in the woods and that he thought the idea was silly. I know that his disdain for such beliefs likely stemmed from his relationships, particularly with my mother. I highlighted the profound absurdity that he could criticize anyone for enjoying drugs with positive intentions when he had been abusing them his entire life with nothing resembling a goal attached. I told him that his use of drugs and alcohol was escapism, so he had no room to judge anyone who used them for growth or exploration of the mind and spirit. We did not speak for a long time after that conversation.

My life included many well-planned and meticulously-executed plans to acquire and experience any substances that could provide a pathway to the meta-conscious. Because I took most of these journeys alone, I spent significant time preparing myself, emotionally and mentally, to be in control of the journey. One could never prepare for some of the experiences I had. When I discovered DMT, it became the most regular and consistent form of exploration. In my junior year at Georgia Tech, I developed a friendship unlike any I had before. I met Siddhartha at a house party. Sid was a freshman, and he approached me, joint in hand, offering no formal introduction, simply sat down next to me on the red couch and handed me the joint. I took it from him, and we shared the first of many numbers, and conversations, that night, in the midst of a rowdy gathering. He, somehow identified me as a "friendly," and decided to share space with me, understanding later that our spiritual connection was older than time. Sid was out of place at a technical school, and eventually left to search for wisdom by "walking the earth," much to his parents' disdain. In the few months we shared, Sid introduced me to a method of synching oneself with the spiritual realm much faster and more effectively than I had known was possible. He would disappear for days at a time, and return with strange stories of visions and understandings that he has experienced. On one such return, after a profoundly overwhelming trip, he presented me with an opportunity to try smoking DMT on my marijuana, and promised to "babysit" while I "blasted off," which is a common description of how the trip takes hold, quite accurately. The substance itself is not addictive, but the experience, for a weekend explorer, can become an infatuation. Some, more open-minded, cultures have been extracting DMT from certain plants for thousands of years, in different forms and potencies, but the result is always the same: the intensity of the trip allows one to connect with the universe, or the divine, in ways that are inaccessible otherwise. Gurus and ascetic pioneers have referred to the experience as "temporary enlightenment," and some of the most profound philosophical discoveries have been made during or surrounding trips involving DMT. In the 1960's, American psychedelic explorers also found the substance to be of great purpose. Some posit that it was never as popular as LSD, Psilocybin, or Mescaline, because, when smoked, the pure DMT experience lasted as little as five minutes, and rarely longer than 20, earning it the title: "the businessman's trip," because it could be done recreationally with little to no time constraint. Other substances could be enjoyed throughout one's day, and were more aligned with "lifestyle," rather than purposeful participation and discovery. More recently, there has been a revival of mainstream hallucinogenic drug use, including "psychedelic tourism," attracting a broader range of explorers into the world of introspective journey. Much of the success in Silicon Valley includes stories of "micro-dosing" various substances to aid in peak process functioning. Others have learned, borrowed, or stolen, the method of brewing plants containing DMT with others containing MAOIs in a tea, called Ayahuasca, allowing the digestive system to metabolize the hallucinogen, and producing a significantly longer trip. The experience has been so popularized, that one can book Ayahuasca excursions online, and they can be experienced locally, hosted by self-proclaimed Shamans and guides. I never participated in group sessions of drinking Ayahuasca, which often causes hours of vomiting, and can be quite dangerous. Sid eventually quit school, released his passion as a visual artist, and, as of our last interaction, was creating inspired, albeit difficult to understand, paintings and sculptures, that he sells, or gives to anyone who will take them. His method of creation is to manifest visions through Psychedelic intoxication, immediately create a related image, emotionally detach from the creation, and then offer to give it away. The entire process is very similar to sand art, whether on the beach, or by Buddhist Monks: Temporary, representing the impermanence of our experiences and the universe. I still see Sid regularly, because he is my primary source of DMT and is my trusted spiritual guide, when needed. I enjoy DMT for the brief and overwhelming encounter it provides. The most profound journey I ever took lasted just over ten minutes, but I explored the outer reaches of the solar system, had a years-long conversation with a deity that I still have yet to identify, saw my own death, immediately followed by my birth, and witnessed the creation of a star, in real-time. I could sense movement that is not possible in the physical realm in which we exist, and learned that our brains are some of the simplest mechanisms of our existence. When I returned to earth from that experience, I had emotionally aged many years and gained the wisdom of ancient beings. Because I went on these trips alone, I never had to explain them to confused audiences like others that I have watched. My experiences are mine, alone.

As the sound of the felled water particles reverberate in my mind and time begins to spool back up to casual speed, I understand that my years of psychedelic training are how I am tolerating the experience of my mind's present disintegration. I witness the colors, sounds, and sensations without question, having long since accepted that if my mind is providing an experience, it is for a reason. This realization provides a new and advanced level of acceptance about my situation. I am stuck in this space but I have prepared myself for mental-collapse for many years. The delusion of control and deliberation regarding the chaos of existence is one of the greatest tricks of the mind, and the most convincing argument for the existence of God that

I can fathom. Only an omnipotent God could generate a universe beyond our understanding, that operates by so complex a formula that its inhabitants would be allowed to believe that they possess any control within it or the ability to understand it.

This may be a good time to speak to God. But I have never spoken to God, actively, because my relationship with The Spirit is nestled in the experiences that represent its presence. The red light has now completely faded. The space above my pantry is completely dark.

My vision is not perfect, but I do not need glasses for driving or reading. I wear glasses when working on my computer for good measure, but I can see very clearly most of the time without aid. Just as I am about to maneuver my hand so that my head can descend back into the pantry, I notice a light at the concrete apex. It seems distant, out of focus, as if filtered through some translucent material. I cock my head like a perplexed puppy and squint my eyes in the direction of the light. I don't see it now. I look around again, wondering if it may be a hallucination. The area is completely dark. There is no light coming from behind me, so it is not a reflection. I scan around again and confirm that I have been here long enough to have outlasted the end of the red sunset glow that has been emanating through the opening. I am accepting the assurance that my mind is fucking with me when I see it again. It is coming from the location of the light source. I have been here long enough to know exactly where that location is in the space. This is a dim white light. It is so faint that it could easily be one of the floating manifestations of the eyes experienced when you close them hard or suddenly, but is more real, not superimposed like visualizations. Even though my brain has recently generated images that consistently supersede reality,

I am sure that I am seeing this light. Instead of second-guessing, this time, I stare and squint right at it. I can't seem to get it into focus and it disappears again. I do not look away.

"Not this time. I see you. What are you?"

A few breaths later, it appears again. It is not sudden, there is a gentle re-appearance. I am almost sure, though, that it has shifted slightly into the inverted crevice between the slabs at the top of my crude roof structure.

I know this light. It flickers, winks at me. The feeling suggests some seductive history, as if encouraging my brain to remember the amazing night of love we had so as to prevent an awkward encounter when it crosses the room full of people and offers cordialities and I am forced to admit that I do not recall its name. I feel a sense of peace, but as I squint and tilt my head once more, it fades into and out of visibility in a brief moment and I know what it is.

It is a star.

I can see a star.

My bloody and parched mouth falls open. I stare, bewildered, at the place where it is coming from. I look, long, at the tiny speck of beautiful white light. I am instantly fascinated by how bright it is, yet also almost invisible. I could easily have left and never seen it. It generates just enough residual light to identify the edges of the hole that it shines through. I can see the location clearly now and I know that it is definitely moving through the hole. I am sure because its distance to the nearest imperfect edges is changing, but also because I believe in science. I can't look away. My brain won't let me lose sight of it. I estimate by its rate of travel and general path, that I will be able to watch it for a few more minutes. I decide that I cannot force it into focus because the refraction of light through a densely particulate-filled atmosphere is distorting the image. The flickering I see is the normal and expected behavior of a distant star and the primary clue when determining if an object in the night sky is a planet, star, or other alien object. The various interferences in the path of light across so vast a distance generates a twinkle. With the added atmospheric distortion, this star presents as a dim, barely-visible, flickering object. I also decide, in my newly found great and unchallenged wisdom, that its disappearing act is caused by passing clouds. I am entranced by the star. It is my star. In this moment, I love this star and consider it my most refreshing experience since the event. While I am confident that the light entering my room is from the outside world, I have not actually seen outside in almost two weeks. I experience daylight entering the room, but it does not provide any imagery that transports my mind to the world that I remember. I can look at this star and recall many times that I have stared up at the stars. I can feel sand below my feet from beach nights. I can smell the remnants of a campfire from seeing stars through the trees before bed on camping trips. I imagine that I can feel a breeze across my skin. I stare at the light and juxtapose the faces and presences of people that I have watched stars with in my head. I think about times that I have seen a beautiful night sky and told my son, wife, parents, friends, or strangers to look up. The nostalgia from the beauty of this tiny light overwhelms me.

My body begins its slow-animation of sensations that I have been experiencing from extreme pain. I feel something in the high center of my back. It starts between my shoulder blades as a tingling. I almost don't recognize it because of the other sensations that I am experiencing. I have been burying so many physical sensations that my mind is confused when it feels something new. Once I acknowledge the feeling, it starts to spread. It does not feel like recent burning sensations, this is a novel tingling. My first reaction is that it is not pain. When it reaches my shoulders and wraps around toward my chest, my muscles tighten. It feels like acute hyperventilation, only specifically recognizable in the places where it manifests. As it spreads both directions within my spine, I feel a rush across my scalp. The feeling breathes into all of my previous injuries as it passes them, tells my mind to ignore that sensation, and focus only on the new concern. As my brain digests this strange idea, I feel excitement. The only way to describe the emotion is: excited. I suddenly want to scream and run. I scream the automatic word in my rescue vocabulary: "help!"

This time, my voice is louder than I remember and sounds strange, higher-pitched, and more separated from the rest of me, yet aggressive and intimidating. I think that if I heard this voice on the street before the event, I would be concerned for the person and equally afraid to find them, for fear of what could cause such emotion. The scream only intensifies my excitement. My muscles twitch and my breathing increases in depth and frequency. I feel my muscles saturate extra blood and begin to pump themselves.

I am not afraid. I stare at the star slowly drifting through the hole, as it threatens to leave my vision soon. This anticipation also exacerbates my excitement. I want that star. I know that it is mine and has shown itself to me for a reason. This is a sign. I want it. I want to hold it in my hands and feel its warmth. My muscles start to take control and I want to climb in and fight my way out. I am experiencing the most overwhelming adrenaline rush that I have known. I have never been so aware of how the hormone affects me, but in my controlled environment, I am capable of a type of focus and self-awareness that I never thought possible. This is adrenaline. I know that many survivor stories refer to adrenaline as one of their weapons in the arsenal of unbelievable victory, and I latch onto this opportunistic concept. The feeling consumes my body and my mind. I will get up into this space and I will find a way out: No more calculating or planning. My right hand is in front of me, forearm deep in the hole shared with my neck. I pull my arm down and grab the edge of the drywall ceiling at the best leverage point and yank downward. A large piece of the material breaks free and folds down, still hanging onto the ceiling by its paper backing. I reach close to where my neck is and repeat. I succeed after two pulls, and tear off another, smaller, piece. I repeat, this time more toward my right side. I succeed in the first try. I have doubled the span of the opening in four attempts. I reach across my body and repeat the effort in front of my left shoulder. I have less leverage, but pull off a piece in three yanks of the material. I consider using the flashlight to calculate my entry, but the adrenaline wins and I feel confident that I can now lift my emaciated body by my arms into the space and then proceed to bring my legs up. I push my entire right arm up and keep it elevated while I lean toward the right to allow my left arm access. I get both arms up and inside the hole with my head and start to push up onto my toes on the crude platform below.

"Now we're doing it!"

The words explode from my mouth as I invert my arms to get my palms flat onto the top side of the ceiling on either side of my head. I do not sense any shaking, trembling, or weakness. My body seems fully prepared to execute this feat. My hands find positions on either side, my shoulders fully in the hole. I am at the top of my height, considering the slight angle that is required to penetrate the opening.

"Better do it now before this wears off."

It seems the voice is coming from somewhere else, but it is mine. I recognize it as my other complex, the "wiser" visitor that has been joining me.

I breathe deep and close my eyes. It is absolutely dark in the space, so this is nothing more than a rehearsed practice I use when preparing for a challenge. I will have to jump off of my toes as best I can. The planning seems simple, my confidence is very high, and I am overtaken by a sense that I can, absolutely, do this. In the midst of picturing the assumed-necessary movements, my body begins to move. I drop slightly at the knees while relaxing my shoulders to allow slight descent. Then I explode upward with my knees and hips. When I sense weightlessness, I transfer attention and energy to my arms and hands. When I feel the pressure in my arms, I push in a relatively equal explosion with every muscle in my upper body to bring myself up into the ceiling space. It happens fast, and as I enter the hole and pass the point where I know I've made it, my head hits the concrete slab ceiling within the new attic space of my pantry that is falling away behind me. I can sense where it is so I ignore the impact and begin to lean forward and pull my buttocks up, in, and then push them out in order to sit. This motion requires great concentration and is calculated and recalculated every time I strike my head and have to adjust at my hips forward to compensate. Just as my arms begin to shake, my ass finds the edge of the hole and I shift some weight to it. I am slumped over, chest almost to thighs, with the very edge of the hole supporting the very back of my ass cheeks. My hands are out and below me, still pushing on either side.

I did it.

I am inside the escape hatch.

I am frozen in this position. I can't see the star any more, so I picture it in my mind. It is so beautiful. Its hazy white glow winks at me and drifts in and out of sight, beckoning me. I sit and breathe, thinking about the star. I want that star. I feel entitled to it. I am sure that it appeared in that hole to tell me that "this is the way out." I have full faith in the prophetic nature of its sudden and magnificent manifestation during my near hopelessness. I am also confident that there is something or someone out there that I need to find and enjoy my star with. I want, so desperately, to find someone to share my joy with. I have experienced moments in my life where I wish that my partner, or my child, or a friend, could experience something that I discovered while alone, but I preserve that desire in a strange little box in my mind that comforts me. I hold all of these solo memories in a guarded and personal place. I long to share them with someone now. I also feel like the mental container where I hold those personal memories is at capacity, so I am compelled to share everything I am presently experiencing and its contents need to be unloaded, somehow. The star is obviously the guiding light to that relief. Also, just like when you have a desperate need to urinate or defecate, the urge increases in intensity as the identified target location approaches. Your body begins to prepare for the release as it realizes the relief is near. My body does the same thing now, emotionally. I am crying, from the belief that I will now find my way to companionship. This new idea, whose authenticity or accuracy is never questioned, is manifested with total confidence. This challenge, getting into this space, will lead me to a way outside, which will lead me to my tribe.

I do not assume the tribe will be the same that I built in my adult life, or that it will resemble any tribe I have been part of before. I just need a companion.

My loneliness is too much.

As my breathing calms, I listen for sounds of hope. I hear absolutely nothing. I can't even hear the water above or below me. I have just made so much noise that I will need to refocus on my environmental sounds again. The adrenaline is still generating a pumping sensation in my muscles, most notably in my pectorals, but has lost its peak intensity, and I am beginning to focus and think again. The past moments start to seem distant and foggy, like some sort of dream memory. I see the actions in my mind with a vignette-style edge-blur. For a moment, I'm not sure that I am actually in the ceiling, and I take a moment to feel around. I determine that I did actually accomplish this goal and now I need to find a way out. I know that I need to bring my legs up. I reach in front of myself, still slumped forward, and feel around on the other side of the hole. I don't have space to lift my legs, so I start to lean to the left. I reach up with my right arm to utilize the nearest slab above for support and guidance. As I lean left, I extend my upper body away from my thighs and begin to bring my right leg up into the hole. When I clear the entrance, I extend my leg until it hits something solid. I am sure it is the toilet, so I take great care to pull back and guide my foot to the right side of the object. Then I start to lean the other direction, to the right. I switch arms, bringing my right arm out to my right side and to find leverage and my left hand up to the slab. I bend my waist back down, cross the divide, and simulate the movement in the transverse direction. I bring my left leg into the hole, extend to the toilet, and then guide it to the left side. I continue leaning to the right, enjoying the hip extension. Now that I am fully inside the attic, I begin to relax. I become aware of this relaxation because I am suddenly aware of other feelings outside of my adrenalized muscle and dermal sensations. The pumping in my chest eases and I sense my breath and pulse slowing. I am in a strange position, lying on my right side, still bent forward at the waist. My right leg is down, my left foot still elevated, because my hip does not want it to fall to the side any further. I sense that my ass is barely in the location it needs to be able to relax, and so my midsection, hips, and buttocks are tense and unsettled. I decide to adjust more. I need to sit up and shift closer to the toilet where I remember the tallest point of the concrete roof/ceiling is, to give myself more vertical clearance. I start to move to the right of the hole, while sitting up and pulling my right leg toward me. My upper-body muscle systems hurt from the recent demand. This discomfort will perpetuate and continue, I know that I am only just beginning to physically realize the overexertion. Trying to shift your body in tight quarters requires acute and precise movements. I'm still operating in total darkness, figuring that the time it takes to illuminate the space, only to see what I have already studied, is an act of frivolity, so I continue to feel my way toward what I assume will be a less awkward position and simultaneously bring me closer to the opening in the concrete ceiling where I expect to find freedom. I regularly shift my gaze up toward the opening above, hoping to see my star, but it never appears, but the opening itself is visible because of a light source beyond that dimly illuminates its perimeter. It could be the moon. It is so faint that I continually wonder if it's real. I keep shifting and opening up my body through tiny adjustments. I decide that the hole will be within reach if I can just get to my knees. I find the toilet bowl and the concrete slab to my right. I withdraw my knee until it is under me, laying my shin and top of my foot on the sheet rock, as far to the right as I can. I extend my body upward from there, bringing my left leg around behind me, prepared to bring it up to the other leg. I get my legs under me, and continue to raise my torso, being careful not to put too much weight on the toilet. I guide my hand up to the opening above, and I can feel air pouring in. I see it in my mind, like the smoke from dry-ice, moving like liquid, in a cascading waterfall over the crude edges of the concrete and into the room. The physical sensation of the air on my hands also brought the horrid smell back to my mind. I stick my fingers up into the jagged opening and begin feeling around and pushing against it in every direction. The broken face is rough, gnarly. I find places to press against all three sections. Nothing budges. I push harder against the slab face closest to me, beginning to feel frustrated that my way out is not more obvious now that I have succeeded in reaching my target location. In my quelling angst, I push hard, and reveal a disaster that I never considered as a possibility.

I feel the drywall split under my right knee first, as a sudden drop, then the whole board gives way. I do not experience any slow motion during the fall. It happens quickly, and is messy, terrifying, and extremely painful. In the darkness, I have no idea what I am striking while I fall, I can only feel the various impacts. I even lose all sense of gravity and I can't tell which direction I am falling. I just continue striking things with different parts of my body and I can sense material all over and around me. I know when I reach the ground, because gravitational-awareness returns. The final impact is on my right leg, receiving the majority of the impact with the side of my knee. I am conscious as I fall, but when the falling concludes, I lose consciousness.

## CHAPTER 17

Day unknown.

Every journey, eventually, leads to this place.

I retract into a smaller physical space.

My ability and desire to explore and seek escape dissipates.

My mind remains my lone haven and any lingering delusion of control fades into oblivion, as I watch my own sunset, helpless.

I awaken on the floor of my pantry. It is no longer dark. I am face down and I begin taking inventory of myself and my situation. I have not moved. I open my eyes and recognize that I am face down on my right cheek. I note that my right arm is above me. My face hurts. My eyes hurt as I open them. Everything is blurry, I cannot immediately determine my location or position in space. I recognize that part of the shelving is in front of me and seems to be laying across me, with the white wire close to my face. I can see the wall beyond and my eyes struggle to focus on any single object. This could be from the strange depth of vision that is confusing me, or simply from shock. The pain I sense in my face is my eyes. It begins to creep backward into my head in a sickening, spreading, sensation, like thick paint dripping down a wall. The pain drips into my head and begins to nauseate. My nerves start sending sharp and disruptive signals from all over my body. I am incapable of pinpointing any location, but each signal comes to my brain with a cringing and wincing that tells me something is wrong. It is going to take a while to process all of this. I am aware of pain and discomfort, but I, almost immediately, become aware of some type of disappointment that tints my physical experience. When I was last conscious, I was excited, full of hope and anticipation. Now I am on the floor again and all of that is gone. I imagine that the hopeful version of me is dead, lifeless, lying in the ceiling, left to die, alone, and miserable. I left all of that up there. I can't even wish for those feelings to come back.

They're gone.

He's gone.

I can barely even find the desire to go through the painstaking process of evaluating my injuries or figuring out what happened. I am on the floor. I fell from 12 feet above, where I was on my knees above the ceiling, so my body and head fell close to 15 feet. I consider the number of objects that could have broken my fall on the way down and understand, immediately, that this is likely a horrible situation. It could be worse that I hit so many things and sustained multiple injuries, but it also may be a blessing that I didn't fall straight down. A fifteen foot fall can be fatal.

Although... Maybe that would have been better...

Pain rushes to my head. I recall striking my head on the way down. I know my shoulder suffered some tremendous impact and that I landed on the side of my knee. I start with those places. My head hurts something awful. The pain throbbing in my skull pumps a colorful show into my vision every time it pulses. A red and orange blur radiates from the outer edges of my vision into my central focal field and I lose the ability to focus for a moment each time the pain inflates. It is a steady pumping. I try to think about my right shoulder. My right arm is over my head. I don't recognize anything significant there. I decide to wiggle my fingers in my right hand and they all respond. They also deliver the message that they are touching things that feel like dust and debris. I can also feel the warped luxury vinyl plank of the pantry floor. It feels cool. I shift attention to my right knee. I am slightly twisted and recognize this as I divert attention to my leg. My legs are out to my left side, so my right knee is on the ground. I feel nothing there. I can actually identify my left leg and decide to wiggle my toes. They respond, I can feel them move inside my leather shoe. I can even sense that my sock is wet and feels pretty disgusting. I decide to move my other arm, which is extended beside me. I find the shelving that is laying across me and I am able to move my left arm freely and with little pain. My chest is what hurts from this movement. My arm reports soreness, but I remember this same feeling following my lift into the ceiling, and I am confident in the cause. I shift the shelving slightly, but it just falls against my left shoulder, so I decide to not worry about that right now. I try to find my right leg again. I try to move my thigh, but get no response. I try to find my toes, but get no response. I decide to press my left leg, which feels like it is on top of my right leg, down onto its supporting member. As soon as I press my left leg into the leg beneath, my whole world spins. I can immediately feel the tilt of my space, my vision becomes instantly clear, and then I lose consciousness. I do not feel anything from my right leg.

I awake again in the same position and through the same process upon opening my eyes. After a few moments of confusion and frustration with my eyes and their refusal to focus, my attention goes straight to my right leg, directly to my knee.

There it is.

There is the problem that is causing me to go into horrible shock.

There is the pain.

This is the pain that I know. This pain is everything that I expect. The beginning of it is just my nerves saying "here I am." They do not give me any specifics, just a warning that "something is wrong down here, and we are not quite sure how to explain it with these simple electrical signals." I start to shift my body and the pain materializes with further clarity. I start to roll my left shoulder back so I can bring my right arm under me and maybe move my left leg off of my right. I lift my left leg while rotating my shoulders and pull my right arm under my body, hoping to roll onto my back. My right leg screams at me, but I keep going. I keep connecting with objects around me and I can't really make out what they are, but I assume they must be the shelving pieces that were my scaffolding. I twist my upper body and roll onto my back. I lift my left leg and lay it down beside the right. My foot hits the wall or door and I cannot fully extend my leg. This tells me where I am on the floor. When body movement forces my right leg to shift, I feel everything in my knee explain, in broad strokes, that I have done something horrible. The feeling that reaches my brain from my knee is one of anger, resentment, and accusation. My knee expresses profound fury with me for whatever I have done. This is angry pain. This is new pain. Everything in me wants to escape it and I become flush with discomfort. I feel my skin crawl and my stomach lurches. I feel sweat beading on my forehead. I notice that I am biting down again. All I can do is feel my knee. It is horrible. I want to escape the pain and my reaction is to move the leg that suffers, as if it were a cramp that I need to stretch.

The slight movement responds with a feeling that something is shifting or moving inside of my leg that should not be. I become nauseated and start to lose consciousness. I try to relax the leg to avoid what I am feeling, which causes it to shift and the pain floods my head.

I am out... Again...

When I come to, it is the pain in my leg that jolts me awake. It is unpleasant, but I do not have to go through the slow and tedious process of figuring things out this time. This is it. I can see now, in a somewhat well-lit space, that the shelf I was using as my platform is on top of me, and the one being used as the supporting leg is behind me. I am crammed between the leg-shelf and the door. The spice rack on the door has fallen off and is leaning to the left. It looks wrong, but I can't care. I want to sit up, so I grab the shelf that is across my chest and push it up. Every motion generates a response from my right knee. I don't know if I am moving it or if it is simply that painful. I push up with my left arm and set the shelf end beside me on my right, so that I can push up more and lean it against the adjacent wall. It takes a bit of convincing and some awkward maneuvering to find the right balance, with a couple of incidents of it starting to fall and me catching it. Once it is in place, I begin to attempt a basic sit-up. I use my arms to help and fight through the immense pain. As I bring the upper half of my body vertical, the room spins and I go lightheaded. I have not eaten for days and now I can't remember when I last drank water. I am now sitting upright and trying to stay this way while alternating sensations of vertigo and pain overwhelm me. I can't focus on anything and I lose the ability to make plans. I begin dragging my body backward with my arms and pushing off with my left leg until I find the back wall and the corner where I have been keeping empty cans. I lean against the wall and suddenly, without any hint of its coming, vomit down my chin and chest. It is pathetic and seems to be nothing more than bile or stomach acids. It burns my chin slightly and I reach up to wipe my, now more-than-stubble-covered, chin with my right hand. I actually feel a bit of rejection from my right shoulder in the process. My knee throbs in response but as I become still again, the intense pain softens into a throbbing, and I am relieved that I can breathe and lean back. I am wet. My face is wet. I look at my right hand after wiping my chin and see blood again. There are also small hairs in the blood. My meager facial hair, that barely grows anyhow, is now also falling out. I touch my head, feel blood and experience pain where the existing, unhealed laceration festers. I realize that I have no identifiable hair on my head and know that I have reopened the cut. There is so much blood. I visually search my surroundings and realize that I am actually looking to see if there could possibly be some other source of blood in the room, because the amount that is on my shirt, my hands, and that I can feel on my head seems like too much to have only come from me. I picture my scenario as a movie set for a moment and pretend that the scene is almost over. There must be a bucket of fake blood somewhere and the director of special effects is squirting it on me from just off-camera. I imagine what the anticipation on set right before the director says "cut" must be like. I yearn for that relief. I pray that the moment I am in, that this disgusting scene is about to be interrupted by someone yelling "cut!"

Everything falls away as I cycle into that selfish prayer. I find it odd, as I transition out of reality, that the hallucination of a movie set, as an escape from my current reality, is the trigger-moment initiating my acceptance of prayer as an option and of God as a presence in my nightmare.

I pray.

I close my eyes and embark on the most mindful and deliberate prayer session of my life.

"God, I know you can hear me, and I have questions."

No one answers, and before I can feel disappointed, I catch myself, and accept that it cannot work this way.

"God, you don't have to answer me, but I need you right now."

Still no response.

"I guess it is ludicrous that I would give You permission not to answer me the first time I genuinely ask for You, but I guess I am acknowledging my acceptance of Your position."

"I have accepted the suffering of life. I have also accepted that death is imminent for all living things. I understand and appreciate how temporary my present existence is. I also appreciate how insignificant I am in the grand-scheme of the universe, time, and space."

"What I am struggling with, right now, is why the suffering I am experiencing is necessary. What lesson am I to learn from this? What lesson do I represent for others if they could witness and testify to the trial I am presently undertaking?"

"The last time we communicated, you explained to me, without words, that my insignificance is actually purposeful. You showed me, with your divine injection of knowledge, during that moment of bliss, that chaos is real, and everything, across all time and space, is connected. I accept that truth. I accepted it then and I changed my life to better serve the universe, having been blessed with that key knowledge."

"I am one of the few that has been presented with that information. I am one of the few entrusted with that wisdom. That is the truncated version of the gospel that was delivered to me that day. I have never taken that for granted."

One of the most rewarding trips I have taken was to a desolate beach in North Carolina, in the spring. I was compelled to take the journey. I knew that I required the ocean and the night sky. I felt that the universe was calling me. I acquired a small amount of very pure DMT from my trusted spiritual guru, packed a small bag, my tent, basic camping supplies, some food in a cooler and grocery bag, and a case of bottled water and drove to the beach in North Carolina. I knew there were campgrounds in this particular section of the Outer Banks, because I had camped there with my father when I was a teenager, which was terrible. We were eaten alive by mosquitoes and barely left the tent. My father and I planned the trip for four nights on that adventure, but left the third morning. On my recent trip, I did not reserve a campsite beforehand, because I felt this trip was some divine calling, meaning there should be no need for such preparation. This was the part of these trips that bothered Samantha the most. She did not always know where I was going, I did not have a cell phone for much of my absence, and I could not explain what the plan was. I also brought back only general stories of mythical adventures in the wilderness and I can admit that it would probably be difficult to accept the information as truth. But if I had told her the actual truth, the entire truth, she would have believed and accepted it even less.

The campgrounds were closed when I arrived in the middle of the night, so I slept in my car, outside the gates, until the local sheriff woke me early in the morning to ask me why I was sleeping in my car. I explained to him that I decided to finish the drive when I was a few hours out instead of stopping at a hotel, but had not planned for a late night arrival. He was not impressed by my story, or my lack of planning, but the campground employee opened the gate while we were speaking and waved me in. I asked the officer if I could leave, to secure more appropriate accommodations, and he reluctantly obliged. I wasn't worried, he would never have found my tiny bit of powdered DMT, nor would he have known what it was. I planned my spiritual trip for the first night, having had just little enough sleep to create general delirium, which is a perfect mental foundation, and found a quiet place on the beach to execute my anticipated experience.

A good trip is absolutely dependent on "set" and "setting." You must begin the experience with a positive mindset, occupy the appropriate physical setting to manifest positivity, and ensure that it is capable of maintaining a calm and comforting environment. This journey was perfect in every way. The night was cool, not cold. The wind was gentle and soft, but strong enough to keep the bugs off, blowing in from the sea with a perfect smell and taste. The sky was magnificently clear, so I lay in the sand, in the eave of the dune, where the light from houses would not interfere with my view of the stars. I waited and meditated for hours before my spiritual adventure. I never know how long the preparatory time lasts, because I take these trips without devices or worldly possessions. This time, I wore a pair of board shorts and kept a pair of sandals nearby. I had nothing else except the pipe with which to smoke the substance, the herb that would act as the vehicle for burning, a lighter, and small vial of DMT. I had utilized this substance in my process no less than

100 times before that night. I was very confident in the purity of the batch and the source from where it had been procured. I had practiced this process in the care of my guru many times and in the care of my wife once. I had never used DMT recreationally, but purely as a spiritual practice. DMT had become my preferred method of communicating with the spiritual realm and experiencing the universe from a psychedelic plain. I had tripped on DMT alone a few times, and typically preferred a caretaker, because the intensity of it could be so profound that it can be frightening. I knew this time was going to be different, and so I planned to be alone.

I know that I could have died from the many solo experiences I undertook in my life, but I had also accepted this possible fate early in life, and was not afraid of death. If death chose me while I was exploring profound spirituality and discovering universal truths, it was no accident. After this night, I trusted even more that it was all God's plan. DMT consistently provides a path to discovery within the mind that unlocks explanations about our place in the universe. It also removes time and space from one's reality and allows seemingly impossible travel and exploration within mere minutes of relative time in this dimension. Experiencing supernatural and profound discovery is normal and expected, and why I plan these trips.

That night was different. My experience was unlike any before and has not been replicated since. I have always been non-religious, so my spiritual nature is not connected to any one deity. I believe in God and that all of the Gods and Deities of all religions, or most of them, are "real." I have spent intimate time with many of them, but I had never been overtaken and administered to by the "One God" that many religious guides speak of. The universe does not have a hierarchy, so this is not the "Boss God" or anything ridiculous like that. The "One God" I refer to is the manifestation of knowledge, wisdom, and omnipotence of all the universe in one entity. This manifestation is inexplicable until experienced. The experience is one of instant understanding upon exposure. Communication is not in any language or delivery that we experience elsewhere. The information relayed resembles an emotion rather than data. When God presented themself to me, I experienced an instantaneous understanding of what it is and an immediate ingestion of knowledge beyond anything one can learn from experiences in our own existences. When you are in the presence of The Divine; you know it. When it shares Wisdom with you: you understand it. If you return to the dimensional existence from which you came: you remember everything. The challenge lies in understanding it, explaining it, or deciphering what to do with it. There is no possibility of ignoring it, disagreeing with it, or questioning it. If you are presented with this knowledge from God, you accept it as a gift. It would not be presented to any being that could do otherwise.

That is omnipotence.

I returned to earth and this dimension having experienced eons of input and having traveled light years of space, with barely ten minutes having elapsed on earth. The entire journey was a hallucination, but I had met God. I returned with a sense of peace that can only be delivered by The Divine. I immediately understood the curious look that true spiritual experts of any religion display. I now understand that they have this same knowledge that brings me great peace. I understand why the priest welcomes death. I understand why the monk goes peacefully to the next realm through meditation at the end of this physical manifestation. I now comprehend serenity and I grasp a certain truth.

Until now, I have never spoken *to* God.

Now I understand that I must manifest that relationship, because I know God may be the only thing that can provide the answers that I seek.

"Why am I suffering like this?"

"I know that pain, and all other sensations of the body, are tethered to this worldly existence. But I also remember that it is critical to my overall existence to experience all of these worldly sensations while I exist in this realm, because they bear crucial information for subsequent and simultaneous experiences and relationships. I also know that my present experience provides some pathway to others in this realm. I accept the vitality of 'oneness' and the dangers of allowing any manifestation of 'aloneness'."

There it is.

God, as we understand Him, is within each of us. Therefore, The Great Wisdom that you seek when asking God big questions, expecting a direct answer, is usually already there, within you.

"I understand. Thank you. My physical suffering is temporary. The pain that I am enduring now is nothing more than a fleeting hallucination that only exists in this physical body. All of that suffering is left behind when I leave this body."

"The suffering that is my present lesson is the 'aloneness'."

I breathe out a deep sigh of relief.

*My physical pain is nothing: my actual suffering is loneliness.*

The Great Knowledge includes an understanding that chaos is real. All things, including energy and light, in the universe, throughout all time, across all universes, and dimensions, existences, and planes within those realms, are connected by a unifying force. The only complete understanding of that force, and the blueprint of interconnectedness, is the explanation of God. Therefore: I cannot be alone here, or anywhere.

"Correct."

I open my eyes, and see my mother again.

"You finally understand."

"How could I have been so stupid, mother?"

"You're not stupid. You're human, right now, whether you want to be or not."

"But the pain is so much. I don't want to be alone."

"It's interesting that you had to go through this to understand that. You have always looked for opportunities to be alone. You have always wanted to be left alone with something to experience it fully. You were never awkward, or a 'loner', but it has been your design."

"I know that. Even my spiritual journeys have been, essentially, alone."

"No they haven't."

"I get that now, but..."

"No 'but'! You have never taken a single step alone in this life or in your entire existence. You cannot. You are literally composed of and connected to all things, across all time and space. You, and every other sentient being that suffers the delusion of 'aloneness', are mistaken."

"Why did I seek to be alone then?"

"Because the discovery of truth often resides in the experience of a failure to accomplish the non-truth. This is why duality is so important. You always knew in your soul, deep within your purity, and in the breath, your spirit, that you could not be alone. But to actually believe it, you had to prove it."

"I don't want to suffer like this any more."

"I know. That is the only real challenge left before you, isn't it?"

Then she was gone.

I am crying. I think I am awake, but I can't actually tell. I do not feel any pain, so I decide that I am not awake. I am not dropping tears of sadness. I am also not afraid any more. I stare across the room, where the bust of my mother was speaking to me, with all of her profound wisdom. I realize that I am staring at an empty space. I feel a whimper-like inhale and my lip quivers. I taste blood. I smell the horrible smell, but it seems far away. The blank space before me begins to change colors and I see the oil-and-water-like backdrop take form. It materializes quickly this time. It is beautiful, like blood. The sub-material is a deep red and the oily substance that is forming multitudes of spirals and shapes is an even deeper red, almost black toward the center. It is beautiful to witness. I am temporarily mesmerized by the patterns and complexities. My vision begins to adjust its focus out of the swirls, and the grand oak tree emerges. At first, it is red and twisting like the liquid backdrop. Then it chooses its location, not quite in the center of the image, but perfectly placed. The tree is not symmetrical, and it is very realistic in its asymmetry. I am, again, impressed by how realistic it is already, and then it begins to take on the textures and colors of a real tree. The leaves are the yellowish colors that indicate the beginning of autumn. This tree represents the present time. This tree could exist in the outside world, in autumn, in a field, somewhere in Georgia. The lighting is from behind me and accents the natural beauty of the oak and all of its imperfections. There are nodules and gnarly places on the trunk. There are awkward, twisted limbs, and branches that have thin spots where there are not enough leaves. The leaves are not uniform. The tree seems very real, but it is not moving. The only way that I know, right now, that it is not real, is because it is not moving. I am instantly bothered by this. I am suddenly uncomfortable after just feeling very calm.

I finally exhale.

I feel the calm return as my breath escapes, providing a breeze that causes the tree to stir. Now the image becomes so real that I want to stand up and walk over to it. I breathe deeply again and watch the leaves shift and spin as the breeze passes through its limbs.

"You *are* the breath. You *are* the breeze."

I feel more tears on my face. I understand that I am suffering for a reason, but I can't understand what that reason is. I know that I need to accept that I cannot understand. There is great acceptance required in my current situation. I understand that the tree is telling me something, and has been communicating with me all along. I understand and accept that my mind is generating this life and this tree, so that I can accept that life is a manifestation and not a reality. I close my eyes, even though the image before me is so beautiful. I accept that it should be gone when I open my eyes, but when I do, it is still there. It is even more majestic and perfect in its imperfection than I remember, even from just moments ago.

"You can't make it go away. You have to let it go."

This voice is familiar. It is coming from all around me. The voice is harsh in my ears, but also somehow comforting. I am slightly confused by the message, but I am also concerned by what it may be suggesting.

"Stop trying to make things happen and simply let them happen."

This time, the voice has changed to my wife's. It is clearly Samantha's voice. I look around and again feel the tears on my face. I sense my shaken demeanor and know that I am suffering less from physical pain now. Her voice sends me into a pain spiral that spawns from loneliness. I want to see her. I want to touch her.

"Please come to me. Even if I can't feel you, why can't I see you?"

"One thing at a time. We can't rush this part."

"What part? What do you mean?"

"Stop trying to force it. You can't squeeze this understanding out of the tube."

"Tell me what to do."

"Relax."

I must manifest peace now. It is Samantha's voice, but it is my inner-voice that is guiding me. My subconscious knows that I will listen if it is her voice. Again, I breathe deep and exhale slowly. The tree responds as it did before. I repeat this process, but on the second attempt, I focus on finding a rhythm-of-breath that does not allow any space, or pause, between the end of the exhale and the beginning of the next inhale, and vice-versa. This is an old trick that helps when I struggle with meditation. I find flow quickly and lose myself in repetitive occurrences, harnessing the force. I open my eyes and see that my perfectly-regulated breath is providing a gentle, steady breeze across the tree. My individual breaths before were sudden bursts of wind, but this is steady and realistic.

"Now, let it go."

On my next exhale, I say goodbye to the tree from deep within my heart. I say goodbye from a place of profound gratitude and appreciation. I feel the acceptance of something finding a conclusion, closure. I experience this gratitude in much the same way that an ancient hunter would thank his kill for existing and allowing him to nourish himself and his family. I experience a deep and genuine gratitude for this tree, and as I accept this as the appropriate emotion, I see a single leaf fall from the tree and float to the ground. It is beautiful. My breath causes it to dance in midair, all the way down. I intently watch the entire process and experience a sense of relief as it settles, very gently, onto the unknown surface at the base of the tree. I have reached a full-meditative state, because my breath never stops its rhythm throughout this event. I am no longer thinking about my breath or myself, but it sustains. I scan the tree during its next acceptance of my breath and I manifest the same gratitude, but now with extreme deliberation, tainted with the knowledge of purpose, not just its potential. I exhale and the tree gently releases all of its leaves, simultaneously. The image is so real that I almost halt, but I accept it, and witness thousands of leaves in the beautiful and chaotic dance from my breath-wind all the way to the ground. It is a magnificent display of how creative our minds can be, even more so when unforced and unintentional. Each leaf has its own path and changes with its own timing. They all release from the tree in unison, but they reach the ground at different times. This representation of chaos lingers in my mind, providing even deeper clarity to the knowledge I already possess. Each leaf, from the same source, at precisely the same time, because of its unique characteristics, experiences a different, unique path, and ends at the same general conclusion, but never at exactly the same time.

Chaos reveals itself.

I understand.

I understand the impossible-to-comprehend.

"You are free."

This time it is my voice and the words are from my lips. I close my eyes, and when I open them again, I am back in my pantry.

"Samantha?"

"I'm here."

"Why can't I see you yet?"

"You ask so many questions! Just be here."

"Right. Be here now."

"I did not say 'now', did I?"

"No. I guess you didn't."

"You need to focus on that."

"Focus on..."

I do not finish my question. This makes sense. I do not need to ask. The answer is in the question: "now" represents time. My next problem is time.

Time is a manifestation of the human condition. We assume it is necessary to measure and explain everything. I must understand and accept that the delusion of time has disturbed my experience long enough.

I am hurting, spiritually, from loneliness. I miss my tribe, my team, my people. I miss my wife. I miss my friends. I miss my son.

"Nathaniel, I really wish I could see you. I would trade anything to hug you and tell you that it's going to be alright."

"Really? Anything?"

The room fades away and my son is suddenly before me. This time, the background is total darkness. I think it is the whole Nathaniel, but there is a strange light that only allows me to see his head and the shadowy silhouette of his body. He is sitting in front of me, smiling. I want to reach out to him, but my body does not respond.

"Don't waste time with that nonsense. I am right here. Just accept that, ok Pops?"

"OK son. That is great."

"You said you would 'trade anything'?"

"I would! I would give anything to be able to hold you right now!"

"You would trade our entire life together up to now, for one hug?"

My jaw drops and I am speechless.

"I don't think I could experience all of the joy and wonder that our life together gave me from one hug. No offense, Pops."

I don't say anything, because I am so shocked at the wisdom that my 11-year-old son has just laid on me.

"I think your desire to hold me, or see me one more time, may be a bit selfish, and that's ok, but I want to work through that with you, if that's alright?"

"Yes, please."

"Every moment you experience is a tiny grain of sand. If your whole existence, your entire purpose, were simply to count every grain of sand on a beach, would you rush to finish the job?

Or would you take the time to study and understand every single grain?"

"I guess that would depend on the reason for counting them."

"There is no reason for the task, it is simply what you do."

"I think I would like to try to complete the task, but I also understand what you are saying."

"Do you, though? Because any existence is the same as that task. There is no reason or explanation for existing, for living, for experiencing, it is simply what we do. Do you take time to enjoy and experience the journey with depth and understanding? Or do you measure the experience against some vain attempt to complete it? Do you focus on every experience within it?"

"How do you..."

"Never mind that. Why are you experiencing this loneliness?"

"Because I am struggling and I am alone. I miss you and I want to be with you again. I want to know if you're ok."

"The experiences that you share with other souls are not measured by the time you are with them. Nor is the mutual existence measured by the number of times you are with them. It can only be measured by the quality of the experiences that you share."

"Of course!"

"So, why would you want to see me again, like this? What if you got that wish? What if I were suddenly in this room with you?"

"I feel like that would be amazing!"

"Except then you would have to watch me suffer with you in this same physical world. Do you think you would be able to protect me from the suffering you are experiencing? You don't want me to feel like you do right now, do you?"

"Fuck no!"

"So, what do you really want?"

"I guess I am afraid. I must feel like I need to control something to find comfort right now. I guess I feel guilty that I couldn't protect you or save you from the event. I think I just want to know that you're alright."

"Do you think I survived the event?"

"What? Why? I don't understand."

"C'mon Pops! You are a really smart guy. Do you have any reason to think that I might have survived?"

"The only evidence that makes it a possibility is that I survived. I have no other reason to think you could have."

"If I did, wouldn't you be able to pretty easily conclude that I am likely suffering the same, similar, or a worse fate than what you are going through?"

"I mean... I guess it's the only information I have, so... yes, unfortunately. You would likely be going through this, or something much worse."

"Do you want that?"

"Of course not! How could you say that?"

"Well, you have already said that you want me to be here."

"No, I said I want to hug you."

"Those are selfish, worldly wishes. If they came true, it would mean that I would have to be here. So, if that came to be, you would be facing my suffering also."

"I know. I'm sorry."

"Don't be sorry! I'm not here to make you feel bad! I'm here to help you navigate the next part of your journey to peace... and it's closer than you think now."

"Thank you."

"You're welcome. But remember this part in a little bit."

"I will, but why are you saying that?"

"Because you are about to feel like you lost the only chance you had to escape and possibly find other humans out there. Deep inside, you actually wish that you could escape and find me. If, because of some horrible twist of evil fate, you were able to escape from this room, and I had survived, and you were able to find me, somehow still alive, can you even imagine what state I might be in? Have you considered all of the horrible things that you might find?"

"No, and I really don't want to."

"Then remember that when you are using it as an excuse."

"Why would that be an excuse?"

"It will be. So ... Remember."

"I will."

"Promise me!"

"Ok! Ok! I promise... shit!"

"Good. Now, I need to tell you something that will hurt and help."

"Go ahead."

"But after you understand and accept this, I have to go."

"Wait.. why?"

"I don't know. But it must be for a good reason."

"Can I just look at you for a minute first?"

"Sure. It's pretty cool that I can just show up here and look great, huh?"

"It really is. You look totally fine, but I can't see you very well."

"That's how hallucinations are, Pops. Otherwise, how could you tell them from reality?"

"Sometimes I don't want to."

"Well, that would be a different problem."

"Right... Ok. Now, what do you need to tell me? 'Hurt and help' is a strange concept, but I am willing to try. My part is to understand and accept?"

"That's right."

"Well, I can't promise, but I will try."

"That's fine, it doesn't matter, you will."

"This is strange. Just tell me."

"Ok: I didn't survive... Neither did Mother... Neither did Sugy... Neither did anyone, really."

"But..."

"Does that hurt?"

"Yes, of course it does. I have been holding onto some hope that maybe you survived."

"But now you understand that is actually a cruel and selfish wish, don't you?"

"I do."

"So, you understand that no one that you love survived this? You really understand?"

My eyes fill with tears. I don't want to know this. I guess I already know, but hearing my son say it is very difficult. No one wants to lose their child. No one wants to lose their loved ones. I lower my head and cry for a bit. I let my sobs push tears down my face. I shiver a few times. I cry, breathe, and I cry again. I start to deny the truth and shake my head to remove that doubt. I look up again and Nathaniel is leaning toward me. The image is so real, the hallucinated light has even maintained its location and I can now see more of his body. He is wearing what appears to be a black t-shirt. He is looking at me with comforting eyes.

He is smiling a soft, gentle smile. His entire demeanor says "look at me, it's ok."

"Do you understand?"

"I do. I don't like it. But I understand."

"Now the good part."

"Please give me something good now."

"If you can truly accept that I did not survive the event and you feel confident that anyone who did survive the event would suffer a horrible and slow death, there may be some comfort in knowing that none of us are going through this."

I do not answer and simply stare at him. I stare at his deep and thoughtful eyes. He is delivering this news to me with such unbelievable poise and confidence.

"None of us are suffering. This suffering only exists in this world, in this physical dimension. I am feeling none of that."

I absorb that last part slowly. I take it into my mind like tasting a fine wine. I let the words run over my eardrums and swirl around in my brain before tasting them with my mind. I let each particle of information wash over me before absorbing them into my soul and spiritually digesting them.

"I am here to deliver that comfort to you. It really is okay. When someone passes from this existence, it is the people left behind that suffer, not the traveler."

"... Not the traveler..."

"That's right. The traveler leaves all of that behind."

"All of you have traveled across?"

"Across... Within... Behind... However your brain needs to understand it, sure."

I lean back. I look at his face and feel his sympathy. He smiles a bit wider, satisfied with the unspoken knowledge of my acceptance.

"Gotta go, Pops!"

"I love you, son."

"I know you do. I love you too."

"What did this have to do with time?"

"Ah... I would not trade anything for the time that we already experienced together. But we aren't done. You just have to finish this journey. But you aren't missing anything. Think about the leaves, how they fell through chaos, each with its own path. There is no time. There is no clock measuring what you are not experiencing with all of us. That's not how it works. You are still here for a reason."

"What is the reason?"

"Ha! You think an 11-year-old would know that?"

"Very funny."

"I know."

I blink and he's gone.

I am overwhelmed by the sadness that he is gone. I stare at the wall across from me for a long time. I stare at the door frame that contains the pantry door which is held fast by immeasurable forces on the other side. I stare at the fallen spice rack shelf that is leaning precariously against the door. I stare until I start to feel my body again. I reach down to my right knee. I am wearing my pants, so I can't see the damage. The khaki denim hides the trauma. I touch the side of my knee and feel the taught flesh beneath the material, swollen and injured. The feeling of swollen skin is distinct. It does not hurt to touch the surface though my jeans, so I open my hand and wrap my palm and fingers around the outside of my knee and begin to increase pressure until I feel it respond. The pain is intense. I have a decent hold, with my fingers on the underside of the knee. I start to lift, attempting to gauge the level of trauma sustained. As soon as my knee begins to bend, the pain runs through my body and my head falls back. I let go, instinctively, and my knee drops to its original position. This movement is more than I can take. I bite down, feel my teeth give way, then scream. As I open my mouth, I feel a tooth fall into my mouth. I tongue it to my lips and spit it out. I run my tongue around my bloody mouth and find another, barely hanging on, and force it free. I spit this one out also. Neither have any significant velocity and only manage to fall over my chin to my chest. I feel blood run down my chin.

I lean my head back against the wall under the bottom shelf and close my eyes. I have to do something, but I fear that I may actually be stuck, right here, this time. I don't think trying to move is a good idea, so I decide to rest. The pain in my knee is the only thing I can think about. It eventually begins to subside, and I fall asleep sometime shortly after the pain begins its retreat.

## Chapter 18

I awaken in total darkness. I sense that I am moving. It is very disturbing. How could I be moving? There is a noise, but I can't place it. I am on my right side and there is something in my mouth. I try to reach up to my mouth, discover that my hands are behind my back, and I can't move them. I try for my feet, but they are also bound together. Suddenly, the movement becomes unpredictable and I am tossed around. I feel centrifugal force pulling my body toward my head. I roll further onto my chest and face and then the force releases me back to my original position. It is pitch black, but I close my eyes again anyhow. The sound is familiar, it is road noise. I hear an engine. I am in a car. I am bound at the wrists and ankles and likely gagged, and I think I am in the trunk of a car. I try to gauge the speed, but it is difficult to determine. The last turn was not too bad, and the exhaust and engine do not seem to be at a high RPM, nor do they seem to be doing any extreme accelerating or decelerating. I try to wiggle my hands free, but they will not budge. I try to shift, but realize that it is pointless, there is very little space for me in here. Then we turn the other direction and my body is pulled toward my feet. The sensation feels like all of my blood is being forced out of my head and into my legs. It is strange. I always imagined that being in the trunk of a moving car would be painful and uncomfortable, but because of my state, I do not move much, and just lay there, wondering what is happening. I listen for voices, but I hear nothing else except the road noise. There is a distinct moment where I stop trying to free myself, I stop worrying about getting out or getting free, and I feel the vehicle hit the brakes quickly and release, then do it again, each time, throwing me further into the trunk. Then the brakes tap... tap again, and then slam. I hear the screeching of tires and I am thrown violently into the back of the seats, forced into the deepest part of the trunk. I can feel the end that I am in fishtailing and can sense the rear tires have lost traction in the skid. It feels like I am floating. Then there is impact, and just before I can experience the inevitable death or violent reaction, I awaken in my pantry.

I have been told that you cannot actually die in your dreams, but this is the first time I have come close enough to be considered empirical evidence of that theory. I am jolted awake, sweating and breathing heavily. I am terrified, but instantly recognize that I am also in pain. The pain is so intense it is generating waves of nausea. I accept that I need to do something. I can't just sit here and suffer. I look for the water container. I do not immediately locate it, and I have to endure some shifting to see that it was knocked over and into the front corner during my episode. This does not surprise me. The floor all around it is wet. The water has pooled in two places that I can see from here. I lean forward and reach for the container that is now on its side. I can't reach it. I sit back and bring my left leg over my right, keeping it away from the assaulted knee, and point my toes, in their shoe, toward the container. I can just reach it. I start working it back toward me, and only stop twice when I accidentally brush my right knee a bit and have to work through the pain before continuing. I get the container close enough, send my working leg back across, and lean forward to retrieve the cereal container by hand. I stand it up, and while I am leaning into the room, I study the puddles and marks in the dirt on the floor to determine where the drops are striking. As I am looking, a drop falls beside my right shin. This is definitely a different location than where it was falling to before I climbed into the ceiling, and I realize that I have shifted the objects in the ceiling during my failed escape attempt. I place the container directly in the drop location and sit back. I am lucky the toilet didn't fall into the room, because that could have been the end of my water supply, or worse. I watch a drop fall into the container. I lean forward again, and wince in pain. I dip my hand into the larger of the two puddles on the floor and bring it to my face. I rub my face with the wetness. It feels good. I repeat this process and even lick my hand after the third time, just to get a little bit of water in my mouth. I swallow hard and feel instantly sick. I lean back and watch the drops in the container. I count to pass the time. I try to estimate seconds again and reach 72, 75, and 64 between drips. I need medicine. I look to where my bag should be. It is covered in dust. I bring the bag over to my lap with a lazy dragging method. I brush the dust off the top of my ridiculously expensive briefcase and open the main compartment. I take out my laptop. I open the cover and press the power button: it does not respond. I feel disappointment and try again: no response. I thought I still had battery left, even if just a little. I try a few more times and then toss the object into the room, screen still open, to my left, with complete disregard for the result. I reach into the bag again and retrieve my personal cell phone. I know that I have intentionally saved some of the remaining battery in this device. Maybe I have opened up enough of a hole in the ceiling now so I can find a satellite signal. I press the power button on the side and it does not respond. I try again with the same result. I shake the thing violently and try again: nothing. I remember hearing that these devices are never really off and now I know that is true. I intentionally saved some battery and it still died in my bag. Either that, or some other stimulus has caused both items to die. I try once more, with a squinted face and a bit of hope, but it does nothing. I exhale and toss it to my left also. These items, for all of their expensive and addictive qualities, do virtually nothing for someone in a survival situation once the battery has been exhausted. I explore the bag a bit more. Pens, pencils, some paper. I find the pill bottle and shake it. There is still a good bit of supply within. I know the pills are going to eat me up with nothing in my stomach, but the cycle of eating and vomiting to try to get pills down sounds worse. I find one of each, an ibuprofen and an omeprazole, and gather enough saliva and blood in my mouth to swallow both. I almost choke on one of them, likely because I have been swallowing so little material. Again, I can feel every millimeter of movement as the pills make their way through the length of my esophagus. I grab the water container and hastily drink the tiny bit that has gathered in the bottom. I replace the container for collection and lean back, hoping that maybe I can keep these pills down. If not, and I regurgitate, I will just keep taking them. Maybe if I can digest any part of them, it will provide some relief. I feel around in my bag and in the other compartments. I find the last compartment and acknowledge what is inside. I have not even unzipped this small inside pocket yet when I accept that my pistol is inside. I look away for a moment and consider this discovery. I examine the weapon through the expensive material and note the placement and direction of the grip and muzzle. I locate the second magazine in the same pocket, still without opening the actual compartment. I look away again. Finally, I unzip the pocket and reach in where my black, Glock 43X is resting comfortably, securely. I take it out of the bag with my right hand and move the bag to my left side. I hold the pistol in front of me and admire its design. I set it down, still in my right hand, on my right thigh. I stare at it for a moment, acknowledge how it fits perfectly in my grip, with a natural aesthetic, then I turn my gaze straight ahead. Before the sickness can take me, I close my eyes and fall quickly back to sleep again.

I dream that I am on a long beach. I see someone up the beach from me, in the distance. They are just a silhouette, a human figure, but I know that it is Samantha. I call to her, but nothing comes out of my mouth. I start to walk toward her, waving my arms. She seems to be standing at the water's edge, likely a half-mile from me. I keep calling to her, but I can't make any sound. It feels like I am making sound, but nothing happens. I can't fully focus on her, but I know it is her. Then I am afraid. I cannot explain why I am afraid, and nothing else has changed. I start to run to her. Because of the distance, her image is shaking too much while I run, so I have to stop and look at her location to determine progress. I do this twice, running, as hard as I can, for about 20 seconds, then stopping to look, but I never get any closer. I keep doing this, and try to call out to her. I never get any closer and no sound ever comes out of my mouth. I start to feel panic and run harder, this time without stopping to look. When I decide to stop and look I trip and fall instead. Just as I am about to land in the sand at the water's edge, arms out to break my awkward fall, I awaken in the pantry.

I am sweating, shaking, and terrified. This dream scared me for no logical reason. The sweating and shaking is from pain. I reach down and feel that my knee has swollen enough to fill my entire pant leg. It has filled the space and is throbbing. I also recognize that the room is almost dark. I look up to the hole, where I can see the entire toilet and all the way up to the concrete slabs. The light entering from the source is turning a deep red again. I look down and realize that I am still holding my gun. I lift it, instinctively eject the magazine, catch it with my left hand, set the magazine in my lap, and rack the slide to ensure there is no round in the chamber. The chamber is clear, so I reload the magazine and set the pistol on my left thigh this time.

I take inventory.

I made it through this last sleep without vomiting the pills I took, but they seem to have no effect on the pain. I decide to take two more ibuprofen and one more omeprazole. I get the bottle from my bag, count out the pills, and settle for three ibuprofen instead, because: fuck this pain. I lean forward and grab the water container that has now collected a mouthful, telling me that I could easily estimate the time I was asleep, but I don't care any more.

*Time is a delusion of the human mind.*

I take all four pills at once with two swallows of the water and return the container to its location. I could also probably estimate what day it is now, but when I start to think about my last point of reference, my brain decides that it doesn't care about this either.

*Time is a delusion.*

I take inventory of my pain. I pretend that I am my own doctor and consider my level of pain on a scale from one to ten:

with one being "no pain at all," and ten being "the worst pain you have ever felt in your entire life." I think for a moment about my pain, and again, my brain decides that I don't care to waste energy on this, so I stop thinking about it.

*Pain is a delusion of the human mind.*

I consider how many pills I might have left to help me cope with the pain I am experiencing. I think there may be ten or more. I then consider how the pain in my knee presently prevents me from doing anything other than just sit here. I consider trying to eat, even though I feel no hunger. I know that I will likely die of starvation soon if I don't eat and how painful it will be to waste away like that. I recall how I felt when I was trying to force food into my body recently, vomiting and struggling as a result. I consider this type of suffering and if it is worth the result. I am sure that my body is being poisoned by the water I am drinking and the air I am breathing. I am certainly showing telltale signs of radiation poisoning. I am certainly experiencing the signs of exposure to a post-nuclear-event environment. This slow torture is, without a doubt, far worse than simply perishing in a sudden, fiery explosion. I recall tales of how the heat from a nuclear blast is so intense that the victims may experience the incineration before losing consciousness or dying, and their brains may continue to experience the horror for moments afterward. I wonder for a moment how it is even possible that I survived this, but my brain decides that it has no desire to waste energy on this futile exploration.

*Pain is a delusion.*

I consider that there are likely other survivors, somewhere. I have no evidence of any near me. I have not heard anything representing human existence since the generator died a few days into my ordeal. I consider the state of the world if I am the only survivor in the general vicinity. Also, if I was not directly exposed to the blast, somehow, other survivors may have already succumbed to their injuries, if less protected during the event. Also, if they are alive and capable, they are likely forming groups and some horrifying new world order is unfolding in the shattered remains of our society. My loneliness will find little relief in that world, in any potential scenario.

*Suffering is a delusion of the human mind.*

I trust that the illusion of my son before me, as the deliverer of critical information, was correct in convincing me that neither he, nor any of my other loved ones, survived this. My loneliness is driven wholly by my selfishness and desire to share this struggle with others. I accept that my wish to have my wife and son is to ease my pain, but I had not considered the selfishness involved until he explained it so eloquently, yet harshly. Therefore, the immense suffering from my loneliness will find no relief from escaping this room.

*Suffering is a delusion.*

The difference between an "illusion" and a "delusion," is that an illusion is a misperception of the mind, which includes hallucinations. A delusion is a dangerous and deceptive concept or idea.

*Time, pain, and suffering are all delusions of the human mind.*

I have never experienced the pain that a severely depressed person feels. I have never considered suicide to be a viable solution to any problem. I have experienced suicide from the perspective of one of the souls left behind that is made to suffer by someone else's attempt to escape their perceived suffering. I consider that decision one of the most selfish and cowardly choices a person can make, and I maintain that position, even now. I do consider euthanasia to be a humane and viable option in particular, extremely rare situations. I feel that when disease or decay has rendered a body as nothing more than the vehicle of physical suffering, and there is no pathway out, that an act of mercy should always be considered.

*Mercy is the ultimate form of Grace. Grace is courteous goodwill, an act of tolerance, acceptance. Mercy is the compassionate manifestation of Grace, when punishment and harm are possible.*

I consider these concepts while I stare at my pistol and wonder if I am expected to show that same Mercy to myself. I question whether my own assisted suicide, at this point, could be considered selfish. I try to consider any possible way that my death could be seen as selfish or inappropriate, and I come up empty.

I remove the magazine again and set it down. I rack the slide and check once more. It is empty. I replace the magazine and set the pistol down again.

"God, is this wrong?"

"I don't think that is something you can ask."

It is Samantha.

"Why not? Isn't God the ultimate authority on morality?"

"Of course. But you have free will for a reason."

"My mind is too tired for this. Can't you just tell me what to do?"

"I can. But I won't. Besides, I am only an illusion of your mind."

"I know."

"I think it is more important that you have convictions that guide your actions."

"What does that mean?"

"That means that you are actually the ultimate authority on morality."

"How can that be?"

"Because, if you have deep convictions about a behavior, you will believe that your actions, in support of that behavior, are justified. Even if your morality is driven by the fear of being judged by some great being, having convictions will support your choice."

"I don't think that anyone should be expected to suffer like this."

"I agree. Pain like this is cruel and you are finding no relief."

"I don't care about the pain. It's the loneliness …"

"I see. But you have been visited by many creations of the mind so real that you can barely tell the difference. So, why are you still lonely?"

"Because I know that you are all just my mind convincing my brain to execute emergency self-preservation techniques."

"That is correct. But then why are you so calm now? You seem so peaceful."

"Because I think I know what to do."

"Well... be careful, my love."

"I am talking about killing myself. How, exactly, am I to exercise caution in that act?"

"Well, I guess I don't want your action to inadvertently cause more pain, instead of providing relief, so don't fuck it up."

"Oh... that's a good point."

"Now: I love you. Be confident in your convictions."

"Okay."

"You don't *have* the wisdom. You *are* the Wisdom."

"I love you too."

The room has gone completely dark again. This time, I do not sleep. I am calm. I am at peace. I stare into the darkness for a long time. I think about the most beautiful art I have ever seen in-person. I think about sunsets that I have seen. I picture the faces of people I love the most. I remember pain on the face of a stranger and I accept that she is no longer feeling that pain. I picture the trees of the Georgia mountains. I consider the pines of the deep forest. I remember the majesty of the redwoods in northern California. I stare into the dark and run through the many experiences this existence has provided and I consider never being able to experience them again. I think about sex. I think in great, specific, detail about sex that I have enjoyed. I immerse my imagination into the bond felt when you make love to someone. I consider that the part of that bond that is supernatural and most incredible is likely a universal truth that exists between spirits beyond this physical world. I consider the sense of unity that I feel when I reach spiritual connectedness with another soul, even when they don't realize it has occurred. I consider the people that I have encountered in this life that I had shared spiritual space with in other dimensions or realms outside of this one. I decide that earthly experiences, while intense and important, are not the experiences that pervade our existence across the space-time continuum. I can leave all of those in this world. I will take the best part of them with me through the rest of my infinite journey.

In the total darkness, I rack the slide, quickly, calmly, to load a live round into the chamber, and point the pistol directly in front of me, as if aiming at some imaginary perpetrator, but with absolutely no animosity. I breathe in, bring my finger to the trigger, and pull in one smooth motion. The pistol fires precisely as expected. I have fired this weapon so many times that there is no shock or surprise from the report. I acknowledge that it is very loud in this confined space, and my ears ring for a good time after. I keep my weapon pointed where I fired with a steady hand for a few breaths. This act was to ensure that the weapon is performing as expected, to prevent the possibility of failure in my final effort, just as Samantha requested. I have no remorse. I shot the imaginary enemy before me and I have no remorse.

I consider my convictions. I think deeply about my stance, on my decision, and I inject others into my position to determine if my choice remains the same no matter who plays the main character in this act. I spend significant time playing over these fantasies in my mind, but my conclusion and the outcome are the same in every scenario.

I have no sense of time, nor do I wonder at all about it.

I accept my convictions and all physical pain melts away.

I understand that my suffering is temporary.

I realize that free will is a gift.

I acknowledge that I keep my sidearm as a last resort, but also as my most comforting tool for survival. It will now become the vehicle of truth in the absolution of my greatest act of mercy.

Survival is intentional, driven by hope and a desire to endure. I could continue to fight, heal, hurt, and struggle in this space, in a seemingly endless cycle. I could find hope once more and chase the illusion again.

It is the energy between us that provides true happiness.

Love and companionship bring ultimate joy.

Serving one-another offers peace and pure satisfaction.

I have decided to remove all remaining delusions and any obstacle preventing my peace.

I raise the barrel of the pistol to my right temple, lift my elbow to ensure proper alignment, calmly move my finger to the trigger, and squeeze, in the same smooth motion, with complete confidence.

-

**END**

-

If you or someone you know is struggling with substance abuse, self-harm, or thoughts of suicide: Seek help immediately. If you or someone you know is in crisis, Call 988.

Please speak to someone.

Check on your loved ones.

https://www.samhsa.gov/
https://www.wannatalkaboutit.com